AF471142

A Sugarloaf Wedding

ROSEMARY WHITTAKER

A Sugarloaf Wedding

Rosemary Whittaker

Also by Rosemary Whittaker

A Sugarloaf Valentine
A Sugarloaf Mix-Up
A Sugarloaf Surprise
A Sugarloaf Christmas
A Sugarloaf Easter
A Sugarloaf Secret
A Sugarloaf Summer
A Sugarloaf Appeal
A Sugarloaf Adventure
A Tale of Two Christmases
A Boxful of Christmas
The Christmas Cookie Club
The Cinnamon Snail
Sunshine State
The Wattle Birds
The Feijoa Tree
The Villa Mimosa
Making the Effort

Copyright © 2025 by Rosemary Whittaker

All rights reserved. This book or any portion thereof may not be reproduced or used in any manner whatsoever without the express written permission of the publisher except for the use of brief quotations in a book review.

First printing, 2025

ISBN-13: 978-1-922651-80-8

This book is a work of fiction. Names, characters, places, and incidents are the product of the author's imagination or are used fictitiously. Any resemblance to actual events, locales, or persons, living or dead, is coincidental.

 Stopwatch Publications

www.rosemarywhittaker.com

Coverdesign including elements from 100 Covers, viktorijareut, lemono, NastyaSigne and ramonakaulitzki.

For my wonderful readers - who have supported and encouraged me from the first page of book one to the final page of book ten. I wouldn't be here today without you, and I'm so grateful to you all.

Chapter One

'You can't say no!' insists Isabella. 'I've brought you to The Wild Horse especially to ask you, and I'm picking up the tab.'

'Of course you are,' I agree. 'Where else would I find the money for a place like this? Certainly not on what you pay me.'

She lays her hand on mine and gives me a pitying smile.

'You and I have been through this several times, Georgia. Lily and I pay you far more than you're worth on the open market, and we top up your pay with free cake. If we were to add up what you eat each day and subtract it from your more than generous wages, you'd owe us a considerable sum by now. But we're kind enough to overlook that. In return, I'd like you to consider my very small request.'

'It isn't a small request!' I exclaim. 'It's a huge ask. Setting aside the time I'd have to give up, there are several other factors to consider. For instance, what would I wear?'

'I'm not sure,' she says. 'We can discuss all that sort of thing once you've agreed to do it.'

'I'm not agreeing to anything so unreasonable without knowing all the facts! Even assuming I agree with your selection of clothing – which is vanishingly unlikely – there are plenty of other things I want clarified before I say yes. Are you taking out any kind of insurance policy? I won't be legally responsible for anything that may – and almost definitely will – go wrong.'

'That won't be necessary,' she says. 'If everyone plays their part properly, no insurance company ever needs to know about it.'

'At least one million pounds' worth of cover!' I insist. 'Uncle Harry can draw up a specific clause for it.'

Isabella lays down her spoon and eyes my chocolate soufflé lovingly. I move my plate out of her reach and stare her down.

'Fine,' she says. 'I'll take whatever actions Uncle Harry deems fit. Does that satisfy you?'

'It removes one of my many doubts. But I refuse to commit myself to anything until I've had a proper chance to consider it. Couldn't you find anyone else for the job?'

'I could find plenty of people. But I want you. Goodness knows why, but I do.'

'Which puts me in a powerful bargaining position,' I point out.

Isabella sighs. 'How about this? I allow you full creative control over all sartorial decisions as they relate to you. I take out whatever insurance cover suits the situation and promise to fully indemnify you against any and all situations that may arise. And I buy you another chocolate soufflé. Is that enough for you?'

I waver. The soufflés at The Wild Horse are delicious. But I'm eager not to throw away my negotiating power prematurely.

'Two soufflés,' I say. 'To be consumed either today or on a future occasion of my choosing. And I want my title changed.'

Isabella assumes what she considers to be a patient expression. 'And we were so close to an agreement! What's your particular objection to your job title?'

'It's demeaning.'

'No, it isn't! I should point out that Lily hasn't kicked up any of this fuss.'

'She's the maid of honour,' I say. 'The clue is in the name. Honour! It shows how important she is. But you want me to be your bridesmaid – a maid to the bride. I'm sure you can see my problem with that – especially when the bride happens to be you.'

'Chief bridesmaid,' she corrects me.

'Is that supposed to make it better? The chief part is ok. I'm happy to keep that word. But I refuse to be a maid to anyone – particularly my older sister.'

'The title of bride has already been taken,' she says. 'And the position of maid of honour has been filled. What do you suggest?'

'I have no idea. That isn't my problem. It's your wedding. You need to think about it some more and come up with a title that befits my status. Run your list of alternative suggestions past me, and I'll select the most acceptable one.'

'And then you'll say yes?' she asks.

'Possibly.'

'Georgia!' she says in a warning tone.

I clasp my hands together. 'I will! Or should that be "I do?"'

'Either works for me,' she says. 'As long as you agree to be my chief ... something or other.'

'I'll await your list with interest.'

'It isn't easy getting married,' she complains. 'There's so much to do, and so many lists to make. Today was supposed to be the simple part. I thought I'd invite you out to lunch, briefly make my request, and that would be another thing ticked off.'

'I was ticked off,' I say. 'Anyone calling me a maid of anything ticks me off.'

I catch her eye and grin. 'Thanks for asking me, Issy. I'll try to do a good job. I'll set several alarms and do my very best not to oversleep that morning.'

'There'll be no chance of that!' she says. 'I'll have the entire household up at dawn. No one will oversleep on my wedding day!'

'I find that all too easy to believe. Still, it will all be over soon, and we can go back to our usual boring existence.'

'You have several more months of this,' she warns me. 'As my chief brides-whatever, you'll be heavily involved in every single thing that happens between now and then.'

'You didn't mention that just now! You said it was a teeny-tiny favour, and I would hardly notice I was doing it.'

Isabella smiles. 'I may have under-exaggerated a little, which is a first for me. But only a very little. Any slight effort required on your part will be more than made up for by all the fun you'll have.'

'How have you not realised by now that I don't do your kind of fun?'

'You do now! I'm willing to bet that by the time my wedding day arrives, you'll have done plenty more things you thought you didn't do.'

'Wedding day!' I say. 'That sounds so strange.'

'In the abstract, or only when the words are connected to one of us?'

'The second one. To me, you'll always be the obnoxious older sister who spent all her time bossing me around while we were growing up. And now you'll have someone else to boss around. You must be delighted about that.'

She shakes her head sadly. 'As you and Lily have reminded me so many times, Jon is one of those annoying people who have a mind of their own and are far less easy to manage than one might hope.'

'Practice makes perfect,' I say consolingly. 'The main thing is that I'm getting rid of you.'

'It's sad to think that idea supersedes the incredible honour I'm doing you by inviting you to play such an important part in my wedding.'

'Nothing is signed yet,' I warn her. 'And if my second chocolate soufflé doesn't arrive soon, nothing ever will be.'

She waves to the server. 'Another one of these as quickly as you can, please. There's a lot riding on it!'

'I suppose I should be flattered,' I say. 'Including me in your wedding party seems more important to you than I expected.'

She smiles. 'It's the only way I'll know exactly where you are and what you're up to on my special day. I want you under my eye at all times.'

'If I agree to undertake this onerous task, I'll perform it with all the grace and efficiency everyone has come to expect of me. I know how much you like to complain about everything, but you'll have to look elsewhere for a scapegoat this time.'

Isabella leans across the table and gives me an impulsive hug.

'Careful!' I say. 'You almost landed in my souffle. There would have been no coming back from that. I would have withdrawn my reluctant consent to supporting you through your ordeal, and the entire wedding would have had to be cancelled.'

'No one is cancelling this wedding,' she says, resuming her seat and picking up her spoon. 'It will be the event of the year – the decade, even. It's a day that will go down in Honeywell history. Parents will tell their children about it for generations to come, and there will be ballads sung about it at village meetings. I can faithfully promise that no one will forget exactly where they were or what they were doing on the joyful day that Isabella Campbell got married!'

Chapter Two

I pick up a sheet of paper and tick off their two names. Then I tuck the paper safely under my pillow. Isabella has told me many times over the years that nothing would persuade her to spend any more time in my bedroom than she absolutely has to. The next time she comes over for dinner, I'll casually mention my sheets need changing, and I haven't had time to do my laundry. So, if she has a moment to spare, I'd be most grateful. That should guarantee she doesn't go anywhere near my room in the foreseeable future.

When she lived at home, she used to stand in my bedroom doorway, pointing out everything that needed to be put away and suggesting a long list of ridiculous tidying systems she'd seen on breakfast television. She never attempted to implement any of them, so I could easily ignore her. But I want her to stay out of my room until the wedding, and the best way to ensure that is to invite her in – preferably with a bright and welcoming smile.

It's been strange not having Isabella living at home for the past twelve months – even though I've spent many years encouraging her to move out and leave the rest of us in peace. Encouraging may not be the correct word. That implies a generally positive conversation, and ours were anything but.

Instead, I adopted a fairly robust approach, sending her every real estate listing I could find. When that had no effect, I started printing them out and leaving them next to her breakfast plate each morning.

Sadly, the pictures of these must-view properties all ended up smeared with butter and marmalade. It considerably lowered their street appeal, and Isabella showed no signs of visiting any of them. Eventually, I took matters into my own hands, booked her a string of viewings, and put them straight into her calendar. She did her best to avoid them for a while. But I persisted, and she finally took the hint and found herself a flat she liked.

I'm glad I didn't have to involve Jon in the process. I'm very fond of him, and I expect him to become a model brother-in-law after a little training. But the sisterhood demands we keep this sort of thing between ourselves, without relying on men or giving them the impression their opinion is either required or appreciated.

Isabella moved into her own flat a year ago. As I regularly inform her, she's incredibly grateful to me for finding it for her.

It's been far quieter here since she left. Mum says she doesn't miss our morning skirmishes over the last piece of toast, but in an odd kind of way, I do. I've always enjoyed a challenge, and there are few things more challenging than being related to Isabella Campbell. Almost no one could have coped with it as well as I have, and I'm determined to make sure she never forgets it.

And I still have to put up with her on a regular basis. I work at least three days a week at the bakery, and I'm also on call for emergencies, which occur more often than you might think. Lily sometimes has to leave early or take time off to deal with a child-related issue, and I'm happy to cover for her on those occasions. She never takes me for granted and always tells me how grateful she is.

Isabella is another matter entirely. Her definition of a crisis covers an alarmingly wide range of possibilities, and the frequency of these so-called emergencies has only increased since she became engaged just before Christmas.

Jon chose his moment well. He took her to dinner at The Wild Horse and asked the server to hide a Haribo ring in her chocolate mousse. He told me later he had no confidence Isabella would eat her dessert slowly enough to notice a genuine ring, and he didn't want her choking on it. In the event, she became so enthusiastic about the idea that she had to be restrained from talking to the chef about making Haribo Surprise a permanent part of the menu.

It took Jon a while to explain the significance of the ring, and even longer for Isabella to stop laughing. But she must have said yes at some point, because the pair of them turned up the following day with her wearing a beautiful ruby-and-diamond engagement ring and carrying a bag of Haribo she'd insisted Jon buy for her on their way over. She told us diamonds might be forever, but they're completely useless for keeping your blood sugar up.

And now she's getting married! Not only that – she's insisting I'm an integral part of it. I did my best to persuade them to elope to Gretna Green on the grounds that it would save them a great deal of money and stress and be a lovely story to tell everyone afterwards. But Isabella can be very stubborn when she chooses, and not even my powers of persuasion could convince her this was the ideal solution for all of us. In desperation, I even offered to pay for their petrol, but my impassioned pleas fell on deaf ears.

So, here we are, right in the middle of wedding preparations, although I haven't entirely given up hope of persuading the pair of them it would be more romantic to be married in a hot air balloon somewhere over the Pyrenees, or among the penguins of Antarctica.

Lily and Abby have promised to help, so I won't have to fend off my sister's bizarre suggestions and inexplicable enthusiasms single-handedly. And it's only until August. After that, she's Jon's problem. The main thing is to get her safely to the altar and off on her honeymoon before she remembers how easy her life was when she lived at home and starts to wonder whether she acted too hastily in moving out.

My phone pings again. I'm tempted to ignore it. I suspect it will ping more regularly than I'd like over the next few months. But there's always the chance it may be something non-wedding-related – like a four-for-the-price-of-one pizza deal or an email from my chocolate-of-the-month club. I flip it open to check. I should have gone with my first instinct and dropped my phone in the bin. It's a WhatsApp message.

> *Natalie: Do we have a name for this group yet? If not, could I nominate The Flour Girls?*

I frown as I read this. The participants need to understand that this group is strictly business-related, and not to be used for general chit chat and unnecessary frivolous emojis.

> *Meghan: I love it! I was going to suggest The Sprinkle Sisters, but yours is much better.*

I'm about to compose a suitably business-like message when my phone pings again.

> *Grace: Shouldn't it be The Whisk Takers, in honour of the time Isabella nearly burned down the kitchen trying to caramelise a crème brûlée?*

> *Olivia: Ah yes! The great caramel conflagration. Lily wrote and told me about it last Christmas. She said the whole village was talking about it for weeks.*

I can still picture Isabella's hurt look as she insisted she was only testing out the bakery's smoke alarms.

> *Victoria: I heard Isabella offered to take selfies with the fire crew. But they said too many people put those pictures into unauthorised calendars, so they'd have to politely refuse.*

> *Georgia: Thank you for joining the group. I know how busy you all are, so I think we should keep this focussed on wedding-related stuff. The idea is that you all get together and plan a surprise event for her before the wedding.*

> *Natalie: I'm surprised Isabella is planning to get married on dry land. I was expecting her to make her vows either skydiving or snorkelling over the Great Barrier Reef, with the bridesmaids swimming along behind, holding a bouquet of goggles.*

It's hopeless. Before I can jump in and exercise my function as moderator, they're off – exchanging reminiscences and recollections of their time in Honeywell. Those who haven't yet met each other in person are busy introducing themselves and telling the group about the role Isabella played in them getting together with their partners.

Despite my frustration with their lack of focus and organisation, I can't help feeling a flicker of pride at hearing some of these stories. Isabella may be my annoying older sister, but it's clear she's touched all these people's lives in a positive way. And now they're keen to return the favour.

Seen in that light, it's quite a nice thing – although I may need a new phone by the time the wedding is over. My current one is prone to overheating on a regular day. If this level of messaging continues, it may give up entirely.

I cheer up when I remember I can charge it to the bakery as a business expense. At least, I can try. Isabella is surprisingly difficult about some of my claims. She thinks being an accountant makes her some sort of an expert when it comes to expense accounts and legitimate deductions. Personally, I think she makes it all up as she goes along, but I've given up mentioning this because she only ever hears what she wants to hear.

If she really won't allow me to charge a new phone to the bakery, she can buy me one out of her own money to thank me for undertaking the arduous task of getting her safely to the altar. It isn't everyone who would accept such a difficult assignment, and I'm trying not to think of everything that could go wrong along the way. I manage all right during the day, but the list of potential catastrophes keeps me awake for at least five minutes every night. That may not sound like much, but I value my sleep. It's hard-earned, and extremely well-deserved. Especially since I started working at The Sugarloaf Bakery.

I look at my screen again. There are already too many messages to keep up with, and I have to be at work in half an hour. I'll leave them to get on with it. Maybe they need one good chat to get it out of their systems. After that, we can adopt a more businesslike stance and keep communications to an absolute minimum.

> *Georgia: I have to go to work now. I'll catch up with you all later.*

No one responds. They're too busy exchanging Isabella stories. Most of the women seem to have heard the more extreme ones, but a couple of them are asking for more details. I sigh and close my phone, but not before switching it to silent. It looks as though it's going to be an extremely long seven months.

Chapter Three

'Good morning!' says Lily cheerfully as I open the bakery door.

'I wouldn't count on it,' I say, pulling off my jacket and tossing it at the row of pegs. It misses and lands on the floor in a crumpled heap.

'You'll get it one of these days,' she says with an encouraging smile.

'I know I will. It's all in the wrist. I almost hit my target yesterday, but this jacket is slightly thicker, and the extra weight threw me off.'

'You sound exactly like your sister.'

I frown at her. 'I thought we had an agreement about that.'

'Sorry,' she says. 'I usually remember, but sometimes the pair of you make it difficult. I'm sure you'll hit one of the pegs soon.'

'I'm not aiming for just one of the pegs – I'm aiming for mine. If a thing's worth doing, it's worth doing properly.'

'When are we taking down that New Girl sticker?' she asks. 'Or at least scribbling over it and writing something more permanent?'

I pick up my jacket and hang it on the correct peg. 'Don't you dare! The only thing that keeps me going on Isabella's more difficult days is the knowledge that this peg is temporary. No employee who's used it has stayed here for long. And that's exactly how it should be.'

'You've been working here for quite a while,' Lily points out. 'But only part-time.'

She switches on the coffee machine. 'That's technically true, but we've had to ask you for extra cover so often, it may as well be full –'

I hold up my hand. 'Let me stop you right there! This is not and never will be a full-time job. It's a stepping-stone on my way to something else. If I didn't believe that, I'd curl up in a corner and die.'

She smiles. 'Some people might take that personally, but not me. I've enjoyed having you working here, and I'm not anxious to lose you. Even if we're only a stop on your journey to your final destination, I'm happy you've chosen to spend some time with us.'

'It was more Isabella's choice than mine. But thank you. It's been a lot of fun.'

'We aren't Martine's,' she says, handing me a carton of milk, 'but we do our poor best.'

I pull a horrified face. 'Just as I thought those memories were fading, you have to bring them up again. I nearly had to go into therapy after working in that awful clothes shop. Only the fact that Isabella is too mean to include private health care for her employees has prevented me from seeking counselling.'

'You appear to have dealt with it very well,' she says. 'Isabella and I were saying only the other day how nicely you've fitted in here. Our customers won't know what to do if you leave. Who will advise them about their cake and coffee choices?'

I finish frothing the milk and pour it carefully over the espresso. 'I have them pretty well trained by now. They know not to order a plum slice with a flat white because it's too bland, or to risk a Victoria sponge and black coffee because the bitterness overwhelms the delicate sweetness of the cake. And I can still pop in now and then to make sure things are running smoothly.'

'We'd be very grateful,' she says. 'We've only run this bakery for ten years, so we're almost complete beginners.'

'So I tell Isabella whenever I see her. Speaking of whom, where is she? Has she overslept again?'

'She's having her hair cut,' says Lily. 'She'll be in soon. By the way, I've set up that messaging group you asked for.'

'I know you have. My phone hasn't stopped pinging all morning.'

'You can mute the notifications if they're bothering you.'

'But what if it's something important, and they need an immediate answer?'

Lily surveys me with amusement. 'You're taking this chief bridesmaid's job far more seriously than I expected.'

I help myself to a meringue. 'I wouldn't say that. But when I agree to do something, I like to do it properly. And there are so many things that could go wrong. What if someone stands up during the wedding ceremony and objects? It's very possible one of Jon's relatives may make a last-ditch attempt to save him. There may be a massive family feud over the seating arrangements, or Isabella may say the wrong name during the vows. You know how scatter-brained she can be. That's why I tried to refuse the assignment when she first asked me.'

'So she told me. But you agreed in the end.'

'Only because she wouldn't shut up about it. And because she offered me extra chocolate souffles.'

Lily selects an orange spice macaron and takes a bite. 'I don't believe a word of it. About you trying to refuse the job, I mean, not the chocolate souffle part. I have no trouble believing that. You just wanted to make Isabella beg.'

I give her a reluctant smile. 'It may not be too awful.'

'It will be wonderful,' she says. 'It's lovely that you two have such a good relationship these days.'

'I wouldn't go that far. But we don't fight as much as we used to. That may have something to do with the fact Isabella no longer lives at home, so there's less for us to fight about.'

'There's more to it than that,' she says. 'You coming to work at this bakery was the best thing that ever happened to you both.'

'To Issy, perhaps. The jury's still out on me. But I like most of our customers, and you and Abby are anyone's idea of perfect work colleagues.'

'Thank you.' She takes a sip of her drink. 'Delicious, as always. I hope you don't leave too soon. Our customers have grown used to a certain standard of hot drinks. Isabella and I can make perfectly acceptable coffee, but we can never get it as good as yours. What's your secret?'

'I could tell you, but then I'd have to kill you. Speaking of coffee, I just have time to clean the machine before the Silver Surfers arrive.'

'Make sure you keep your phone out of sight when Isabella gets here,' says Lily. 'This chat group is supposed to be top secret, and she's surprisingly observant when you don't want her to be.'

'I've changed my code in case she knows the old one, and I'll keep it switched to silent while I'm at work. I suggest you do the same.'

She pulls out her phone and switches it on. 'Are you serious? That's what we're calling the group – The Flour Girls?'

'Not my idea,' I say. 'I wanted a more businesslike name – one that expressed how important it is to get this thing done properly and to a high standard.'

'Isabella should be touched you're so committed to this.'

'I don't want anything to go wrong,' I say. 'It's essential to get her safely married off. Otherwise, she might decide to come back home. I live in constant dread of that.'

She smiles. 'Isabella has been living in her own flat for more than a year. I don't think you have too much to worry about.'

'A year is nothing. You know how volatile my sister can be. I often wake at three in the morning wondering whether I've heard her key in the door. She's always so impulsive. She may decide at any moment she's had enough of living by herself and doing all her own cooking and cleaning. That's when she'll realise how easy she had it when she lived with us. From there, it's only a small step to her selling her flat to the highest bidder and slinking back home, and then we'll never get rid of her.'

'I think Jon might have something to say to that,' says Lily.

'Not if they're not yet married. When he and Isabella first got together, I thought he might exercise a steadying influence on her, but he's been a huge disappointment in that regard. He thinks everything she does is wonderful and lets her get away with far more than is good for her. But if we can get her down the aisle and pass her over to him permanently, all that may change. So, that's what I'm determined to do, even if I have to lock the church doors to prevent her escaping.'

She drains her mug. 'There's very little danger of that. I've never seen Isabella as happy as she's been since she and Jon got together.'

'She has been annoyingly cheerful since meeting him,' I agree. 'And just when I thought she couldn't become any more irritating, she went and got herself engaged. The prospect of the next seven months is almost unbearable. I'll need years of counselling to get over it.'

Lily doesn't look as sympathetic as I'd hoped. 'You'll have a fantastic time. We all will. Isabella will be so excited with whatever it is the Flour Girls end up planning for her.'

'Are you sure this isn't a mistake?' I ask. 'She may not want any surprises.'

'She'll love it.'

'I'll take your word for it. But if she doesn't, I'll drop you in it quicker than Bernie can eat a biscuit. I'll tell her you set up the whole thing, and you threatened to fire me if I refused to go along with it.'

'Isabella won't believe that,' she says. 'She insists all hirings and firings go directly through her.'

'Then I'll say you threatened me with a written warning.'

'Again, she won't believe you. Written warnings are her thing, not mine.'

I finish wiping the nozzle and throw down the cloth. 'All I'm saying is that I intend to take full credit for everything that goes right and disclaim all responsibility for anything that goes wrong.'

'Duly noted,' she says. 'I'm not too worried. Isabella isn't one to insist on everything being perfect. She just wants to get married to the person she loves, surrounded by all her friends and family.'

'Not good enough. If my name is to be anywhere near this wedding, it needs to be a complete success. I have a reputation to uphold.'

Lily looks less impressed than I'd hoped. 'If you say so. I'm glad you've cleaned that machine, by the way. The Silver Surfers are headed this way, and it looks as though there are more of them than usual.'

Chapter Four

The door opens a minute later, and the Silver Surfers pile in, talking and laughing. I do a quick headcount to check we have enough milk for everyone. Bernie is with them as always, and I know we have lactose-free milk for his puppuccino because I restocked it three days ago.

'It's a cold one out there!' Mabel greets us, pulling off her bright pink coat to reveal a vivid green two-piece beneath. 'I almost called for a taxi, but Edie insisted the mutt was dying for a walk, so I gave in as usual. If I go down with double pneumonia in the next few days, we'll know exactly who's to blame.'

'If you go down with double pneumonia,' says her sister, 'it will be because you insist on prowling around the house in the early hours looking for snacks.'

'So does Bernie!' protests Mabel. 'And you never tell him off for it. I almost tripped over him in the pantry the other night. There was I, doing my best to act like a responsible housemate and not wake anyone up. Bernie didn't have any such qualms. He was sniffing around his food bowl in case it had magically refilled itself during the night.'

'I hope you didn't give him anything,' says Phyllis. 'Edie says it upsets his stomach if he eats at the wrong time of day.'

'Nothing upsets that dog's stomach!' proclaims Mabel. 'He has the digestion of a teenager. I wish I still did.'

'I'll make you a pot of tea,' I say before she and her sister can start arguing. 'The usual for everyone else?'

'Go on, then,' says Phyllis. 'It's easier than thinking of something new to order.'

'How do you remember what we all like?' Barb asks me. 'Do you write it all down in a special notebook?'

'I've memorised our regular customers' orders. Don't forget I've been working here for quite a while.'

'I wouldn't have said we were in here often enough to count as regulars,' says Ivy.

Lily and I exchange smiles. If these women spent any more time in our bakery, they'd have to start paying business rates.

I make the drinks while Lily sorts out the cake orders. It takes a while, as there are so many of them.

'Is this a special meeting?' I ask as I hand Phyllis her latte and Mabel her pot of Earl Grey.

'Not really,' says Barb. 'I told Mary I was coming here this morning. She mentioned it to Mabel and Edie when she bumped into them, and they told Ivy.'

'The village grapevine!' says Lily. 'It's a powerful thing when used correctly. And Honeywell has a particularly effective one.'

'Better than a telegraph system,' agrees Phyllis. 'How else would we get all our news and find out who's doing what? It isn't as though the national papers are interested in our goings-on.'

'There's the village website,' I say. 'That's always good for keeping in touch with current activities.'

'And the arts centre,' says Lily. 'Almost everyone is in there each week for one reason or another.'

'I know I am,' says Mabel, taking a large bite of her plum slice and nodding approvingly.

'Me too,' says Ivy. 'There are so many classes to choose from that I've had to limit myself or I'd be out every single night.'

'What's wrong with that?' asks Barb. 'I love keeping busy. I don't have anyone to talk to at home except my cat, so this place and the art classes are the best parts of my week.'

'I'm glad our bakery is such a valuable part of your life,' says Lily.

Mabel looks around the cafe. 'Where's the third musketeer?'

'Abby?' asks Lily.

'I'd almost forgotten about her!' says Mabel. 'She's usually in the kitchen making delicious plum slices. I meant the other one.'

'She who must not be named?' I ask. 'I'm glad that's finally catching on. I've been trying to make it happen for years.'

'Who must not be named?' asks Isabella's voice, and I sigh. I might have known she'd appear the minute we started talking about her.

'The new prime minister of Liechtenstein,' I tell her.

Isabella shrugs off her coat and hangs it on her peg. I notice she doesn't try to compete with my amazing coat-throwing skills in front of all these people. I don't blame her. She has terrible aim. I have no idea how she beats Jon at crazy golf. My private theory is that he allows her to win, but I don't often say that to her because it inevitably leads to a long diatribe about the art and science of wielding a golf club and dealing with the loop-the-loop.

'Why are you discussing Liechtenstein's prime minister?' she asks.

'I thought Georgia was talking about Isabella,' says Phyllis, starting on her second piece of key lime pie. I make a mental note to cut off supplies if she says anything further to embarrass me.

'Isabella is the fourth musketeer, not the third,' says Ivy.

'Poor Abby,' says Isabella. 'Tucked away in the kitchen all day like Cinderella – with none of you remembering she's there.'

'Whereas she's the powerhouse of our entire operation,' says Lily.

Isabella picks up a plate and dumps a couple of doughnuts onto it. 'Abby's a valuable part of the process, but we're all a cog in this particular machine. Some of the cogs are equally – if not more – important than others, while different cogs are less essential.'

She looks at me when she says this. I return the stare, waiting for her to blink first. She always does, especially when she has a plateful of cake demanding her attention.

Mabel laughs. 'When are you two going to admit you both do a great job here?'

'When Isabella gives up doughnuts for Lent,' I say.

Isabella's mouth is too full for her to make one of her usual snarky answers, so I seize the opportunity to change the subject before she can swallow.

'We've been talking about the arts centre,' I say. 'It seems to be pretty popular with everyone here.'

'I thought I might try memoir-writing next,' says Barb. 'Phyllis has signed up for that too.'

'Great idea,' says Lily. 'I'd like to read them when they're finished.'

'I've signed up for a dance class next month,' says Ivy. 'It's called *Dance like no one's watching!*'

'That sounds amazing,' says Isabella. 'Maybe I'll sign up for that one too.'

'No need,' I say. 'I used to see you gyrating around the living room when you thought you had the house to yourself. If you take my advice, you'll sign up for a class called *Dance like someone definitely is watching, and they're judging you for making them feel seasick.*'

'How about you?' Lily asks Mrs Ogilvie. 'Are you taking any classes at the moment?'

'I'm starting a macramé class next week,' she says. 'I'm very much looking forward to it.'

'Are you going along too?' I ask Mabel.

'I considered it, but apparently the mutt doesn't enjoy being left by himself, so he would prefer us to select different classes. It's surprising how many opinions that animal has, and how many of them happen to coincide with what my sister wants.'

'What are you doing instead?' asks Isabella.

'I thought I'd try my hand at pottery as soon as I've finished chair yoga. I have a feeling I'll turn out to be extremely talented at pottery. If not, I'll tell everyone I've done my pieces in the modern style, and they don't understand art. It's what most artists these days seem to do.'

'What will you be making?' I ask her. 'Pots and vases?'

Mabel pulls a face. 'Goodness, I hope not! I'm hoping we'll get on to the human figure fairly quickly. I'm planning to make some lovely statues to put in our garden this summer.'

'Like gnomes?' asks Lily.

'Only if they don't turn out as well as I hope. I'd like to make a couple of models to represent me and Edie. I plan to call them Double Trouble.'

'And I've already told you I refuse to display some ridiculous statue of me for everyone to laugh at,' says Mrs Ogilvie.

Mabel shrugs. 'Then I'll put the statues in my half of the garden. The mutt and I can have tea out there and admire them, while you sit stubbornly in the house and sulk.'

'You could make a statue of Bernie,' I suggest.

'No, I couldn't! We don't want him getting delusions of grandeur. It's bad enough that you've pandered to his vanity by making him your bakery mascot. His head would explode if I made him the subject of one of my artistic creations.'

Mrs Ogilvie sets down her cup of tea and turns to Isabella. 'I thought you were going to have Bernie's portrait painted? You mentioned it quite a while ago, and I've been wondering ever since when you plan to make a start.'

'I think I remember that conversation,' says Isabella with a faint blush. 'As I recall, it was only a suggestion. I don't believe we had any concrete plans.'

'You told us you were trying to decide whether to go for a full-length portrait or just a head shot,' says Mrs Ogilvie.

'That sounds like a concrete plan to me,' I chip in. 'What an excellent idea! You should move ahead quickly with that, Isabella, before you get too busy with the wedding plans.'

'How are the preparations going for that?' asks Ivy.

'Swimmingly,' says Isabella. 'My sister and Lily are in charge of most things, which means –'

'Not even close!' I interrupt before she can sweep on in her usual manner and commit me to more than she should. 'I've agreed to be your chief bridesmaid, as long as you come up with a less demeaning term for it. Abby is your other bridesmaid, and Lily is your maid of honour. We'll perform those duties to the best of our abilities, but we aren't organising your whole wedding for you. That's your job.'

'It's a bit of a grey area,' begins Isabella.

'It's entirely black and white.'

Ivy laughs. 'I love watching you two trying to get the better of each other.'

'I'm just clarifying the facts,' I say. 'My sister tends to blur the details. It's something I'd like her to overcome.'

'Georgia is supposed to be my chief bridesmaid,' says Isabella. 'If she doesn't want to be involved with all the duties that job normally entails, maybe we should change her title to simply bridesmaid.'

I pull out a carton of Bernie's milk and open the tab. 'We'll do no such thing. Chief is the only part of my title of which I approve. If I lose that, you'll be looking for someone else to carry your train for you.'

'We'll discuss it later,' she says.

'It will be a brief discussion. And completely one-sided.'

I scoop Bernie's foam into a paper cup and hand it to Mrs Ogilvie. 'There you go. Just the way he likes it.'

Mabel grins at Isabella. 'That's told you!'

Isabella sighs. 'It's very difficult working alongside a family member. But I believe it's made me a better person.'

'Not noticeably,' I say. 'So, about this portrait?'

Isabella casts me a look I have no difficulty in interpreting as a precursor to one of her written warnings. I give her my blandest smile in return.

'I'd think twice about that portrait if I were you,' Mabel advises us. 'No one needs to see the mutt's face whenever they walk into the bakery.'

I catch sight of Mrs Ogilvie's disappointed face and notice Isabella looking in the same direction.

'The portrait is a wonderful idea!' she says. 'I'm so glad you reminded me, Mrs Ogilvie. What with one thing and another, it's been a busy couple of years, and several things have slipped my mind.'

Mrs Ogilvie's face lights up. 'So, you'll arrange it soon?'

Isabella nods. 'We'll get around to it as quickly as possible.'

'It's up to you, of course,' says Mabel. 'And no doubt you know best how to run your own affairs. But don't come crying to me if you lose half your business over it. Just the thought of looking up and seeing that furry little face staring down at me is enough to put me right off my plum slices.'

Chapter Five

I arrive home from work absolutely exhausted. I've said it before, and I'll say it again – my job would be a million times easier without our customers. On the other hand, it would far less fun, so I wouldn't really trade. But I'm looking forward to dinner, a quiet evening, and a long hot bath before bed.

'There you are!' Mum greets me as I open the front door. 'I was about to call to remind you Isabella and Jon are eating with us tonight.'

I groan. 'I thought that was tomorrow.'

'They're driving down to Cornwall tomorrow to spend a few days with his parents,' she says. 'Jon wants them to get to know Isabella better before the wedding. They aren't in the best of health – especially Jon's mother – so they don't travel up here very often.'

'I wouldn't have thought it was the best idea to force someone who's not in the best of health to spend more time than necessary with Isabella.'

Mum smiles. 'Don't be so silly. They've met her a few times now, and Jon says they love her.'

This doesn't seem likely, but I'm too tired to argue.

'Do I have to eat dinner with you all?' I ask. 'Can't I take a tray up to my room?'

'Of course not. Issy has a long list of things she'd like to discuss with you.'

'I'll bet she has, but that wish is very much not mutual.'

'Have a shower and get changed,' she says. 'You'll feel much better for it.'

I consider making a dart for the door and driving over to the Red Lion for dinner. I can tell Nathan to pretend I'm not there if anyone calls. But Isabella is more than capable of guessing where I've gone and setting out in search of me. More likely, she'll send Jon, while she stays here in the warm, eating all the hors d'oeuvres. I saw a tray of mini sausage rolls in the fridge this morning. That decides it. Isabella isn't getting her hands on those.

I shower and change into a clean top. The one I was wearing today has several patches of white icing on it. I'm not opposed in principle to looking like a gingerbread person, but I'm not up for any of Isabella's very unfunny jokes this evening.

I arrive downstairs just as the doorbell rings.

'Can you get that?' calls Mum from the kitchen.

I open the door to find Isabella standing on the doorstep, beaming at me. Two men are standing behind her. I recognise the first one as my brother-in-law-to-be. I don't recognise the other. He's muffled up in a thick coat and scarf, and he has his hood up. I assume Isabella and Jon realise he's there, but it's possible they don't. Maybe they think he's someone I've invited.

That's how a lot of these scams succeed. People crash a wedding or special event by walking in behind a genuine guest, then spend the evening eating all the sausage rolls and rifling through the house for valuables. This thought makes me irrationally annoyed. I've had a long day, and most of those sausage rolls are mine.

'Who are you?' I demand.

Jon gestures for the man to step inside. I keep the door half-closed.

'I thought it was just the two of you,' I say.

'Georgia, this is Michael Reynolds,' says Isabella. 'Michael, this is my delightful sister, Georgia. Are you planning to let us in, or would you prefer us to freeze to death out here?'

I reluctantly open the door wide enough to admit all three of them.

'I was checking you knew who he was,' I say, taking the coat Jon hands me and slinging it over the banister rail.

'Very wise,' approves Jon. 'You never know who might turn up on your doorstep on a night like this. You can't afford to take any chances.'

'That's what I thought. Crime is supposed to be on the rise in rural areas.'

'How rude!' says Isabella. 'I only knocked over one traffic cone.'

'I wasn't talking about you. I wanted to make sure your companion was actually on tonight's guest list.'

I turn to face Michael. He's pulled off his coat and scarf and looks far less sinister than he did on the doorstep. He's just under six foot tall, with tousled brown wavy hair. I can't decide whether he's deliberately styled it that way or if it's the fault of his thick hood. His eyes are calm and steady, with a hint of humour lurking in their grey depths.

'Nice to meet you,' I say. 'Are you one of Jon's friends?'

'My best friend,' says Jon. 'Which is why he's kindly agreed to be my best man.'

'So, that's why you're here?' I ask.

Michael grins at me. 'Unless you have any family silver hanging around.'

'Our cutlery is all nickel-plated, and very, very well-used. Don't forget Isabella used to live here.'

Mum bustles into the hall. 'You're here!'

She swoops on Isabella and kisses her before hugging Jon.

'This is Michael,' says Isabella. 'Jon's best man.'

'How lovely,' says Mum. 'I've been looking forward to meeting you, Michael. I hope you like chicken chasseur?'

'It's one of my favourite meals,' he tells her.

Isabella catches sight of my face and laughs.

'You should have said you're allergic to all poultry dishes,' she tells Michael. 'My sister doesn't like the competition.'

'I've made plenty for everyone,' says Mum. 'Come into the living room. It's chilly out here.'

'Not as chilly as it is outside,' says Isabella. 'If Jon hadn't brought his ice scraper, I'd still be stuck to the car door handle.'

I refrain from telling her she's welcome to go and try the car door again and follow her into the living room, where Dad is sitting by the blazing log fire, reading a newspaper.

He jumps up when he sees us and kisses Isabella. He shakes Jon and Michael's hands and offers us all a drink.

'I thought you'd never ask,' says Isabella. 'I'd like a glass of ginger wine, please. A large one.'

'I'll take a ginger ale, if you have any,' says Jon. 'I have to drive later, and it's treacherous out there.'

Dad pours their drinks, and I turn to Michael. 'What can I get for you?'

'Are you sure?' he asks. 'I thought you hadn't yet decided whether I was a burglar.'

'The jury's still out on that. But Jon seems willing to vouch for you, so I'm prepared to give you the benefit of the doubt.'

'In that case, I'll have a whisky.'

I pour us both a drink, and he follows me over to the fire. 'I've heard a lot about you.'

'I get that quite often. My sister is fond of traducing my reputation all around the county.'

'She's only told me good things,' he says. 'As has Jon.'

'He's always so polite. I keep wondering when it will wear off. I'm fairly sure he's still terrified of our family and determined to stay on our good side. But that won't last.'

'I'm sorry to disappoint you,' says Jon, 'but I've never been scared of your family. You've all made me feel very welcome.'

'That's because my parents are so relieved to be getting one of us off their hands,' I say. 'The most expensive one too, which is a bonus.'

'Well, isn't this nice?' says Mum, taking the glass of sherry Dad hands her. 'All the family together for once. When you've finished your drink, Georgia, would you mind helping me dish up?'

'Certainly,' I say. 'I'll make sure Isabella gets that extra-small dinner plate Daisy painted for her birthday.'

'It's a side plate,' says Isabella.

'It's a dinner plate,' I insist. 'I measured it against our side plates, and it would give you an unfair advantage during any afternoon tea party. It's definitely supposed to be a dinner plate. And as your goddaughter made it for you, I'm sure you'll want to use it tonight.'

'You shouldn't tease her,' Mum tells me when we reach the kitchen. 'Isabella has a lot on her plate at the moment.'

'Not if I have anything to do with it.'

'Very funny. But I remember the lead-up to my wedding. It was surprisingly stressful, and I wasn't working full time like she is.'

'I'm working too,' I say. 'And you don't see me getting worn out with it all.'

'Maybe you will when it's your own wedding,' she says, handing me a colander. 'Can you please drain those vegetables and tip them into the serving dishes?'

I reach for the pan of beans. 'I don't intend to get married. It seems like a lot of unnecessary stress. Although eloping has always seemed quite fun.'

'A few months ago, I'd have said you were wrong,' says Mum. 'But now we're in the thick of it, I'm starting to wonder. And this isn't even a big wedding. Only around one hundred people so far.'

'That feels like a big wedding to me. I'm not sure I even know one hundred people.'

'It all adds up,' she says. 'There's the family on both sides, and all of Isabella's and Jon's friends. And she's planning on inviting half your customers.'

'That's because they'd invite themselves if she didn't. I can't imagine the members of the Silver Surfers or the poker club agreeing to be left out of things.'

'I've asked Isabella for the final guest list,' she says. 'But you know what she's like. She keeps changing her mind.'

'I thought you weren't getting involved? Isabella told me she wanted you and Dad to come as guests so you could celebrate finally getting rid of her.'

Mum picks up the potato masher. 'Could you please decant the gravy into that jug? Isabella said she wants us to enjoy the day, and so we will. But I'd like to keep an eye on everything and make sure it's going to plan. Isabella has a terrible habit of leaving things until the last minute. I don't believe she's even thought about dress-shopping yet.'

'She hasn't told me what she wants me to wear either. She'd better not try to palm me off with some monstrosity just to make herself look good.'

'Isabella would never do that,' she says. 'You're both very nice-looking girls. Neither of you will outshine the other.'

'I'm not talking about outshining her,' I say. 'But I refuse to prance up the aisle wearing something that looks like a Victorian lampshade.'

'I'm sure you'll both find the perfect dress,' she says. 'Can you carry those plates through to the dining room and ask everyone to take their places? And please try to make Michael feel welcome. It must be nerve-wracking coming to dinner when everyone else knows each other, and you're the odd one out.'

Chapter Six

Michael may be the odd one out, but he doesn't seem particularly nervous. Mum has placed him between me and Isabella.

'I'm sorry about that,' she apologises to him when we're all sitting down. 'I don't know what I was thinking when I sat you between my two daughters. You'll have to do the best you can. And there's plenty more food in the kitchen.'

'If you're referring to Isabella,' says Michael, 'I've eaten with her before. She, Jon and I had dinner together only last week.'

'Did you have to pick up a takeaway on the way home?' I ask. 'Jon should have warned you in advance. Isabella sits there, looking all sweet and innocent. The next thing you know, your chips have disappeared, and Isabella is looking like a particularly contented python after an enormous meal.'

'We didn't have chips,' says Isabella. 'And it wasn't my fault Michael couldn't finish his second dessert.'

'I don't even recall ordering it,' says Michael. 'But you assured me I did, so I put it down to a temporary memory lapse.'

She helps herself to a large portion of potato. 'Georgia's a fine one to talk! I grew up having to master the art of speed-eating. The first few years of my life were fine. Then she came along, and life became a constant struggle for survival. Due to possessing particularly neglectful parents, I had to adopt the rules of the jungle if I wanted to stand a chance of growing into the healthy and balanced adult I am today.'

Jon pats her hand. 'Never mind. It's only a few months until I rescue you from all that. I'll have it written into our vows that we'll never live more than fifty metres from a food delivery route.'

'Are the pair of you writing your own vows?' asks Mum. 'How sweet.'

'Of course, we are,' says Isabella. 'It's important to get things clear right from the start. I realise wedding vows aren't legally binding. But they're made in front of witnesses, which ought to mean they're more difficult to wriggle out of.'

'I suggest you impose a word limit,' I tell Jon. 'If I know Isabella, her list of vows will increase each month, until we have to add an extra hour onto the ceremony. The vicar won't like that. His fee is only supposed to cover the regular wedding service.'

'That shows what you know!' says Isabella. 'Jon and I aren't getting married in church, so the vicar can rest easy.'

'No one tells me anything,' I say. 'When did that happen?'

'We planned to tell you all about it this evening. We're getting married at Willowmere Hall! They've had a cancellation for the middle of August, and we swooped in and signed up for that date!'

'An actual cancellation?' I ask suspiciously, 'or did you nobble the people whose booking it really was?'

She reaches for the dish of beans. 'What a suspicious mind you have. I wouldn't dream of doing such a thing. As it happens, the happy couple has decided on a destination wedding in Mauritius. Apparently, it's the dry season there in August, and it will make it more convenient for their honeymoon.'

'But far more expensive for their guests,' says Dad.

'Maybe they come from a rich family,' says Isabella, 'and the cost isn't a problem. The important thing is they called the hotel and cancelled just as Jon and I were looking around. It's almost impossible to hold your wedding at Willowmere Hall. They're usually booked up for at least three years ahead.'

'So, why were you looking around in the first place?' I ask. 'Were you planning on postponing your wedding until they could fit you in?'

Jon takes Isabella's hand. 'Not a hope. I'm anxious to get her down the aisle before she changes her mind.'

She beams back at him. 'I won't do that. But people should stop saying down the aisle. I'll be walking along the lawn towards the rose-draped arbour. And towards the start of our new future.'

'We were at Willowmere Hall because I've been project managing some of the hotel's recent renovations,' says Jon. 'It never occurred to me that Isabella might like to be married there. But I noticed a wedding brochure lying around, so I picked it up and took it home with me. It looked like an amazing place to get married, and Isabella agreed at once when she saw the pictures. So, I asked the manager if we could take a quick tour. As luck would have it, we were standing next to the rose arbour when the cancellation phone call came through. It was snowing, so there were no actual roses, but he assured us there will be plenty by August.'

'Are you certain you want roses?' I ask. 'I imagined the pair of you taking your vows under an awning of marshmallows.'

'Don't even think about it!' says Jon as Isabella opens her mouth to speak. 'The birds would strip it bare in seconds. And think of the mess if it rained.'

'That's a point,' I say. 'What happens if there's a thunderstorm? Do we have to stand outside getting wet? If so, you'll need to offer free flu shots to all your guests the week before. It seems only fair.'

'Willowmere Hall has a beautiful room inside, overlooking the gardens,' says Jon. 'It won't be quite the same, but it should still be pretty good. And I'd marry Isabella in a broom cupboard if I had to. Or in a leaky tent in a hailstorm.'

'Either of those could easily be arranged,' I say. 'Just say the word. As the chief bridesmaid, I consider it my duty to make all reasonable adjustments to the arrangements.'

'We're getting married at Willowmere Hall,' says Isabella. 'We've already put down a deposit, so it's all sorted. Thank you for your kind offer, though. I'll bear it in mind for when it's your turn.'

I pull a face. 'If I get married – and it's a huge if – it won't be in a garden full of roses and marshmallows. I'm not sure where the ceremony will take place, but somewhere far more interesting than that. While my fiancé and I are skydiving, perhaps, or in a haunted lighthouse in the middle of a thunderstorm.'

'You appear to have given this some thought,' says Michael, passing me a dish of carrots.

'Not really. I'm just saying I don't want to go down the conventional route. I'm a little surprised Isabella has chosen to do that. I expect it's Jon's influence. He's a bit of a stick-in-the-mud.'

'It comes of being a project manager,' says Jon. 'We're all dull and reliable and obsessed with colour-coded timelines. It's too late to change me now.'

'I don't want you to change,' says Isabella. 'You're perfect just as you are.'

I groan. 'The sooner we get you two married, the better. All this lovey-dovey stuff is unnatural. It will soon wear off when you wake up to the realities of married life. You'll be filing for divorce in no time.'

They beam at each other, clearly not taking any of my words of wisdom on board. I give up. There's no talking to people who think they know it all. I decide to concentrate on my meal instead.

'Don't listen to her,' Mum advises Isabella. 'Your father and I have been married for more than forty years, and we're still very happy.'

'Never more so than when your eldest born finally moved out?' I ask.

'It's your turn to fly the nest now,' Isabella tells me. 'Mum and Dad deserve a bit of peace after all these years.'

'I'm working on it. But you'll have to offer me more hours at the bakery before I can afford a place as nice as yours.'

'Or you could open your own bakery,' suggests Jon.

'No, she couldn't!' objects Isabella. 'Not in this area, at least.'

I help myself to more potatoes. 'Are you afraid of the competition? You can rest easy. I have no intention of setting up a rival business while your attention is distracted. Running a bakery is your thing, not mine.'

'But you work in one,' says Michael.

'Temporarily. It's important that everyone is very clear about that.'

'And Isabella's mind won't be elsewhere for long,' says Mum. 'By September, all this wedding stuff will seem like a dim and distant memory.'

'I hope not,' says Isabella. 'I want people to be still talking about my wedding ten years from now.'

'At least you have a venue booked,' I say. 'I was starting to think you'd never get around to it, and you'd end up being married on a street corner.'

'So, what's next?' asks Mum. 'The dress?'

'Dresses plural,' I say. 'I refuse to have mine selected as an afterthought.'

'It's a pity we can't recreate our triumph from the fundraising ball a few years ago,' says Isabella. 'Lily, Victoria and I went as the three Graces. We were a smash hit. We didn't win a prize, but that was because the Silver Surfers got together and went as the cast of Cinderella. Mavis Sotherby made a wonderful Prince Charming.'

'Poor Victoria tore her costume and ended up dressed as Jack and the Beanstalk,' adds Mum.

Isabella gives a snort of laughter. 'I'd forgotten that! And Matthew still chose to be with her. It must have been love.'

'Would you still want to be with Isabella if she turned up at your wedding dressed as Jack?' I ask Jon.

He smiles. 'She could come as the troll under the bridge, and I wouldn't care.'

'That's the Billy Goats Gruff,' I say. 'You're mixing up your fairy tales.'

'I felt like Red Riding Hood the first time I met Jon,' says Isabella. 'There I was, tripping along the high street with my box of cakes –'

'And literally tripping over with them,' I say. 'Lily told me the full story one day at the bakery. Our customers were most amused.'

'Lily needs to remember where her loyalties lie,' she says. 'As do several of our customers.'

'Why?' I ask. 'Do you propose to ban them?'

'The thought has crossed my mind once or twice. I can't give our customers a written warning – more's the pity – but I could bar them from the bakery for a few days.'

'Remind me again how you make that business work,' I say. 'I suppose it's mostly been Lily.'

'They make a great partnership,' says Mum. 'And I know you've been a wonderful addition to the team, Georgia.'

Isabella and I look at each other with the same horrified expression.

Jon laughs. 'Time to change the subject before one or both of them spontaneously combusts.'

'I'm just saying how nice it is to see them getting along so well at last,' says Mum. 'But I promise not to mention it again tonight. Is everyone ready for dessert? I've made an apple pie and a sticky toffee pudding, so no one will go hungry. Long years of experience have taught me that a good choice of desserts is the secret ingredient for a peaceful family evening.'

Chapter Seven

It isn't until we're sitting in the living room drinking coffee that I have time to talk to Michael properly. Most of the dessert course was taken up with Isabella's enthusiastic description of the flowers she plans to have at her wedding, and the existential significance of various colour palettes.

'So, what do you do when you're not working in the bakery and acting as a volunteer wedding planner?' Michael asks me.

'I'm not the wedding planner. I'm far too smart to have fallen for that. I've agreed to be the chief bridesmaid. That's the extent of my duties.'

'I'm not too familiar with the duties of a chief bridesmaid,' he says. 'Never having been one. What are you expected to do?'

'As far as I can tell, I have to help Isabella with all her plans, however ridiculous they may be, and keep the other bridesmaids in order.'

'Isn't there only one other bridesmaid?' he asks.

'Yes, but Isabella's also having a maid of honour and a flower girl. They'll need keeping under control too.'

'The maid of honour is Lily, isn't it?' he asks. 'I met her a couple of months ago at Isabella's flat.'

'That's right. She's Isabella's business partner, and Daisy is her daughter. She'll make a beautiful flower girl. She's old enough to know what to do. Her younger brother is going to be a ring bearer.'

'How does he feel about that?' asks Michael.

'It's difficult to tell. I believe some sort of bribe has been employed, but Isabella won't tell me what it was in case I demand the same thing.'

He laughs. 'It sounds as though your heart isn't in this.'

I relent. 'I don't really mind. It was nice of Issy to ask me. But I'm not really one for dressing up in frilly clothes and posing for endless photographs.'

'Maybe it won't be frilly,' he suggests.

'I wouldn't bet against Isabella continuing the fairy tale theme and deciding to dress me up as Little Bo Peep.'

'Isn't that a nursery rhyme?'

'That makes it even worse. It gives her far more possibilities to choose from. And she's bound to go for one of the duller ones, rather than something exciting like Little Miss Muffet.'

'With you as –?' he asks.

'The spider, of course. At least I could reuse that outfit at Halloween. I'm unlikely to want to wear some huge meringue-like monstrosity again. Which is ironic, as meringues are some of my favourite cakes.'

'Isabella said you'll get to choose your own dress,' he consoles me. 'So, you'll have the chance to veto anything you hate.'

'Isabella says a lot of things. But she usually ends up getting her own way.'

He looks at me in some amusement. 'I barely know you, but I wouldn't bet a month's salary on your giving way without a fight.'

'I wouldn't bet a month's salary on anything,' I say. 'Especially considering the amount my sister pays me. I need every penny of it to pay my bills. If it weren't for the perks of my current job, I'd have handed in my notice long ago.'

'What did you do before that?'

'I worked in a hideous dress shop in Christchurch. My employer was pretty hideous too. She had no people skills whatsoever, and she treated her staff like unpaid interns.'

'I take it that's not the case in your current job?'

'Isabella is a surprisingly good employer,' I admit. 'And Lily's there to bring her back to earth whenever she's struck by one of her more bizarre ideas.'

'I hardly dare ask,' he says.

'Last autumn, Isabella decided we should do something for Oktoberfest. You know – the German beer festival. The bakery isn't licensed to sell alcoholic drinks, but Isabella thought we could all dress up as Bavarian barmaids and serve pretzels and bratwurst. Goodness knows why. Thankfully, Lily put her foot down, so I didn't have to.'

'Evidently, your sister likes to be creative,' he says.

'You don't have to be polite. My sister is a walking hazard sign.'

'And yet she seems to run a successful business.'

'It's a mystery,' I say. 'To be fair, half the inhabitants of Honeywell are just as eccentric. Maybe that's why the bakery does so well. That, and the fact everyone loves cake.'

'Speaking of which,' says Isabella, walking past carrying a box of mint chocolate thins and setting it down on the coffee table, 'we have to decide what to do about my wedding cake.'

'*You* have to decide,' I say. 'That isn't one of the bridesmaid's duties.'

'I told you up front those duties would be flexible – just as they are in the bakery. Lily and I perform any and all tasks required of us. We don't refuse to clean up Bernie's puppuccinos when he's been a little too over-enthusiastic with them, simply because we're successful business owners.'

'No, you tell me to do it. And then you tell me I've done it wrong.'

'Staff training is crucial,' she says. 'It's the key to any well-run business. That may be why Cath struggled so much with Martine's.'

'Is that the clothes shop where you used to work?' Michael asks me.

'It is. To be fair to Cath, it wasn't so much a lack of staff training that caused the place to run at a loss. It was the staff she employed – by which I mean me. I can't pretend my heart was entirely in the clothes-selling business.'

'Especially those particular clothes,' agrees Isabella. 'They looked as though they'd been designed by a blind-folded contestant on some bizarre reality sewing show.'

'Cath forced us to model them sometimes,' I say gloomily. 'Lucinda still has a photo of me wearing an emerald-green jumpsuit, with one leg longer than the other. It was confusingly labelled as Safari Chic.'

Isabella gives a crack of laughter. 'Why have I never seen that picture?'

'Because I told Lucinda that if you ever laid eyes on it, I'd post one on Instagram of her wearing a burnt-orange, faux-leather pinafore dress with the word VIBE spelled out across the front in sequins.'

'And yet you refused to wear a simple Bavarian outfit,' she says. 'The workings of your mind are a complete mystery to me.'

'Coffee?' says Mum, bustling in with a tray. 'What are you all talking about?'

'You should have asked Georgia to make the coffee,' says Isabella. 'She's surprisingly good at it.'

'She's also off duty,' I say. 'She has to be at work by eight o'clock tomorrow morning, while certain other staff members are jaunting off on their holidays.'

'Would you say jaunting?' asks Isabella.

'I would.'

'I'd say it was more gallivanting, but you may be right. I'll have to ask Jon. He's the one doing most of the driving, so it's up to him to pick which style suits our journey best. Maybe we'll go with zooming.'

'Not in this weather,' says Mum. 'You will be careful on those roads, won't you? They only salt the larger ones, and there's more snow forecast tonight.'

'I'll drive slowly,' promises Jon. 'If need be, we can find somewhere to stay for the night on the way there.'

'Or we could sleep in the car,' says Isabella. 'I've always wanted to do that.'

Jon catches Mum's anxious look and laughs. 'I promise I'll look after her. And I'm not sleeping in the car. There's barely enough room for one, let alone two of us, to stretch out.'

'You could send ahead Isabella on the train,' I suggest. 'And meet her there tomorrow night.'

'No, he couldn't,' says Isabella. 'I've seen *Murder on the Orient Express*. I was too scared to take a train for years after I saw that. Jon and I will be fine driving down there together. We aren't as irresponsible as you think, Mum.'

'I don't think you're irresponsible,' says Mum. 'Just a little prone to act without thinking first.'

Isabella drops a kiss on the top of her head. 'But Jon isn't. Stop worrying about me all the time and turn your attention to Georgia instead.'

'I'd prefer she didn't,' I say. 'I'm capable of sorting out my life without anyone's help.'

'What do you plan to do when you finish working at the bakery?' Michael asks me. 'You said it was only a temporary job.'

'I have some ideas, but I'm not quite sure yet. How about you? What do you do?'

'I'm a civil engineer. Jon and I met soon after we graduated from university. I was working on a building in Southampton, and he was the project manager. We spent several weeks working there, and the pair of us hit it off, so we stayed in touch. I moved to this area last summer, so we've seen more of each other than when I lived in London.'

'You can't paint, can you?' I ask, suddenly remembering one of my more pressing problems.

'You mean houses?'

'I mean dogs.'

He raises an eyebrow. 'What kind of dogs were you hoping I could paint – and what colour were you expecting me to paint them?'

'I don't mean painting the dogs themselves. I mean painting pictures of them. One dog in particular.'

'He's a cavoodle called Bernie,' says Isabella. 'Georgia has kindly undertaken the task of getting his portrait painted in order to relieve me of that duty. At least, I hope she has. I really don't have time for anything extra at the moment.'

'Georgia wouldn't be doing it for you,' I say. 'She'd be doing it for the elderly woman who's depending on a promise you once made, then promptly forgot all about.'

'It was supposed to be a joke,' she pleads. 'I didn't expect her to take it so seriously.'

'Well, she did. So, someone has to sort it out for her.'

'I'm sorry to say I've never painted anything more complicated than my bedroom walls,' says Michael. 'How about you, Jon?'

'Isabella's already asked me. I can't even draw a recognisable stick person. The boys are happy to give it the portrait a go, but I wouldn't depend on anyone recognising the dog in question when they've finished.'

'How are the boys?' I ask.

'Thriving. They've both shot up at least a foot during the past year. They're about to start secondary school, and they're excited about that. Ali is back at work now and doing much better. She's just had an offer accepted on a house with a much larger garden. Everything seems to be working out well for them.'

'Will the boys be in the wedding?' I ask.

He laughs. 'As page boys, you mean? Isabella suggested it, but the idea didn't go down too well, even when she offered to let them dress up as secret agents, complete with earpieces and briefcases. I'm sure we'll find a role they're happy with. We've promised not to make them dress up in dinner jackets or anything they aren't comfortable in.'

He looks at his watch. 'We should be going. Isabella and I have an early start tomorrow, and we have to drop Michael off on our way home tonight.'

'I'd love you all to stay longer,' says Mum. 'But I think you're wise. You need a good night's sleep before your journey.'

'Thanks for letting me into the house,' says Michael as I hand him his scarf and coat. 'I'd have spent a cold evening sitting on the doorstep waiting for my ride home if you hadn't.'

'You're welcome,' I say. 'I was just being cautious. I'll recognise you another time.'

He smiles at me. 'I'd offer to walk you home, except you're already here.'

'And staying here. I'm not half as keen on snow as I was when I was younger.'

'I am!' says Isabella. 'I'm hoping there'll be time for us to make a snowman when we get home.'

'Good luck!' I tell Jon, who laughs as he walks her to the car.

'Don't miss your ride,' I say to Michael. 'Isabella is quite capable of forgetting how many people she brought with her and driving off into the night without a second thought.'

He shakes hands with Mum and Dad. 'Thank you both for a great evening. It was lovely to meet you both. You too, Georgia. I very much look forward to seeing you again.'

Chapter Eight

To my relief, the messaging group calms down a little after the first week. I'm glad I followed my instinct to allow them to blow off some steam before I gently turned their attention to more practical issues. It's amazing how many people see weddings as exciting and joyous occasions, rather than the nightmare of organisation and satin-based trauma they really are.

The next time I check in with the group, the talk has turned to the subject of a possible meet-up. I'm not sure why. They'll see each other at whatever they plan for Isabella's wedding. But when I mention this, I realise I'm in the minority, so I decide not to argue.

> Grace: *It sounds like fun, but it's a bit of a logistical problem. We all live in different places.*
>
> Meghan: *Maybe we could meet somewhere central – like London?*
>
> Natalie: *Is there a colour theme for this wedding that we should take into consideration for whatever we decide to do?*
>
> Georgia: *Isabella hasn't mentioned it, but that doesn't mean there won't be one. It would be just like her to*

forget to tell anyone about it until the day before. I'll ask her the next time I see her.

Grace: Can you also ask her if there's an overall theme?

Georgia: People have themes for weddings?

Alix: Of course! There are hundreds of possible wedding themes.

I almost drop my phone. What fresh hell is this?

Georgia: I thought the wedding itself was the theme?

There's a flurry of answers. I quickly skim through them. They all seem to be saying the same thing – the wedding is just the setting. The theme can be anything from fairytale castles to Jane Austen recreations to Pirates of the Caribbean extravaganzas.

Olivia: And that's just off the top of my head. Will does quite a bit of wedding photography. You wouldn't believe some of the themes he's told me about.

Natalie: We attended a regency-themed wedding last year. Luke and I had to wear period costumes. He looked very dashing, but I spent the whole evening worrying about falling out of my dress while we were dancing. That time period isn't nearly as glamorous as it seems in the movies.

Time to put a stop to this and lay down some guidelines before they all get too carried away.

Georgia: It definitely won't be a regency theme. In fact, I doubt there's a theme at all. Isabella's never mentioned anything about it, and she talks about her wedding non-stop.

Grace: Is the wedding being held at the bakery?

Georgia: What makes you ask that?

*Meghan: That was my first thought too. Hasn't Isabella
suggested it?*

*Georgia: Never. It's far too small for one thing, and I
doubt we're licensed for weddings. Isabella would
probably give me a written warning if I proposed any
such thing.*

This is a huge mistake. They're off again, talking about all the
written warnings they managed to collect while working at the
Sugarloaf. I try to interject a few times to bring them back to the
subject in hand, but it's no good.

These women don't have the faintest understanding of how
weddings are supposed to work. They're over-enthusiastic and
undisciplined, and worryingly prone to wandering off topic at the
slightest provocation. I mentally cross off wedding planner from
my list of possible future careers, then catch sight of the time and
grab my car keys.

I arrive at the bakery with fifteen seconds to spare, which I
count as a win.

'Sit down and catch your breath,' advises Lily. 'There's no
need to rush.'

'That's not what my sister says. She threatens a written
warning if I'm not standing at my post the moment our first
customer walks down the street.'

'Isabella isn't here yet. She called to say she has to sort
something out and will be a little late.'

'Of course, she did. And, being Isabella, she'll get away with
it. I don't suppose it occurred to you to tell her she's on her final
warning due to incessant lateness?'

Lily hands me a bag of coffee beans. 'I'm afraid it didn't. Your
sister doesn't take kindly to that sort of thing. As she's a part-
owner of the business, there isn't much I can do about it. Besides,
I arrive late or leave early far more often than she does, and
Isabella never says a word about it.'

I measure out the beans and drop them into the grinder. 'She probably welcomes the extra unsupervised time in the shop. Less competition for the almost-out-of-date cakes. What would you like to drink?'

'Cappuccino, please.'

'Coming up. I'll put a stopwatch on your foam if you like.'

'Not wedding bells?' she asks. 'That seems more appropriate.'

'I'm trying to avoid talk of this wedding for a couple of hours. Did you see this morning's group chat?'

She pulls out her phone. 'Goodness! I've missed a lot. Would you like to sum it up for me before Isabella arrives?'

'I'm not sure I could. It's mostly about dresses and themes and colour schemes.'

'I'm looking forward to it all,' says Lily. 'And so are you, really.'

She ignores my derisive laugh and carries on. 'Isabella has asked us to play two of the most important parts of her wedding. It's quite an honour, don't you think?'

'Aren't the bride and groom the two most important parts? There wouldn't be much of a wedding without them.'

She takes a sip of her drink. 'But Isabella wants us there to support her, and I intend to do my best to do just that. As I'm sure do you.'

'I don't like to fail at anything I set my mind to, so I suppose you're right. You'd better put your phone away before Isabella arrives. You know how she likes to appear just when she's least expected – or wanted! I can't think how she does it. Maybe the arts centre is offering some sort of tactical manoeuvring classes.'

She drops her phone into her bag. 'I can see some customers heading this way. Don't mention the chat group to them.'

'I'll be far too busy working to have time for gossiping with our customers,' I say virtuously. 'I leave all that to you and Isabella, while I get on with the actual work of running this place. By the way, you have part of a stopwatch on your top lip. It may be deliberate, in which case you should feel free to leave it there. But I thought you might like to know.'

Chapter Nine

'What ho!' Mabel greets us the moment she's through the door.

Our staff handbook doesn't contain instructions for dealing with customers who burst into the shop sounding like P G Wodehouse characters. I make a mental note to raise this omission with Isabella. The more things I can find to keep her busy during the coming months, the less time she'll have to bother me.

'Good morning,' I say. This feels like a nice, neutral greeting that will neither offend the customer nor end up earning me a written warning from the despot who currently employs me.

'It's snowing again,' says Mabel, pulling off her scarf and tossing it over the back of her usual chair. 'I offered to bring the mutt with me, but Edie thinks he has a slight chill, so she's keeping him in front of the fire for the afternoon. Goodness knows why! He seems fine to me. She's probably roasting him some lovely marshmallows at this very moment.'

'I could make you a hot chocolate with cream and marshmallows,' I offer.

'What a splendid thought. I don't suppose you could add a little something?'

'Like extra foam?' I ask, and she snorts.

'I meant something out of a bottle. You must keep some medicinal brandy or rum around the place. Isabella is always talking about your well-stocked first aid kit. I assume that's what she means.'

'She's never mentioned any bottles of spirits to me,' I say. 'Maybe she's already drunk them. I could add some cinnamon or nutmeg if you like. Or I could check her office to see whether she's hiding a bottle in there.'

'Good idea,' says Mabel, settling herself more comfortably into her chair. 'What do you say, Phyllis?'

'It doesn't matter what Phyllis says,' interrupts Lily. 'No one will be searching the medical kit or Isabella's office for anything. We'd have the licensing enforcement officers in here before you'd even opened the cap. Isabella and I would be lucky if we only got away with a massive fine.'

'The Red Lion treats its customers with far more respect,' says Phyllis.

'But they don't sell plum slices and meringues,' I say. 'And they don't make pretty pictures for you on the beer foam.'

'True,' says Mabel. 'And they're at least a five-minute walk from here. We'll stay and give you our custom today. But remember we have alternatives.'

Lily only laughs. I make two hot chocolates and add a picture of a bottle for Mabel and a smiley face for Phyllis.

'I hope that makes up in some small way for your disappointment,' I say, setting the mugs in front of them.

'I can't drink at the moment, anyway,' says Mabel. 'I had an ear infection last week, and I'm still on antibiotics. My GP threatened me with all sorts if I mixed them with alcohol. I don't know what the medical world is coming to. There was none of this nonsense when I was a girl. They handed out those things for everything that ailed you, then left you to get on with the rest of your life exactly as you pleased.'

'You drank brandy and rum when you were a girl?' I ask.

'I did not, Miss Impertinent! You know perfectly well I meant the antibiotics. But you're just like your sister. If she can twist anyone's words, she will.'

'My mother used to rub whisky on my gums when I was teething,' says Phyllis. 'Everyone did that with their babies in those days.'

'So they did,' says Mabel. 'I'll have to remember that the next time my dentures are chafing. I'm sure Edie keeps a bottle somewhere about the place, although she always denies it. She's more of a sherry drinker. I expect she's having one right now. She says it's the perfect drink for a winter's afternoon.'

'How about Bernie?' I ask.

'I wouldn't put it past her to offer him a quick snifter too. I've often been tempted to do the same at three in the morning when he's prowling around the house looking for someone to disturb. Usually me. Speaking of the mutt, Edie was asking me again at breakfast about this so-called portrait of him.'

'That's Isabella's project, not mine,' says Lily. 'I'm surprised your sister even remembered it. It happened so long ago. From what I remember, Mrs Ogilvie and Bernie were in the bakery one day, and Isabella made a joke about intending to have his portrait painted. Only Mrs Ogilvie didn't realise it was a joke, and she took it seriously. She thought it was an excellent idea. Isabella didn't have the heart to tell her the truth, so she brushed it off, and she's been kicking the can down the road ever since.'

'She'll have to stop kicking it now,' says Mabel. 'Edie's obsessed with the idea. She was telling the Silver Surfers all about this portrait at our last meeting. Maybe one of you can mention that to Isabella the next time you see her.'

'I'd love to,' I say. 'But she seems to have delegated this particular task to me. And for reasons I currently forget, I didn't refuse quickly enough.'

'Do you know any painters?' Phyllis asks Lily.

'Not unless you include my two. They're very fond of painting, although not always in the correct place. They generally prefer to paint all over themselves or the walls. Luckily, my parents don't seem to mind, so Jack and I give them most of our craft supplies and let them get on with it.'

'I was wondering whether someone at the arts centre could do the painting for us,' I say.

'Now, there's an idea!' says Phyllis. 'There are plenty of volunteers working there. I could ask one of them for you.'

'Thanks, but I was thinking of going to the Red Lion for lunch today. I could pop into the arts centre afterwards and check the list of classes and contact numbers.'

'You'll have to find the right artist,' Mabel warns me. 'None of your post-modern stuff. Edie's a traditionalist at heart. Strange though it may seem to you and me, she's bound to want a picture of the mutt that actually looks like him. In her shoes, I'd be searching for someone specialising in Cubism or Abstract Expressionism. The more abstract, the better in the furry menace's case. But you'll never get that sort of thing past Edie. Take it from me and don't waste your time.'

'I'll look for the most conventional possible artist,' I promise. 'And I'll tell them to send their bill to Isabella. It's about time she learned that words have consequences.'

The door opens, and several more of the Silver Surfers troop in, shaking the snow from their boots.

'It's a small world,' says Mary, sitting down next to Mabel, who's busy arranging her mini marshmallows into an artistic pattern on her saucer.

'It's an even smaller village,' says Phyllis. 'That may be why we all keep bumping into each other.'

'You didn't mention you were coming up here this morning,' says Barb. 'We'd have come with you if you had.'

'What's the difference?' asks Mabel. 'The odds are that we'll all bump into each other at some point each day. It's like that bridge.'

'What bridge?' asks Ivy.

'I'm not sure. But they say if you stand there long enough, the whole world passes by. It sounds rather like this bakery.'

'If you wait by the river long enough, the bodies of your enemies will float by,' says Barb.

Phyllis looks startled. 'What enemies?'

'It's an old saying,' explains Barb.

'I've not heard that one,' says Mabel. 'But I like it better than mine. We could wander down to the water meadows after we finish here and see whether it's true.'

Ivy pulls a face. 'It's a bit cold today. I think we should wait until the summer.'

'Your call,' says Mabel. 'But don't blame me if all your enemies have floated away by then.'

The door opens with a loud crash, and Isabella appears. 'Sorry I'm late. It's snowing out there!'

'Is that why you're late?' I ask. 'You got trapped in a snowdrift and have only just fought your way out of it?'

'It's only an inch deep,' she says, unwinding her scarf and dropping it onto the counter.

'I can imagine you getting lost in a far shallower snowdrift than that,' says Phyllis.

'People have so little faith in me,' sighs Isabella. 'I didn't get lost in the snow, and nor was I building a snowman. I was at the florist's shop, talking about possible flower arrangements.'

'I thought the wedding wasn't until late summer,' says Mabel.

'August,' says Isabella. 'But there's so much to do. I have a checklist as long as my arm. And I've made another one especially for Georgia.'

I scowl at her. 'You'd better not have. As chief bride something-or-other, my duties are clearly delineated, and no one is allowed to add to them. The same goes for Lily. We have enough to do without you deciding you'd like us to source the lace for your veil from an elderly woman who lives on the top of a Swiss mountain and only spins on a moonlit night when the edelweiss is in full bloom.'

'I wouldn't dream of it,' says Isabella. 'Although it would have been nice if one of you had offered. I'm not sure I'll even be wearing a veil.'

'All brides wear veils,' objects Mabel.

'Get with the times!' Phyllis advises her. 'Brides today wear all sorts – jumpsuits, capes, torn jeans. Ivy sent me a link to a woman on Instagram who got married in a wetsuit.'

'I saw that one,' I say. 'She was married underwater on a coral reef. Very romantic – although the groom looked as though he'd like to change his mind if he weren't already ten metres down and busy trying to dodge an enormous grouper.'

'That's the problem with themed weddings,' says Barb. 'One minute you're exchanging vows in full scuba gear, the next you're being photo-bombed by a passing stingray.'

'I'm definitely not planning on wearing a wetsuit,' says Isabella. 'Although I'm open to most other things.'

Lily sighs. 'The last time you said that, we ended up with a mariachi band at Daisy's christening.'

'They were delightful! And very enthusiastic. Anyway, I've promised not to wear a wetsuit – although I do like Phyllis' suggestion of a cape.'

'You're engaging in holy matrimony,' I say, 'not charging up the aisle like some bridal superhero. Think of your husband-to-be's feelings.'

'Jon's fine,' she says. 'And not half as stuffy as you. He suggested last night we had a crazy-golf theme for our wedding.'

'Please tell me you're joking.'

'I am not. We decided there could be a hole shaped like a church, with the ball rolling up the aisle and ending up at the altar. The guests could have personalised scorecards instead of orders of service, and we could cover the chairs in artificial grass. You, Lily, and Abby could dress as matching caddies in polo shirts and tartan skirts.'

'How about you?' I ask. 'What's the well-dressed crazy golfing bride wearing this season?'

'Maybe a spotted white organza dress with green trim? I'd have to think about it.'

'You could hand out little chocolate golf balls as wedding favours,' I suggest. 'And put up a scoreboard next to the altar with the results of your last five games.'

'I'm not sure the hotel would go for that one,' says Isabella. 'But I applaud your lateral thinking. It's good to see my chief bridesmaid finally taking her duties seriously.'

Chapter Ten

I walk over to the Red Lion for lunch. What Isabella always refers to as Shelley's game pie is excellent at any time of the year, but it's particularly welcome on a bitterly cold winter's day. I finish with a large helping of sticky toffee pudding and custard.

Isabella and I have had many arguments about this. She insists that crème brûlée is the perfect companion to game pie. The last time we had what she calls a friendly discussion about this, she told me I had an uneducated palate and should be ashamed of myself. In return, I told her I was acquainted with several toddlers who knew far more about food than she did. And from there, we descended into personal insults. Why anyone wants to date her, let alone spend the rest of their life with her, remains a constant mystery to me.

I push open the door of the arts centre. With any luck, there will be a suitable person here to ask about this portrait. It's so typical of Isabella to make a silly joke, not thinking about the consequences. I'm glad Mrs Ogilvie has the memory of the proverbial elephant. Isabella may think twice in the future before she makes ridiculous promises. It's unlikely, but stranger things have happened. Like her finally leaving us all in peace and moving into her own place, or meeting her soulmate and deciding to marry him.

I didn't see that one coming. I thought Isabella was one of those people who remains permanently single by choice. But it appears that, contrary to all expectations, Jon is her kryptonite. I suppose it happens to the best of us – and Isabella is very definitely not the best of us. But she's my sister, and I did once tell her I owe her a favour, so I'd better do what I can to help her out now. I wonder whether this counts as making us equal – me sorting out her Bernie problem in return for her giving me a job when I needed one. Knowing Isabella, it won't, but there's no harm in asking.

I hear voices upstairs, punctuated by the occasional burst of laughter. I look at the timetable pinned on the noticeboard. The laughter must be coming either from the acting improvisation or the beginner's watercolour class. On the face of it, the drama class seems the most likely bet. But I've seen some of the pieces produced by the watercolour enthusiasts, so it could easily be their teacher.

I walk upstairs as quietly as possible, in case the acting class is busy developing a break-in scene. The last thing I need is for its members to get carried away and decide to incorporate me into it. I don't want them becoming over-excited and improvising defensive weapons out of a tambourine and a yoga mat. Isabella would never let me hear the last of it.

I walk past the drama room. A voice I'm almost sure I recognise as Ivy's is telling everyone how devastated she was when she opened that letter by mistake and discovered her husband – the love of her life – had been cheating on her for the past five years with the local vicar. I wonder whether Bob is in this class. I'd love to know what he thinks about his own nefarious goings-on.

The painting class is being held in the front room. Apparently, a north-facing art studio is the most desirable for serious students of art. I'm not sure the beginner watercolour attendees count as serious, but that's not really my business. I poke my head around the door. Five people are sitting at their easels, staring at a vase of snowdrops standing on a small table.

A fair-haired man of about my age is giving them instructions.

'Let the light guide your brush,' he says. 'The shadows are just as important as the flowers themselves. Don't be afraid to get it wrong. The paper isn't judging you.'

I notice with amusement that Bob is one of the art pupils. It's a good thing this place is well built, and the walls are thick. It would be a shame if he overheard all the things his wife was saying about him in the adjacent room. The pair of them seem to enjoy a very happy marriage, and it would be nice if it stayed that way.

The tutor looks up and sees me. 'Are you here for the watercolour class? You're a little late, but I'm sure we can find you somewhere to sit.'

'I'm definitely not!' I say.

It occurs to me this may sound rather rude. I don't want to give the impression this class isn't how I dream of spending my afternoons. But neither do I want this man thinking I'm some budding artistic genius who's too shy to come in and needs some gentle persuasion.

Mary turns her head and smiles at me. 'Hi, Georgia! I didn't know you were an artist on top of your other talents. I suppose I should have guessed. It isn't much different to those beautiful foam pictures you do for us.'

The tutor looks interested. 'Foam pictures? Is that some sort of acrylic medium?'

I choke back a laugh. 'Mary's talking about coffee. I create pictures on the lattes and cappuccinos in the local bakery.'

'You're a barista?' he asks.

'Only because I didn't get good enough A levels to get into law school.'

Seeing his confused look, I add, 'I was making a pun on barrister.'

'I see. Well, now that you're here, what can I do for you?'

'I wanted to talk to you about a picture. But it can wait until you're free. What time does this class end?'

He looks at his watch. 'We have another half hour to go.'

'Great! I'll get myself some more lunch and come back then.'

Bob grins at me. 'Don't eat all the sticky toffee pudding!'

'Please don't let me distract you from your art lesson,' I tell him coldly. 'You look as though you need all the help you can get.'

As I walk back down the hallway, someone who sounds exactly like Phyllis is proclaiming at the top of her voice that they can take her crown, but they'll never take her heart and courage. I totally get it. That's pretty much how I feel about meringues.

I return to the Red Lion where, just to annoy Bob, I order myself another helping of sticky toffee pudding.

Victoria brings it out to me. 'I thought this might be for you. Our new server came into the kitchen looking really confused. He said he'd served a portion of sticky toffee pudding to a tall, blonde woman with curly hair, who paid her bill and left. Half an hour later, there she was again, sitting in the exact same chair and ordering the same thing!'

'Tell him he doesn't need to consult a psychologist just yet,' I say. 'Both those women were me.'

'So I surmised. I realised that either you and Isabella must have visited the pub in quick succession, or one of you had come in twice. That's why I brought out your pudding in person, so I could find out which it was.'

'On second thoughts, it might be more fun to tell him he's seen the ghost of the Red Lion,' I say, digging into the custard to check there's a suitably large-sized helping of toffee pudding underneath it. 'Inform him that she only appears on special occasions.'

'Such as lunchtime?' she asks.

'Or dinner time. Any mealtime, really. She isn't a high-maintenance ghost.'

'Does she have a name?'

I consider. 'Arabella Crumble. She passed away two hundred years ago in a tragic trifle-related accident.'

'What sort of accident?' interrupts Victoria.

'How should I know? Maybe she was leaning over the dumb waiter to see which puddings had been placed on it, and she fell in. Since then, she's haunted the place with surprising persistence. People smell the scent of warm custard in the middle of the night and hear the gentle creak of a dessert trolley coming down the landing.'

'We don't have a dessert trolley,' she says.

'That's what makes it so spooky. Last Valentine's Day, Arabella turned up at the bar and wrote rude messages on all the chocolate tarts in raspberry sauce. To this very day, the staff puts out a small dish of Eton mess every evening after closing. Not because they're scared, but because it's never a good idea to annoy a ghost.'

'If I closed my eyes, I might think you were Isabella,' she says.

'Well, you'd be wrong. Her ghost stories are nowhere as good as mine. Are you planning to repeat this one to your server?'

'I am not. He looked worried enough when he believed he'd just had a case of déja vu. Goodness knows what he'd do if he thought a ghostly apparition really stalked this pub.'

'Just to be safe,' I say, 'I think you should continue to leave that Eton mess out for Arabella each evening.'

'Let me make it clear that we won't be leaving anything on the bar for the benefit of wandering spectres. If I were the Campbell sisters, I'd stay safely at home in the warm.'

I push away my plate. 'Don't say I didn't give you a heads-up. I'd better be going. There's someone I want to talk to. But if you wake tomorrow morning to find a threatening message scrawled in caramel on your pillow, don't blame me. Remember, I'm the one who tried to warn you.'

Chapter Eleven

The classes have finished by the time I get back to the arts centre. Groups of people are coming down the stairs, talking and laughing.

'Hello, Georgia,' says Ivy when she sees me. 'You missed an excellent drama lesson.'

'I didn't miss it,' I say. 'I wasn't signed up for it in the first place.'

'You should have been. I haven't had so much fun in a long time.'

'I'm pleased to hear that, but I don't need any more drama in my life. I have far more than I can handle already. Don't forget I work at The Sugarloaf Bakery!'

'You make a good point,' says Barb, who appears to be yet another member of the Honeywell wandering minstrels. 'There always seems to be something going on over there.'

'I'm also involved in Isabella's wedding,' I say. 'That's more drama than one person should have to experience in a lifetime.'

'Is your sister being difficult?' asks Ivy.

'Not exactly. In some ways, it would be easier if she were. Whenever I ask her about something, she either says she doesn't care or she hasn't decided. It's impossible to get a coherent answer out of her.'

'She's in love!' says Barb. 'It has that effect on people.'

'I can't imagine it having that effect on me. It's as though meeting Jon has driven everything else out of her mind, and now she's scattier than ever. There's no reason why someone who's getting married shouldn't behave normally.'

Ivy laughs. 'We'll remind you of that when it's your turn.'

'You'll have a long time to wait,' I say. 'Falling head over heels in love and marrying doesn't feel like my thing. I've reached this stage in my life without it, so it looks as though I'm immune. It all seems most undignified. Isabella has lost whatever grip she used to have and now spends most of her time mooning around after Jon. I wouldn't have believed it of a sister of mine.'

'How the mighty have fallen?' asks Barb.

'Exactly!' I agree, pleased to find her so quick to understand. 'There's no hope for her, but that's no reason for me not to maintain proper standards. Hopefully, she'll come to her senses after she's married and start behaving like a reasonable human being again.'

'At least she isn't behaving like a Bridezilla,' says Barb. 'Have I got that term correctly?'

'You have,' says Ivy. 'There was a woman on Instagram having an absolute meltdown because her shoes hadn't been dyed the right colour. You wouldn't believe the way she was carrying on!'

'Send it to me!' says Barb. 'I love that sort of thing. It sounds so much fun.'

'We didn't behave like that in my day,' says Ivy. 'The man proposed, and we said yes. Then we bought a dress and booked a venue. Our mothers told us we'd never be happy with the man we'd chosen, and we got married anyway. Simple and traditional.'

'Your mother told you not to marry Bob?' I ask, surprised. 'I'd have thought you two were perfectly matched.'

'We are,' she says. 'It was just the tradition back then. It wouldn't have felt right without it.'

'My mother told me when I married Doug that she gave it six months,' says Barb with a reminiscent smile. 'I was delighted to prove her wrong.'

'I'm glad to hear it,' I say. 'How long were you married?'

'Eight months!' she says proudly. 'And I only hung on for the final two months to annoy my mother. He was a drinker and carrying on with the local barmaid.'

I glance in the direction of the pub, and she laughs. 'It wasn't a much younger Shelley, if that's what you're thinking. Doug and I were married in Coventry. After I threw him out, I moved back to Honeywell where my family lived. I met John soon after, and we were married for forty very happy years until he died.'

'I'm confused by these stories,' I say. 'Are you saying we should listen to our mothers' warnings or not?'

'It depends on the mother,' says Ivy. 'Hi, Bob. We were just talking about your mother-in-law.'

'And weddings,' says Barb. 'How have your parents taken the news of your sister's engagement, Georgia?'

'With great relief. Anyone would be relieved at the prospect of finally getting rid of Isabella. I doubt my mother will be issuing any last-minute warnings and providing a getaway car.'

'Not like yours!' Bob tells Ivy. 'If I remember correctly, she told you it would never last, gave you the numbers of several good divorce lawyers, and suggested you take a taxi to the station right before the ceremony.'

'And offered to pay for it,' agrees Ivy.

'I'm happy you proved her wrong,' I say. 'If for no other reason than that it's always nice to prove people wrong. It's one of my favourite things.'

'Georgia was telling us she never intends to fall in love,' Ivy tells Bob.

He smiles at me. 'Is that right?'

'Never say never. But I can promise that if the worst ever happens, and I do accidentally lose my mind – I mean my heart – I won't carry on in the same undignified way as my sister. I have better things to do with my time.'

'Our tutor appeared to be very struck with you,' he says.

Ivy's eyes light up. 'That good-looking blonde one?'

'I'm certainly not talking about the woman who subbed in for him when he had the flu,' he says. 'She was no fun at all. She told us that perspective is not a matter of opinion and made us paint in silence for the rest of the lesson. She was very critical.'

'I must have missed this Adonis,' says Barb. 'Which is most unlike me. What's his name?'

'David,' says Bob. 'He was asking if we knew who you were, Georgia. He seemed very keen to find out. We pretended none of us had ever met you before.'

'Quite right,' I say. 'There's no sense in giving out unnecessary information to strangers. Why did he want to know my name? I told him I'd be back after the class had finished.'

'Maybe he thought it was a Cinderella situation,' suggests Barb. 'A beautiful young woman turns up, then disappears, never to be seen again. And no one knows who she is.'

'You should have told him her name,' Ivy reproves Bob.

'No, he shouldn't,' I say. 'Information is power. That's always been my motto.'

'I thought I could sell it to him later in exchange for a better grade,' says Bob.

'They grade your art?' I ask, surprised.

'I have no idea. But after what Moira said about my brushwork, I'm not taking any chances.'

There's a clatter of feet on the stairs, and the other members of the art class appear, followed by the tutor I saw earlier.

Ivy winks at Barb when she sees David. 'I told you he was good looking.'

'Hello again,' says David, catching sight of me. 'I wondered whether you'd be back.'

'We were just leaving,' says Ivy, taking Bob's arm.

'So soon?' I ask.

'We're off to your bakery for lunch,' she says, ignoring my sarcasm. 'Maybe we'll see you there later?'

'There's a strong possibility you will. But I'm not due back for another twenty minutes, so you'll have to put up with inferior foam on your first round of lattes.'

'We can wait,' says Bob. 'Please don't hurry on our account.'

He casts a meaningful look at David, and Ivy gives a tiny snort of laughter.

'I won't,' I say. 'Before I return to the bakery, perhaps I'll pop upstairs and look at your snowdrop painting, Bob. I may even take some photos for Ivy to put on Instagram.'

Is it my imagination, or has he turned slightly pale? It serves him right for trying to embarrass me in front of David.

'I'll send Ivy a list of hashtags,' I add. 'It would be a shame for those pictures not to be shared as widely as possible.'

She grins and takes his arm. 'Come on, Picasso. I'll buy you one of Abby's quiches for lunch while you impress me with stories of your artistic triumphs.'

'And you can tell Bob about your latest improv scene,' says Barb. 'I'm sure he'd like to hear all the details.'

'Traitor!' says Ivy. 'See you later, Georgia.'

'What was all that about?' David asks me when they've gone.

'Just the usual married people stuff. She tells the world her husband is having an affair with a barmaid and threatens to stab him, while he spends his time painting flowers, oblivious to everything going on around him.'

'Bob's having an affair?' he asks.

'I very much doubt it. I happened to overhear what was going on in the room next to yours when I passed by. And by "happened" I mean I stopped and listened in as closely as possible. It's always good to have blackmail material on our customers in case we need to keep them in line.'

'Where do you work?' he asks.

'At The Sugarloaf Bakery on the high street. Do you know it?'

'I'm fairly new to this area. I live in Christchurch. But I'll be sure to visit you.'

'What do you do for work?' I ask.

'I'm a teacher.'

'An art teacher?'

'Maths.'

I can't help pulling a face, and he laughs. 'You'd be surprised how often I get that reaction when I mention what I do for a living.'

'I'm not sure I would. So, what are you doing here?'

'Volunteering. I've always enjoyed painting, and a friend of mine at school mentioned they were looking for volunteers for the classes at the Honeywell arts centre. I thought it would be a good way of getting to know people.'

'So, you enjoy painting,' I say. 'But are you any good at it?'

A flicker of amusement passes over his face. 'That's not really for me to say.'

'But you can draw things that are recognisable?'

'Again, that's in the eye of the beholder.'

I'm starting to find this guy a little frustrating. Modesty is all very well, but surely he knows whether or not he can draw properly.

'How about a horse?' I ask. 'Or a dog? Would I recognise what they were supposed to be?'

'I expect so. Why do you ask? Are you thinking of taking my class? You'd be most welcome. You could pop along next week if you're free. There are a couple of places left. By which, I mean I could find two more chairs and tables. I'm happy to have as many people attend as possible, but the latecomers will have to sit on the floor.'

'Floor art sounds like it may be the next big thing,' I say.

'So, will you be attending next week?'

'That isn't why I asked about your art skills.'

'Are you checking my credentials for the oversight committee?'

'I don't think there is any oversight committee,' I say. 'Just Mavis Sotherby and the parish council. The reason I'm asking whether you can draw is because I'm looking for someone to paint a portrait of a dog, and the arts centre seemed the obvious place to begin that search.'

'I see. Whose dog is it?'

'One of our elderly customers. She adores Bernie, and my ridiculous sister told her a while ago we were thinking of having his portrait painted to put up in our bakery. She was only making a joke, but the customer took it seriously, and now we have to make good on the promise.'

'I see,' he says again. 'But why are you trying to find someone? Your sister's the one who made the joke. Why isn't she the one running around fixing it?'

'Usually, I'd agree with you. But she's getting married this year, and it's as much as she can do to cope with that. Isabella isn't what you might call a natural multi-tasker.'

He leans against the stairs and shifts the bundle of papers in his arms. 'What type of portrait are you after?'

'How many types are there?'

'Quite a few,' he says. 'First, you have to select the medium. That could take a while. Then you have to decide on the pose. Does the owner have a view on that?'

'I imagine she does. She has strong views on everything to do with Bernie. So does her sister, but they're rather different views. Let's say they don't always share the same perspective on their dog. That wasn't meant to be an artistic pun, by the way.'

'There are other things to consider,' he says. 'How cooperative is the dog likely to be?'

'That depends on who you're talking to. If you ask his owner, she'll tell you he's a perfect angel, and butter wouldn't melt in his mouth. If you ask her sister, she'll tell you he's a demon from hell. I imagine the truth lies somewhere between the two.'

'Maybe it would be simpler to paint the picture from a photograph,' he says.

'So, you'll do it?'

He laughs. 'There must be plenty of people around here who are far more artistically talented than I am.'

'You're the only one currently offering painting classes. I checked.'

'Any port in a storm?' he asks. 'I'd need a few more details before I agreed to anything.'

'I can get you as many details as you like. This is a paid commission, by the way. I've already told my sister she's footing the bill. It may teach her the value of stopping to think before she speaks. It's unlikely, but stranger things have happened.'

'Why don't you give me your number?' he says. 'I'll send you the questions I'd like to have answered, and you can ask the people concerned. Then I'll take you to dinner, and we'll talk about this some more.'

'Or I could text you the answers,' I say.

'Don't you eat dinner?'

'I eat more dinners than most people. But there's no need for you to put yourself out.'

He smiles. 'I'm not putting myself out. I'd very much like to have dinner with you, and this seems like a convenient excuse.'

'Oh,' I say, somewhat taken aback.

'So, what do you say?'

I consider this. It wasn't what I was expecting when I came over here today. But if there's a chance of sorting this out, I'd like to get it done. There's plenty to do before the wedding, and it would be nice to tick something off my list before the real chaos begins.

'Fine,' I say. 'You send me the questions, and we'll arrange a time to meet. I should get going now. I have precisely three minutes before I start my afternoon shift, and one of my employers is a tyrant who's always looking for an excuse to fire me!'

Without waiting for him to answer, I shoot off down the hall and run towards the high street. Dinner engagements are one thing. Being late for work is quite another.

Chapter Twelve

I arrive at the bakery with only ten seconds to spare, but I don't care. Ten seconds is ten seconds, and a lot can happen in that time. A rocket launch can be aborted, an important document can be signed, or Isabella can start yet another kitchen fire. The point is that I'm here on time, which means no one has any grounds for giving me a written warning. And when I say no one, I mean Isabella.

To be clear, I have no objection to written warnings in general. I've found several uses for them, such as folding them into bookmarks, swatting flies, fanning myself dramatically on hot days, and decoupage. In fact, I encourage them – and the more ridiculous, the better. But only for those things I haven't done.

It's a matter of pride for me to avoid legitimate warnings – the kind that Isabella could claim some kind of justification for, even if no reasonable person would. I may not wish to work in a bakery for the rest of my life, but while I'm there, I'm determined to perform my job properly. It's the first time I've ever felt that way about anything, and it would be a pity to mess it up.

Naturally, Isabella isn't present to observe my meticulous time-keeping. That would be far too much to expect. She's like Macavity – the cat in that annoyingly long poem we had to read at school. Whenever you reach the scene of crime – Isabella's not there.

However, a group of Silver Surfers is, and they're making great inroads into Abby's new batch of strawberry tarts. I glance at the chill cabinet to make sure there are plenty of tarts left. I wasn't here when they came out of the kitchen this morning, and it's imperative there are enough left for my quality control test.

'Isn't that a little late?' asks Lily when I mention this to her.

'Not at all. A retrospective test is almost as valuable as a prospective one. If and when Health and Safety calls, we can assure them a member of staff has personally monitored the integrity of the ingredients.'

'When you two have finished jabbering,' says Mabel, waving her cup at me, 'I'd like another pot of tea, please.'

'This is your fault,' I tell Lily. 'You've pandered to your customers over the years, and they've come to believe they're the most important part of this business.'

'They are,' she says.

'But they shouldn't know that. A professional outfit would have trained their clientele to understand we're doing them a favour by providing them with cake and hot drinks. They ought to be delighted to wait in line for hours on the off-chance of being seated. When we double our prices overnight, they should be posting reviews on the village website, telling everyone how exclusive we are, and what a privilege it is to get a table for two at the Sugarloaf. They should be referring to us as the Ritz of the South.'

'The Ritz *is* in the south,' argues Ivy, brushing pastry crumbs off her sleeve.

'Not for long,' I say, spooning tea leaves into a pot. 'The famous London hotel may struggle on for a while, but it will eventually be forced to close its doors, acknowledging the fact there's a new and better place available for afternoon tea – and one with which they have no chance of competing.'

Lily laughs. 'You paint a vivid picture. But, as you say, we haven't trained our customers properly, so it's too late now for us to become the Ritz of the New Forest.'

'Edie and I visited The Ritz once,' says Mabel. 'I treated her to afternoon tea there for our eighty-third birthday. By rights, she ought to have treated me back because it was a joint birthday, but I didn't dare push it. She was so busy worrying about leaving the hound with Angela Carson for the day and complaining about the no-mutt policy at the hotel that I thought I'd better pay for everything so she had no excuse to pull out.'

'Was it any good?' asks Barb.

'It was no Sugarloaf Bakery, but we had a wonderful afternoon. I remember walking into the Palm Court for the very first time. It was all mirrors and marble columns, with a glass ceiling that made you feel as though you were having tea outside on the lawn. It was worth the money for that alone.'

'You could put one of those glass ceilings in here,' Phyllis tells Lily.

'No, we couldn't. We'd never get planning permission.'

'Now, there's a can't-do attitude!' Mabel chides her. 'I doubt Monsieur Ritz approached his original project like that. I see him sweeping into the office one morning, waving his plans for the new glass ceiling and threatening to fire anyone who mentioned the words "planning" or "permission." Quite right too!'

'Our local council doesn't really work like that,' says Lily.

'Then they all need firing and replacing,' says Mabel. 'Imagine if we could recreate the Ritz experience right here in Honeywell. It would save us all a trip to London. You could have a piano in the corner just like theirs.'

'There would be no room for any tables if we did that,' says Ivy.

'Don't you start being defeatist as well!' says Mabel. 'We could have a very small piano. Or a mouth organ for when the place is really busy.'

'I think Mabel's right,' I tell Lily. 'There's no point in setting our sights too low. I vote we start practising right away. You and

Isabella can institute appropriate rules and insist everyone follows them. Ladies must wear hats whenever they drop in here for a cup of tea, and there will be no admittance for gentlemen without jackets and ties.'

'That's you done for!' Ivy tells Bob. 'I don't think you even own a jacket and tie now you've retired.'

'I have my funeral suit,' he says. 'And I think my old dinner jacket is somewhere around, although I'm not sure I can still fit into it.'

'Your suit will be fine,' I say. 'Add a trilby hat and pop a carnation in your buttonhole and you'll fit in perfectly with the new clientele we're seeking to attract.'

'We?' asks Lily.

'You and Isabella,' I correct myself. 'I'm just an underling – here to do the menial and degrading jobs neither of you wants to do.'

'And don't you forget it!' she says. 'You and Mabel paint a pretty picture, but unless you plan to fund all our renovations, we'll stay as we are, thank you. We already have a no-bare-feet policy. That will have to do.'

'Your call,' I say. 'But I think you're missing a trick. Mabel and I have offered you the benefit of our expert advice, and you're turning it down without even thinking about it. That's hardly the mark of a business guru. Here's your tea, Mabel. One extra lemon slice, just as you like it.'

'Lovely,' she says, pouring herself a cup and taking a sip. 'This is easily as good as the Ritz.'

'What were their cakes like?' asks Phyllis. 'Did they have any plum slices?'

Mabel shakes her head. 'They did not, which was a definite strike against them. To do them justice, they had an awful lot of other things. Edie and I ate until we almost burst.'

'You did,' says Mrs Ogilvie. 'I enjoyed a pleasant sufficiency.'

'And then tried to hide a smoked salmon sandwich in your handbag to take home for the mutt because he loves them so much,' scoffs Mabel. 'But you caught the server's eye and thought better of it. Still, it was a birthday to remember all right.'

'It was,' agrees her sister. 'Although I was worried we might be asked to leave when you dropped that cucumber sandwich and announced it was all the chef's fault for making it too slippery.'

'You should always speak truth to power,' says Mabel. 'I expect they paid more attention to the quality of their cucumbers after that.'

'How about their scones?' asks Ivy. 'Were they as good as Abby's?'

'No one's scones are as good as Abby's,' says Mabel. 'But I must say the ones at The Ritz came a close second. I didn't own a mobile phone in those days or I'd have taken lots of pictures. You could have blown them up and pinned them on the cafe wall for inspiration.'

'Speaking of putting things on the wall,' says Ivy, 'how did you get on with David after we'd left, Georgia? Weren't you going to ask him about painting a portrait of Bernie?'

'I opened negotiations,' I say.

'But did you close the deal?'

'He told me there were several questions he needed answering first,' I say evasively.

'What sort of questions?' demands Mabel. 'It's a straightforward enough commission. Can you paint a recognisable picture of the mutt – yes or no? It isn't a creative brief to portray a member of the royal family. Although the way my sister carries on, it may as well be.'

'I don't know what questions he'll have,' I say. 'He's going to think about it and send them over to me.'

'And then no doubt he wants to meet you to discuss them?' asks Phyllis.

'That's the plan.'

'Here?' asks Ivy.

'He wants to have dinner with me. I expect we'll go into Christchurch.'

'It's about time we had another romance at the bakery,' says Barb. 'It's been ages since the last one.'

'You mean Isabella?' I ask. 'That wasn't really a bakery romance. She and Jon met at the arts centre.'

'Don't split hairs,' she says. 'It all counts. And the Silver Surfers did their bit to get her and Jon together.'

'Did you?' I ask. 'I thought they managed it all by themselves.'

'We were standing by,' says Ivy. 'We had all kinds of plans in case the pair of them messed it up.'

'Please don't make any plans for me,' I say. 'My life is challenging enough without adding any further complications. Have you forgotten I'm the chief bride something-or-other at the upcoming wedding of the decade?'

'It's called multi-tasking,' says Mabel. 'Something every modern woman needs to learn how to do. To be fair, we had to do it when I was young too, but it didn't have a fancy name back then. We just called it getting on with things.'

'I multi-task!' I protest. 'I'm working at the bakery several days a week, on top of coping with all Isabella's unreasonable demands for her wedding. I'm surprised I've lasted here for as long as I have.'

'You've enabled us to get some much-needed work-life balance,' Lily tells me. 'Before you arrived, Isabella and I were covering the entire operation by ourselves, with occasional help from temporary staff when we needed it. But none of them worked here for more than a few months. If you decide to leave, we'll be advertising for someone to work here at least three days a week. We've grown accustomed to regular time off and holidays.'

'Isabella certainly has,' I say. 'She and Jon are always going off on camping trips. They took the boys to Scotland during the Christmas holidays. They booked a cabin, so it wasn't as bad as it might have been, but it isn't my idea of a relaxing holiday.'

'Ollie and Toby are lucky to have Isabella in their lives,' says Barb. 'She's a natural with them, and it gives their mum a break.'

'And the rest of us too,' I say. 'But not too much of a break because there's always work here for us to get on with. Our customers are so demanding, and my employers just allow them to get away with it. If I owned this place, I'd run things very differently.'

'Would you ban dogs?' asks Mabel. 'You'd have my custom for life if you did.'

I look down at Bernie, lying in a patch of sunlight, his legs twitching as he chases imaginary rabbits through the snow.

'Your custom is extremely valuable,' I tell her, 'and I'd do almost anything to retain it. But that would be a step too far. Bernie is an important part of this place. No wonder he persuaded Lily and Isabella to make him their mascot.'

'I'm disappointed,' she says, 'but not surprised. Far too many people are taken in by that dog. It's a mystery why, but that's the way it is. And now you've talked that poor man into painting his portrait, it will be too late. Once your customers have seen his ridiculous face grinning down at them from the wall, no one will have the heart to ban him. It's a crying shame, but it's a burden I'll just have to bear.'

Chapter Thirteen

David picks me up from The Lodge on Thursday evening.

'I thought we could eat at Allesandro's,' he says. 'It's a nice little Italian restaurant in Christchurch. I go there fairly often, and you told me you didn't have a strong preference for any particular cuisine.'

'I don't,' I say, climbing into the front seat and marvelling at the non-frayed seatbelt. Months of travelling to and from work in my battered old hatchback have made me forget that cars with working features exist. This one even possesses cup holders. Life can hold no greater luxury.

He turns the key, and I'm impressed by how smoothly the engine purrs into life.

'We have a twenty-minute drive ahead of us,' he says, pulling away from the crossroads and starting off towards Christchurch. 'Just enough time for you to tell me something about yourself.'

'You already know the most important thing. I work at The Sugarloaf Bakery.'

'That's work, not personal.'

'It's what I spend most of my time doing. So, it counts. How about you?'

'I've never worked in a bakery. Perhaps I should have suggested something more original for this evening. It didn't occur to me that taking a baker to a restaurant might be like bringing sand to a beach party.'

'I'm not a baker,' I say. 'We leave all that sort of thing to our pastry chef. Even if we didn't, I'm always happy when someone else cooks for me. It gives me the opportunity to send my food back and complain that it's cold or not properly seasoned. Customers sometimes do that to us at the bakery, and it looks like fun.'

Is that a faint look of alarm on his face? I harden my heart and continue. 'And I can shout insults at the chef. I've always wanted to do that.'

'Was that my beeper?' he asks. 'I forgot to tell you I'm on call this evening.'

'You're a maths teacher. They don't have out-of-hours emergencies. And don't bother telling me you feel the first faint stirrings of appendicitis. I had mine out as a child, and I'm well acquainted with the symptoms.'

'How about leprosy?' he asks.

'Don't you want to have dinner with me? You can always turn around and take me home. The turning's just coming up.'

He laughs. 'I would love to take you to dinner. But I'd prefer it if you kept the cutlery-throwing and yelling to a minimum.'

'I'll do my best. But it will depend to some extent on the service and the quality of the food.'

'In that case, we should be safe. I had a lobster ravioli the last time I was there that wouldn't have been out of place in the *Piazza San Marco*.'

'Have you visited Venice often?' I ask.

'Never. But I went to the Venetian resort in Las Vegas a few years ago. It was just as good.'

I somehow doubt it, but I'd prefer not to get into an argument before the evening has even started.

'There's a car park down here,' he says, turning into a tiny, cobbled street. 'You don't mind walking a few hundred metres, do you?'

We walk down several small alleyways until we reach the main road.

'It's just along there,' says David. 'And we're right on time for our reservation.'

He holds the door open for me, then walks over to greet the receptionist. '*Buona Sera!*'

The receptionist, who doesn't look much older than sixteen, blinks at him. 'Excuse me?'

'*Buona Sera!*' repeats David. 'It's Italian for Good Evening.'

The boy's face clears. 'I thought you said banana syrup, and I don't think we do that here. Although I could ask Chef if you like.'

I give an involuntary snort of laughter, then quickly turn it into a cough as the boy turns to look at me.

'Sorry,' I say. 'I choked. On a –'

I was about to say breadcrumb, which is always the first thing that comes to mind when someone tells you they've choked on something. But we haven't yet been served. I consider reaching across to the nearest table, grabbing a bread stick, and cramming it into my mouth just so I can choke on it. But I've promised myself to behave this evening, so I decide against it.

'Dust,' I finish weakly. 'I swallowed some dust.'

Both of them regard me as though I've announced my sincere belief the moon is indeed made of Stilton, and I'd like a piece of it with my dinner.

'Table for Beaumont,' says David at last.

A server bustles up before our youthful host can spontaneously combust with confusion.

'Good evening!' he says. 'My name is Mario, and I will be serving you tonight.'

We follow him over to our table. It's at the far end of the restaurant and has a view over the old castle.

'Do you think that receptionist is here on work experience?' I ask David in a low tone.

I gesture towards the reception desk, where the boy is now busy greeting an elderly couple – and, by the looks on their faces, doing his absolute best to confuse them.

'Maybe it's take-your-son-to-work day,' he suggests.

'Or the real receptionist is blind drunk in the kitchen at this very moment, and there was no one else available to stand in for him at a moment's notice.'

It feels a little unkind to cast aspersions on the character of this unknown and probably mythical man, so I add, 'Or he may be suffering from a severe bout of food poisoning. Someone may race out of the kitchen at any moment, calling, "Is there a doctor in the house?" If no one rises to the occasion, I'll summon up my memories of my last health and safety training session, leap from my chair and shout, "Yes!" On the plus side, the day will be saved, and our meal will almost definitely be free.'

'I've never been in a situation where anyone has shouted that,' says David.

'There's a first time for everything. Restaurants are the perfect place for all kinds of disasters, especially when steak is on the menu. An over-cooked, rubbery steak is a potential choking minefield. Although that may be less of a risk in this type of restaurant. Pasta, even al dente, is slippery enough to slide down without too much danger of obstruction.'

'After an evening with you, I may never want to eat in a restaurant again,' he says.

I'm about to argue the point, but I recollect in time I'm in a lovely restaurant with a man from whom I need a favour. So, instead of giving in to the temptation to tell him everything I remember from last season's finale of Britain's Worst Chef, I scan the menu.

'The cacciatore looks good,' I say after careful thought. 'I think I'll order that. How about you?'

'I'll have the risotto. You can never go far wrong with rice dishes.'

Mario brings us a basket of bread and pauses to take our order.

'How do you like the bread?' David asks me.

'Georgia works in a bakery,' he tells Mario. 'I'd like her opinion of the ciabatta.'

I can guess what's going through Mario's mind right now. No one wants to hear that someone is judging their work, even when that person is off the clock. It's like an Ofsted Inspector sitting at the back of a Sunday School lesson taking careful notes.

'I'm off duty tonight,' I tell Mario. 'Not that I'd be judging your bread even if I weren't. I couldn't bake a loaf of anything if my life depended on it.'

He looks a little confused, but nods and smiles before taking our orders and moving away.

'I thought you'd like this place,' says David. 'The owner is Italian, so he has the honour of his national cuisine to uphold.'

Our food arrives a few minutes later.

'*Grazie!* says David as the server places the dishes on the table.

'*Prego!* says Mario.

'Are you checking whether he's really Italian?' I ask David after he's left.

'Not at all,' he says. 'I was simply being polite. I thanked him, and he said I was welcome.'

'Did you learn Italian at school, or have you travelled much in Italy?'

'I've never been to Italy,' he says. 'I prefer places like New York or San Francisco.'

I take a gulp of my wine and search for a different topic of conversation.

'So, how has the rest of your week been?' I ask at last. 'Have any unusual incidents happened at work?'

'Plenty of unusual incidents. But I try not to talk about work when I'm not there. I don't want to turn into the sort of bore who thinks what they do is more fascinating than what other people do. I decided early in my career never to become like that.'

'Would the same principle apply if you were a pilot?' I ask. 'You'd be having dinner with a group of people or chatting at a cocktail party, and someone would ask how your week had gone. Would you pretend you hadn't flown anywhere interesting? Or would you say something cryptic so your fellow guests spent the rest of the evening speculating about which countries you might have visited?'

I warm to my theme. 'It would be even more difficult if you were an astronaut. You could hardly remain anonymous if you were floating around the International Space Station each day on live TV, trying to pretend you'd bumped into the console on purpose, and it wasn't you who'd set all the alarms off.'

'But I'm not a pilot or an astronaut,' says David, looking slightly confused. 'Most of what I do is routine. And I don't like to talk about my pupils out of school.'

'Most of what airline pilots do is routine too,' I say. 'Or that's what I hope for whenever I board a plane. It's one of those jobs where the fewer interesting things that happen the better.'

'How was your chicken?' asks a voice, and I return to reality to find Mario standing next to our table.

'Excellent,' I say. 'Very authentic.'

'*Vorrebbe vedere il menu dei dessert?*' he asks.

'Mario was asking whether we'd like to see the dessert menu,' says David.

'I would,' I say. 'Do you have any recommendations?'

'Our chef makes his own tiramisu,' says Mario. 'He won a prize for it last year at the New Forest Local Spoon awards.'

'That's impressive. I'll try that.'

David closes his menu. 'So will I. *Due tiramisu, per favore. E un caffe latte.*'

'I was just ordering myself a coffee,' he tells me kindly. 'What would you like?'

I'd like to ask for a cappuccino, but I don't want to appear to be joining in with this pseudo-Italian conversation.

'Black coffee, please,' I say.

'*Un café nero,*' David translates, and I give a tiny choke of laughter as I catch Mario's eye.

I can't seem to help myself. There's nothing intrinsically ridiculous about speaking someone else's language. But David isn't an Italian speaker, so it feels forced and performative. It's like those people who make a massive deal out of having the wine poured out for them to taste, when the closest they've ever been to a decent vintage is a carton of Tesco's finest.

Mario leaves, and I scrabble around for something to say that doesn't include the words, 'So, are you going anywhere nice for your holidays this year?'

'My godfather always told me to speak Italian or French in the appropriate restaurants,' David tells me. 'He says it ensures better service.'

'It's a good thing we didn't go for Mongolian food this evening,' I say somewhat flippantly.

I'm relieved to see him smile. 'That's what Google Translate is for.'

Our desserts arrive. I feel an impulse to say *Merci* or *Danke Schön* just to confuse matters, but I restrain myself.

'These look wonderful,' I tell Mario, just as David chimes in with, '*Grazie mille.*'

I cram a mouthful of tiramisu into my mouth before either of them can notice my fit of the giggles.

David takes a rather more restrained spoonful and tastes it. It looks as though he's rolling it around his palate – assessing the mouth feel, the taste, and the aroma. It makes a certain sense. Tiramisu contains dark rum. But you can taste it equally well by shoving it into your mouth and swallowing it. Still, each to his own. As long as he's enjoying it, that's all that matters.

'Very good,' he says at last. 'The rum blends perfectly with the bitterness of the chocolate, and the chilled cream gives a great finish.'

'Have you had any more thoughts about that portrait of Bernie?' I ask. 'It would really help everyone out if you were able to do it.'

He looks faintly embarrassed. 'Perhaps I should have mentioned earlier that I don't really do portraits. I enjoy watercolour painting, but I mainly stick to landscapes and still lifes.'

'So, why are we here?' I ask a little too bluntly.

He smiles at me. 'It was the only excuse I could think of on the spur of the moment. I wanted to have dinner with you, and I didn't think it would improve my chances if I refused your request out of hand.'

I'd like to give him a piece of my mind, but I'm too tired. I've had a busy few days, and I feel as though I could lie down and sleep for a week. I would usually offer to split the costs on a first date, but David has got me here under false pretences, so the least he can do is pay for my meal.

He waves for the bill, and I find myself hoping he doesn't refer to it as the *conto.* I'm relieved that he doesn't say anything more to Mario as he reaches for his credit card and scribbles his name.

We say goodbye to the teenager at the desk and stroll back towards the water.

'Would you like me to drive you straight home?' David asks when we reach the car. 'Or would you prefer to come back to my flat for a nightcap? It's only a couple of minutes' walk from here.'

'I have an early start at the bakery tomorrow,' I say. 'I should be getting home.'

'Of course.' He opens my car door for me. 'It's a good job I only had a small glass of wine with my meal. Otherwise, there was enough rum in that tiramisu to put me over the limit.'

'I doubt it,' I say, settling myself into my seat. 'They used the good rum, and that stuff is expensive. They wouldn't have been sloshing it around without using an accurate measure.'

He swings the car through the narrow streets and carefully navigates the roundabout that leads to the road to Honeywell. There isn't much traffic on a Sunday evening, and it only takes us fifteen minutes to reach Little Compton.

He pulls up outside the house, jumps out, and comes around to open my door. 'This is where I wish you a –'

I freeze, willing him not to say it.

'*Buona notte!* he finishes, and it's as much as I can do not to grimace.

'That means –'

'I got it from context,' I say.

He looks at me for a moment, as though unsure what to make of this. Then he takes a step forward and quickly kisses my cheek.

'Thank you for dinner,' I say. 'I'm sorry you can't help us with the portrait.'

He has the grace to look slightly ashamed. 'Perhaps I should have been more upfront with you about my painting skills. But I had a lovely evening, and I hope we can do it again soon.'

I watch him climb into his car and drive away. I hope I wasn't too rude to him. It isn't the worst crime in the world to invite someone to dinner, and I can't remember when I last had an evening out. Judging by my less-than-stellar performance tonight, it may be quite a while longer before I get another opportunity.

Chapter Fourteen

'Well?' says Lily as I push open the door on Monday morning.

'Well, what?' I ask.

'I'd like a flat white,' she says. 'And an update.'

'Are you sure you wouldn't prefer a *latte*? Did you know *latte* means milk in Italian? If you're looking for something a little stronger, I could pour you a *vino*. That means wine.'

'I know what *vino* means,' she says. 'Why are you treating me to an impromptu Italian lesson so early on a Monday morning?'

'No reason,' I say, frothing her milk as I wait for the coffee to brew. 'Would you like a picture on your foam? I could do you a gondola.'

'No, thanks. How did dinner go?'

'It was fine. Nothing earth-shattering, but the food was good, and David was very pleasant company.'

'That's all?' she asks.

'Unfortunately, he doesn't feel up to the task of producing a professional portrait of Bernie.'

'What a shame,' she says. 'Why didn't he tell you that at once?'

'Because he thought I might not agree to go out with him if he did.'

'Would you have?'

'I'm not sure. I don't have much time for dating right now, and I don't think David and I are quite on the same wavelength.'

'No spark at all?' she asks. 'Not even a tiny, almost invisible one?'

'If it was invisible, I wouldn't have seen it.'

She sighs. 'I said "almost" invisible. And you might have felt it even if you didn't see it. From tiny sparks, huge conflagrations can grow – if the fire is properly nurtured and fed.'

'The only sparks last night came from the candle on our table. There would have been a lot more if I'd leaned forward and accidentally caught my sleeve in it. But I stayed safely on my side of the table, so disaster was averted.'

'No tender holding of your hand while staring deeply into your eyes?' she asks, disappointed.

'I'm afraid not. I've never been a fan of that sort of thing. How are you supposed to eat your dinner with someone clutching on to you for dear life? It isn't too difficult with something like pasta, but cutting up a steak or a chicken breast one-handed isn't ideal. It can be done, but it makes a bit of a mess.'

'I agree,' she says. 'But it's disappointing to discover you aren't a fan of romantic moments.'

'I've never been too keen on that "eyes meeting across a crowded room" trope. I'd prefer to get to know someone a bit better before deciding they're my soulmate. Even that's no real guarantee. Love is a lottery, and we have far less control over it than we like to think.'

'But you'll never find true love if you don't go out on any dates,' she says. 'And behave yourself properly while you're on them.'

'I'm an excellent date!' I protest. 'I always use my knife and fork correctly and remember to say thank you for a pleasant evening. But I rarely find myself wanting to see people again.'

'Don't you find first dates exciting?' she asks. 'I used to. There's always so much potential.'

'I enjoy dating, but I'd far rather be single than end up with the wrong person. My mother always told me it was better to travel alone than badly accompanied. The older I get, the more I think she was right. Being with the wrong person is more trouble than it's worth, which is why I won't be taking things further with David.'

'What really happened?' she asks.

'I found it difficult to think of things to talk about. I never do when I'm with the right person. And I kept fixating on unimportant things.'

'Such as?'

'He insisted on talking in Italian to the server.'

Her lips twitch. 'Hence the *latte* and the *vino* this morning?'

'I told you I was being petty. Why shouldn't he speak Italian in an Italian restaurant?'

'No reason at all,' she agrees. 'You sound horribly judgemental. No wonder the date didn't go well. That poor man. Anyway, we can't stand around all day talking about your love life. I need to change the water in all the vases before our first customers arrive. Those snowdrops are looking a bit sad.'

Before I can answer, the bell jangles, and I turn to see Ivy and Mabel standing in the doorway.

'How did your dinner with David go?' asks Mabel almost before she's through the door.

'I'll tell you all the details if you each buy a dozen loaves of bread,' I say.

'That's no way to treat our customers,' says Lily. 'They know they're welcome to drop in here at any time of the day or night with no obligation to buy anything.'

'Not at night,' I object. 'We close at five-thirty, and we don't want a bunch of ne'er-do-wells hanging around outside of business hours.'

'The dinner didn't go as well as it might have done,' Lily tells them.

'What a shame!' says Ivy, dropping into the nearest chair and looking expectantly at me. 'What went wrong?'

'It wasn't all bad,' says Lily, who appears to have appointed herself my official spokesperson. 'In fact, Georgia has decided to give him another chance, in case she judged him too hastily.'

'Georgia has decided no such thing!' I say.

'She and I were just discussing the subject of flowers,' Lily goes on. 'I was about to explain to her that love is like a delicate blossom. Some flowers spring up overnight, overwhelming us with their bloom and beauty. Others are shyer and take their time. They peep out between their more confident cousins, trying to pluck up the courage to bloom. And when they do, they're often the most beautiful and long-lasting of all the flowers. Georgia is considering whether her relationship with David falls into the latter category.'

I make a derisive noise. 'Lily may be wondering that, but no one else is.'

Mabel is looking confused. 'Have I missed something here?'

'Not at all,' I say. 'I was about to check the sell-by-dates on those fruit slices when you arrived. Shall I make your drinks first?'

'What a good idea,' says Ivy. 'And perhaps a couple of cookies might go down well with them. Dealer's choice.'

'Or should we say *biscotti?*' asks Lily.

I make a pot of tea for Mabel, a latte for Ivy, and a flat white for Lily. I'm reasonably sure she won't know the Italian word for that. I place a selection of chocolate chip cookies onto a plate and carry it over to their table.

'*Grazie,*' says Lily.

I frown. 'You aren't helping your case here.'

'I'm sorry. I don't seem able to help myself.'

'So, is David doing the portrait or not?' Mabel asks me.

'He feels the task requires a greater degree of professionalism and dedication than he can currently offer.'

'I can understand that,' she says. 'Most people would feel the same way. We may have to stick to a photograph of Bernie – heavily edited, of course. The Silver Surfers could help you with that. Mavis Sotherby is a dab hand with Photoshop. She may be able to reduce the red gleam in his eyes and soften the ferocious snarl.'

'I haven't given up on the portrait yet,' I say. 'There must be other people locally who would jump at the opportunity of making a name for themselves. By the way, I was thinking of going over to The Red Lion for lunch today if anyone would like to join me?'

'I'll need you to take an early lunch break,' says Lily. 'I have to go out at one o'clock.'

'Not a problem,' I say. 'It lowers the possibility of Victoria's game pies selling out. She told me the other day that Isabella goes in at least once a week to check the quality of her pies hasn't diminished since Shelley stopped making them. Victoria said she feels like one of Da Vinci's students being ordered to paint the Mona Lisa's twin sister.'

'Why would anyone ask their students to do that?' Ivy asks with interest. 'And why Mona Lisa's twin sister? Why not her cousin or her aunt?'

'Why shouldn't the Mona Lisa have a twin sister?' asks Mabel. 'They're far better than the usual kind.'

I drop my head in my hands. 'I wish I'd never started this conversation. Whatever possessed me to mention the Mona Lisa? I'd forgotten how literal you all are.'

There's a general shout of laughter.

'We're enjoying the opportunity to wind you up,' says Ivy. 'It's important to demonstrate that you and your sister don't have the monopoly on being ridiculous.'

I open my mouth to speak, then close it again. There are various situations that call for someone to be a grown up. And this is obviously one of them.

Chapter Fifteen

A few weeks later, I arrive at work to find Isabella and Lily deep in discussion as they leaf through what I immediately recognise as a bridal magazine. There's a picture on the cover of a woman wearing a white dress and looking radiant. We have several similar magazines at home. Mum likes to glance through them in the evenings for ideas, which she insists on sharing with me and Dad, whether we like it or not.

'What's in the latest issue of Bridezilla Weekly?' I greet them, closing my eyes and hurling my jacket in the general direction of the pegs.

I decided last week that the reason I'm unable to hit my peg with reasonable frequency is because I've been overthinking it. I read somewhere that professional basketball players are told to switch off their brain and allow their gut to take over. Apparently, it increases their accuracy by over eighty percent. I've been using the same tactic for several days now – admittedly without success. But it's the only plan I have, so I'm sticking to it.

'I'm not a Bridezilla,' says Isabella, retrieving my jacket from the coffee machine and hanging it on its peg. 'I was showing Lily pictures of flower girls, in case she likes any of the dresses for Daisy.'

'Isn't it more relevant whether Daisy likes them?' I ask. 'She seems to be a young woman with a mind of her own.'

'She is,' says Isabella fondly. 'But I wanted to run them past Lily first so we don't overwhelm Daisy with too much choice.'

'She said on Sunday that she wants to wear her gardening dungarees,' says Lily in a resigned voice. 'Apparently, they're her very favourite clothes. Luckily, we were at my parents' house for lunch, so Dad distracted her with trifle before it turned into an argument.'

'Dungarees are a great idea,' I say. 'Lily and I could join in with the theme and go as a couple of scarecrows.'

'No, we couldn't,' says Lily. 'I get very few opportunities to wear a nice dress these days, and I intend to make the most of this one.'

I shrug. 'Your call, but I think you're mistaken. Isabella could organise the entire wedding around a horticultural theme. It would be a great talking point.'

'My wedding *is* the talking point,' says Isabella. 'I don't need any extra themes.'

'You're very wise,' says Lily. 'Jack and I attended a friend's wedding last year. The invitation said it was a rustic theme, so half the guests turned up wearing checked shirts and jeans. They were rather taken aback when the wedding party arrived in smart suits and ties.'

'So, what did the invitation mean?' I ask, confused.

'They had wildflowers in Mason jars, fairy lights strung everywhere, and hand-painted wooden signs. You know the sort of thing.'

I pull a face. 'I'm thankful to say I don't. That invitation sounds most misleading. As far as I'm concerned, the bride and groom got exactly what they asked for. Please tell me you wore a gingham dress with puffed sleeves and looked like an extra from Little House on the Prairie?'

'I did not,' says Lily. 'Jack's mum knows the mother of the bride, so she managed to clarify what the invitation meant before Jack had time to buy himself some steel-capped boots and a flannel shirt and go full-on lumberjack. He seemed quite disappointed. He said there was no point working in forestry if he was never allowed to look the part.'

'Doesn't Jack work in an office?' I ask.

'Mostly, yes. But I gave him a wooden sign saying *Timber Zone* for his birthday and told him he could hang it on his office wall to remind him of the man he might have been.'

'Love is a beautiful thing,' I say.

'It is indeed,' says Isabella. 'And how better to demonstrate that to the world than through a compost-themed wedding?'

'Rustic,' Lily corrects her.

'You've told us you aren't having a theme,' I remind Isabella. 'I think we should stick with that decision.'

'But I need a dress,' she says. 'Which is why you, Abby and Lily are coming out with me on Saturday afternoon to help me choose one.'

'What about the bakery?' I ask. 'Saturday is one of our busiest days. You aren't planning to close it?'

'Definitely not. Our customers would never forgive us. Lily's mum has offered to help out, and Shelley is giving Victoria the afternoon off so she can look after things here. She knows how to use the till and the coffee machine, and Angela makes an excellent cup of tea. I'm planning to have a word with some of our regular customers to warn them to be on their best behaviour. No throwing scones around or forming impromptu conga lines.'

'That was only once,' says Lily. 'Dancing Queen came on the radio while the Silver Surfers were here. The rest was a foregone conclusion.'

'Once is too often,' says Isabella. 'As I shall make plain to our more high-spirited clientele. I expect your mother and Victoria to keep the customers in check. If not, I've told them where we hide the pepper spray.'

'I'd offer to stay and help,' I say, 'but you may choose something awful for me to wear if I don't come with you.'

Isabella sighs. 'You have so little faith in me. I have excellent taste in dresses, which is more than I can say for someone who spent several years working for the establishment known as Martine's.'

'We offered the very latest in cutting-edge fashion to the style-challenged octogenarian,' I protest. 'I assumed you'd want to start there to see what Cath is offering this season.'

'It's tempting,' she says. 'But I may stick to the more traditional bridal boutiques.'

'That's probably wise. I may be barred, anyway. It wasn't explicitly mentioned on the day I walked out, but there was a certain look in Cath's eye that made me think it may not be wise for me to set foot over the threshold again.'

'So, that's all sorted!' says Isabella. 'We'll meet here at lunchtime on Saturday, have a quick bite of something to keep our energy up, then set out in search of the perfect dress. We have an appointment at Chez Colette at two-thirty.'

'Unless I can come up with a plausible excuse before then,' I say.

She frowns. 'Don't make me give you a written warning!'

'No one makes you give out those things. It's all your own doing. If you ask me, it's more of a compulsion than a considered decision, and I advise you to get the better of it before it gets the better of you. People always think they can control these things. By the time they realise they're in too deep, they find themselves standing on street corners at three in the morning, handing out written warnings like confetti to all the passers-by.'

'Speaking of confetti –' she says.

'We weren't. And neither will we be. We're trying to focus on buying you a wedding dress. One thing at a time, Isabella. You have to learn to prioritise.'

'Maybe you're right,' she says.

'I'm always right. That's why you made me your chief bridesmaid.'

'I thought you didn't like that title?'

'I don't. I'm still waiting for you to think of a better one.'

'I have far too many things on my plate as it is,' she grumbles.

'We're all more than aware of that. But what does that have to do with you thinking up my new job title?'

'Have you had any ideas about what you'd like to be called?' Lily asks me.

'That's Isabella's job. It was part of our initial agreement.'

Isabella rests her chin on her hands and stares into the distance. It's difficult to tell whether she's wrestling with the problem at hand or thinking dreamily of Abby's coffee eclairs. She adopts the same expression for both.

'Chief Vow Witnesser,' she suggests at last.

'I'm not going to dignify that,' I say.

'Commander of the Confetti? Head Dress Wrangler?'

I sigh. 'Now you aren't even trying.'

'We'll have to find something suitable for Isabella to wear first,' says Lily. 'Or there will be no dress to wrangle.'

'That's irrelevant now that I've lost my head dress wrangler,' says Isabella.

'Vow Vigilante?' suggests Lily.

I consider this. 'I like the vigilante part. We could work with that.'

'Keeper of the Bouquet?' says Isabella. 'Glitter Guru?'

'I've been very patient until now,' I warn her. 'But that won't last.'

'I'll give it some more thought,' she promises. 'Meanwhile, could you please make me a cappuccino? All this wedding talk is exhausting, and I need something to wash down Abby's cherry Bakewell tarts.'

'I'll make you a macchiato,' I say. 'I've already told you that cappuccinos pair best with milder flavours.'

'Remind me again whose bakery this is supposed to be?' she grumbles.

I ignore this and flip the switch on the coffee machine. She'll appreciate the wisdom of my decision once she tastes the correct combination. I rarely put my foot down while I'm at work, but this is my specialist subject, and I refuse to be overruled.

I'm just spooning foam over the espresso when the shop door opens. I don't turn around to see who it is. There are two other members of staff in here, and I'm at a crucial stage of the ladling process.

'Hi, Michael!' says Isabella. 'I didn't expect to see you here today.'

'People rarely expect to see me,' says Michael. 'I'm like the Spanish Inquisition.'

I turn around, holding the mug out to Isabella. 'Hello again. Are you here for one of our superb coffees, or were you looking for something to eat? We have some freshly baked cupcakes.'

'I decided to drop in and see this bakery everyone's been talking about,' he says.

'Who's been talking about it?' asks Isabella, apparently delighted by the thought that news of her business has spread far and wide.

'You, mostly,' says Michael. 'And Ollie and Toby, of course. I can't think why I haven't been in here before.'

'Now that you're here, what do you make of it?' she asks.

He looks around the shop and cafe. 'It's great. Much larger than I expected.'

'What can we get you?' I ask him.

'What do you recommend?'

'We have some pistachio meringues. They go nicely with a flat white. If you're after something more substantial, we have blackcurrant and apple turnovers. Perfect with a pot of Darjeeling tea.'

'The meringue sounds good,' he says.

I measure out the coffee beans before selecting a meringue for him.

'I've given you the biggest one we have left,' I say. 'I'm sure there were some much larger ones when I left here last night, but Isabella turned up before me this morning, and the rest is history.'

'This one is fine,' he says. 'Did you say you're making me a flat white to go with it?'

'That's right. It's a winning combination.'

'What's the difference between a flat white and a latte?' he asks.

I glance over at Isabella. 'Would you like to take this one?'

She clears her throat. 'It's difficult to explain to a non-aficionado.'

'Give it a go!' I encourage her.

'Well, one of the drinks is flatter. Obviously.'

'Flatter?' asks Michael.

'It's all to do with the hierarchy of the foam,' she says vaguely. 'There's no exact specification.'

'I think you'll find there is,' I say, laying Michael's mug in front of him.

Isabella dismisses this with a wave of her hand. 'Not one that universally applies. Some cultures don't even acknowledge the flat white. To answer Michael's question – it's all about milk texture. Lattes have looser foam and more flounce, whereas flat whites are tighter.'

'Tighter?' Michael echoes.

'Denser,' she corrects herself. 'The milk proteins undergo a more rigorous transformation during the heating process.'

I smile. 'And there was me thinking it was simply a case of using microfoam and employing a smaller ratio of milk to coffee.'

Michael raises an eyebrow. 'To clarify – a flat white is flatter, but tighter, and wholly unacknowledged in some regions of the world?'

'Exactly!' says Isabella. 'I'm sorry my sister wasn't able to explain it to you more clearly, but she hasn't been working here as long as I have.'

He takes a sip of his drink. 'Whatever the exact explanation –'

'And no one really knows what that is,' says Isabella. 'Coffee-making is an art, not a science.'

'I was going to say it tastes excellent,' he says. 'Hats off to the barista.'

'Isabella may be a little shaky on the fundamentals of fine coffee,' I say, 'but she's excellent at making tea. If you want some boiling water poured into a nice pot of Earl Grey or spiced chai, she's your woman.'

'Don't patronise me!' says Isabella huffily. 'You think I don't notice, but I do. I'm going to the kitchen to talk to Abby about Saturday afternoon.'

'What's happening on Saturday afternoon?' Michael asks when she's gone.

I roll my eyes. 'We're choosing a wedding dress. Apparently, it's a mandatory excursion.'

'Don't you like dress-shopping?'

'That kind of thing was knocked out of me during my time as deputy sales assistant at Martine's. But it's one of my current duties, so I'll have to grin and bear it as best I can.'

'I'm glad it's not one of the best man's duties,' he says. 'It isn't, is it?'

'I have every faith in Jon to choose his own outfit without any fuss and to dress himself on the day. Your duties are far lighter than mine. All you have to do is sort out his stag night and try not to let the ring bearer lose the ring.'

'Not even that,' he says.

'You mean you are planning to lose the ring?'

'I am not. But Jon and Isabella are having a joint stag night and hen party, and they're organising it themselves.'

'It had better not involve camping.'

He smiles. 'I have no idea what the pair of them have planned. Jon wasn't too forthcoming when I asked. But I'm sure whatever it is will be great fun.'

'I wish I had your confidence,' I say. 'I suppose the bridesmaids will have to be involved.'

'I expect so. But that sort of thing happens closer to the wedding day, so you don't have to worry about it yet.'

He pushes back his chair. 'I should be going. It was nice to see you again. Have a good time on Saturday. I look forward to hearing how you all got on.'

I pick up his cup and wipe his table. 'If you switch on the news on Sunday morning and hear about the mysterious disappearance of two bridesmaids and a maid of honour, you'll know that Isabella has finally driven us to change our names and flee the country.'

Chapter Sixteen

I haven't visited the arts centre since my dinner with David. It wasn't the best evening of my life, and I'm aware I may not have behaved like the perfect date in his eyes. Then again, I have no intention of changing my behaviour to suit someone else. If I ever meet anyone and settle down, they'll have to like me for what I am, not for what they hope I may become.

Isabella is lucky in that way. She's met a man who knows her through and through and loves everything about her. As much as I tell everyone it's a complete mystery how my sister has talked someone into marrying her, I'm happy for them both. They appear to be very well-suited. Jon is perfect for her. He's calm and grounded, and he gives her space to be herself without allowing himself to be pushed around too much.

I still think they should have eloped. It would have made it far easier for the rest of us. I sigh as I think of all the things that still need to be done before we finally pack Isabella and Jon off on their honeymoon to whatever ridiculous location the pair of them have settled on.

Today is Friday, and I decide to call in at The Red Lion for lunch. I'm not working again until two o'clock, which gives me plenty of time to enjoy a generous helping of pie and chips. To my annoyance, the sticky toffee pudding has sold out, but I make do with a more-than-acceptable slice of apple tart with whipped cream. It does us all good to get out of our ruts occasionally.

Victoria stops by my table as I'm drinking my coffee.

'I was hoping to run into you,' she says. 'I could have put something on the group chat, but it moves so fast I was worried my message might be lost.'

'It's a mystery, isn't it? You'd have thought that once they'd got their Isabella stories out of their system, things would have quietened down. But there are hundreds of new messages each time I open my phone. What did you want to talk to me about?'

'I thought we should discuss our upcoming London trip. The Flour Girls want to meet up and get to know each other properly before the actual wedding. And it seems easier to plan a wedding surprise for Isabella if we do it in person.'

'I'm already having to go dress shopping on Saturday,' I plead. 'Going to London feels above and beyond the call of duty. Do they really need me to be there?'

'Not if you hate the idea. But Lily's on board with it. I saw her last night at the pub quiz, and she thought it sounded great. Abby too.'

I sigh. 'I suppose I ought to go if they are. It wouldn't look good for the chief bridesmaid to duck out.'

'Are you still calling yourself that?' she asks. 'I thought you were hoping for a more suitable title.'

'I am. But so far, no one's come up with one. Isabella, of course, keeps making ridiculous suggestions. Keeper of the Lip Gloss was her last one. I'll take chief bridesmaid over that any day of the week.'

'We're planning to meet in London on Friday 27th if that works for you,' she says.

'I'll have to talk to Lily about it. It might look strange for the three of us to take the same day off. Isabella's bound to wonder what's going on.'

Victoria smiles. 'Lily has that covered. She's planning to tell Isabella the bakery needs some rewiring done that day. The electricians aren't sure how long the work will take, and it will too noisy for your customers.'

'That's quite ingenious,' I say. 'But Isabella does the accounts. Won't she want to know why we haven't received a bill?'

'Lily has apparently made up the name of a company who supposedly do this sort of work as part of an apprenticeship training scheme. All the bakery has to do is supply the cakes and hot drinks.'

'That's the least believable thing I've ever heard!' I say.

She shrugs. 'Lily has already printed an agreement on the firm's letterhead. Technically, that counts as forgery. But as the company doesn't exist, it doesn't matter too much.'

'I still think she's on shaky ground,' I say. 'But she may get away with it. Isabella can't concentrate on anything except her wedding these days. She's been far more distracted than usual. She even said no to the last piece of carrot cake the other day. Lily was quite worried about her.'

'I can imagine. So, you'll come to London with us?'

'Unless Isabella decides that closing the bakery would be the perfect opportunity to order me to perform an all-day stock-take. That would be just like her.'

'If she does, tell her you'll eat all the spare eclairs to save you having to count them. That ought to make her think twice.'

'Is that what you did when you worked at the bakery?' I ask.

'I didn't have to. I only worked there for a few months.'

'Oh, that's right. Yet another member of staff my sister recruited, then failed to retain. It's happened surprisingly often over the years.'

She laughs. 'That's a little unfair. I was only employed because Isabella broke her leg. She and Lily made it clear from the start it was a short-term thing, but I didn't care. It was an absolute lifesaver for me, and I'll always be grateful to them both for giving me a new start. I believe it was the same for everyone else who's worked there over the years. They may not have been as desperate as I was, but everyone except Abby was employed for a short period, and they all knew that when they signed up.'

'I imagine it was the only way my sister could persuade them to join her staff,' I say. 'If any of those women had been told up front they'd have to work with Isabella indefinitely, they'd have run a mile.'

'It's a great place to work, and you know it. She and Lily are wonderful employers. I love working at the Red Lion, but I still miss The Sugarloaf Bakery.'

'It's a complete mystery to me,' I say. 'But I'll take your word for it.'

'You do a great job there. They'll be sorry to lose you.'

'That won't be for a while yet,' I say. 'We have this wedding to get through first. We're going wedding dress shopping on Saturday. Then there's this brunch thing in London. And Jon and Isabella have something secret planned for their joint stag and hen dos. I'm already losing sleep wondering what that will be.'

'And there's Bernie,' she says. 'Have you got any further with getting his portrait done?'

I clap my hand to my head. 'I'd completely forgotten about it. I'm as bad as my sister, and that's saying something.'

'Have you at least decided what kind of picture you want?' she asks.

'Provided it looks like Bernie, I don't think Mrs Ogilvie will care.'

'The most important thing about a portrait is the eyes,' she says. 'If you get those right, everything else follows. Or so our school art teacher used to tell us.'

'I didn't know you studied art.'

'I was encouraged to give it up as quickly as possible. If I possessed even a smidgen of artistic talent, I'd have offered to help you out before now.'

'It's a pity more people aren't offering painting classes at the moment,' I say. 'Modern dance and dramatic improvisation aren't too helpful when it comes to producing recognisable portraits of dogs.'

'You could search for a photo of a cavoodle in an appropriate pose and get someone online to copy that,' she suggests. 'I'd never dare say it to Mrs Ogilvie, but don't all dogs of a similar breed look pretty much the same?'

'I said the same thing to Lily, but she told me any dog owner can recognise their dog in a line-up. Apparently, it's like babies. They all look exactly the same to me, but Lily insists she could identify hers within seconds of meeting them. It sounds dubious to me, but she's adamant. It seems to be the same with dogs. She insists Mrs Ogilvie would know in a second if it wasn't a picture of Bernie. I'll just have to keep looking for a local artist.'

'The arts centre offers all kinds of creative classes,' she says. 'How about asking people to produce a representation of Bernie? You could turn it into a competition. The entry that best portrays the spirit of Bernie wins a prize, and the finished piece will be displayed somewhere in the bakery.'

'You want me to commission a Bernie-themed art-off?'

'Why not?' she asks. 'It could be fun. Sculptures, collages, felted miniatures, interpretive sock puppets – whatever people want to do.'

I imagine a roomful of enthusiastic retirees brandishing glue guns and googly eyes.

'I hope no one makes a picture of Bernie out of spaghetti or something equally unflattering,' I say. 'Mrs Ogilvie wouldn't like that at all. She's always telling us how much dignity he has.'

'You'll have to tell her it's a concept that symbolises the connection between people and their pets. I'm sure you can think of a believable explanation.'

'It could work,' I say. 'But if one of the budding artists sculpts Bernie out of papier-mâché and he ends up looking like Scooby Doo, someone else will have to explain it Mrs Ogilvie.'

'You can select the winner,' she reminds me. 'I'm sure there will be plenty of highly creative entries.'

I finish my coffee and hand her the cup. 'It's a great idea, thanks, and it would solve at least one of my problems. If the others agree, I'll put up a notice at once.'

Chapter Seventeen

We set off from the bakery after lunch on Saturday. Isabella tries to stop and issue last-minute instructions before we leave, but Lily and I refuse.

'Victoria and Mrs Carson are perfectly capable of keeping the business afloat for a few short hours,' I tell Isabella.

'But what if they aren't? You know what some of our customers are like. The moment Mabel realises we aren't here, she's bound to think up some scheme or other. We may arrive at work tomorrow morning to find the till is empty and half our stock has disappeared with no explanation.'

'I'm not sure what you imagine will happen,' says Lily. 'Remember that Victoria worked for us fairly recently. She's on to all Mabel's tricks.'

'But your mother isn't,' says Isabella. 'And you know how nice she is. Mabel only has to announce it's her birthday, and our policy is to offer free cake and drinks to the birthday girl and all her friends, and that's our entire week's profits wiped out.'

'Not if Mrs Ogilvie is with her,' I remind her. 'If it's Mabel's birthday, it has to be hers too, and I don't see her going along with that sort of scheme.'

'And Mum knows which date it is,' says Lily. 'Don't you remember her holding a party for their eightieth birthday?'

'That was ages ago!' says Isabella. 'And those Silver Surfers are crafty. Your mother may not put two and two together quickly enough.'

'Victoria is aware we have no such policy,' says Lily. 'And my mother isn't half so much of a pushover as you think. She may be nice, but she managed to raise me and Ben, and she spends lots of time with Daisy and Ethan. She's capable of asserting herself when she needs to.'

She opens her car door and pushes Isabella into the passenger seat. 'The bakery goes along fine when you aren't there. There's no reason that shouldn't be true today.'

'Let me at least send them a text!' begs Isabella.

Lily closes the car door and rolls her eyes at me. 'If she's like this now, what will she be like by the time we arrive at the wedding boutique?'

'With any luck, she's getting it all out of her system,' I say. 'She was exactly the same with holidays when we were young. We'd barely closed the front door before she was demanding to go back and look for all the things she'd forgotten to pack. My mother was almost as bad. She spent the first hundred miles of every journey convinced she'd forgotten to switch off the oven and all the taps. She was also sure she'd left every single window wide open as an invitation for all the local burglars to stop by. I'm surprised we ever left Little Compton at all.'

'What are you two talking about?' asks Isabella as I climb into the back seat next to Abby and fasten my seatbelt.

'Holidays,' I say. 'And how difficult it was to get you to leave the house. You're a lot better about that nowadays. Is that because you and Jon usually go camping, and you no longer have enough space to pack the entire contents of your wardrobe as well as the larder?'

'It's because I've matured,' she says. 'And I've become the chill, laid-back person you all know and love.'

No one answers. Isabella seems to take our silence for enthusiastic agreement. She leans back in her seat with an air of pleasurable anticipation.

'Will they give us some cake at the bridal shop?' she asks. 'I'm starving.'

'I hope not,' I say. 'I wouldn't put it past you to drop it all over whichever dress you're currently trying on. Then you'll have to buy it, whether you like it or not.'

'The website says they'll offer us champagne,' says Lily.

'It's a start,' says Isabella. 'But you should have slipped some cakes into your bag to keep us all going if this takes longer than we expect.'

'It won't take longer than I expect,' I say. 'If you find a dress at the first shop we visit – or even the fifth – I'll be amazed.'

'That's the fun of this sort of thing,' says Lily. 'No one wants to walk out of the shop with the first dress they've seen.'

'Why not?' I ask. 'It's just as likely to be the dress of your dreams as any of the others you see. Isabella should understand that. It's a simple matter of probability.'

'I often buy the first thing I see,' says Isabella. 'But not until I've tried on everything in every single shop I visit. Then I buy the original item because I've conclusively proved to myself it's the absolute best.'

I groan. 'Is that what you're planning to do today?'

'I've never been shopping for a wedding dress before. How can I predict what will happen?'

'As long as you don't get cake all over the dresses, I'll be happy,' says Lily. 'And I'm prepared to go shopping with you as many times as you need until you find exactly what you're looking for.'

'I'm not,' I say. 'This is a one-shot deal. Imagine what our customers will get up to if we keep taking off like this.'

Lily catches my eye in the mirror and frowns. 'Don't set her off again.'

'It's true, though,' says Isabella. 'If we go dress-shopping a second time, we'll have to go in shifts.'

'Or close the bakery entirely,' says Abby.

'We're already doing that at the end of this month,' says Isabella. 'Lily tells me we need some plumbing or something done.'

'Rewiring,' says Lily.

'That's right. I offered to help organise it, but she told me to leave it all up to her, so I am.'

'You have enough to do with the wedding,' I say, and she sighs.

'That's very true. I'm using that day for the menu tasting. Jon's taking the morning off work and coming with me.'

'Why am I invited to go dress shopping with you but not to the menu thing?' I ask. 'I would have thought you'd be grateful for my discerning palate and talent for pairing flavours.'

'You're welcome to come along,' she says. 'But you told me you were busy that day.'

Too late, I remember why we're closing the bakery on false pretences. I rack my brain for some suitable reason to give her.

'I'm meeting an old friend in London,' I say. 'Otherwise, I'd have loved to be there.'

'And I'll be off visiting my great aunt in Somerset,' says Abby.

'And Lily will be supervising the electricians,' says Isabella. 'She's promised to keep a close eye on them and make sure they don't break anything while they're fixing whatever it is that needs doing. What is it again?'

Lily casts me an agonised look over her shoulder, and I grin back at her.

'Lily told me it was the power supply to the refrigeration units,' I tell Isabella.

'That's right,' says Lily. 'They said if we didn't fix it soon, there was a risk of it shorting out and causing a fire.'

'I'm glad you called them in,' says Isabella. 'What made you think of it?'

'It came up during our routine annual inspection,' says Lily, not meeting anyone's eye.

Isabella seems satisfied with this explanation, so I change the subject before she can ask any further questions. I'm willing to bet

Lily and Abby have as little electrical knowledge as I do, and I'm all out of inspiration if she pursues the subject further.

'I was talking to Victoria recently,' I say. 'She suggested that if we can't find a suitable artist to paint Bernie's portrait, we should turn it into a village-wide competition. We could put up a notice in the arts centre inviting people to come up with different representations of him.'

'Like what?' asks Isabella.

'We needn't be too specific. We can ask the contestants to use whichever medium they prefer to catch his likeness.'

'That's a good idea,' says Lily. 'The watercolour class could try their hand at painting him, and the pottery class could make a model of him.'

'Suzanne Cowen teaches knitting for beginners,' says Abby. 'Some of her pupils might like to have a go at making stuffed Bernies.'

'Isn't there a mosaic class on Thursdays?' asks Isabella. 'Bernie would be the perfect subject for that. I'm almost sure they found a Roman mosaic in Pompeii with a picture of a dog on it. The title was *Cave Canem.*'

'No one needs to beware of Bernie,' says Abby. 'He's such a friendly little thing.'

Isabella laughs. 'Far too friendly, Mabel says. She's always bemoaning the fact he'd make a useless guard dog. It's a pity there's no film class at the moment. They could take some footage of Bernie and turn it into a short movie. They could sell the rights to a television company if it turned out well.'

'*The Pawprentice,*' I suggest.

'*I'm a Dog – Get Me Out of Here!* says Isabella. 'Although Mrs Ogilvie wouldn't like him having to do the trials. How about *Come Dine with Bernie?* He'd enjoy starring in that. He could have all his little friends over for a three-course meal while Mabel did a sarcastic voice-over. It could be the surprise hit of the season.'

'He may prefer a slot on *Strictly Come Barking,*' I suggest. 'Mrs Ogilvie is always telling us how graceful he is.'

'*Or Top Mutt*,' says Abby. 'Bernie tries out a new car each week and gives his thoughts on it.'

'Mrs Ogilvie would never sign off on her precious dog appearing on a television show,' says Lily. 'She'd be far too worried about the crew not appreciating the wonder that is Bernie.'

'I'll bet she'd allow him to make a guest appearance on *The Only Way is Bernie*,' says Isabella. 'This competition idea could be the solution to all our problems. Good thinking, Georgia. Can we leave it to you to arrange it all?'

'If you want it done properly. There's no use asking you to do anything these days. Your naturally brief attention span has shrunk to almost nothing since you got engaged.'

'It happens to everyone,' says Lily, pulling into a parking space near the bridal boutique. 'Are we all ready for the this?'

'As we'll ever be,' I say, unfastening my seatbelt.

Isabella is already out of the car and hurrying towards the shop.

'I'd better go and keep an eye on her,' says Abby.

'It's nice that she's so excited,' says Lily.

'It's still not too late for her to elope,' I say. 'It would save us all a lot of time and worry. I'd be willing to drive them to Gretna Green myself.'

'Nonsense,' she says. 'It's going to be a beautiful wedding, and you'll enjoy it very much. I promise.'

'I'm sure you're right.' I pick up my bag and plaster a smile on my face. 'Let's go and talk necklines!'

She laughs and links her arm through mine as we follow Isabella towards Chez Colette. The shop bell tinkles cheerfully, as if unaware of the chaos about to unfold.

'Bridesmaid mode officially activated!' I say. 'What could possibly go wrong?'

Chapter Eighteen

It's like walking into a different world. Outside is cold and grey, and it's started to sleet again. In here, it's bright and warm and very, very shiny. It feels like diving into a snow globe.

Light bounces off the racks of dresses, reflecting off the sequins and rhinestones like a fairy-tale disco ball. The air smells faintly of roses and vanilla, and the carpet is cream and ankle deep. It must be a nightmare to clean, especially on a day like this. Soft music is playing in the background. It takes me a moment to identify the tune as *I'm Getting Married in the Morning*. It feels a little optimistic when we haven't even chosen the dress.

The proprietor surges forward in a whirl of enthusiasm and delicate perfume. She's wearing a pastel pink suit, and her hair is swept up into a neat chignon. Her two assistants stand demurely in the background. One of the women is wearing a pale blue suit, and the other a mint-green dress with matching jacket. Between the three of them, they look like a dish of sugared almonds. I feel suddenly scruffy in my jeans and thick sweater.

'Welcome!' says the owner of the shop in a hushed yet thrilling voice. 'I'm Colette Valentine. It's such a pleasure to meet you all. We're here today to make your dreams come true.'

We glance at each other. Someone has to speak. The silence is growing uncomfortable.

'Thanks,' I say at last.

'We had another booking after this,' says Colette. 'But unfortunately, the other bride has had to cancel, which means we can offer you our undivided attention for the next few hours.'

She gestures towards her assistants. 'These two lovely ladies will assist you today in your search for perfection. Fleur and Elodie – please take our customers' coats and their drink orders.'

The woman in green steps forward, and we hand her our jackets. The woman in blue disappears briefly and returns carrying a golden tray bearing five champagne flutes.

'I can offer you something soft if you'd prefer,' she says.

Champagne sounds great to me. It may help me through the upcoming ordeal. I suspect the reason they're offering it for free is to cloud Isabella's judgement and make her reach for her credit card, but that's her business.

'Alcohol works for me,' I say, reaching for the nearest glass.

Apparently, it works for everyone else too, as they all pick up a glass and take a sip.

Colette takes the last one and lifts it to Isabella. 'To fairy-tale moments!'

I almost choke on my champagne – which tastes remarkably like cheap prosecco – although I'm not about to ruin the moment by saying so.

Isabella beams back at her. 'I love fairy tales!'

'Doesn't everyone?' asks Colette with an arch smile.

'My favourite is Rumpelstiltskin,' continues Isabella, 'Especially the bit where he stamps his foot so hard it almost goes through the floor. But I've always loved the one about the three little pigs. It's very motivational for people like me who are trying to get on to the property ladder.'

Colette looks taken aback. 'I was thinking more of Sleeping Beauty or Cinderella.'

'They're alright,' agrees Isabella. 'But not half as much fun as the big, bad wolf or the Frog Prince.'

The woman in green speaks for the first time. I'm not sure whether she's Elodie or Fleur. Colette neglected to identify them when we first met, and it feels too late to ask.

'I'm sure your prince was never a frog,' she says coyly.

'Possibly not,' says Isabella, 'although he is very keen on swimming.'

Colette's bright smile has slipped a little during this conversation. She seems to realise this and quickly hoists it back into position.

'What a fascinating discussion,' she says. 'But what I'd really like to ask you about is your vision for this wedding. For instance, do you have a theme?'

'Not really,' says Isabella. 'Just a general marriage sort of thing.'

Colette's smile stays firmly in place. 'How about the reception? Are you thinking whimsical, rustic, old-time glamour, timeless elegance, or something completely different?'

'Definitely!' says Isabella.

'Definitely what?' asks Colette.

'All of those sound great.'

The woman in the green dress glances at the one in the blue suit. Neither of them speaks, but it's clear they weren't prepared for this when they got out of bed this morning.

Colette tries again. 'Where are you getting married?'

'Willowmere Hall,' says Isabella.

'A lot of our brides choose that venue,' says Colette. 'It's so wonderfully romantic. You'll be in excellent hands.'

'We were very lucky to get it,' says Isabella.

'Have they discussed themes and ambience with you?'

'Not really, but we're doing the food tasting on the 27th, so maybe they'll talk about it then.'

Colette gives a trill of laughter. 'Let's hope so, or you may find yourself walking down the aisle without any cohesive theme at all!'

'It sounds like glue,' says Isabella. 'I appreciate your warning, and I'll be sure to discuss it with our wedding co-ordinator when we meet her.'

Colette inspects her critically. 'You have a wonderful figure. You'd suit almost any style of gown. I had a bride a few years ago who was organising a Gone With the Wind theme. She, of course, was Scarlett, and her husband-to-be was Rhett. The bridesmaids made beautiful southern belles. She had eight of them. We had their dresses custom-made by a designer – each in a different colour. They looked like a flock of exotic birds as they walked down the aisle. Everyone was most impressed.'

'I love that idea,' says Isabella. 'But I only have two bridesmaids, so it may be difficult to get the same effect.'

She gives me and Abby a considering look. 'You two could go as a pair of budgies if we ordered you blue and green dresses.'

Colette brings us back to reality, or whatever passes for reality in my sister's world. 'So, no theme, then?'

'Not yet,' says Isabella. 'But I promise I'll give it some thought.'

Colette clasps her hands and assumes a playful expression. 'Are we ready to try on some dresses?'

'Absolutely!' says Isabella with enthusiasm.

'Unless you'd like something to eat first?' asks either Fleur or Elodie. The one wearing the blue suit, anyway.

'I'd love something to eat!' says Isabella. 'It's been ages since lunch.'

Colette gestures towards her assistants. 'Would you do the honours?'

They produce two bowls, which they set down on a table next to us.

'Champagne truffles,' says Colette, 'and tiny dried apricots. We like to provide a lighter option to go alongside the chocolates. Many of our brides are watching what they eat.'

'Quite right too,' says Isabella. 'I always watch what I eat. It's most important.'

'I can see you do,' says Colette with an approving glance at her figure. 'Your wedding is the most special day of your life, and you want to look your best.'

Isabella takes a champagne truffle and pops it into her mouth. 'These are amazing!'

She chooses a second one and hands the bowl to me. I grab a chocolate and bite into it.

'You're right,' I say. 'These are delicious.'

'We may need some more of these,' Isabella tells Colette. 'There are four of us, remember?'

She takes another one before passing the bowl to Abby.

Colette watches her in horror. 'These truffles are made with fresh cream, dear.'

'I can tell they are,' says Isabella. 'That's what makes them taste so good.'

'Would you like to try the apricots?'

Isabella shakes her head. 'I don't think so, thank you. I've never been a huge fan of dried fruit. But that shouldn't stop the rest of you. I'm happy to finish these truffles by myself.'

'Not a hope,' says Lily, taking the bowl from her. 'Dress shopping is hungry work – especially with someone like you. I need to keep up my energy.'

Colette looks as though she's about to pass out with horror at the scene before her.

'Are you sure this is wise?' she asks anxiously. 'Some of our dresses fit extremely snugly. The corseted tops in particular are quite unforgiving.'

Isabella helps herself to the last truffle. 'Those were lovely, thank you. I feel in much better shape for trying on dresses now.'

Colette's expression indicates that Isabella won't remain that shape unless she changes her eating patterns in the very near future. But she doesn't comment further.

'Before you try anything on,' she says, 'I need you to answer a few questions.'

'Go ahead!' says Isabella. 'As long as they aren't about the names of mountain ranges or the major exports of small nations, I don't mind giving it a shot.'

Colette looks puzzled. 'I meant about your personal style.'

'That should be easy enough! I'm all ears.'

Colette picks up a piece of paper and glances down at it.

'We already know where you'll be getting married, so we're aware you're looking for a dress that embodies the spirit of class and romance. Let's try something more specific. Would you say you're more of a minimalist bride or a fairy-tale princess?'

Isabella frowns. 'Are those the only two options?'

'For now,' says Colette. Is it my imagination or is her tone rather less cheerful than when we arrived?

'I'll have to pass on that one,' says Isabella. 'What's the next question?'

'How would you like to feel on your wedding day?' asks Colette.

Isabella considers this. 'Married?'

The blonde assistant giggles, then claps her hand over her mouth as Colette glares at her.

'What are my options?' asks Isabella.

Colette glances at her list. 'Romantic, sexy, comfortable, elegant, feminine, sophisticated, or classic?'

'Those all sound good to me. Do I have to select only one of them?'

Colette's smile doesn't falter. 'It would be very helpful if you could.'

Isabella turns to us. 'Which one should I choose?'

'Whichever you like,' says Lily. 'It's your wedding day, so you should have exactly what you want.'

'But I don't know what I want,' says Isabella. 'I keep thinking I do, but then someone suggests something different and I start wondering whether those ideas are better.'

'Perhaps, as time is getting on, we should move on to the silhouette,' says Colette. 'I'm sure you have some ideas about that?'

'Lots!' says Isabella. 'Can you quickly remind me what types of silhouette there are?'

Colette consults her list again. 'Let's start with the classical A-line, the ballgown, the mermaid, the tea-length gown, and the sheath.'

'Those all sound lovely,' says Isabella.

'You wouldn't like to narrow it down a little?' asks Colette, a hint of desperation in her tone.

'Not really. I was thinking about a princess cut too.'

'Do you have any preference as to neckline?' asks the woman in the green dress.

'I definitely want one,' says Isabella. 'But I'm not sure which shape.'

'You're being incredibly unhelpful,' I tell her. 'You must know which type of neckline you don't want, even if you haven't yet fixed on the one you prefer.'

'Remind me of my choices again?' she says.

'Sweetheart, V-neck, high-neck, off-the-shoulder, boat-neck, halter, or plunging,' rattles off Colette, who doesn't appear to be having as much fun as she expected.

'Not plunging,' says Isabella with the air of someone who thinks she deserves a gold star for being so decisive.

'How about sleeve length?' asks Lily. 'It's a summer wedding, so you could choose a strapless dress if you like.'

'That might not be so good for dancing,' says Isabella. 'And I intend to do lots of that.'

Colette makes a note on her pad. There's a note of relief in her voice. 'So, we've ruled out strapless.'

'Unless it's a really nice dress,' says Isabella. 'In which case, I might consider it.'

'Let's assume you won't,' I say, anxious to move things along a little. 'What are your sleeve preferences? Long or short, spaghetti or cap, bishop or bell?'

Isabella looks impressed. 'You seem to know a lot about sleeves.'

'You're always leaving those bridal magazines lying around the house. I've picked up quite a bit by osmosis.'

She nods. 'All those sound lovely to me.'

I wonder whether Colette has ever thrown any brides out of her shop. Even if she hasn't, it's looking increasingly likely she may make an exception for Isabella.

'Should I assume you haven't narrowed down your choice of fabric either?' she asks.

'Something comfortable,' says Isabella. 'I'll have to wear it all day and during the evening reception too.'

'And I take it you're equally open to all types of embellishment,' says Colette in a resigned tone. 'Beads, sequins, seed pearls, diamanté?'

'Very open,' says Isabella. 'Willowmere Hall has the most beautiful chandeliers in their ballroom. I'd quite like to outshine them if I can.'

Colette claps her hands together, and her helpers hurry forward. I'm not sure why she needed to do that. They're only standing a few feet away. But perhaps it gives her an illusion of authority in a situation that's fast spinning out of her control.

'Fleur, Elodie – I'd like you to make an initial selection of dresses for Miss Campbell and carry them through to the changing area.'

She turns back to Isabella. 'I assume you're wearing appropriate undergarments to try on a wide variety of styles?'

'Oh yes!' says Isabella. 'I'm wearing the matching Winnie the Pooh set my goddaughter gave me for my birthday. It's very sweet. It's a pity no one will see it on the day, but you can't have everything.'

I take her arm and guide her towards the changing room. 'I think you need to stop talking before you get us all banned from here.'

Chapter Nineteen

Colette looks at her watch a couple of hours later and gives us a tight smile. 'I'm devastated to have to tell you this, but your appointment is over. We're about to close.'

Isabella doesn't seem to realise that Colette's tone is anything but devastated.

'Oh, no!' she exclaims. 'We're only just getting started!'

Colette visibly flinches. I glance around the changing room, which looks as though a blizzard has hit it. Every surface is buried under an avalanche of dresses. Fleur and Elodie began by putting away each dress once Isabella had tried it on. But no sooner had they done so than Isabella wanted to see it again, and they quickly gave up.

I reach for a tiara balanced precariously on the back of a chair and hand it to Colette.

'It's a pity time got away with us,' says Isabella. 'But you can't rush bridal inspiration. I've almost narrowed it down to my favourite fifteen dresses.'

Colette makes an indeterminate noise. 'Perhaps you'd like to book a follow-up appointment?'

'I'd love to!' says Isabella. 'We haven't even thought about veils yet. Maybe we can extend the next appointment a little? Three hours doesn't feel like nearly enough time.'

'To you, maybe,' says Lily.

'Would you like any help putting away the dresses?' I ask Colette, who gives a tiny shake of her head.

'Thank you, but no. My assistants know where they all go.'

Fleur and Elodie give us less than loving looks as they scoop up armfuls of dresses and carry them back to the shop.

'We seem to have made rather a mess in here,' says Isabella. 'I can't think how we managed it. I didn't try on that many styles.'

'Forty-two,' says Abby. 'I counted.'

'You surprise me. I wouldn't have thought it was more than twenty.'

'Are we any further forward?' Lily asks her.

Isabella considers. 'I've ruled out the one with the fishtail. At least, I'm almost sure I have. It has a lovely neckline, but I might not be able to dance in it as well as some of the others.'

'You seemed quite keen on that dress with the puffed sleeves,' says Abby.

'It was beautiful,' agrees Isabella. 'But it was a little plainer than I had in mind. I really liked the one with the embroidered bodice and the trumpet sleeves. It felt almost mediaeval. If I wore that, I could pretend I was a princess uniting two rival kingdoms after years of war.'

'I thought you got on well with Jon's parents,' I say. 'And Mum told me she and Dad had a very enjoyable meal with them the last time they were here.'

'But they may have a spectacular falling out at some point,' she says. 'And then I could wear this dress. I could walk down the aisle with a falcon on my wrist and a herald in front of me, proclaiming that I came in peace.'

'Would Abby and I still have to dress as budgies?' I ask. 'I don't think they're too keen on falcons, and with good reason.'

'Maybe ravens?' she says. 'It would give my wedding a Game of Thrones vibe. You love that show!'

Colette holds the shop door open and smiles at us in a determined manner.

'So lovely to meet you all!' she says brightly. 'Do come again. Although we tend to get booked up very quickly for these appointments, so I can't promise anything.'

'I'll book early,' promises Isabella. 'Thank you for a wonderful afternoon. See you soon!'

I hustle her out of the shop before she can torture the poor woman any further.

'We'll need to take a taxi home,' I say. 'We all drank quite a lot of champagne – including you, Lily.'

'There's no need for that,' says Isabella. 'I've made appropriate arrangements.'

'They'd better not include me walking home,' I tell her. 'It's freezing cold, and it's started to snow again.'

'No one will be walking anywhere. I wonder where they are?'

Before I have time to ask who she means, I notice Jon waving at us from the opposite side of the road. I'm surprised to see Michael is with him.

'Jon will drive Lily's car,' says Isabella. 'She's insured for any driver. We can all meet at Alessandro's.'

'The restaurant in Christchurch?' I ask. 'You didn't tell me anything about this.'

'Didn't I? It must have slipped my mind. You don't have any other plans, do you?'

'I do, actually.'

'What?' she asks, surprised.

'Just plans.'

'You didn't mention anything about them earlier.'

'There are plenty of things I don't mention,' I say. 'Especially to you!'

'Do you have a date?' Lily asks me.

I flush. 'It isn't that sort of plan. I just have a few things I need to do this evening.'

'Can't you put them off?' begs Isabella. 'I've booked a table for all of us.'

'How many people are coming?' I ask.

'I'm meeting Jack there,' says Lily. 'And I believe Chris is joining us too.'

'Why am I always the last to know about anything?' I grumble. 'Does the word *chief* mean nothing to you?'

'It's more of an honorary title,' explains Isabella. 'Designed to make you feel important without conferring any actual power.'

'You could have explained that when you asked me to do it. I would have said no.'

'Why do you think I didn't tell you? Come on, Georgia. You've never yet turned down the offer of a free meal. Jon and I are paying for the three of you to thank you for giving up your afternoon for me. Couldn't you do some of those other things later?'

'I suppose so,' I say reluctantly. 'But I can't stay out too late.'

Michael and Jon have crossed the road to join us.

'Your keys, please,' Jon says to Lily. 'I can tell from looking at you all that champagne has been consumed.'

'We could report Colette under the Trade Descriptions Act,' I say. 'Her website said champagne, and she served us cheap prosecco. However, after spending an afternoon with Isabella, I've decided she deserves our pity rather than our censure.'

'I was a delight!' says Isabella. 'I said please and thank you, and I ate all the truffles she brought us. What more do you want?'

Jon takes her arm. 'I'm sure you were the model client. Why don't I drive you and Lily to the restaurant? Abby and Georgia can go with Michael and show him the way.'

'Chris is picking me here in a minute,' says Abby. 'He wanted to bring our car so we can stop off on the way home and see my parents.'

'It looks as though it's just us,' Michael tells me. 'Do you know the way?'

'Georgia ate there very recently,' says Isabella. 'She can't have forgotten already.'

'I've been running the heater, so it's nice and warm,' Michael tells me as we reach the car.

'I'm already warm,' I say. 'Colette had the heating turned up high. I was wearing a thick sweater, but I soon regretted it.'

'I suppose they don't want the bride to be cold while she's trying on dresses,' he says. 'Or the rest of you, for that matter.'

'Chance would be a fine thing. We didn't get around to the other members of the bridal party. Isabella has to choose her dress before the rest of us get a look in.'

He smiles. 'Do I take it she didn't find one today?'

'You do indeed. Not that any of us were expecting her to. If there's one quality my sister is definitely not known for, it's decisiveness.'

'So, this was just a preliminary skirmish?' he asks.

'You could put it like that. I gained the distinct impression that the woman who owns the shop would be happy never to see us again.'

'I'm sure that's not true. Which way do I turn at the roundabout?'

'Left. And I wouldn't be so certain about Colette. Isabella can be a lot to cope with if you haven't met her before. Someone should have warned the staff what they were in for.'

'How bad could it have been?' he asks.

'Let me see! First, we got into a discussion about fairy tales, during which Isabella ended up talking about the three little pigs. Then came the questionnaire about styles – just to narrow things down a little. Isabella isn't really into narrowing things down, so that didn't go too well. She spent several minutes working her way through a bowl of truffles while explaining to Colette that every single style she suggested sounded better than the last. Finally, she tried on almost every dress in the shop – several of them more than once – all the while discussing parrots and crows and eagles, while Colette made confused notes on her jotter. I'm pretty sure the final note was instructing her helpers to call the emergency services and pretend there was a fire.'

'It sounds as though you all had a wonderful time,' he says.

'Except Colette.'

'I expect she's seen much worse.'

'I hope you're right, but it's difficult to imagine how.'

'Do you have another appointment booked?' he asks.

'There was some talk of it, but I won't be in the least surprised if Isabella finds they're fully booked up when she calls. I know they're keen to make sales, but there must be limits.'

'Isabella said you've eaten at this restaurant recently,' he says. 'I hope you don't mind going there again so soon.'

'Not at all. It was lovely, and I didn't get to try half the things I wanted to. But I should warn you we may be greeted at the door by a twelve-year-old wearing his father's jacket and tie.'

'Isn't that illegal?' he asks.

'Twelve may be a slight exaggeration. Possibly, he's reached his mid-teens by now and has simply retained his extraordinarily youthful looks. He'll be grateful for them when he's older. David tried to speak Italian to him, which was a mistake. He may not have started studying for his GCSEs yet.'

'David?' he asks. 'Is that your boyfriend?'

'He volunteers at the arts centre. I asked him about painting a portrait of one of our customers. He invited me to dinner so we could discuss the commission more thoroughly. In the end, he decided the specifications didn't match his skill set and turned it down.'

'That's a shame,' he says. 'Was your customer very disappointed?'

'Not noticeably. He ate a biscuit and lay down under a table to go to sleep.'

'He –? Oh, I remember now. You're talking about a dog.'

'I am indeed.'

'You confused me when you referred to him as a customer.'

'Bernie is one of our very best customers,' I say. 'Rain or shine, he comes to the bakery several times a week for a dog biscuit and a puppuccino. He's often the only thing that stands between the staff being paid that week or going hungry.'

'No one would ever go hungry in a bakery,' he says. 'You'd be some of the safest people in Honeywell in the event of a zombie apocalypse.'

'What a cheering thought. I suppose we would. I wouldn't put it past Isabella to sell tickets to a few lucky people so they could shelter in there with us.'

He smiles. 'I'll remember to head in your direction the moment the news hits.'

'You won't be able to afford our ticket prices. I'm afraid you'll have to take your chances with the zombies.'

He pulls into the car park. 'I can't say I'm not disappointed.'

'I understand your feelings, but it will be every person for themselves on that day. It seems fairer to mention that upfront and give you the chance to make your own preparations.'

'Don't think I'm ungrateful,' he says. 'I'm even more keen to scope out Alessandro's now. I'd like to find out whether they're likely to adopt a more welcoming policy than The Sugarloaf Bakery when the awful day comes.'

'I'm sure you can talk the Maitre d' around,' I say. 'Just slip him a fifty-pence piece to buy himself a comic and some chewing gum, and you'll go straight to the top of the list.'

Chapter Twenty

Isabella and Jon are waiting for us when we arrive. Sadly, the twelve-year-old isn't. Instead, we're greeted by a man of about fifty, who directs us to a large table at the back of the restaurant.

'Your friends have already arrived,' he says. 'Your server will be with you directly.'

Michael nudges me as we walk to our table. 'I wouldn't put money on you winning any guess-the-age competitions.'

'That wasn't the boy wonder,' I say. 'As you're well aware.'

'Not necessarily. You don't appear to be short-sighted, but I was about to suggest a trip to a good optician.'

'You made it!' says Isabella.

'Did you think we wouldn't?' asks Michael.

'I thought your chances were about fifty-fifty. I know what it's like to drive somewhere new with only Georgia to give you directions.'

'So, you were willing to risk us never arriving?' he says. 'That wasn't very friendly of you.'

'Isabella was hoping we'd end up in Portsmouth,' I say, pulling out a chair and sitting down. 'Then she could have eaten whatever she'd ordered for us.'

Michael sits next to me. 'A good plan, but between my careful driving and Georgia's excellent directions, here we are.'

'And I was here only a few weeks ago,' I remind Isabella. 'Even I can remember back that far.

'Ah, yes,' she says. 'Dinner with David. Of all the weak excuses to ask someone out, that was the weakest.'

'It was a business dinner,' I say.

'And how much business did you transact?'

'That's hardly the point.'

'I didn't see your expense claim for this so-called dinner,' she says.

'That's because David paid.'

'You see!' she says triumphantly. 'It was a date.'

'It really wasn't. If you hadn't made such a rash promise about Bernie in the first place, I wouldn't have had to go at all.'

'Didn't you enjoy your dinner?' Jon asks me.

'The food was excellent, and we had a lovely time. All I'm saying is that it wasn't a date. If you must know, I'm not dating at all at the moment.'

'That seems rather extreme,' says Isabella.

'Not really. I have more than enough going on in my life without adding any extra stresses. I'm choosing to concentrate on those things for now and avoiding unnecessary complications.'

I reach for a piece of bread and cram it into my mouth.

Isabella touches my hand. 'I'm sorry, Georgie. I was only teasing. You know how carried away I get.'

I smile back at her. 'No one knows that better than me.'

'The other members of your party have arrived,' says the server, laying a menu by each place.

Abby and Chris appear, closely followed by Jack and Lily.

'I thought you'd got lost,' Isabella tells Jack. 'After all the champagne Lily drank this afternoon, there was a strong possibility she'd tell you we were meeting in Brighton.'

'Two small glasses,' says Lily.

'And it wasn't even champagne,' I add.

'You aren't letting that one go, are you?' asks Isabella.

'Ordinarily, no. But after what you put that poor woman through, I've decided to be the bigger person.'

'I expect Colette is lying in a darkened room right now,' says Abby, 'holding an ice pack to her head and questioning her life choices.'

'I don't see why,' says Isabella. 'We spent a delightful afternoon with them all.'

Lily, Abby and I exchange glances, but none of us speaks.

Jon lays a hand on Isabella's. 'I imagine that, charming as everyone finds your company, it could be a little overwhelming for someone meeting you for the very first time.'

'Were those really their names?' I ask.

'Whose names?' asks Michael.

'The women in the dress shop. It seems improbable they were really named Colette and Fleur and Elodie.'

'That's what I thought,' says Isabella. 'Maybe those are their professional names. When they're at home, they're called Janet, Peggy and Maud.'

'Or they chose their profession based on their names,' I add. 'Like Usain Bolt becoming a sprinter. When you think about it, what other course was open to him?'

'Or William Wordsworth becoming a poet,' says Isabella. 'Imagine how much the world would have lost if he'd been called Bill Spreadsheet.'

'I wouldn't work anywhere that expected me to change my name to impress the customers,' I say.

'We've dodged a bullet there,' says Lily. 'Isabella and I originally considered introducing you to our customers as Madeleine Crumb.'

'Or Cherry Ganache,' adds Isabella. 'I'm glad we didn't suggest it before you signed your contract.'

'I don't have a written contract,' I say. 'You and I agreed from the start it would be best not to formalise anything. I can walk out any time I like, and there's nothing you can do about it.'

'But you won't,' she says. 'You love working at The Sugarloaf Bakery. Everyone does.'

'It's better than working at Chez Colette,' I admit. 'Although she does serve lovely champagne truffles.'

'Not to her staff,' Lily reminds me. 'They stood well back and watched with awed respect as Isabella and you got on with it. Although Colette seemed worried about Isabella bursting out of her dress on the big day.'

'She'd have to choose one first!' I say.

'I've narrowed down my choices considerably,' says Isabella. 'Why are you all laughing?'

'No reason,' says Abby. 'Here comes our food. Make sure you don't eat too much pasta or you'll have to buy a wedding dress with an elastic waist.'

'What a great idea,' says Isabella. 'I don't believe Colette showed me any of those today. I'll have to mention it to her the next time we visit.'

'You don't really plan to make me go through all that again?' I ask.

She waves a slice of pizza at me. 'Don't pretend you didn't enjoy this afternoon because I wouldn't believe you.'

'It was quite fun, in an odd sort of way.'

She looks pleased. 'I told you it would be. It's a shame that none of you will be there for the menu tasting. We could have made a day of it.'

'Aren't you coming to that?' Jon asks me. 'It sounds right up your street.'

'I wish I could, but I've arranged to go to London to meet a friend.'

'And Lily will be at the bakery, supervising the trainee electricians,' says Isabella. 'And Abby is visiting her great aunt in Somerset.'

'Your great aunt?' asks Chris in a surprised tone, then gives a sharp gasp as Abby elbows him in the ribs.

'I've been meaning to get down to see her for ages,' says Abby.

'Are you going with her?' Isabella asks Chris.

He looks at Abby. 'Am I?'

'That's up to you,' she says. 'I'm not in charge of your timetable.'

'Which date is the menu tasting?' asks Michael.

'The twenty-seventh,' says Jon. 'You're welcome to come along too. I'd value the opinion of my best man about the food we plan to serve.'

Michael shakes his head. 'Any other day would be great, but I'm booked up then.'

He looks at me. 'As it happens, I'm also going to London. Would you like a ride?'

Lily gives a tiny choke of laughter, then shoves a large mouthful of risotto into her mouth to cover it.

'I'll have to leave quite early,' I say. 'I've arranged to meet my friend for brunch.'

'That suits me,' he says. 'I don't have to meet my client until two o'clock, but I'm happy to drive you up there at whatever time you prefer.'

I glance at Lily, who's still apparently engrossed with her risotto. Then at Abby, who's staring at a picture on the wall as though she's never seen anything so beautiful. I can't think of any good reason to turn down the offered ride, except that we were all planning to take the train up to London together.

The best thing may be to accept now and find an excuse to cancel later. Or I could take Michael aside at some point, explain what's going on, and ask him to give us all a ride. The important thing is that Isabella doesn't discover we're all headed for the same place. What happens when she's safely out of the way is none of her business.

I make a note to discover exactly how long this menu-tasting is supposed to last. We don't want to arrive at work on the 28th to discover Isabella was only at the hotel for an hour before rushing back to the bakery to check the electrical work was going to plan. Lily would have some explaining to do if that were to happen. And possibly a written warning to contend with too.

'That's very kind of you,' I tell Michael. 'I'd love to travel with you. Don't worry about bringing me home again that evening. I've already worked out the train times.'

'I'd love to,' he says. 'But I have to stay up there for a couple of nights.'

'I still think you should have postponed your London trip,' Isabella tells me. 'How can you bear to miss out on tasting all that delicious food? There'll be cakes to taste as well.'

'Isn't Abby making your cake?' I ask.

'I wanted her to, but the hotel employs their own pastry chef, and they insist on us using him.'

The server clears away our plates and hands us a dessert menu.

'I can't decide between tiramisu and apple crisp,' says Isabella.

'Who don't I order one, you order the other, and we can share?' suggests Jon.

'That's very romantic,' she says. 'But it might be even more romantic if we ordered two of each.'

'No Haribo surprise?' I ask.

'I checked, but they aren't serving it,' she says. 'I can't think why not. It's the perfect dessert to end any meal.'

The server pulls out his pad to take our orders. Chris and Abby go for the gelato sharing plate, while Lily and Jack stick with the always reliable tiramisu. I wonder whether this is how all couples become when they've been together for a while. Do their tastes gradually merge until they're unable to make independent decisions? I hope not. It seems a most undesirable state of affairs. I can't imagine spending the rest of my life with one person. But if that ever happens, I want to be sure my dessert choices remain my own.

'I'll have the pavlova,' says Michael. 'How about you, Georgia?'

'The chocolate mousse,' I say.

I love pavlova, but I refuse to get sucked into this coupley thing everyone else seems to have going on.

'So,' says Jon. 'Marks out of ten for this afternoon's entertainment?'

'Ten!' says Isabella. 'At least.'

'Nine,' says Lily. 'I'm subtracting a point for the place being overheated. Otherwise, I had a great time.'

'Eight,' says Abby. 'I didn't mind the heat, but I thought they could have offered a greater variety of dresses with pockets. It constantly shocks me how men's garments are bristling with them, whereas most women's clothing is lucky to have a place to put a spare key.'

'Very true,' says Isabella. 'I'll raise that issue with Colette the next time I see her.'

Michael grins at me. 'I expect you're looking forward to that conversation.'

I try not to laugh. 'I signed up for this, so I'm determined to finish it.'

'You aren't a quitter,' agrees Isabella. 'I used to think you were, but you've more than proved me wrong over this past year.'

'Praise indeed!' I say.

'You haven't given us your score for the afternoon,' Michael tells me. 'We need your marks too so we can calculate an average.'

I'm tempted to give it two out of ten because of how boring it is to watch someone else try on clothes. But I catch sight of Isabella's excited face and relent. I don't want anything to take the shine off her wedding.

'They lost a mark for their choice of music,' I say. 'A little too much whimsy and not enough cynicism for my taste. But they made up for it with the truffles and the free drinks. I'm inclined to give them a solid nine out of ten.'

'Excellent!' says Isabella. 'I'm so glad you enjoyed it. We'll do it again as quickly as possible.'

'Maybe you should pace ourselves,' says Jon. 'Recover from this afternoon first. Getting married is a marathon, not a sprint. There's plenty of time for everything that needs to be done. It would be a shame not to stop and enjoy it sometimes.'

'Well said!' agrees Isabella. 'It's lots of fun being engaged, and I'm not eager to change that too soon.'

'August!' I say before she can get any ideas about postponing the wedding. 'That's what I've committed to, and that's what we're doing.'

'You're right,' she says. 'And the married part should be quite fun too, even if there's rather less cake and champagne.'

'There will always be cake and champagne,' says Jon.

Isabella looks more cheerful. 'Do you promise that?'

'I'll add an amendment to my vows the minute I get home. At this rate, they'll be longer than the telephone book.'

'Five minutes,' I say. 'Maximum. You don't want the congregation falling asleep halfway through your vows. By which, I mean me.'

'Agreed,' says Michael. 'I'll make a note to bring a stopwatch and an air horn in my suit pocket. I believe it's one of the chief duties of the best man.'

Chapter Twenty-One

'How did the shopping trip go?' Phyllis asks me on Monday morning. 'Did Isabella find the dress of her dreams?'

I stop frothing the milk and turn to face her. 'What do you think?'

'Is that a trick question?' she asks Mabel. 'I never know how to answer those.'

'It may be a riddle,' says Mabel. 'If four women go into one dress shop, how much fabric should they purchase if each woman requires two and three-quarter yards?'

'That's more of a mathematical problem,' says Phyllis. 'A riddle is something entirely different – such as, "What costs a fortune, causes lots of arguments, and will have to be altered again in three months?"'

'A new kitchen?' hazards Mabel.

Phyllis sighs. 'Why would the answer be a new kitchen when we're discussing Isabella's upcoming wedding?'

'She and Jon may be planning some renovations before they move in together,' says Mabel stubbornly.

I set Phyllis' mug in front of her. 'Perhaps I should save us all some time before Mabel starts talking about underfloor heating and boiling water taps. The answer is no. Isabella did not buy a dress. On the plus side, she almost drove an innocent bridal shop owner to leave the profession and take up a less demanding career in either air traffic control or bomb disposal.'

Phyllis laughs. 'I'm sure it wasn't that bad.'

'We left Colette sitting with her head in her hands, contemplating all the decisions that had led her to that moment.'

'Was she really called Colette?' asks Mabel. 'It sounds like a made-up name to me.'

'That's what I said!' I tell her. 'The other two were called Fleur and Elodie. It somehow seemed too good to be true.'

'Still, I expect you had fun,' says Phyllis.

'So much fun that Isabella had to buy us all dinner afterwards to revive us.'

'You'll have enjoyed that,' says Mabel. 'I never thought I'd meet anyone who ate as much as your sister until you came along. I've often asked Edie how this bakery makes a profit with the pair of you working here.'

'That's funny,' I say sweetly. 'Lily says the same thing about you. With the number of free plum slices you talk Isabella into giving you, she tells me it's a constant wonder she's not forced to sell the bakery to pay off their debts.'

'You could put it into public ownership,' says Mabel, unabashed. 'That's what all the big businesses do when the directors have been caught with their hands in the till or stealing from the pension funds. They float it with an IPO and allow the members of the public to buy shares to raise the money they need.'

'That's a good idea,' says Phyllis. 'I'd buy shares in this place if it ever went public.'

'I'd be careful if I were you,' I say. 'I hear that profits aren't all they could be. There are too many unscrupulous people talking the gullible proprietors out of free plum slices.'

'How do you know about IPOs?' Phyllis asks Mabel.

'I watched a programme about it when the hound was ill. I had to mutt-sit him while Edie was out.'

'Is Bernie alright?' I ask. 'I hadn't heard he was under the weather.'

'Oh, this was a while ago. And I wouldn't describe it as under the weather. He happened to sneeze once or twice, and Edie was all for calling out the emergency vet. I persuaded her to wait for a day and see how he went. But she wasn't happy until she had him tucked under a heated blanket in the sitting room, with a nice marrow bone to keep up his strength. She doesn't treat me half so well when I'm sick.'

'You have to be careful with colds,' says Barb. 'I had an aunt who insisted on going out on a winter's day when she had a cold, and she ended up with double pneumonia.'

'There's no chance of that with the mutt,' says Mabel. 'He stayed by the fire all day, with Edie cooking all his favourite foods to "tempt his appetite" as though he was a heroine from one of those old books who developed consumption at the drop of a hat.'

'It's nice that Mrs Ogilvie looks after him so well,' I say. 'If people have pets, they ought to make them a priority.'

'But not their sisters, apparently,' says Mabel dejectedly.

'Sisters are all the same,' I assure her. 'They don't know a good thing when they've got it.'

'So, yours is no further forward with thinking about her dress?' asks Phyllis.

'No, but I have more immediate problems. There's this Bernie thing, for one. I need to put up a notice in the arts centre about the competition.'

'It's an excellent idea,' says Ivy. 'Bob and I have already started talking about what we plan to do for it. He isn't very confident with his watercolour skills, but he's working on them.'

'I didn't help when I threatened to post pictures of his work all over the internet,' I say. 'Please tell him I'm sorry about that, and I'll never do it again. I'm sure Bernie would look lovely in watercolour.'

'He'd look even lovelier behind a screen,' says Mabel.

'Are you entering the competition?' I ask.

'I expect so. Edie will never let me hear the last of it if I don't. I'm thinking of making a display piece out of all the things of mine he's destroyed – an old shoe, an odd sock, a mangled cushion. You know the sort of thing. I could call it Shattered Objects – an Ode to Impermanence.'

'It's lucky your sister can't hear you,' I say. 'You'd be in the doghouse if she was here.'

'Very funny,' says Mabel. 'Edie would have me sleeping in the summerhouse if she could. She's always saying the mutt would like his own bedroom.'

'You lead a very hard life,' I say. 'Abby has made a coffee and walnut cake, if you'd like to try a slice?'

She cheers up at once. 'That's why we come here. The quality of the service is second to none. What would we do if you ever shut down?'

'You'll find out on the 27th,' I say. 'Have you heard we're closing that day?'

'I saw the notice on the village website,' says Phyllis. 'Electrical work, isn't it?'

'Something like that,' I say evasively.

'Best to get it done sooner rather than later,' says Mabel. 'Otherwise, you'll be toasting more than just bread in here. And mind you get a certificate when they're finished. Some of these cowboys don't have the faintest idea what they're doing. You'll need written evidence for when you sue them later.'

'I'm sure Lily and Isabella don't use cowboys,' says Phyllis. 'Is Mike Adams doing the work for you?'

'I'm not sure who'll be here,' I say. 'But I promise you'll be equally as safe afterwards as you are now.'

This at least is the truth. Why did Lily have to make this so complicated with her ridiculous story about free electrical work? Couldn't she have said we were temporarily closing down because of a rat infestation?

It's with a feeling of relief that I hear the shop bell ring. It's Isabella, and she's holding an umbrella.

'It's pouring out there!' she announces. 'It makes a change from snow. That's the beauty of our British climate – the weather is never the same two days running.'

'I wish it would make up its mind,' grumbles Mabel. 'The sun was shining when I left home, and I didn't bring my umbrella.'

'We have a couple of spares in Isabella's office,' I say. 'People sometimes leave them behind, and we don't always know who they belonged to. We can lend you one if you like. Otherwise, I'm sure someone can give you a ride home.'

'I'll call Bob,' says Ivy. 'He isn't doing anything particular today. He'll run a shuttle service for us if need be.'

'Isn't Bob busy perfecting his watercolour techniques all ready to win the big prize?' I ask. 'If I were him, I'd be practising every day. I'd start with something small, like an ant or a cockroach, and slowly build up through the species until I reached dogs.'

'I'm sure Bob has better things to do with his time than paint the mutt,' says Mabel. 'I'll bet you regret making that daft suggestion now, Isabella.'

'Not at all,' says Isabella. 'My deputy is handling everything admirably. I'm planning to offer her a promotion upon the successful conclusion of the competition.'

'To senior manager?' I enquire, but without much hope.

'I was thinking more of a post as my personal assistant,' she says. 'You could organise my life for me and take on the responsibility of ensuring my creative ideas come to fruition.'

'I'll pass, thanks. I have plenty of other things to keep me busy. As should you. The coffee machine needs cleaning, and it's your turn.'

'I'm sure I did it last time,' she says.

'And I'm equally sure you didn't. I've made a rota we can consult if you don't believe me.'

She sighs. 'I can't clean it now. Our customers may want to order more drinks. You should think more about customer service and less about your overly-rigid timetables. Flexibility is the name of the game in the bakery business. Wouldn't you agree, Lily?'

'I've told you already that I refuse to get in the middle of your arguments,' says Lily. 'No good can come of it. Would anyone like another drink?'

'Not me,' says Mabel. 'I should be getting back home. Edie always makes a terrible fuss when she's been to the dentist. She huffs and puffs and demands soft foods. It must be where the mutt gets it from.'

'I've messaged Bob,' says Ivy. 'He'll be here in a couple of minutes to drive us home. I think I'll take an Eccles cake for him. He loves those.'

'Have you all remembered about the 27th?' asks Isabella. 'I'm putting a card in the window, but I wanted to make sure all our regular customers were notified personally.'

'We'll need to find a new place for our morning coffee that day,' says Mabel. 'Does anyone have a suggestion?'

'You can go for one day without cake,' says Isabella. 'It will be good for you.'

'That's rich coming from you!' says Ivy. 'But I'm not sure I can. Mabel's right. We should look around for an alternative venue.'

'Is the idea of customer loyalty quite dead?' asks Isabella in a despairing tone. 'It's a one-time thing! And you don't come in here every single day. You can easily arrange your schedule around our closure.'

'I don't like being tied to a rigid timetable,' explains Mabel. 'I go where the fancy takes me. It's the beauty of being retired. No one can tell me what to do any longer.'

'I can't imagine anyone ever telling you what to do,' I say. 'Retired or not.'

'You may be right,' she says. 'But that doesn't solve the problem of what we should do on the 27th.'

'Couldn't you buy two cakes on the 26th and take one home with you?' asks Isabella. 'That way, you'll still have something for your morning tea while we're closed.'

'But the second cake won't be as fresh as the first one,' says Phyllis. 'It seems an unnecessary expense for a sub-standard product.'

'Why don't we offer our regular customers a special deal on the 26th?' suggests Isabella. 'Two cakes for the price of one. In return, you must promise not to look for another establishment.'

The women glance at each other.

'I suppose that might work,' says Ivy in a grudging tone.

'It's better than nothing,' agrees Mabel. 'Fine, you have a deal. Although you drive a hard bargain.'

'It's only for one day,' says Isabella again. 'I think we're being more than fair. Is that Bob's car I see drawing up outside?'

I wait until they've left before turning to Isabella. 'You didn't even see them coming, did you?'

'What are you talking about?'

'Our customers,' I say. 'They've just performed what I believe the movies refer to as a grift.'

'No, they haven't. It was a straightforward deal. I gave them something they wanted in return for them giving me something I wanted. Fair exchange is no robbery.'

'But two cakes for the price of one is,' says Lily. 'They were definitely trying it on. Those women have no more intention of going elsewhere than of climbing Everest. They were just having fun with you and seeing what you'd fall for.'

Isabella sinks into a chair. 'I would never have believed it of them! Why didn't one of you step in and put a stop to it?'

'I was unwilling to exceed the bounds of my limited authority,' I say.

'And I was enjoying the spectacle,' Lily adds. 'It isn't often anyone gets the better of you, but Mabel and co seem to know how to do it.'

'I'm shocked and appalled,' says Isabella. 'Do we have any lemon tarts left? I need something to help me recover from the realisation our customers are prepared to treat their benefactors in such a callous way.'

'Georgia ate the last one,' says Lily.

'And I didn't even pay for it,' I add. 'Which is far more impressive than a two-for-one deal.'

'Then I'll have a few macarons instead,' says Isabella, leaning back in her chair and closing her eyes. 'They at least have never let me down in my time of need. I wish I could say the same for the rest of you.'

Chapter Twenty-Two

Michael picks me up from Little Compton on the 27th. I offer to meet him somewhere more convenient, but he refuses, telling me it's barely out of his way.

'It's a lovely morning for it,' he says when I open the car door. 'I've double-checked the directions, so you don't have to worry about us getting lost.'

'I'm not half as bad at reading maps as my sister would like you to think,' I say. 'Although there's no point in telling Isabella that. It's nice for her to think she's better than me at something. It rarely happens, so I expect she wants to make the most of it.'

He laughs. 'You two crack me up. You're almost carbon copies of each other.'

'We are not! If we didn't share the same surname, no one would ever suspect us of being related.'

'That won't be a problem after August,' he says. 'Or is she keeping her own name?'

'As far as I know, they're planning to double-barrel their surnames so that Isabella becomes Phillips Campbell and Jon becomes Campbell Phillips. I told Isabella it would be a lot easier for them both to keep their own names, but she said it was more romantic this way. I have no idea whether she was joking. Either way, I don't want to know the answer, so I'm leaving her to get on with it.'

'They seem very happy,' he says.

'They do. It's quite sweet, really. I thought she and I would be single forever. But it appears fate had other ideas for Isabella.'

'Maybe it does for you too,' he says.

'I doubt it. Not for a long time, anyway. There are plenty of things I want to do before I worry about settling down.'

'So, what are you doing in London?' he asks.

'Meeting a friend. Several friends, in fact.'

I glance at him, wondering whether to tell him the truth. It would be a relief not to have to make up any more ridiculous stories.

'Can you keep a secret?' I ask.

'What sort of a question is that?'

'It seems a straightforward one to me,' I say.

'That's because you haven't thought about it. It's like that puzzle where you meet one person who can only tell the truth and another who can only tell lies, and you have to decide which question to ask in order to find out the answer you want.'

'How is it like that?' I ask.

Michael reaches into the glove compartment and hands me a tin of travel sweets. 'You'll notice I came prepared,' he says. 'You asked me if I can keep a secret. If I'm the kind of person who really can keep one, I'll say yes. And if I'm the kind of person who can't, I'll still say yes because I'll be keen to hear what it is.'

'So, where does that leave me?'

He smiles. 'I'm not sure. You'll have to choose for yourself whether you want to share your deep, dark secret with me.'

I select a sweet and hand him the tin. 'It's neither deep nor dark. It's just a little complicated.'

'It's your call,' he says. 'Which door will you go through?'

'Fine,' I say. 'I'm tired of trying to keep up with all these stories. I'm meeting Lily, Abby, and all the women who've worked at the bakery since Lily and Isabella bought it. When

Isabella first started planning her wedding, Lily asked them all if they'd like to do something as a secret surprise for the bride.'

'That sounds like a great idea,' he says. 'If a little complicated.'

'It's turned out to be far more difficult than we imagined. For one thing, they all live in different parts of the country. So, we've had to find a way to meet up and make plans.'

'Hence the trip to London!' he says.

'Exactly. We're meeting for brunch to talk it over and decide on something definite. Maybe Lily will come up some ideas.'

'Or you will,' he says. 'You strike me as a very competent person.'

'Not a word that's usually applied to me.'

'I can't think why not. You're helping to organise this wedding.'

'I'm not doing much,' I say. 'I'm pushing back on as many things as I can to prevent any possibility of mission creep. Isabella is great, but she suffers from an excess of enthusiasm that needs keeping in check. It isn't really her fault. I believe it's more of a medical condition, for which there's no known treatment.'

'As Jon's best man, I think I should warn him.'

I select another travel sweet. 'That's your call, but Jon's a smart guy. If he doesn't know what he's getting into by now, he deserves everything he gets. I wonder how he and Isabella will get on at the menu-tasting today. If our wedding dress trip is anything to go by, the staff will end up dazed and bewildered and reconsidering their choice of career. Meanwhile, Isabella will return home pleased and satisfied, declaring the whole day a complete success. But as long as I don't have to pick up the pieces, I don't care.'

'You'll be in London,' says Michael. 'Many miles from the scene of the crime. Now I know why you refused to change your plans the other day so you could attend the menu tasting with Jon and your sister. It surprised me a little because it seemed right up your street.'

'It is,' I say. 'But this London thing was arranged before I heard about the other thing. It wasn't easy finding a date that suited everyone.'

'Where are they all coming from?' he asks.

'All over the place. I can't remember exactly where everyone lives, although there are four of us from Honeywell.'

'Four?' he asks.

'Victoria used to work at the bakery too.'

'I don't think I've met her.'

'She works at The Red Lion these days. But she came to Honeywell in the first place to fill in for Isabella when she broke her leg, and she decided to stay.'

'So, all these women have worked at the Sugarloaf over the years?' he asks.

'That's right. There's been a rather high staff turnover since they first opened their doors. I used to assume no one wanted to work for Isabella for long. But that theory doesn't hold water. Lily set up a group chat, and none of them will stop using it. They seem to have surprisingly happy memories of working with my sister. It's probably a case of traumatic recollections fading over the years, but they all insist they look back with great fondness on their time in Honeywell.'

'I remember reading about these mass hallucinations that occur from time to time,' he says. 'Collective delusions, I believe they call them. Psychologists believe they're responsible for the vast majority of UFO sightings.'

'I thought those often turned out to be weather balloons? They did in *The X-Files*.'

'I doubt your former members of staff remember their time at the bakery fondly because of weather balloons,' he says.

'You make a good point. But whatever the cause of this delusion, these women all seem to be suffering from it. The only thing we can do is go along with it and hope the traumatic memories don't resurface when they're faced with the actual reality again.'

Michael glances at the GPS. 'We leave the M25 in a minute. I should have you at your destination in about twenty-five minutes. Unless we hit any major traffic works, you should be right on time.'

'I'm very grateful,' I say. 'The other three decided to travel up last night and enjoy a well-deserved night away, which means I would have had to make my own way this morning. This is far more fun – and a lot warmer.'

'Didn't they invite you to go with them last night?' he asks.

'They did, but I had other things to do.'

'Hot date?'

I laugh. 'Why is that everyone's first assumption? I had some … paperwork to finish.'

'Your employers make you take work home?'

'Not yet. And please don't put that idea into Isabella's head when you see her. This was something else. It's a private project.'

'It must have been important for you to miss a night out in London,' he says.

'It was.'

I don't elaborate on this. What I choose to do in my spare time is my business, and I have no plans to share it with anyone else.

'Will you be ok taking the tube after I drop you off?' he asks.

'I'll be fine,' I assure him. 'It makes no sense for you to drive into central London. The traffic will be awful, and there's the congestion charge too. Anyway, I love taking the tube. Going to London for the day was one of my favourite things to do when I was young. Our parents would take us to a museum, and then on to Harrods for an ice cream.'

'Just the one?'

'At those prices, yes. But it was an enormous treat, and Isabella and I looked forward to it all year.'

'I hope you have an equally good time today,' he says. 'Here we are at the station.'

I unbuckle my seatbelt. 'Thanks for the ride.'

He smiles at me. 'I've rarely enjoyed a drive as much as this one. We'll have to do it again sometime.'

Chapter Twenty-Three

I arrive at the Goreston hotel with a few minutes to spare. Lily pushes her way through the crowd towards me, with Victoria close behind her.

'Hi, Georgia!' she says. 'The rest of the group should be arriving any minute. I wish you'd been able to come with us yesterday. We went out for cocktails and then to the theatre.'

'Maybe next time.'

She laughs. 'Is that a dig at your sister?'

'In what way?' I ask.

'I thought you were suggesting her marriage to Jon won't last, and we'll be back here in a few years, doing it all again.'

'I missed a trick there. I meant that I'll join you the next time you organise a night away. As long as it's after June.'

'Don't you mean August?' she asks.

I flush. 'I got my dates muddled up for a second.'

'That's understandable, We all have a lot going on.'

There's a commotion near the doorway, and we turn to see several women enter the lobby. Lily rushes over and hugs them all, then beckons for me to join them.

'Georgia, you've met everyone except Natalie – at least briefly. Everyone, you remember Georgia? She's the chief bridesmaid, which means she'll be keeping you all in order.'

'I'd have known who you were even if we hadn't met before,' says Meghan. 'It's like looking at a clone of Isabella.'

'But younger and more attractive?' I ask.

'You even sound like her!' says Natalie. 'It's lovely to meet you. Isabella often mentioned you when I was working at the Sugarloaf.'

'I'll bet she did,' I say. 'And I'm sure none of it was flattering.'

'It's difficult to remember the details after all this time,' she says diplomatically.

'I stayed at your house once,' Olivia reminds me. 'It was when I first came to Honeywell and accidentally ended up working at the bakery.'

'How does someone accidentally end up working anywhere?' asks Grace. 'Did you wander in for a cream tea, then absent-mindedly pick up a cloth and start wiping down the tables?'

'Not quite,' says Olivia. 'I was on my way to the Purbecks when my car broke down near Honeywell. Will gave me a ride into the village so I could get something to eat. I met Isabella there, and the rest is history.'

'Isabella is a force of nature,' agrees Lily. 'I only planned to work at the bakery for a few months while I looked for a new job as an office manager. But without me quite knowing how, Isabella talked me into buying the place with her.'

'There's a useful word I've discovered when dealing with my sister,' I tell them. 'No!'

'I've tried that,' says Lily. 'Isabella never hears what she doesn't want to hear.'

'She does if you follow it up by turning on your heel and walking away.'

'Maybe it's different when you're related to her,' says Olivia.

'What are we doing first?' asks Natalie.

'Brunch!' I say with decision. 'I'm starving!'

'You really are Isabella's sister,' says Olivia. 'Do we know where we're going? There are rather a lot of us just to walk in and expect a table.'

'I've booked a table at The Brunchery,' says Lily. 'It's only a few minutes' walk from here.'

It's a bright sunny day, and my spirits lift as we walk. I've been cooped up inside most of the winter, so it's good to be outside in the cool spring air. We arrive at the cafe five minutes later, and the server guides us towards a table at the back of the room.

'I wonder whether they think this is a hen party?' says Alix. 'They may prefer to tuck us away out of sight so we don't disturb the other customers with our antics.'

'We're a respectable group of current and ex-bakery employees,' says Lily. 'Antics are not on the schedule.'

'How disappointing,' says Meghan. 'And after I came all this way.'

'Feel free to dance on the table,' I say, 'but not until after we've eaten. It's been ages since I had breakfast.'

'Isn't brunch supposed to be a substitute for both breakfast and lunch?' asks Grace.

I give her a horrified look. 'You mean they expect us to combine two meals and pretend that's just as good as eating them separately?'

'It's an all-you-can eat brunch,' Lily reassures me. 'And we have plenty of time. I expect you'll survive.'

The server sets glasses of orange juice in front of us.

'Champagne is extra,' she says. 'But you can order as many soft drinks as you like. The waffle station is open until twelve, although we recommend you start with the savoury dishes. You're welcome to order from the à la carte menu or help yourselves from the buffet.'

Olivia picks up a menu. 'I'd love to try the avocado toast.'

Our server scribbles down the order. 'And for the rest of you?'

Everyone places their orders for a variety of dishes.

'And for you?' the server asks me at last.

'I'd like the truffle scrambled eggs and the mushroom ragu on toasted sourdough, please.'

'That's two separate dishes,' she says.

'I know. I was thinking about adding the three-cheese omelette, but I don't want to be too full for waffles.'

She raises an eyebrow and leaves the table.

'How have you and Isabella survived working at the bakery at the same time?' asks Alix. 'Have you had to institute some sort of rationing system?'

'They often work different shifts these days,' says Lily. 'But it's put quite a strain on Abby.'

'Nothing puts a strain on Abby,' says Alix. 'I've never known anyone so calm under pressure.'

'I reserve my melt-downs for the privacy of the kitchen,' says Abby.

'I once hid in there,' says Meghan. 'Between the freezer and the wall. It was extremely uncomfortable.'

'I'm glad to say I've never felt the need to do anything so undignified,' I say.

'How do you tell the pair of them apart?' Grace asks Lily, and laughs at my indignant frown.

'Very easily,' says Lily. 'They're both wonderful in their different ways. But if I were really struggling, I'd ask them both to make me a cappuccino and conduct a blindfold test.'

'Who would win?' asks Natalie.

'How is that even a question?' I say. 'I would! Isabella still doesn't know the difference between a cappuccino and a flat white. Luckily for her, neither did our customers until I arrived. They do now, which is why they always ask me to serve them. It drives Isabella up the wall. I've several times caught her practising when she thinks she's alone. But it's no good. You're either born with that gift or you aren't.'

'So, the art of brewing fine coffee isn't genetic?' asks Alix.

'Not at all. You either feel the milk, or you don't. That kind of intuition and timing can't be taught.'

'This avocado toast is amazing,' says Olivia.

'These eggs are pretty good too,' I say. 'And the mushroom thing.'

I eat in silence for a while, listening to them all talking and laughing. I thought they'd have run out of Isabella stories by now, but that doesn't appear to be the case. I can't think how she ever made time for work with all the extra things she appears to have got up to. But the bakery is humming along nicely, so presumably she did.

And our customers are happy, despite their threats to take their custom elsewhere today. They were as good as their word yesterday afternoon and insisted on Isabella fulfilling her promise to sell them two cakes for the price of one. To no one's surprise, Mabel demanded to buy four for the price of two, telling us she was redeeming her sister's share of the offer too. How many of those cakes Mrs Ogilvie will ever see is anyone's guess. But that's between the two of them.

'How was your drive up here?' Victoria asks me during a break in the conversation.

'Great, thanks. It was nice not to wake up early to take the train. I can never get a decent seat, and everyone's always grumpy because they've had to wake up so early.'

'Didn't you come up last night with the others?' Meghan asks me.

'I had a thing I needed to do.'

'She had a better offer,' says Abby. 'Jon's best man offered to drive her up here. I noticed he didn't offer to bring the rest of us.'

'That's because he didn't realise any of you were coming,' I say. 'And by the time I found a time to speak to you without Isabella overhearing, you'd all decided to travel up the night before.'

'We invited you too,' says Victoria. 'But you said you were doing something else. Were you out with Michael?'

'I was not. I had something else planned that I couldn't get out of.'

'He's very good looking,' says Abby.

'And single,' adds Lily. 'You could do a lot worse, Georgia.'

'Nothing doing,' I tell her. 'I'm far too busy. And someone has to fly the flag of joyous singledom. You're all letting the side down in a big way.'

Natalie grins at me. 'Isn't there a tradition about the best man and the chief bridesmaid?'

'No, there isn't! This is real life, not some stupid rom-com.'

'Rom-coms aren't all stupid,' says Meghan. 'I've always loved Sleepless in Seattle.'

'It's a ridiculous movie,' I say. 'Who falls in love with someone they hear on the radio? For all she knew, he could have been a serial killer.'

'No, he couldn't,' says Grace. 'Or they wouldn't have let him on the radio. I'm sure they check that sort of thing before they allow people on the air.'

'They didn't have time to check anything,' argues Alix. 'One minute, that little boy called in. The next thing they knew, they were talking to Tom Hanks. But that's ok – everyone knows he's not a serial killer.'

'But he wasn't being Tom Hanks,' says Olivia. 'He was playing an architect or something.'

I throw up my hands in frustration. 'You're as bad as our customers! This is exactly the sort of conversation I can imagine Mabel having with Phyllis. I'm used to it with them, but I expected better from you.'

'Are you talking about Chef Mabel?' asks Grace.

'I'm talking about Mrs Ogilvie's sister.'

'That's the one. She once pretended to be a famous Australian chef to throw a television crew off balance.'

'I haven't heard about that,' says Natalie. 'But it's something I can imagine her doing.'

'I'll tell you the full story sometime,' says Lily. 'In the meantime, if everyone's had enough to eat, maybe we should get down to business?'

Chapter Twenty-Four

Everyone turns towards us, and Lily gestures to me. 'The floor is yours – or should I say the table?'

'What do you want me to say?'

'Whatever you like. You're the chief bridesmaid.'

'But you're the maid of honour,' I argue.

Victoria laughs. 'Did you bring us all the way to London so you two could sit here and play Wedding Top Trumps?'

'That wasn't our original intention,' I say. 'But it sounds like fun. I used to love playing Top Trumps. I'll bet the chief bridesmaid card would outperform all the others. Crisis management skills – ten points. Bridal drama deflection – eight points.'

'I wouldn't be so sure,' says Lily. 'The maid of honour would have strong multi-tasking points too. Especially if she had experience raising Daisy and Ethan. Ability to produce tissues, Band-aids and safety pins at a moment's notice – nine points. Chaos control – ten points.'

I smile triumphantly. 'But I know how to zip up a dress one-handed while clutching a glass of champagne in the other – although don't ask me how. Game, set and match to the chief bridesmaid.'

'How about us?' Natalie asks me.

'You're welcome to play too, but you don't stand a chance. When it comes to speed, strength and staying power, it has to be between me and Lily. None of you lasted at the bakery for more than a few months, whereas we've both stayed the course and have the scars to prove it.'

'I've worked with Isabella for ten years, while you've only been there for a year and a half,' says Lily. 'Nine points on the matron of honour card.'

'But I lived with her for decades before that,' I counter. 'Twenty bonus points to the chief bridesmaid.'

'I still think The Flour Girls may turn out to have some surprising strengths,' says Olivia.

I give her a pitying smile. 'Such as what – group chat engagement? You're more likely to lose points for refusing to stick to the subject.'

'I've noticed you're always trying to drag us back to discussing practicalities,' says Grace.

'Without much success,' I remind her.

'Only three points to Georgia for group chat moderation,' says Lily.

'You're the one who set it up!' I protest.

'Exactly,' she says. 'Ten points for initiative and organisation. I could do this all day. I've worked with Isabella for the past decade, and I have two young children. It takes a lot of effort to out-argue Daisy. But practice makes perfect, and my skills improve every day.'

'I've noticed Isabella can't out-argue her goddaughter either,' I say. 'Daisy runs rings around both of you.'

'I don't think Isabella really tries,' says Abby. 'She thinks whatever Daisy does is wonderful, and she sees it as her job to encourage her in everything.'

'I'd love to have a godmother like Isabella,' says Victoria. 'Mine always gave me the impression she expected to be summoned to the police station to bail me out any day. The worst thing I ever remember doing was cutting my fringe with the kitchen scissors. But the way she carried on, you'd have thought I'd stolen the crown jewels and attempted to flee the country.'

'Mine was a bit like that too,' says Grace. 'She used to postpone promised outings with me until "trust had been re-established." I can't imagine Isabella ever doing that.'

'Neither can I,' says Lily. 'I live in daily fear of her deciding to teach Daisy essential life skills like hot-wiring a car and how to talk your way out of a speeding ticket.'

'You have a few years before you need worry about that,' I console her.

'I hear Isabella has some extra children in her life now,' says Natalie.

'Toby and Ollie,' I say. 'They're Jon's nephews. Their father died a couple of years ago, so he spends quite a bit of time with them.'

'I'll bet they love Isabella,' says Grace.

'They do,' I agree. 'And she adores them. It's lucky Jon is usually around to keep the three of them in check.'

'Are they in the wedding too?' she asks.

'Definitely,' says Lily. 'Although they were very much against the idea of being page boys in little velvet suits. The exact details haven't yet been decided.'

I sigh. 'That's turning out to be the motto of Isabella's wedding. "The exact details haven't yet been decided." I wish she would decide on a few things. It's already March, and she still hasn't chosen a dress or shoes or flowers.'

'With any luck, she's deciding on a menu as we speak,' Lily reminds me.

'I wish I had half your confidence. But she's finding it extraordinarily difficult to make up her mind about any of the details. Isabella's usually so decisive. Unnecessarily so, one might say. She's never had the slightest difficulty in telling me what to do. But the minute she started planning this wedding, she seemed to fall to pieces.'

'It is odd,' says Lily. 'I expected her to present us with a long list of requirements, and all we'd need to do was help her tick them off the list. But she doesn't seem to have any requirements at all, which makes everything far more difficult.'

'There's a happy medium to be struck between bossing everyone around and keeping your options wide open until the last possible minute,' I agree. 'I suppose it will all work out in the end. These things usually do. But I hope we don't have too many repetitions of the bridal shop disaster.'

'I laughed so hard when I read about that on the group chat,' says Meghan. 'I wish I'd been there to see it.'

'You'd have been more than welcome to switch places with me,' I say. 'Or Colette, for that matter. She looked as though she'd rather be anywhere else.'

'I loved the story about Scarlett O'Hara and her bevvy of bridesmaids,' says Alix.

'Apparently, they all looked like emus,' I say.

'Parrots,' Abby corrects me.

'Colette said tropical birds,' says Lily. 'What made you think they looked like emus, Georgia?'

'I must have been thinking of the parasols,' I say. 'Don't southern belles carry those everywhere they go?'

'And fans,' says Natalie. 'In case something shocks them, and they're tempted to swoon.'

'The only shocking thing about this wedding will be if Isabella settles on something and sticks to it,' I say. 'Poor Colette. She didn't stand a chance.'

'Did I tell you that Isabella called to make another appointment with her?' Lily asks me. 'Colette told her she was fully booked until late next year.'

'I'm not surprised. How did Isabella react?'

'She was disappointed, but she said there were plenty more bridal shops in the area, so she could easily move onto the next one.'

'I can hear the noises of shutters being pulled down all over the New Forest,' I say. 'Colette will have put out the word on the bridal shop grapevine not to accept a booking from anyone of the name of Campbell.'

'Do bridal shops really have a grapevine?' asks Abby.

'They're bound to,' says Lily. 'People in similar professions always stick together. That's why they form guilds. I expect everyone in the country who sells wedding dresses keeps a blacklist of time-wasters.'

'And brides who smear makeup all over their dresses while they're trying them on,' says Olivia.

'And the ones who find their perfect dress, then decide they can find it cheaper online,' adds Meghan. 'Those brides probably subscribe to a monthly newsletter called Say No to the Dress.'

'True,' agrees Lily. 'And the bridal boutiques run a Facebook page called The Veil of Shame.'

'Whatever the Facebook page may be called,' I say, 'we can safely assume that Isabella's name is all over it – including any pseudonyms she may have adopted. I remember her entering a radio competition when she was about fifteen. She was desperate to win an inflatable outdoor hot tub, so she called herself Mrs Higgins and told the presenter she lived in a two-bedroomed flat with her five young children. Isabella thought she'd have more chance of winning if the radio host took pity on her and decided she deserved a break. It didn't seem to occur to her they were far more likely to offer the prize to someone with a garden.'

'Did she win?' asks Victoria.

'No, but she got one of the runner-up prizes. It was a garden gnome doing yoga. Salute to the sun, if I remember correctly. Who knows where the presenters thought Mrs Higgins would put it? Isabella stomped outside in disgust and dumped the gnome in our garden pond. The goldfish were most surprised.'

'I must visit your pond the next time I'm over,' says Lily. 'Isabella never told me about that.'

'I expect she was too embarrassed. I fished it out the following day and put it on the bookcase in her bedroom, along with a note from the gnome saying, "You have made a powerful enemy today." I have no idea what she made of it, but I noticed she carefully dried him off and put him back in the garden with all the other gnomes, so I hope she heeded his warning.'

'Your poor mother,' says Natalie. 'How did she cope with the pair of you?'

'She's a strong woman,' I say. 'But it must have been a relief to her when Isabella finally moved out. I noticed she didn't take Sir Grudgewick the gnome with her when she left.'

'You named him?' asks Abby.

'He named himself. He used to leave threatening notes lying around the house for Isabella to find. She never knew when the next one would appear. With any luck, it cost her a few nights' sleep.'

'Fascinating though this discussion is,' says Lily, 'we aren't any nearer to deciding what we want to do to surprise Isabella.'

'You're right,' I say. 'We're all as bad as she is.'

'I think some sort of pre-wedding surprise is a great idea,' say Olivia. 'But it can't be anything too strenuous. I don't know whether this is an appropriate moment to mention it, but I'm expecting a baby in September.'

Everyone converges on her and hugs her. She emerges from the scrum at last, laughing and smoothing her hair.

'How far along are you?' asks Lily.

'I've just had my twelve-week scan. Everything looks good. Will is over the moon at the thought of becoming a father.'

'Do you know whether it's a boy or a girl?' asks Alix.

'No, and we don't intend to find out. I was a little worried when I found out the baby was due in September, but there should be a full month between the wedding and my due date.'

'Wouldn't it be exciting if you went into labour during the service?' asks Meghan.

'No!' Olivia and I say simultaneously.

'It isn't likely for a first baby,' says Lily. 'But Victoria's boyfriend will be at the wedding, and he's a doctor.'

'Matthew is an orthopaedic specialist,' I say. 'He won't know anything about babies.'

'I'm sure he'd know what to do in an emergency,' says Victoria.

'So, this pregnancy rules out us taking Isabella on a pre-wedding ski-jumping weekend?' I say. 'I can't tell you what a relief that is to me personally. I'm all for something low-key and civilised.'

'How about an afternoon tea?' suggests Grace. 'That would be right up Isabella's street.'

'I love it!' says Natalie. 'What could be more appropriate for Isabella than cake?'

'You don't think she gets enough of that in her everyday life?' asks Meghan.

I laugh. 'The words Isabella and enough cake have never appeared in the same sentence before, and probably never will again. It's a great idea. What did you have in mind?'

'We could all come down to Honeywell a day early,' says Olivia. 'Would we be able to use the bakery for the afternoon tea?'

'I don't see why not,' says Lily. 'I doubt Isabella will be working the day before her wedding.'

'She doesn't work much on any other day,' I say. 'So, that's probably a safe prediction.'

'You could close the bakery a little earlier than usual,' says Victoria. 'One of you could call Isabella and ask her to come over on some pretext or other, and we'd all be waiting there.'

'She'd love that,' I say. 'Cake, and the chance to catch up with you all. It's exactly Isabella's sort of thing.'

'I could make most of the food,' says Abby.

'We can prepare some of it at the pub,' says Victoria. 'Shelley is bound to be on board with the idea.'

'The rest of us can provide the decorations and champagne,' says Alix. 'We can each bring something with us and set it up when we arrive.'

'Great idea!' says Meghan. 'We can decorate the bakery with balloons and banners. It would be lovely to use fancy china and lace tablecloths for the occasion.'

'And fairy lights and candles,' adds Olivia.

'The Red Lion has some lovely tiered cake-stands,' says Victoria. 'I'll ask Shelley whether we can borrow them for the afternoon.'

'And we can sort out some games,' says Natalie. 'Cake-related, naturally.'

'This idea has my vote,' I say. 'We can finalise the details on the group chat. Or you lot can! I'll have enough to do with keeping Isabella under control until her big day.'

'We should order champagne,' says Lily. 'To celebrate Olivia's news and the fact we've finally decided on something.'

The server brings us all a glass of champagne, and an orange juice for Olivia.

Lily raises her glass. 'I'd like to propose a toast. To baby Sullivan. May he or she sleep all night and smile all day.'

'To baby Sullivan!' we all echo.

'And to all of us,' adds Grace. 'The most fabulous bunch of secret supporters any bride could ask for.'

'To the Flour Girls!' I say, raising my glass to them all. 'May they always rise to the occasion and never crumble under pressure!'

Chapter Twenty-Five

I drop into the bakery on Saturday morning. I'm not officially on duty, but I want to hear how Isabella's menu-tasting went.

I find her half-heartedly cleaning the coffee machine while listening to the radio.

'You'll have to wipe harder than that,' I say. 'Otherwise it won't shine, and Lily will give you one of her looks.'

'You're welcome to do it,' she says, handing me the cloth.

'If you'll dig out one of those strawberry tarts for me. I noticed there were several left when I closed up yesterday evening. They'll be reaching their best-before date soon.'

'It's a deal,' she says. 'You're much better at cleaning that thing anyway.'

'I believe that's known as strategic incompetence. Do something badly, then say the other person is better at it and hand it over to them. This is a one-shot deal. Like my flat whites.'

'You can make us both a drink once you've finished cleaning the machine,' she says.

'I'm not being paid to be here today.'

'You're being paid in strawberry tarts. Most people would be more than satisfied with that.'

'It doesn't pay the mortgage,' I say. 'But as I don't have one, I'll let you off this time. The real reason I came in was to hear how everything went yesterday.'

'It was great,' she says.

When she doesn't elaborate further, I stop cleaning and turn to face her. 'That's not very informative. I expected to find you frothing over with excitement – like my hot chocolates.'

She smiles. 'It went fine. I think you'd have enjoyed it. The chef set out a variety of different options for each course and talked us through them all. He paired them with appropriate wines in tiny glasses. By the end of the afternoon, Jon and I were too drunk to walk straight. Luckily, the wedding co-ordinator took notes as we went along.'

She opens her handbag and shows me a printout. 'Apparently, we were very keen on the goat cheese tartlets and the scallops and pancetta, followed by a choice of lamb with mint puree and pan-seared sea bass with lemon butter and seasonal vegetables. I have only the haziest recollection of the chocolate and salted caramel fondant and the blackcurrant posset with rosemary shortbread, but I'm reliably informed I loved those too.'

'It all sounds delicious,' I say. 'I'm glad you've sorted out the menu. And the wines.'

'To tell you the truth, it was all a bit overwhelming. Everything was perfect, but I kept wishing you were there to help me out.'

'I'm really sorry,' I say. 'I wish I'd known. But it would have been difficult to change my meeting with … erm … Alison.'

'I know it would. And Jon pointed out that the more people who came along, the less likely it was anyone would agree on anything. This way, we've signed off on the meal, and we don't have to worry about it again.'

I'm not sure what to say. I'd expected Isabella to be hugely enthusiastic about the food. I decide not to mention this. She seems to have lost some of her bounce over the past couple of weeks. The bridal magazines all warn that the strain of getting married can take its toll on brides, and it appears they're right.

'Why don't you take the morning off?' I suggest. 'I can fill in for you here, and Lily should be in soon.'

'And do what?' asks Isabella.

'Go to a spa?'

She looks at me as though I've grown a second head. 'Why would I want to visit a spa?'

'I have no idea. But I was reading an article in either Brides Behaving Badly or The Bossy Bride that said the bride should be careful to practise self-care in the lead-up to the wedding. Otherwise, she risks having a meltdown and having to be banished to a country retreat for several months to recover.'

'I don't think there's any danger of that,' she says. 'I'm a little tired, that's all. There's so much to think about on top of keeping this place running. I was wondering whether you might like to take on some extra work in the bakery until the wedding?'

'I can't right now. I don't mind helping out on an ad hoc basis, but I can't commit to anything more permanent.'

She frowns. 'I don't see why. You aren't doing anything else.'

'I'm doing all the chief bridesmaid stuff.'

'But that doesn't take up much time. I'm so busy, and you're almost always free. Why wouldn't you take on some extra work when it's offered? I'm sure you could do with the money.'

I try to keep my voice calm. 'I could always do with extra money, but it isn't that simple. I have lots of things going on in my life at the moment. You'll have to take my word for it.'

She shrugs. 'If you say so. In which case, there isn't much point in suggesting I go off to a spa.'

'If you'd like to go home now, I'll stand in here for you.'

She shakes her head. 'I'm fine.'

I finish my last mouthful of strawberry tart. 'The coffee machine is clean, at any rate. Look how lovely and sparkly it is. Remember to tell the customers only to order tea. We don't want it getting messed up again too soon.'

'I'm sorry, Georgie,' she says in a choked voice. 'I shouldn't have taken it out on you.'

My anger disappears at once. I put my arms around her and give her a quick hug. 'It's ok. Brides are allowed to be stressed. All the magazines say so.'

She rests her head on my shoulder. 'They say a lot of things. I've been trying to follow all their advice so we can have the perfect wedding, but I don't feel as though I'm doing a very good job.'

'You're doing an excellent job,' I assure her. 'I'd have run away and jumped on a ferry to the Hebrides months ago.'

'No, you wouldn't. You're more resilient than you give yourself credit for. When you start a thing, you always see it through.'

'I'm not certain that's true. Think of how many jobs I've quit over the course of my misspent life.'

'When you start something that's important to you,' she corrects herself. 'And the Georgia who dropped out of school and didn't stay in the same job for more than three months isn't the Georgia I know today. I'm not sure the current version of you would have quit working for Cath.'

'Steady on!' I say. 'I'd like to think I still have some standards. I'm only surprised I lasted there for as long as I did.'

She gives me a watery smile. 'A surprise in which I'm sure Cath shares. But her loss was our gain, even if neither of us could see it at the time. I can't think how Lily and I ever coped without you. I was telling Jon only the other day that I would never have had time to get to know him properly if we hadn't taken you on here to share some of the load. So, he and I both owe you a lot.'

'That isn't true,' I say, embarrassed.

'Yes, it is. Lily and I were struggling to cover everything by ourselves. It was always much easier with a fourth person here. But we hadn't realised it was ok to employ someone else when there wasn't an emergency. We were both secretly worried that any extra expense would tip us over the edge, even though I did the accounts and knew that wasn't really the case.'

'There's your answer,' I say. 'You were doing the accounts! No wonder you had no idea how much money there was.'

'I'm an excellent accountant! In another life, I'd have won prizes by now for my superb number-work. But I've chosen to serve my community in a far more valuable way.'

I pick up an orange spiced macaron and take a bite. 'I can't argue with that. So, you didn't employ me entirely out of pity?'

'I've never done anything out of pity!' she protests. 'Not for nothing am I known around these parts as Isabella the Merciless.'

She turns the shop sign to Open.

'Not a second too soon,' I say. 'I see Bernie coming along the high street. He's wearing what looks like a new tweed cap and looking extremely pleased with himself.'

'That's his default attitude,' says Isabella. 'Who's with him – Mrs Ogilvie or Mabel?'

'Difficult to tell until they arrive.'

'I'll fire up the machine anyway,' she says.

The shop door bursts open, and Bernie prances inside.

'If I've told you once, I've told you a hundred times it's not polite to push!' says his companion. 'A gentleman always waits for the lady to go first.'

Bernie gives her an amiable grin and looks meaningfully at the basket of biscuits on the counter.

'Good morning, Mabel,' I greet her. 'How are you both this morning?'

'I had to come up here rather earlier than usual,' she says. 'If I'd left the house any later, I'd have run the risk of people seeing Bernie in that ridiculous cap and thinking I had something to do with it.'

'He looks very smart,' says Isabella.

'Like an old-time detective,' I agree.

'More like the evil villain,' says Mabel. 'But I had no say in the matter. You'd think that years of faithful service would entitle me to a say in his day-to-day life, but you'd be wrong. His lordship is still under the care of his personal valet and chef. His other servant's opinion counts for nothing.'

'One biscuit coming right up!' I say.

'This isn't your day for working here,' says Mabel, pulling off her coat. 'Are you covering for Lily?'

I take it from her and hang it on the nearest peg. 'How do you know it isn't my day?'

She settles herself into her chair. 'Oh, please! I memorised your timetable years ago. We all have.'

'I've only been here for one and a half years.'

'Months, then, if you insist on being picky.'

'Did you want to discover when I was on duty to give yourself the best chance of enjoying the perfect drink?' I ask. 'That makes sense. It also accounts for the fact the bakery is always so busy when I'm here. People are saving their pennies for those times they get the most value out of them.'

'The bakery is equally busy when I'm here!' says Isabella.

'You don't know that. You aren't always here when I'm working with Lily. I'm almost sure it's busier on my days.'

'And I'm almost sure I don't see a cup of tea in front of me,' says Mabel. 'Despite having to get up early to sneak the mutt up here without everyone laughing at us.'

'Coming right up!' says Isabella. 'You know I make your tea exactly as you like it.'

'She's right,' I say. 'She almost always gets the hot water into the pot these days, instead of all over the floor. You'll have to excuse her if the lemon isn't as cleanly sliced as mine. We can't have everything in life, and we must all learn to cut our coats to suit our cloth. I'll get you a plum slice. The largest we have.'

'How do you know that's what I want?' asks Mabel.

I pause, holding the tongs open near the tray of plum slices. 'Isn't it?'

'As it happens. But it's never a good idea to make assumptions.'

'Quite right,' says Isabella. 'My sister has a distressing habit of doing that.'

'The sister who isn't meant to be here, yet who dropped in and cleaned the coffee machine for free?' I ask.

'How many sisters do I have?' she counters.

'Just the one, to the best of my knowledge. And she's about to leave and find somewhere to spend the day where she'll be valued and appreciated. Have a lovely day, Mabel. Bernie – your very humble servant!'

Isabella accompanies me to the door.

'I always like to see her off the premises,' she tells Mabel, who grins.

'See you tomorrow,' I say.

Isabella catches my hand and squeezes it.

'Thank you,' she says in a low voice.

'For what?'

'Coming in today. I was feeling pretty down before you arrived. I feel much better now.'

'Wedding jitters,' I say. 'It happens to the best of us. Or so I hear – not having personal experience of the phenomenon, nor ever being likely to.'

'But they've all gone now, thanks to you,' she says. 'Thank you, Georgie. I owe you one.'

'You should get back to your customers,' I say. 'Bernie looks as though he's about to eat his nice new hat if someone doesn't provide him with a biscuit in the next ten seconds.'

Chapter Twenty-Six

'Are you ready for our weekend away?' Lily asks me one day while we're serving lunches at the bakery.

'What weekend?' I ask, trying to remember whether the quiche is for table seven or eight.

'The one Isabella and Jon are arranging. It's at the end of this month.'

'No one's mentioned it to me.'

'Not the date, perhaps. But you knew it was happening.'

I set a quiche in front of a customer, who shakes her head. 'I was the steak pie.'

'I'm sorry,' I apologise. 'I was temporarily distracted.'

I sort out the confusion, then grab Lily as she's heading back to the kitchen.

'Why is this thing happening so early? The wedding isn't until the middle of August. Don't people usually have their stag and hen dos a week or so before the wedding?'

'I believe so, but there are no hard and fast rules about it. And it shouldn't come as much of a surprise to any of us to discover Isabella isn't doing things the conventional way.'

'But why May?' I persist. 'It's awful timing.'

'It seems fine to me. They were planning to do it at the end of July, after the boys broke up from school. But Ali is taking them to Cornwall for a week to stay with their grandparents. By the time they get back, there will be less than two weeks until the wedding. Jon and Isabella thought that might be leaving it too late. They want to be available in case of any last-minute hitches.'

'Aren't the boys free at any other time?' I ask.

'Not really. You know how strict schools are about unauthorised absences these days. Is there a problem?'

I sigh. 'Only that it isn't the most convenient timing for me. How many people are attending this thing? Maybe Isabella won't notice if I'm not there.'

'I think we both know that's not true. She has a habit of noticing everything you wish she wouldn't. And this isn't some relatively minor thing, like not turning up to a family lunch. She'll want her chief bridesmaid there, along with her matron of honour and her other bridesmaid.'

'It's a pity she isn't having ten bridesmaids,' I say. 'There would be such a crowd that my absence would never be noticed.'

Lily smiles. 'It would always be noticed. Isabella has set her heart on making you an important part of this wedding. There's no getting out of it now. I'd have thought you'd be pleased. It shows how far the two of you have come since the days when you spent every waking moment thinking of ways to annoy each other.'

'I haven't given that up entirely. It's always a good idea to keep your hand in. You never know when you're going to need old skills, and it doesn't do to let them become rusty.'

'You can't have much opportunity these days,' she says. 'Isabella no longer lives with you, and she's so busy it can be difficult to find time to see her.'

'Not for me. No matter where I hide, she tracks me down to hand me yet another list of unreasonable requirements to be completed within a ridiculously short time-frame.'

'I thought most things were sorted now,' she says.

'Not really. They've signed off on the hotel and the menu, but there's still so much to be done. Isabella hasn't found herself a dress yet, let alone one for us. If she isn't careful, we really will be marching down that aisle in gardening dungarees. Personally, I'd have no objection, but Isabella might.'

'Didn't I tell you?' she asks. 'My mum's making the dress.'

'How did that happen?'

'Isabella and Jon came over for lunch last week, and she was talking about the difficulty of getting exactly what she wanted. Mum offered to make it for her. She's a brilliant seamstress, and she can make anything she's asked for. Isabella practically burst into tears on the spot. Mum said she couldn't think why Isabella hadn't come to her first.'

'That's great,' I say. 'Maybe not for your mum, but certainly for Isabella.'

'Mum's quite happy. She's known Isabella for a long time, and she knows exactly how to handle her.'

'How about us?' I ask. 'Has Isabella made any decisions about what she'd like us to wear?'

'Mum's offered to make our dresses too if we like.'

'That's incredibly kind of her, but it feels like a huge imposition.'

'She wouldn't have offered if she didn't mean it. Isabella said yes. We just need to find a time to talk to them both.'

'It's a huge relief,' I say. 'I really wasn't looking forward to a string of bridal shop appointments. And that's assuming they even let us through the door. Word has probably spread of the wonder that is Isabella Campbell, and we'll mysteriously find every boutique within a fifty-mile radius is booked out for the next ten years.'

She laughs. 'It wasn't that bad. That story gets worse every time you tell it. Soon you'll be telling everyone that Isabella burned the place to the ground, with all the wedding dresses in it.'

'I won't be telling anyone anything. I'm determined to turn it into a repressed memory and lock it deep within my subconscious. Only the most skilled of psychologists will be able to retrieve it.'

'That sounds healthy,' says Lily. 'You should do that.'

The door opens, and Isabella walks in. She's looking more tired than ever. She's very pale and there are dark circles underneath her eyes.

'Are you ok?' I ask her.

She collapses into the nearest chair. 'I'm fine. I didn't sleep well last night – that's all. I had a dream that I was walking across the lawn at Willowmere Hall wearing my swimming costume and wellington boots.'

'What was the weather like?' I ask.

'How is that relevant?'

'If it was in the middle of a monsoon, you'd be appropriately dressed.'

'I don't think it was raining. There seemed to be a lot of birds around, all trying to eat the buffet. Jon had to keep fending them off with his crazy golf club.'

'So, you were getting married on the driving range of a bird sanctuary?' I ask. 'That makes perfect sense to me.'

She shudders. 'There were holes in my swimming costume. I had to cover them up as best I could with a tablecloth. My wedding co-ordinator was not impressed.'

'I'll make you a drink,' I say. 'Lily refuses to relax her unnecessarily strict rules about adding a little something, but I'll use a double shot of espresso and give you extra chocolate powder.'

'Could you make that two drinks?' asks Lily. 'I didn't sleep well last night either, but for very different reasons. First, Ethan woke up and remembered he'd left a stone egg in the airing cupboard to "hatch". Nothing would do for him but to get out of bed and wander down the landing to check its progress. Unfortunately, Daisy had left a trail of plastic dinosaurs across the floor, and he trod on them. The whole house was woken by his yells of pain. I thought the burglar alarm had gone off. By the time he'd calmed down enough to go back to bed, Daisy decided she'd had enough sleep for one night and was clamouring to go downstairs and make breakfast.'

'It sounds less than ideal,' I say. 'Although there have been a host of similar occurrences in our house over the years. Isabella is too modest to tell you about them, but I'll fill you in sometime when she isn't here.'

'Not unless you want me to tell her the story of the bowling ball,' says Isabella.

'I've already heard it,' says Lily. 'By the way, I was telling Georgia you've fixed the date for the joint stag and hen do.'

Isabella brightens. 'Our Final Fling weekend? We have! It should be great fun.'

'I'm sure it will,' I say. 'Although I'm a little surprised you're holding it so early.'

'It was the only date that suited everyone.'

'You didn't run it past me.'

She takes a sip of her cappuccino. 'I didn't think I needed to. I checked with Michael and Ali, but I already know your schedule. You're either here or you're at home.'

I feel a flash of annoyance. 'I do plenty of other things.'

'But none that I don't know about. All I'm saying is that I knew you wouldn't have any difficulty with the date. And Lily and I have the bakery rota covered.'

'So, you mentioned it to her in advance?' I ask.

'I had to. I wanted Jack to come too, and that meant giving them both enough notice to sort out babysitting.'

Lily notices my expression. 'I think Isabella was so keen for you to be there that she assumed the timing would suit you.'

'You're right,' agrees Isabella. 'I'm sorry, Georgia. That was thoughtless of me. I didn't mean to take you for granted. But you are free, aren't you?'

'I'm not sure. It isn't the best timing for me. I have a few things on around that time.'

Her face falls. 'Are they important?'

'Everything I do is important,' I say lightly.

'But not as important as this weekend. Do you really have other plans?'

This is the moment to tell her that I won't be able to make it. If I say it firmly enough, she'll accept it. Isabella is never unreasonable. I should get it over with, deal with her disappointment, and we can both move on.

But, looking at her eager face, I can't find the words to tell her I won't be coming. This weekend is obviously so important to her. Now that I come to think about it, it's the first time for quite a while I've seen her show so much enthusiasm for the wedding preparations. I can't bear the thought of seeing her face fall when I tell her this Final Fling weekend isn't important enough for me to attend.

And it isn't as though I have anything specific I can point to. Just a general wish she hadn't planned this event exactly when she did. I realise she and Lily are staring at me. Lily looks slightly quizzical, whereas Isabella is watching me with the same expression Bernie wears when he'd like a second biscuit and isn't sure whether someone is going to give it to him.

I take a deep breath and smile back at Isabella. 'Of course I can come to your shindig. I wouldn't miss it for the world.'

Her face breaks into its familiar beaming smile. 'I knew you wouldn't let me down! You never do. I promise you'll have lots of fun. Michael is coming too.'

'I assumed he would be, although I don't see the connection.'

'You and he seem to get along very well,' she says. 'Jon and I were commenting on it only the other day.'

'I get on well with everyone,' I say. 'I'm famous for it. Ask any of our customers which of our staff has the sunniest temperament and sweetest disposition. Every single one of them will say me.'

'I'll do that,' she says. 'If only to see your face when they all vote for me. Seriously, though, I want to thank you both for giving up so much of your time for this wedding. I know it's a lot to ask, and I don't want either of you to think I don't realise that.'

'We're happy to do it,' says Lily. 'Aren't we, Georgia?'

'I don't mind it too much,' I say. 'As long as no one expects me to do anything too strenuous during this upcoming weekend away.'

'I can't make any promises,' says Isabella. 'But I can guarantee we're all going to have a wonderful time.'

Chapter Twenty-Seven

'When do the wedding invitations go out?' I ask Mum one morning at breakfast.

'The middle of May. Isabella has already sent everyone a save-the-date card. She had to be restrained from sending them twice, just in case!'

'Of course, she did. Does she really think anyone is in danger of forgetting her wedding? It's all anyone talks about. Which is to say, it's all Isabella talks about.'

Mum passes me the butter, and I spread it lavishly on my toast.

'I didn't expect her to throw herself quite so whole-heartedly into it all,' she says, and I laugh.

'This is Isabella. She throws herself whole-heartedly into everything she does.'

'That's true,' she says. 'But I didn't quite mean that. What I'm trying to say is that I didn't expect her to be quite so … conventional about it all.'

'Me neither. If I'd ever thought about Isabella's wedding, I would have imagined her getting married on a beach at dawn before snorkelling off to France for her honeymoon. Not getting married at a country house hotel with a formal menu and a master of ceremonies and all that stuff. Still, it's her wedding, and it's up to her what she wants to do.'

'And Jon,' she reminds me with a smile.

I take another bite of toast. 'Him too, of course. But, as with most things, he seems happy to go along with whatever Isabella wants. It's probably the only way anyone can sustain a relationship with her for very long.'

'I think you're being unfair to him,' she says. 'They both seem extremely happy to me. And Jon doesn't give the impression of someone who has no voice in his own relationship.'

'He doesn't. And you're right – they do seem happy. It was obvious from the day they first got together that he was the one for her. I didn't necessarily think they'd end up doing something as conventional as getting married, but it comes to the best of us.'

She smiles. 'And how about you?'

'I have absolutely no plans for matrimony, especially if it means spending hundreds of hours looking for the perfect dress and listening to Colette tell me how the perfect wedding will make all my dreams come true.'

'That was just one afternoon,' she says.

'That's technically true, but it felt like an eternity. Isabella was completely unable to make up her mind about anything. It was most unlike her. I expected her to prance into the shop with a detailed drawing and turn down every single dress that didn't meet her exact specifications.'

'Prance?' she asks. 'Isn't that what ponies do?'

'And Isabella when she's feeling more than ordinarily pleased with herself. But she spent the entire afternoon dithering about one dress after another until she'd almost driven Colette to early retirement.'

'A wedding dress is a big decision,' says Mum.

'Not as big as sinking her life savings into buying the Sugarloaf. And yet that idea popped into her head one day, she talked to Lily the next, and the pair of them were the proud owners of a failing bakery within a few months. Getting married should be far less complicated than that.'

She hands me the plate of toast. 'Technically, maybe. But she's feeling the pressure of all the expectations that surround a wedding. She wants everyone to have a wonderful time, and she's worried about getting everything just right.'

'There do seem an awful lot of traditions and expectations surrounding this kind of event,' I agree. 'It's the sort of thing I hate. This is Isabella's wedding – not a day for everyone else's demands and preferences. Hopefully, all the preferences will be hers and Jon's.'

'I expect they will,' she says. 'But when I asked about you, I wasn't talking about the wedding or your role as chief bridesmaid. I was checking how everything else is going? You have a lot on your plate right now.'

'No, I haven't. I've eaten the last slice of toast.'

She smiles. 'I can make you some more in a minute.'

'Thanks, but I need to get going. I'm due at work in half an hour. I'm doing a couple of extra days this week.'

'That may be why you're looking so tired. Are you trying to do too much?'

'I don't think so. But time will tell.'

She squeezes my shoulder. 'Don't put so much pressure on yourself, Georgia. Everything will work out. It always does.'

I push back my chair. 'I'm sure you're right. Thanks for the breakfast, Mum. Sorry to eat and run like this.'

'If the Campbell girls ever stop eating breakfast, I'll know something is very wrong,' she says, adding in a casual tone, 'Have you seen much of Michael recently? I was saying to Dad last night that he seems a nice lad.'

'He's in his thirties,' I say. 'Hardly a lad.'

'Let's not quibble about that,' she says mildly. 'I was asking how the two of you are getting on?'

'Fine, I think. He gave me a ride to London the other day, but I haven't seen him since then. I'll definitely see him at this stag and hen thing at the end of the month. I realise they had to arrange things around the boys, but it couldn't have come at a worse time for me.'

'I know,' she says sympathetically. 'I hope you find a way to make it work. If not, you'll just have to tell Isabella you're too busy and won't be able to make it.'

'That would crush her. She's set her heart on this weekend away. I don't know exactly what we're doing, but it seems as though it will make a difference to her having me there. So, I've given in with a good grace. At least outwardly.'

She nods. 'You're a good sister, Georgia.'

'Who would ever have thought you'd be saying that to me?' I tease her. 'It's wonderful to think how much Isabella and I have grown up. You must be extremely proud!'

'I've always been proud of the pair of you,' she says.

'I know that, and I'm grateful for it. Isabella and I are lucky to have such supportive parents. But I'm painfully aware I haven't given you much to be proud of so far. Isabella has. She's a qualified accountant, she runs a successful business, and now she's getting married.'

'Stop that!' she says. 'Any parent who judges their children on their qualifications or relationship status isn't fit to be one at all. Your father and I are equally proud of both our daughters, and we always will be. We don't care what you choose to do with your lives, or how long it takes you to make that choice. I've watched you both grow into independent, strong-minded women, and that makes me very happy. Maybe your path hasn't been as conventional as Isabella's, but who cares? You're finding your way now, and you're doing it with a good deal of courage and resolution. Don't ever let me hear you compare yourself to your sister again.'

'I won't,' I promise. 'I can't say the same for our customers. They're always saying how much alike the pair of us are.'

'You look like each other, and you share a similar sense of humour,' she says. 'Otherwise, I don't see much resemblance.'

'And I'm far more intelligent,' I say, quickly making my escape before she can reply.

My phone rings as I arrive at the bakery. It's a nice day, so I stay outside to take the call. I'm not sure whether Isabella has arrived yet, and it may be one of the Flour Girls calling me with an update on the decorations or a suggestion for a game.

'Hello?' I say cautiously.

'Georgia? It's Michael.'

'I thought you might be one of the Flour Girls.'

'I could give it a go,' he says. 'But it sounds as though you have plenty of participants in your group chat without adding another one.'

'What can I do for you?' I ask.

'I thought you might like to have dinner this week. I'm free on Wednesday if you are?'

'I'm afraid I have plans on Wednesday.'

'No problem,' he says. 'How about Friday?'

'I'm booked up Friday too,' I say.

There's a pause. 'I'm free on Sunday,' he says at last.

'I'm not. Isabella has asked the three of us to Lily's house for dinner. Angela wants to take our measurements for our bridesmaids' dresses. Isabella warned us not to eat too much, which I thought was rather a cheek coming from her. I refuse to starve myself just so I can fit into a smaller dress.'

'You obviously have a packed schedule this week,' he says. 'How about next Monday?'

'I'm afraid not. I have a commitment I can't break.'

There's an even longer pause before he speaks again. 'That's too bad. It sounds as though you're booked up for the foreseeable future.'

'I have very little free time right now,' I say. 'I'm afraid that won't change for a while.'

'I understand,' he says. 'I just thought I'd ask. Don't let me hold you up.'

'I really have to get to work. I've made a resolution not to collect more than ten written warnings before this wedding.'

He laughs. 'That sounds overly ambitious to me, but you know best. Nice to speak to you, Georgia. I'll see you around.'

'At this Final Fling weekend, if not before. It seems there's no getting out of it for any of us.'

'Would you want to?' he asks.

'In a heartbeat! But Isabella isn't taking no for an answer, so I've reluctantly signed up. I can't say I'm looking forward to it.'

'I think it sounds like fun,' he says. 'We could team up and win all the games.'

I groan. 'There are going to be games?'

'From what I hear. It's a shame you aren't looking forward to it, but it will soon be over.'

'That's what I'm counting on. I really do have to go now.'

'Of course,' he says rather formally. 'Have a good week, and don't burn the candle at both ends.'

He rings off, and I stuff my phone into my pocket and run towards the bakery as quickly as possible.

Chapter Twenty-Eight

'You're late!' Isabella greets me.

I sigh. Of course, she's here before me. Whenever I'm at work early, Isabella is nowhere to be seen. But the one time I arrive thirty seconds behind schedule, there she is, tapping her watch and looking at me as though I'm back in school and trying to sneak into morning assembly without Miss Flowers noticing and giving me yet another detention for lateness.

'I was here on time,' I defend myself. 'But my phone rang as I was walking from my car.'

'You could have answered it in here,' she says, sounding even more like Miss Flowers telling me that if I had something to say to my friends, I could share it with the entire class.

'I could,' I say, 'but I didn't want to.'

'Was it your secret boyfriend?' she asks.

'I don't have a secret boyfriend.'

'I'm not sure I believe you. You're always busy these days. And, despite me telling you so often that no one would want to date you, you're quite attractive. Our customers are always saying how much you look like me.'

I switch on the coffee machine. 'If your head grows any larger, it won't fit in your veil.'

'Veils are one-size-fits-all,' she says smugly.

'But tiaras aren't. I seem to remember you're wearing one of those.'

She shrugs. 'I wanted fresh flowers, but the wedding co-ordinator thinks a tiara is the only way to go with a veil like mine. Chloe knows far more about these things than I do, so I've agreed.'

'That doesn't sound right to me,' I say. 'You should have whatever you want to hold your veil in place, even if it's a circlet of doughnuts. This Chloe woman sounds awfully opinionated for someone who's there to facilitate what you want. I'd tell her where to go if I were you.'

'I can't do that,' she says. 'Some of my ideas were a little off-the-wall when I started out. I've never thought much about weddings until now. I had no idea there were so many traditions and expectations surrounding them.'

'Whose expectations?' I ask.

'The families, the guests, the staff at Willowmere Hall.'

'They aren't the ones getting married. Is Jon's family putting pressure on you to do things a certain way? Would you like me to have a word with him for you? I'd be happy to.'

'Jon's family is lovely,' she says. 'They haven't said anything about what we should or shouldn't do. But I want everything to be nice for them and for all our guests. I can't bear the thought of letting Jon down.'

'You could never do that. I've heard him say he'd marry you standing on a pile of rubbish at the recycling centre, provided you said, "I do." Strangely enough, I believe he meant it. You have nothing to worry about as far as Jon is concerned.'

'You're right,' she says, looking more cheerful. 'But I still want to show him I can organise the perfect wedding.'

'As long as it's your perfect wedding, and not Chloe's perfect wedding,' I say.

'So, who was your phone call from?' she asks. 'We've established it wasn't from your secret boyfriend, which is rather a disappointment.'

'It was Michael.'

Her eyes sparkle. 'So, not an ex-boyfriend, but a possible future –?'

'Let me stop you right there! I've had just about enough of all this best man and chief bridesmaid nonsense from everyone else. I expected better from you.'

'Why?' she asks.

'I should have said I looked for better, although without much hope. People need to knock it off and find something more interesting to talk about.'

'What did Michael want?' she asks.

'How is that anything to do with you?'

'It isn't,' she says. 'But I miss my career as a matchmaker. I've loved doing it for our staff over the years, and it's left a huge gap in my life.'

'You can still matchmake,' I say. 'Just not for me.'

'Who, then? We haven't had a new member of staff for years.'

She brightens. 'Maybe I should fire you to give us the opportunity to hire someone else.'

'And maybe you won't get the chance. It wouldn't take much at this point to make me quit my job entirely. Then you can matchmake your next member of staff to your heart's content.'

She shakes her head. 'I have so little time for that sort of thing now that this wedding is taking up most of my spare time and energy. But I thought I could fit in some part-time meddling with you. I already know almost everything about you, which is the most time-consuming part. I had to get to know each of our previous staff members quite well before I could decide whether the person they were involved with was a suitable match for them, or whether they were making the most colossal mistake.'

'I have no experience in the field of professional matchmaking,' I admit. 'But surely you should leave other adults to get on with things by themselves, without sticking your oar in.'

'You'd think so,' she agrees. 'But it isn't always that simple. Take Olivia, for instance. You only met her briefly, so you won't remember much about her stay in Honeywell. She got together with a photographer called Will, and I had to nudge things along quite a bit.'

I bite back the urge to say that not only do I know all about Olivia and Will, I also know she'll be exactly thirty-six weeks pregnant by the time the wedding day arrives.

'It sounds as though you know what you're doing,' I say. 'Although I imagine most of those couples would have got together all by themselves without your interference. In return, I'd like you to admit it may be easier to matchmake for strangers than for someone you've known all your life.'

'I can't be sure until I've tried,' she says.

'And I refuse to allow you to try. I hold all the cards here. I don't have to go through with this bridesmaid thing. I could promote Abby to head bridesmaid and just attend as a guest. Not even that, if you get too far out of line.'

'You wouldn't!' she exclaims, and I laugh.

'Very likely not. But you should remember that I could. So, the next time you feel an urge to set me up with another member of the wedding party, please bear in mind you're skating on very thin ice.'

'I'll remember,' she says. 'So, what did Michael want?'

'You're unbelievable!'

'I'm not planning to interfere,' she says. 'But there's so little happening except for this wedding that I need something to divert myself now and then.'

I sprinkle chocolate over our cappuccinos. 'If you must know, he wanted to ask whether I'd like to have dinner with him sometime. But we couldn't find a mutually agreeable date, so we've left it for now.'

She inspects her drink. 'No picture today?'

'Pictures are for those who deserve them, and for paying customers. You are neither.'

'You should have dinner with Michael,' she says. 'It doesn't have to be a date. You've hardly spent any time with him. I think you'll like him when you get to know him better.'

'He drove me to London,' I say.

'And how did that go?'

'Straight up the M3, and on to the M25.'

She folds her arms and gives me another one of her Miss Flowers looks. 'I am still your employer!'

'As I often tell you, that can be remedied at any point.'

'Why won't you meet him for dinner? Don't you like him?'

'He seems very nice, but none of the times he suggested worked for me.'

'How many dates did he offer you?' she asks.

'Three – no, four.'

'Four dates, and you couldn't make any of them? I find that difficult to believe.'

I finish my drink. 'Believe what you like. Not that it's any of your business.'

'You can't be booked up every night of the week,' she says. 'You used to enjoy a bewilderingly active social life. But you told me recently you have no intention of dating for the rest of the year, which means you must have a lot of free evenings.'

'It means no such thing. I have plenty of other things to fill my evenings.'

'Like going out for dinner with Michael?' she asks.

'If this is a specimen of how you behaved to your temporary members of staff, I'm surprised any of them ended up in relationships. It must have been despite your efforts, rather than because of them.'

She laughs. 'I was far more subtle with them than I need to be with you. You and I have never really done nuance, have we?'

'There's quite a large gulf between nuance and your current sledge-hammer tactics.'

Ivy puts her head around the door. 'Are you busy in here?'

'Busy trying to keep my patience with my annoying sister,' I say. 'Otherwise, no. The morning rush hasn't yet started.'

'That's good,' she says. 'I'm meeting a group of Silver Surfers in ten minutes, and I wanted to make sure all the coffee eclairs hadn't been sold. The last time I was in here, you'd run out.'

'I'm sorry about our poor stock-control,' I say. 'That's my sister's purview, not mine. Take it up with her.'

I pick up a tray and go to the kitchen to fetch some cups and glasses for the morning traffic. When I come back, Ivy is telling Isabella all about her entry for the art competition.

'I don't want to paint anything,' she says. 'That's Bob's speciality. He isn't too confident about his brush work, so it seems best to leave him to it. I thought I might have a go at writing a one-act play.'

'About Bernie?' I ask.

'Or starring Bernie?' asks Isabella.

'The first one,' says Ivy. 'Lots of foam, please. That's my favourite part of the drink. I can't really cast Bernie. He might not be up to learning his lines.'

'Mrs Ogilvie is always telling us how quickly he picks up new tricks,' says Isabella.

'I suppose I could give him a walk-on part,' says Ivy. 'But he might catch sight of someone he knows in the audience and rush over to greet them.'

'What's your play about?' I ask.

'I'm not sure. But I'm taking an improvisation class, so I thought a short drama could be a good idea.'

'How about setting it in a laundrette?' I suggest. 'Bernie loves socks. You could make it a modern vignette, with themes of static cling and the existential angst that arises when a sock loses its one true pairing.'

'Which most of Mabel's seem to,' says Isabella. 'You could call it The Spin Cycle of Despair – a ten-minute tragedy.'

'I doubt Edie would be too keen on that,' says Ivy. 'Although Mabel would love it!'

'We can come up with lots more ideas if you need them,' I say. 'How about Bernie and the Biscuit of Destiny?'

'Perfect!' says Isabella. 'A sweeping one-act epic, in which Bernie is forced to journey across the living room, make his way past the vacuum cleaner of doom, and dive under the coffee table of peril to in order to fulfil his quest of meeting the biscuit of his dreams. A high-stakes drama of crumbs and courage.'

'Please don't mention that in front of Mabel,' begs Ivy. 'She'll insist on directing it, and I couldn't cope with that.'

'You could do far worse,' says Isabella. 'She has a natural talent for the dramatic. Remember her star-turn as Chef Mabel in that television show they shot here?'

'I've been trying to forget it for years,' says Ivy. 'But every time I do, Mabel brings it up again. You'd think she'd be ashamed to remember how badly she behaved, but not a bit of it. She's as proud as punch of her dramatic creation. At one time, I think she was hoping to sell the rights to the character. She's finally accepted that's unlikely to happen, but I don't want you reminding her about it and setting her off again.'

'Mabel could act in your play instead of directing it,' I say. 'It could be like Cats, but with all the cast members dressed as different breeds of dogs. I'd love to stay and talk about this all day, but I've promised to help Abby with the lemon tarts this morning. So, I'll leave you in Isabella's more-than-capable hands.'

Isabella gives me a suspicious look. 'Why are you being so polite about me all of a sudden?'

'I'm always polite. Also, I'm hoping you'll let me leave twenty minutes early this afternoon. I have something important to do.'

'Is it wedding-related?'

'No.'

'Then how important can it be?' she asks.

'Not everything in this village revolves around your wedding.'

'Yes, it does. Our customers are constantly asking me for updates.'

'I respectfully disagree,' I say, edging towards the door. 'So, can I leave a few minutes early?'

'We'll see how good the lemon tarts are first,' she says. 'If they aren't just as delicious as the ones Lily and I make, I'm keeping you here until midnight.'

Chapter Twenty-Nine

I meet Isabella and Abby at the Carson's house the following Sunday. I've been here for lunch several times over the past couple of years. The Carsons are one of the most friendly and welcoming families I've ever met, and Angela is an excellent cook.

'It's no wonder you spend so much time here,' I tell Isabella as we're enjoying second helpings of roast beef and Yorkshire pudding. 'I've rarely eaten such perfect roast beef.'

'Are you implying that no one would spend time with my parents if the food wasn't so good?' Lily asks in a reproachful tone.

Isabella helps herself to roast potatoes. 'I apologise for my sister, Angela. She hasn't been as well brought up as I have.'

'We share the same parents,' I say. 'And Angela knows that isn't what I meant.'

'Of course I do,' Angela reassures me. 'It's lovely to have a guest who enjoys my food so much.'

'You have me!' says Isabella in a hurt tone.

'I meant another guest,' says Angela. 'I don't know which of you enjoyed my salmon en croûte the most last month.'

'I did!' says Isabella at once. 'I ate four helpings, and Georgia only managed three.'

'It isn't a competition,' I say.

She doesn't look convinced. 'How else do you measure someone's enjoyment of a dish?'

'I promise I'll try to do better today,' I say. 'Although it seems rather unfair on the Carsons. One Campbell sister at a time might give them more of a fighting chance.'

'I offered to bring a dessert,' says Isabella. 'But Angela was most insistent it wasn't necessary.'

'Perhaps she thought you'd eat it on the way over here,' says Lily. 'And then you'd have no room for your lunch.'

'I always have room for my lunch,' says Isabella. 'While we're on the topic of the excellent dining opportunities this house affords, we should give an honourable mention to the vegetables. These roast leeks are wonderful, Martin. Did you grow the cabbage too?'

'Martin grows almost all our vegetables,' says Angela. 'It's his hobby.'

'I've always enjoyed gardening,' he says. 'And I have a very able helper these days. Daisy could be the next Alan Titchmarsh.'

'It makes a change from the days when she used to trot around the garden after you, digging up everything you'd planted,' says Lily. 'You were so patient with her.'

'It took her a while to grasp the principles of gardening,' Martin says fondly. 'She didn't have much concept of time when she was small. It was very understandable. She liked to help Angela in the kitchen too. They would mix the ingredients for her favourite cookies, pop them in the oven, and twenty minutes later they'd be ready. Why should gardening be any different?'

'That may be why I've never been able to grow anything,' says Isabella. 'I've tried house plants a few times, but they all seem to die within weeks. I may be a little over-enthusiastic with them.'

'Plants like to be given all the ingredients they need for a successful life cycle,' says Martin. 'Which means water, food, and light. After that, they prefer to be left alone to get on with it.'

'My plants had all those things,' says Isabella. 'In fact, I used to double the quantities to make them grow twice as fast.'

He looks amused. 'Why doesn't that surprise me? But gardening doesn't work like that.'

'She sang to them too,' I say. 'I think that's what finally finished them off.'

'I'm sure it was just bad luck,' says Angela. 'You should try again some time, Isabella. Plants are a wonderful hobby.'

'I'm too busy for hobbies,' says Isabella. 'I'm rushed off my feet these days. I rarely have the chance to sit down and eat a proper meal at the moment. What was that noise supposed to mean, Georgia?'

'Nothing!' I say. 'But you should definitely make time for some hobbies. They're good for your mental health.'

'Then why don't you have any?'

'I have hobbies,' I say.

'Such as?'

'Maybe not official ones, but I have plenty of things to keep me busy.'

'You're always saying that,' she says, 'but I can't imagine what they are. Are you secretly building a full-scale model of a nuclear submarine in the garden shed?'

'How would that work?' asks Lily. 'Most garden sheds are quite small.'

'You have to think outside the box,' says Isabella. 'Or in this case, the shed. People build ships inside bottles. You could apply the same principles here.'

'So, you'd build an entire submarine,' I say. 'Then you'd pull a series of strings, and the hull would spring into shape?'

'Why not?' she asks. 'It wouldn't do the shed much good, but Dad's been saying for ages he wants to knock that old thing down and put up a new one. You'd be saving him the trouble.'

'It would be difficult to transport to the docks,' says Lily. 'It might be better to take it down there in its flat-pack form and wait to pull the strings until you'd carried it down to the water.'

'We should write to the navy and offer to sell them our idea,' says Isabella. 'They're always looking for agile and innovative solutions to modern military problems. If we patented it, we could be rich.'

'If you want to find something craft-related to do,' says Angela, 'you could enter the competition at the arts centre.'

'That's a great suggestion,' I say. 'The more entries there are, the more chance we have of Mrs Ogilvie liking one of them.'

'I doubt she'd be too happy with the idea of someone making a Bernie in a bottle,' says Lily.

'I don't see why not,' argues Isabella. 'It isn't as though we'd be using the real Bernie. We could make a tiny model of him and use the little strings to wag his tail.'

'Go ahead,' I say. 'Each entry will be judged on its own merits. We're asking people not to put their names on their entries.'

'But you'd known it was mine and mark it down on principle. Anyway, I have no time to learn new skills. I have a business to run and a wedding to plan.'

'If you've all finished eating, I'll clear up,' says Martin. 'You can go upstairs with Angela and discuss what you'd like her to make for you.'

'Are you sure?' I ask. 'We could help you with the dishes first.'

'Perfectly sure. It's my contribution to this wedding. Everyone has their part to play, even if most of them are behind the scenes. It's like the cogs in a finely-tuned Swiss watch. You don't see them turning, yet each of them has its function, and none of them can work without the others.'

'You may not always see the inner workings of things,' says Lily, 'but sometimes you do. Ethan's current passion is dismantling anything he can get his hands on, just to see how it works. Jack was most put-out when he arrived home the other day to discover Ethan had taken apart the iron and couldn't remember where he'd hidden all the parts.'

'Bless him!' says Angela. 'He's shaping up to be an engineer, just like his uncle. You mustn't discourage him.'

'I have a spare iron in the garage if you need it,' says Martin.

'Thanks, but they found everything in the end,' says Lily. 'They spent a happy evening putting it all back together. I held my breath when they switched it on, but it appears to be working.'

'I hope Jack's enjoying a nice lunch,' says Angela. 'I've kept some beef and potatoes back in case he's still hungry when he comes to pick you up.'

'He's having lunch at the Red Lion,' says Isabella. 'No one goes home hungry from there.'

'Didn't he want to eat with us?' I ask.

'He'd have been more than welcome,' says Angela. 'But he, Jon and Michael decided to eat at the pub together. They didn't want to be in the way.'

'You mean they wanted to avoid any more wedding discussions?' I ask. 'I can't say I blame them.'

'Chris has gone with them too,' says Abby. 'He loves Victoria's steak and kidney pudding.'

'I'm sure they'll have a wonderful time,' says Angela. 'And the children are with Jack's mum today, so that gives us a couple of uninterrupted hours.'

'Not if you don't get moving,' says Martin. 'Leave all this to me.'

'You have the perfect husband,' I tell Angela as we follow her upstairs to her sewing room.

'That's what I always tell him,' she says. 'I think you should show appreciation for your partner, especially when you've been as lucky as Martin and me.'

'Do you show appreciation for Jon?' I ask Isabella.

'I'm marrying him! How much more appreciation could I show him?'

'You could stop hogging the handset when you watch television together,' I suggest.

'It's important for me to keep it because I have faster reflexes and know exactly when to pause the film whenever we need a snack. Jon understands that.'

'He's a lucky man,' I say.

'Isn't he?' asks Angela, not appearing to notice my mocking tone. 'They both are. It's always so lovely when wonderful people find each other. I know they'll be incredibly happy together.'

'Finally, someone who gets me!' says Isabella.

Lily looks at her watch. 'We have one hour and fifty-five minutes before everyone arrives. If you two could put your sisterly feud aside until later, we have work to do.'

Chapter Thirty

Angela pulls down a file from a shelf. 'Let's start by glancing through this so that Isabella can give me some suggestions about what she'd like.'

'Why do you have a collection of wedding dress patterns?' asks Lily.

'They aren't wedding dresses,' says Angela. 'They're just a collection of dress patterns I've gathered over the years. I won't be using any of them for Isabella's actual dress, but it should give me an idea of the sort of shape and design she's after.'

'If you can discover that,' I say, 'you'll be doing a lot better than Colette. All she managed to extract from Isabella was that yes, she wanted a dress, and no, she hadn't the faintest idea what it should look like. That should give you quite a bit of latitude.'

'I don't anticipate many problems,' says Angela, smiling at Isabella. 'I've made her several outfits over the years, so I have a good idea of her measurements and the sort of things she likes.'

'I hope she's wearing more appropriate underwear today,' I say. 'I don't want to be embarrassed a second time by her Winnie the Pooh pants and matching vest. Colette's eyes almost popped out of her head when Isabella pulled off her jeans and sweater to reveal Piglet trotting after Pooh, telling him it was a beautiful day for a walk in the Hundred Acre Wood.'

'I don't know why you're so bothered,' says Isabella. 'None of the guests will see my underwear on my wedding day, so it doesn't matter if I wear hundreds of cartoon characters.'

'There's no need for you to undress today,' says Angela. 'All I want to do is exchange some ideas and talk about what is and isn't possible.'

I throw myself into a beanbag and prepare to be entertained. I'd feel sorry for Angela if she hadn't gone into this with her eyes open. But if she's made clothes for Isabella before, she must know what she's let herself in for.

Which makes it all the more of a surprise when, by the end of the first half hour, the pair of them appear to have reached some sort of agreement. I have no idea how Angela does it. She doesn't argue or push one design over another or offer any definite opinions. But somehow, Isabella narrows her options down and has no apparent difficulty with making a series of decisions that would have felt impossible even a few short days ago.

'You have a promising career ahead of you as a bridal designer if you want one,' I tell Angela. 'You've achieved more in thirty minutes than those so-called professionals did in almost three.'

'I'm not sure I'd like to do this full time,' she says. 'But it's a pleasure when it's for someone you love.'

'What's your secret?' I ask. 'When we were in Chez Colette, it was as much as we could do to persuade Isabella to choose a sweetheart neckline over a round neck, let alone make decisions about sleeves or embroidery.'

'I've always believed that people know exactly what they want,' says Angela. 'You just need to listen to them.'

I'm not convinced, but neither am I about to argue. I only hope Isabella doesn't wander downstairs when we've finished, announcing she wants to scrap all her previous plans because she's now longing to dress as a pirate queen and would love to structure her entire wedding around a nautical theme.

'Now we've sorted out some preliminary ideas,' says Angela, making a few final notes on her jotter, 'how about the bridesmaids?'

I groan. 'I've been secretly hoping Isabella would never decide on anything so you'd never get as far as our dresses.'

'Fat chance!' says Isabella. 'If I have to go through it, the rest of you do too.'

She beams at Angela. 'No offence. You've made this far more painless than I was expecting.'

'None taken,' says Angela placidly. 'Lily never enjoyed doing this, even when she was a little girl. She wriggled and kicked and complained I was sticking pins in her.'

'You were!' says Lily.

'Only because you wouldn't stand still,' says her mother.

'I promise to stand quietly for all my fittings,' promises Isabella. 'I almost never wriggle these days.'

'But you rarely sit still either,' says Lily. 'I've never met anyone so energetic. It makes me feel exhausted just watching you.'

'That's because you have children. Even I admit to the occasional feeling of tiredness after a day spent with my delightful goddaughter and her brother.'

'I thought there was nothing difficult about looking after small children,' says Lily. 'That's what you're always telling me.'

'And I'm quite correct,' says Isabella. 'I said occasionally – not all the time.'

'They often wear me out,' says Angela. 'Martin and I aren't as young as we were. But we love it.'

'Whereas Lily has no such excuse,' says Isabella. 'I've noticed that parents like to play an elaborate game of "my life is worse than yours" when they're around mere godparents such as myself. It always goes the same way. "My life is harder than yours because I didn't get any sleep last night." "No, mine is more difficult because I have a work deadline and a broken washing machine." "Fine – that one wins. Take the card and deal again." It's all most unbecoming if you ask me.'

'I do have a broken washing machine,' says Lily. 'I'm glad that counts as a win in your universe.'

'Did Ethan take it apart to see how it worked?' I ask.

'No, but he found a jar of coins and dumped the lot into my last wash without me noticing.'

'It gives a whole new meaning to the concept of money laundering,' I say. 'Is someone coming to repair it?'

'Dad has promised to swing by later and take a look if Jack and I can't locate the rest of the coins in the filter.'

'It's all part of the rich tapestry of parenting,' says Isabella. 'I'm glad I didn't meet the boys until they were nine. They had far too much appreciation of money by that stage to risk losing any in the wash. They needed their cash for more important things – like bubble gum and trading cards.'

'But not cookies,' says Lily. 'They were lucky their uncle not only met and fell in love with a bakery owner, but one who was happy to hand out free cookies at the drop of a hat in order to buy his nephews' affection.'

'I'm sure Isabella would never dream of doing that,' says Angela.

'There are very few things my sister wouldn't dream of doing,' I say. 'And no, Isabella, that isn't a compliment. But for some strange reason, children seem to love her. Toby and Ollie certainly do, and I don't think it has anything to do with her being their official cookie supplier.'

There's a knock on the door.

'Come in!' calls Angela.

Martin appears with a tray of cups. 'I thought you might appreciate some coffee after all your strenuous work.'

'And Turkish delight?' asks Isabella.

He smiles and hands her the plate. 'Of course. I bought a box the moment I heard you were coming over for lunch.'

'You're the best!' she says. 'I'm always reminding Lily of that. She seems to know it already, but that sort of thing can't be repeated too often.'

He sets down the tray on the nearest worktable. 'I'll leave you all to it. I didn't want to interrupt proceedings, but I'm aware that decision making is hungry work, particularly for some of us. I'll be in the garden if anyone needs me.'

'He really is the perfect man,' says Isabella when he's left. 'I've said it before, and I'll say it again – if I'd seen him first, Angela, you'd have had a fight on your hands.'

'I must remember to mention that to Jon,' I tell her.

'He already knows. There should be no secrets between engaged couples. Or only ones about who ate the last chocolate biscuit and replaced the empty packet in the pantry instead of updating that week's shopping list.'

Angela peers out of the window. 'Martin's going out to his greenhouse.'

Lily smiles. 'Every time Isabella comes for lunch, Dad has to plant a whole new crop to replace everything she's eaten.'

'Could you pour the coffee while I put these notes somewhere safe?' Angela asks her. 'I want to keep them separate from the ones about the other dresses.'

She turns to me. 'Have you had any thoughts about what you'd like to wear?'

'Not really. We've been waiting for Isabella to choose hers first. I imagine we all need to follow some sort of common theme. It might look odd for her to be channelling Queen Elizabeth the First, while the rest of us rock a rural shepherdess theme.'

'I would never do that,' says Isabella. 'Those neck ruffs look horribly uncomfortable. I have no concrete plans for the bridesmaids' dresses, although my wedding co-ordinator probably does.'

'Chloe?' I ask. 'What does it have to do with her?'

'She's working on the overall vibe. That's why she's called a co-ordinator.'

'Up to a point,' I say. 'But it's your wedding, not hers. She's there to facilitate what you want, not what she thinks you should have.'

'I agree,' says Lily. 'She sounds quite bossy with all her vision boards and napkin-folding rules and flow charts.'

'The hotel has a reputation to uphold,' says Isabella. 'Chloe says the reason they're booked up so far ahead is because they pay so much attention to detail and insist on everything being exactly right. She told me the last time we met that perfection is the minimum anyone should expect, and she insists on going above and beyond that.'

'How can you exceed perfection?' I ask.

'I don't know, but she seems to think it's possible. She says she demands high standards from everyone, including the bride.'

Lily, Abby and I exchange looks but don't speak.

'Chloe sounds as though she's very good at her job,' says Angela, handing Isabella a cup of coffee and the cream jug. 'But Georgia's right, you know. She works for you and Jon, not the other way around.'

'That's true,' says Isabella. 'But she's been very helpful in lots of ways. When I first got engaged, all I could think about was that I was marrying the man I loved. It never occurred to me I'd have to plan a wedding, let alone in a place like Willowmere Hall.'

'Don't you want to get married there?' I ask. 'It's not too late to cancel.'

'It's a lovely place, and we were lucky they could take us. But I didn't anticipate everything that goes along with getting married in that sort of venue. I had a vague vision of inviting lots of people and everyone letting their hair down and having a great time. But Chloe has helped me to see that wouldn't be right for this sort of venue.'

'So, get married somewhere else!' I say.

She shakes her head. 'Jon fell in love with Willowmere Hall the first time he saw it. It was his idea to go and see it, although neither of us expected to book it. He was so excited when they said they could fit us in. We both were. And we've paid all the deposits now, so we'd lose a lot of money if we pulled out. All we have to do is make sure the wedding arrangements are appropriate for the venue. I was so grateful when they gave me a co-ordinator. I didn't have many ideas of my own, and I was becoming overwhelmed. That's when Chloe stepped in and helped guide me through it all.'

'That all sounds great,' I say. 'Although I can't help wondering whether one of the reasons you don't have many ideas is because Chloe has so many of her own.'

'I don't think so. As I say, I was feeling overwhelmed, and I was relieved when she stepped in to help me out.'

'Fair enough,' says Lily, shooting me a warning glance.

There's no need. I have no intention of pursuing this further. Isabella's stressed look has returned, and her glow of excitement at having made some decisions about her wedding dress has faded. If everyone keeps raising objections, nothing will ever be decided, and Isabella may end up getting married in her Pooh Bear underwear after all, complete with a matching onesie.

Chapter Thirty-One

The end of May rolls around far more quickly than I expected. There's no real reason it shouldn't. Time, as my high school physics teacher always told us, is linear – which means it flows in one direction, like a river.

He usually followed this up by saying that if we believed he couldn't identify the smell of nail polish just because he wasn't a chemistry teacher, we were sorely mistaken. And if the culprit didn't put it away at once and concentrate on all the valuable things he was trying to teach us, he would keep the entire class in at break time.

So, I stopped painting my nails and did my best to look as though I was listening. At least some of it must have gone in because I now understand how calendars work, and it no longer takes me by surprise when one day of the week follows another.

'Are you all ready for the weekend?' Isabella greets me one morning when I arrive at work.

'Difficult to say. I've packed all the usual things for a disgustingly hearty couple of nights in the heart of the British countryside. But this is your event. Who knows what I'll wish I'd included once the weekend gets off the ground?'

'Off the ground is a very appropriate camping metaphor,' she says. 'I'm delighted to see you getting into the spirit of the thing.'

'I wouldn't go that far. But, having agreed to take part, I'm prepared to do things properly and have fun, whether I like it or not.'

'Look how far we've both come since we were young,' she says. 'I used to say I couldn't imagine spending a week away from the nearest supermarket, and you always refused to have fun on principle. Even if our parents took us somewhere exciting, like a theme park, you wandered around all day looking as though you'd prefer to be anywhere else. Was that really the case, or were you trying to wind everyone up?'

'A little of both. Family trips were never my favourite way to spend time. You were there, for one thing. And forced jollity was never my thing. I was happier wandering around by myself and thinking deep thoughts.'

'There will be no forced jollity at our Final Fling,' she promises. 'It will be genuine jollity. No one will be able to avoid enjoying themselves – even you!'

'Don't count on it, but I promise to behave myself. How many people are coming?'

She counts on her fingers. 'Me and Jon – obviously. Then there's Abby and Chris, Jack and Lily, Ali and the boys, and you and Michael. It will be a good chance for the two of you to get to know each other better.'

'And for Michael to get to know Lily and Abby,' I say, determined to misunderstand her. 'They're in the wedding party too.'

'That's different. You're the chief bridesmaid, and he's the best man. It's important for you to have an excellent working relationship so that my big day proceeds with the utmost harmony and efficiency.'

'Did Chloe tell you that?' I ask.

'No, I came up with it all by myself.'

'No one needs to work with anyone else for the purposes of efficiency. Chloe can manage that all by herself. It's what you're paying her for. Quite a lot, I imagine. These bossy types always negotiate top dollar.'

'I don't know how much we're paying her,' she says. 'It's an all-inclusive package. The hotel sorts out the individual costs.'

'I'd still make her work for her money,' I advise. 'She appears to have overstepped quite a few boundaries so far. If you don't rein her in, I imagine she'll overstep quite a few more before your wedding day rolls around.'

Isabella sighs. 'We've already discussed that. I told you I wasn't well-equipped to be making all these decisions. Chloe was quite taken aback when she and I first started working together and she discovered I didn't have a long list of wishes and demands. Apparently, most brides have been dreaming of this day for a long time, and they begin the process with very definite ideas about the theme and ambience of their wedding. I had a long way to go to catch up.'

'That's nonsense, and you know it. I hope you told her to get lost?'

'Why would I?' she asks. 'I was grateful to her.'

There's no point in getting into all this again. I've told Isabella several times what I think of her wedding co-ordinator, and it's too late now for anyone to tell Chloe what they think of her domineering ways. For all I know, she's right to say that everyone arrives at their first appointment clutching vision boards and swatches, and goodness knows what else. The main thing is that Isabella should be happy with everything, and she's made it clear she is.

If I get married, I'm more than ever determined to do it my way. I hate the thought of someone like Chloe dictating what I may and may not do and telling me she knows best what I want. Having studied wedding etiquette rather more closely than I might have wished over the past few months, I can safely say most of it seems ridiculous.

From what I've observed, the entire industry is nothing but a mass of expectations – most of them dated and unreasonable, and all of them eye-wateringly expensive.

There's nothing wrong with following tradition if that's what the happy couple wants. But there's everything wrong with being pushed into making a string of decisions because what that's the co-ordinator deems most Instagram-worthy.

'Michael has offered to give you a lift over to Fernwood Campsite on Friday evening,' says Isabella, breaking into my thoughts about the dubious ethics of the wedding industry.

'That's thoughtful of him, but I may arrive late on Friday evening. There's something I need to do first.'

'Georgia!' she protests.

'I'll be there as soon as I can. I'm sorry, but it's something I can't get out of.'

'But you've known about this weekend for ages,' she says. 'How often are you invited to your sister's hen weekend?'

'I know you're expecting me to say only once. But if you carry on like this much longer, I'll warn Jon this match no longer has my blessing and strongly encourage him to rethink his personal choices before it's too late.'

'Couldn't you rearrange your thing for another time?' she asks. 'It won't be half so much fun without you.'

'No, I can't. I'll be two hours late at the most. I'm sure you can manage without me for such a short time. I promise to be the life and soul of the party once I arrive – or at least not complain too much.'

'You're being horribly secretive these days,' she grumbles. 'Whenever anyone invites you to do anything, you're always booked up. I'm starting to suspect it's an elaborate ruse to avoid anything related to the wedding.'

'It isn't,' I say shortly. 'I've done everything you've asked of me, and I'm ready to do whatever else you need. In return, it would be nice if you could remember that other people have lives to lead, and your wedding isn't the centre of everyone's universe.'

She sighs. 'I'm sorry. I know I'm being a bit of a diva.'

'You have a long way to go before you reach diva status,' I reassure her. 'But you should retrace any steps you've taken along that path. It's the duty of the chief bridesmaid to offer such advice. Just as it's one of the bride's duties to chill out and tell her chief bridesmaid she's doing a wonderful job.'

Michael calls me later that evening.

'How are you doing?' he greets me. 'I've been trying to get hold of you for hours.'

'I'm sorry,' I say. 'I've been out tonight, and my phone was switched off.'

'My father is always telling me mobile phones are the curse of the modern world, and I should throw mine overboard the next time I'm out at sea.'

'Are you often out at sea?' I ask.

'Almost never. I think it was a figure of speech.'

'I couldn't live without my phone,' I say. 'Especially not at the moment. People are always contacting me with inspired suggestions and brilliant ideas. And by people, I mean Isabella. She expects me to be available around the clock in case some new and wonderful scheme occurs to her.'

'And yet whenever I call you, your phone is switched off,' he says.

'That's a slight exaggeration. I keep it on most of the time, but not when I'm doing something important.'

There's a short pause.

'Got it,' he says. 'Anyway, I have you now, so I should make the most of it before anything more pressing occurs. I wanted to talk to you about next Friday.'

'The thing at Fernwood?' I ask. 'It's the only topic of conversation around these parts. I can't even escape from it while I'm at work. That's one of the many downsides of working with a family member.'

'I'm sure it has its upsides too.'

'You'll have to remind me what they are sometime. Anyway, you didn't call to discuss the trials and tribulations of a career in cake management. How can I help you?'

'I was wondering whether you'd like to go together on Friday?' he asks. 'It makes no sense for us to take more cars than we need. Apparently, it all kicks off around seven o'clock. That feels rather late for a Campbell woman to wait to eat, so I thought we could stop somewhere for dinner on the way. There are lots of nice pubs in the New Forest.'

'That's kind of you, but I told Isabella today I'd be going under my own steam. I can't make it until late that evening. I offered to come first thing on Saturday morning, but she wouldn't hear of it. She seems to think I might make some excuse not to turn up at all.'

'That's a shame,' he says. 'Are you sure you can't postpone whatever it is until another time?'

'Isabella asked me the same thing, and I told her other people have lives as well as her. To her credit, she took it pretty well. I don't believe she's a natural born diva. She's just been sucked into this whole wedding thing. I blame Chloe for that.'

'I'm glad it's not me getting married,' agrees Michael. 'When Jon told me he and Isabella were engaged, I envisioned them exchanging their vows on a canal boat or in the middle of a field at harvest time. I never expected them to go down such a traditional route.'

'I agree, but there's no reason they shouldn't do it properly – or what most people consider the proper way. And they aren't doing everything by the book. They're having a joint hen and stag weekend, for one thing.'

'For which I'm hugely grateful,' he says. 'It's saved me having to organise anything. Work's pretty busy at the moment, and I don't have a lot of free time.'

'Me neither.'

'Don't you work part-time at the bakery?' he asks.

'Why is no one able to accept I have other things going on in my life that are just as important as other people's arrangements? It feels as though everyone else only has to mention they have a lot on at work, and everyone's happy to make allowances for them. But not if you only work four days a week at a crummy bakery.'

'Whew!' he says. 'I'm very sorry. I take it you mean crumby with a b?'

I give a reluctant laugh. 'I didn't mean to fly out at you like that. I'm extremely tired. I should get some sleep. I have an early start tomorrow.'

'I understand,' he says. 'Just for the record, I don't see what you do as a crummy job. I doubt anyone except you does.'

'You may be right. Anyway, I should let you go before I say something I wouldn't want Isabella to hear.'

'My lips are sealed,' he says. 'She won't hear it from me. I'll see you on Friday at whatever time you can get away. Enjoy your date.'

'It's not –' I begin, but he's already rung off.

I set my alarm and move my phone to the far side of the room so I won't be able to reach it without getting out of bed. My days of joyfully sleeping through all my alarms are long gone. Time is at a premium these days, and it will only get worse as the summer draws near.

Chapter Thirty-Two

I pull up outside the Fernwood reception building at ten o'clock on Friday night. I climb out of the car to check whether anyone is still on duty, and Isabella looms up out of the darkness.

'You made it!' she says.

'I told you I would.'

'But all kinds of things might have happened to prevent you. Hop back into the car, and I'll give you directions to our cabin.'

She directs me past a row of lighted buildings and down a stony track, which narrows even further as we get towards the far end.

'They've put us down here, out of sight of all the other visitors,' she says. 'Jon made the mistake of telling them it was a hen and stag weekend. I arrived this afternoon to find a note on the dining table informing us in polite yet firm tones that we were expected to behave ourselves in a becoming manner, refrain from anti-social behaviour, and ensure we kept noise to a minimum after 10 p.m. All damages will apparently be billed to the credit card they have on file. I don't know what they expect us to get up to, but they appear to be bracing themselves for a week-long riot.'

'Instead of hosting a group of thirty-somethings who are attempting to re-live their twenties?' I ask. 'And are far more likely to end up in bed by 9 p.m, clutching a mug of hot cocoa and a packet of indigestion tablets.'

'The cocoa bit sounds alright,' she says. 'But I'm thankful to say I've never taken an indigestion tablet in my life. Have you?'

'Not knowingly. My digestive tract has never yet let me down, and I hope it never will.'

'Words to live by! Here we are. You can park outside the second cabin. We've booked one for the women, and one for the men. It may be a bit of a squash, but we're only sleeping in them, so it seemed a waste to pay for extra cabins. And it will be much cosier!'

'The word "cosy" is doing a lot of heavy lifting here,' I say. 'But I came here prepared to suffer in a good cause, and that's what I'll do.'

'You'll love it,' she says. 'You know you will.'

She picks up my backpack. 'My goodness – this bag is heavy! You're only here for the weekend. What did you pack in here – a portable generator in case we have a sudden emergency? One look at the map would have informed you that we're less than half a mile away from the main road, and the entire site has power and light. Besides, I suspect the staff will patrol this area more assiduously than usual during the weekend, just to keep an eye on us. I told the woman on reception when we arrived that we had two children with us, but I'm not sure she believed me.'

'Where are the boys sleeping?' I ask.

'In with the stags. They're eleven now and rejected with horror the idea of sleeping in a separate cabin with their mum.'

'I hope they'll be ok,' I say. 'Someone ought to check on them every half hour right through the night.'

'They'll be fine. Jon and Michael will take excellent care of them.'

'I meant the men,' I say. 'Two nights of Toby and Ollie would be enough to make even the strongest man quail.'

'Hilarious,' she says. 'I'm happy to say that Toby had his tonsils and adenoids removed last year, so his snoring won't keep the whole campsite awake. The first time I went camping with them, he could be heard from miles away. Not by me, because I slept through it all. But I doubt Jon slept a wink the entire weekend. He was very patient about it, though.'

She points to the nearest cabin. 'We're in there!'

I take my backpack from her and sling it over my shoulder with some difficulty. 'After you!'

The cabin is warm and brightly lit, but completely silent.

'Where is everyone?' I ask. 'Don't tell me this is all an elaborate prank and you've booked us in for a weekend of sisterly bonding? If so, I'm leaving right now.'

'Your mistake is assuming that would be any more acceptable to me than it is to you,' says Isabella. 'The only reason I invited you along this weekend is because there would be plenty of other people here to dilute your extreme awfulness. We've put you in this room at the far end. You're sharing with Abby. If you'd arrived at the proper time, you'd have had your choice of beds. But the early bird catches the worm, which in this case means the lower bunk bed. You're sleeping up there.'

I drop my bag by the window. 'I don't mind. I prefer the top bunk.'

'You may think that now, but you'll change your mind after a strenuous day in the wild. We'll stagger in, completely exhausted. Abby will collapse onto her bed to nurse her aching limbs, whereas you'll have to face climbing the steps of doom. Either that or sleep on the floor.'

'Or outside with the forest creatures,' I say. 'I can always come back inside in an emergency. There are four steps up to our cabin door. I counted.'

'Always a good idea in a new place. You never know when such information will come in useful. You could be chased back to the cabin by a wild beast. Knowing the exact layout could mean the difference between life and death.'

'I was thinking more of returning after an evening of drinking games,' I say. 'But I don't suppose that will be happening with the boys here.'

'It wouldn't have happened anyway,' she says. 'It isn't that kind of weekend.'

'That's a relief. The older I get, the less wild parties appeal to me. Where is everyone right now?'

'At the campfire, roasting marshmallows.'

'And you've delayed me by talking about bunk beds and wild animals? Sometimes, I think you do these things on purpose.'

'Relax!' she says. 'We've saved a bag especially for you. I knew you wouldn't stay here if we didn't.'

'I'm glad to hear you've learned a few things about me over the years. Where is this campfire?'

She points. 'Just down there, near the river.'

I nod. 'The campsite designer clearly put some thought into this. They foresaw the day a bunch of hooligans would book in for the weekend, and they located the cabins accordingly. Very well – lead on! And you'd better be telling the truth about those marshmallows.'

Isabella hands me a head torch. 'I've come prepared. Keep this on you at all times. I can't answer for the consequences if you don't.'

We set off down the hill, passing the boys coming the other way with Ali and Jon.

'Hi, Toby! Hi, Ollie!' I say. 'It's too dark to tell which of you is which, but I recognise your general shape and size.'

'Switch on your head torch!' Isabella tells me.

'I don't want to dazzle everyone. So, are you both having a good time?'

'We were,' says Ollie resentfully. 'But then we were sent to bed.'

'And it's still very early,' adds Toby.

'I'm sorry to hear that,' I say. 'Adults can be so unreasonable. Especially uncles. I won't say all that I could about yours, because I'll soon be related to him. But you have my deepest sympathy. If your mum had any sort of sense, she would have chosen herself very different brother – one who was patient and understanding. The very opposite of your uncle.'

The boys are laughing now.

'That's better,' says Isabella. 'Sleep well. Remember that you'll get your chance of revenge on all the unreasonable adults in your life tomorrow – starting from the moment you wake up. Don't lie in bed, drowsily enjoying the chirp of the crickets outside your window and the merry song of the lark. Leap from your beds and run around the cabin sharing the joys of a spring morning with all your fellow guests.'

'Remind me again while you're marrying my sister?' I ask Jon.

'Because I'm reasonably sure I can't live without her.'

I roll my eyes. 'That may all change by the time this weekend is over.'

We wave goodnight and carry on down the path towards the river.

'I hope Toby and Ollie are still speaking to me tomorrow,' says Isabella. 'I would have let them stay up for as long as they liked. But, as Jon never fails to point out to me, I often fail to consider long-term problems in favour of short-term solutions.'

'Meaning what?' I ask, and she shrugs.

'Who knows? Maybe it means the boys will be crabby in the morning if they stay up all night. But I always remind Jon that tomorrow may never come. So, why not live in the moment and deal with the consequences if and when they arrive? But I can never get Jon and Ali to agree, no matter how eloquently I argue. Perhaps it's a good thing he and I don't plan on having children.'

'You're an excellent aunt and godmother,' I console her. 'Stick with your strengths, and let everyone else do the difficult tasks. It works for you at the bakery!'

'You may be right,' she says. 'And I can give Toby and Ollie extra s'mores tomorrow to make up for tonight's disappointment.'

'Why would they be disappointed?' I ask. 'They're about to snuggle down in their nice, warm beds. I'd pay quite a bit of money to change places with them.'

Isabella turns her head to look at me. 'Is there something going on I don't know about, Georgie?'

'Like what?'

'I have no idea, but you seem permanently tired these days. Every time I ask whether you'd like to meet up, you're always too exhausted or you say you have other plans. Either you're disinclined to spend any more time with me than you have to – which seems vanishingly unlikely – or there's something you aren't telling me.'

'It's the first one,' I say. 'I didn't like to mention it to you before. But now I can admit I'm doing everything possible to avoid having to spend a single second more with you than is strictly necessary.'

Instead of looking offended, she laughs. 'Good one. What's really happening?'

'Does anything need to be happening? I'm tired. That's all.'

'Are you sick?' she asks. 'Seriously, Georgia – have you been diagnosed with something awful, and you don't plan to tell me until after the wedding? I'd far rather know now. If it's serious, we can cancel the wedding and help fix it.'

Isabella and I are getting along far better these days, but we still spend half our time winding each other up and doing our best to score points off each other. That she would offer postpone her wedding for me feels strangely touching.

I smile at her. 'It's nothing like that.'

'I wouldn't be upset,' she says. 'Well, obviously I would. But your well-being is the biggest priority. Jon would say the same if he knew about it.'

'There's nothing to know about. But if it makes you feel better, I promise to call you every single time I sneeze or feel a slight headache coming on. I promise that I'm only a little tired. I haven't been sleeping well for the past few months, and you know how much I love my rest.'

'Some of us need more beauty sleep than others, she says. 'I'm thankful not to be one of those people. My stunning good looks are entirely a result of my strict diet and exercise routine.'

'I've often thought you should write a book,' I agree. 'Have I put your mind at rest, or would you like me to ask my GP for a medical certificate?'

'I trust you without that. But if you aren't ill, why aren't you sleeping? Is it Michael?'

'Are you asking whether he's been calling me at all hours to discuss our joint wedding responsibilities? It's possible, but I always put my phone on silent when I go to bed, so he'd be out of luck.'

'I don't mean that,' she says. 'I'm asking whether you and he —?'

She pauses in what she doubtless considers to be a tactful way and gives me an enquiring look.

'Are good friends?' I ask, determined not to get into this sort of conversation with Isabella, of all people. For a so-called accountant, she's distressingly prone to putting two and two together and coming up with fifty-eight.

'For now, or for ever?' she asks.

'Forever, as far as I'm concerned. And how do you know Michael isn't already seeing someone?'

'He isn't. He would have told Jon.'

'And how do you know I'm not seeing someone?' I ask.

Her eyes widen. 'Are you? Is that why you're so busy these days? When can I meet him?'

'I'll have to check my calendar. How about four o'clock on the thirty-second of June? I think we're both free that day.'

'Very amusing,' she says. 'But I want to know whether you're secretly dating someone?'

'This is neither the time nor the place. I can see the glow of the bonfire. I'd like to get there before they eat the last of the marshmallows.'

'Michael's saving a bag just for you,' she says. 'Marshmallows are Jon's and my love language. Maybe they're Michael's too.'

'What a shame that I'm secretly seeing someone famous,' I say. 'I'd tell you about it in a heartbeat, but his publicist insists on us keeping it under wraps under he's out of rehab.'

'You're impossible,' she says. 'But I'll have the truth out of you one way or another. Just you see if I don't.'

Chapter Thirty-Three

Isabella claps her hands the following morning and calls for silence.

'I hope you all slept well! Only the most rested and alert combatants will make it through today alive.'

'Don't you mean contestants?' asks Jon.

'I said what I said. Now, I need everyone to listen carefully.'

We're standing on a patch of grass outside the cabins. Most of us are rubbing our eyes and looking as though we'd prefer to climb back into bed for several more hours' sleep rather than engage in whatever Isabella has in store for us.

As usual, she's bright-eyed and eager. Most people's energy levels subside as they approach the years of maturity. But Isabella isn't most people. She never has been, and she never will be. I probably wouldn't change her if I could. The jury's still out on that one, but I'm leaning towards letting her stay as she is.

She certainly has her moments – witness our conversation last night. I have no doubt she meant exactly what she said when she told me she would cancel her wedding without a second's hesitation, even if it meant braving the wrath of the awful Chloe. The least I can do is to demonstrate similar – if not entirely genuine – levels of enthusiasm.

I draw the line at letting out regular whoops of encouragement. This is the UK, not America, and almost no one my age has any cheerleading experience. But I can undertake whatever tasks I'm allocated with a reasonable grace and show Isabella how much I'm enjoying myself. One good turn deserves another.

'For this morning's task, we'll be splitting into pairs,' Isabella announces. 'We're using a secret ballot so the organisers can't be accused of rigging the results. I've written everyone's name on a slip of paper and put them in this baseball cap. Jon will draw them out in pairs. I don't expect any grumbling or attempts to swap with other people. The sorting hat will decide your fate.'

'Isn't that hat trademarked?' objects Lily.

Isabella shrugs. 'No one will ever find out. But we can come up with something else if you're worried. Do you have any suggestions?'

'The fedora of fate?' I suggest.

'I meant sensible suggestions,' she says. 'It should be obvious to anyone with the most minimal intelligence that this is a baseball cap, not a fedora.'

'The cap of destiny?' suggests Michael.

'The lucky lid?' adds Abby.

'Not bad,' says Isabella. 'But I was looking for something a little more portentous – like the visor of reckoning.'

'Let's go with that one,' says Jon. 'Otherwise, we'll be here all day, and we won't even start the task, let alone finish it.'

'If we must,' says Isabella. 'But it's important to pay attention to detail – especially today. Anyone who takes their eye off the ball is risking the most severe consequences. Don't say you haven't been warned.'

'Why do we need to divide into pairs?' asks Chris. 'Surely, most ball games are played in teams?'

'Except for golf,' I say.

'Or squash,' adds Lily.

'And bowling,' adds Michael. 'Or tennis.'

'Are we playing tennis?' asks Ollie with interest. 'Bags me and Toby play on the same side!'

Isabella looks as though she's about to suggest today's activity will be for the entire company to take a twenty-four-hour vow of silence – except for herself, of course.

'Give the names a good shuffle,' Jon tells her. 'Then we can begin the sacred pairing ceremony.'

'Like *The Bachelor*,' says Abby. 'You should be handing out roses, not bits of paper.'

Isabella shakes the cap vigorously, and the next few moments are taken up with everyone running around the damp grass, picking up slips of paper.

'With any luck, mine has been lost without anyone noticing,' I whisper to Michael. 'Everyone else will be paired up, and I can sneak off for a full English breakfast at the cafe.'

'And the first name out of the hat is … Michael!' says Jon. 'So, which lucky contestant will be working with you today?'

He dips his hand into the cap again. 'Georgia!'

There's a quick burst of applause.

'Is that for me or for Michael?' I ask. 'It should really be for him, to congratulate him on his luck in gaining such an excellent partner in crime.'

'It's for both of you,' says Isabella. 'You're lucky to have such a complementary balance of skills.'

She winks at me when no one's looking. I glare back at her. I know she has the memory of a goldfish, but she can't already have forgotten about my mystery celebrity boyfriend. I make a note to talk to her later about respecting people's choices – even if the boyfriend is purely imaginary. It's a pity he is. It could have been quite fun to find out what goes on at the awards after-parties – and possibly swipe an unattended Oscar while I was about it.

Jon's voice snaps me back to reality. 'So, that's everyone paired up. And now you'll want to hear what we have planned for you today.'

'You're making a raft!' chimes in Isabella, unable to contain her excitement. 'There's an inlet on this side of the lake that's only about fifteen metres across, and not too deep. Best of all, there's a slight current when the wind is in the right direction. Your challenge is to create a small raft using only materials you can source from around the campsite. The raft needs to carry three two-litre bottles of water without sinking. The winner will be the team who navigates their craft from one side of the inlet to the other, arriving with the same cargo as when it set off.'

'What if several teams achieve that goal?' asks Jack.

'We haven't thought about that,' says Jon. 'To be honest, we'll be surprised if any of you manage it. But that's no problem. If more than one team gets across, the successful craft must sail back again. We'll repeat the process until all but one of the boats has sunk.'

I glance at Ali to see what she thinks of this. I know her boys are strong swimmers, but she may not be too thrilled if they attempt to dive in and rescue their raft the moment it starts to sink.

Isabella notices my hesitation. 'Ali is way ahead of you. Jon and I told her weeks ago what we had planned, and she's borrowed a couple of lifejackets.'

'How about the rest of us?' asks Jack. 'I've been paired with Abby, and I'm not confident she has the extensive resuscitation training I feel I deserve if I accidentally fall in.'

'The water's only waist deep,' says Jon. 'You stand in more danger of your boat becoming stranded than of you drowning.'

'And I do know how to resuscitate someone,' says Abby. 'Isabella's very strict about us keeping our first-aid certificates up to date.'

'Why do Toby and I have to wear lifejackets?' demands Ollie. 'We both have our five-hundred-metre swimming badges.'

'Because you're more important and valuable than we are,' I tell him. 'There are so many people in this wedding party that no one will notice if some of us are still in the hospital during the ceremony. But you're playing a central part in this upcoming ceremony and will be sorely missed if you aren't there to do … what exactly is it you're doing?'

'Making sure Daisy doesn't drop her basket of rose petals,' says Ollie. 'But only if none of our school friends are there to laugh at us.'

I give him an encouraging smile. 'Your friends will have better things to do than watching a middle-aged couple exchange vows to look after each other in their old age and never to steal each other's walking sticks.'

'That's true,' says Isabella. 'And Chloe insists on us keeping the numbers down, so we couldn't have invited your school friends even if we'd wanted to.'

'Why is it any of her business?' asks Jack. 'Aren't you the ones paying for this wedding?'

'Technically,' she says. 'But Chloe doesn't like large weddings. She says it's far better to keep the event exclusive.'

'To be fair,' says Jon, 'neither of us were inclined to argue with her when we realised how much they were charging us per head.'

Isabella nods. 'We expect our guests to eat as much as possible during the reception to make sure we get full value for money. Is that clearly understood, boys?'

They both give her a mock salute.

'Let's get down to business,' says Jon. 'It's ten o'clock now. We suggest you all work until noon, then we'll meet at the cafe for lunch. After that, you can work until three-thirty, when the race will start. That will last for anywhere between seven seconds and an hour, depending on the quality of your various craft. We'll return to our cabins to dry off before enjoying an early dinner at the local pub. We can see where the evening takes us after that.'

'What are the rules?' asks Chris. 'Can we use anything we find around the campsite?'

'That's right,' says Isabella. 'But I'd like to make clear that doesn't include anything you find in the shop. No one may spend any money on this race. We want to discover whether we still retain the skills of our forefathers.'

'Our great-grandfather worked in a coal mine,' I remind her. 'I doubt he did much raft building.'

'But he was self-sufficient in other ways. I'm sure he's passed down some of his inventive genes to his great-granddaughters.'

'Can we scavenge?' asks Jack.

'It depends on what you mean by scavenging,' says Jon. 'If you mean picking things off the forest floor, then yes. If you mean lurking behind the caravans, waiting for people to pack their cars, then sneaking their canoes off their roof racks, then no. Use your common sense, and dig deep. Extra points will be awarded for initiative.'

Michael takes my arm. 'I think we've heard enough. Let's get going. We only have a few hours in which to create the greatest ship that has ever sailed the Fernwood inlet.'

Chapter Thirty-Four

We set off for the lake a little ahead of the others. Behind me, I can hear Ollie arguing with Jon about the meaning of scavenging, while Toby is busy telling Isabella that it isn't cheating to use an air mattress.

'There were loads of them in the pool when Mum took us swimming this morning,' he says. 'They wouldn't miss one. There were some armbands too. I saw them in a bucket outside the changing rooms.'

I can't hear what Isabella answers. Judging by her tone, she's doing her best to disagree with him without pouring too much cold water on his brilliant idea.

'What do you think?' I ask Michael. 'Does removing something from the swimming pool count as scavenging or cheating?'

'It depends on how likely you are to be caught.'

'Are you telling me your morality is based on consequentialism?'

'On what?' he asks.

'The belief that morality should be predicated on outcomes. What matters most is whether the action leads to the greatest good. If you and I decide the greatest good would be served by us winning, then sneaking an air bed or pool noodle to help us achieve that outcome would be a morally justifiable action.'

'Isn't that moral relativism?' he asks.

'Not exactly. Moral relativism holds that a course of action depends on the norms of your culture or group. What would be acceptable in one particular situation and culture may not be in another.'

He frowns. 'So, which situation is this? One where it's fine to raid the swimming pool or one where it isn't?'

'That's not for me to say. Everyone has to decide for themselves. You may prefer to take a different approach entirely. You and I could choose to be moral particularists – holding the view that moral judgement depends on the specific details of each situation. We could tell the judges it's impossible for them or anyone else to generalise about that kind of action because it's based on the unique details of the competition and its context. No one can say the decisions we've made are right or wrong because context is everything.'

'That last one sounds good to me,' says Michael. 'How do you know so much about moral philosophy? Did you learn about it in school? I'm impressed you've retained so much. I've forgotten most of what I learned back then.'

'Not at school,' I say. 'But years of living with Isabella have taught me it's essential to understand the structure of societies and nuclear families and how they should be ordered. Otherwise, you may find yourself moving from deontology towards postmodernism and existentialism. From there, it's only a short step to entropy and nihilism.'

He lets out a low whistle. 'Who *are* you?'

'Someone who just wanted a peaceful weekend and is realising that won't happen.'

'Are you still complaining about that?' he asks. 'There must be some philosophy that teaches you to let go and allow the forces to direct you where they will.'

'You can take your choice from Taoism, Stoicism, and Fatalism. Or we could forget all about it and concentrate on building this boat.'

'That may be best for now,' he says. 'There will be plenty of opportunity for us to discuss the deeper meaning of life this evening over dinner.'

'You can discuss what you like. I'll be too busy eating and trying not to fall asleep in my dessert.'

'Isabella mentioned you were feeling tired at the moment,' he says. 'It sounds as though you enjoy quite a busy social life.'

'It picked up quite a bit in January, and I don't see it calming down for a while.'

He gives me a slightly quizzical look. 'You're always busy when I call.'

'Or to put it another way, you always call when I'm busy.'

'Isn't that the same thing?' he asks.

'A relativist would say it depends on your perspective. Both statements can be true, but they reflect different points of view.'

He bursts out laughing. 'I feel as though I'm talking to a debate team. Are you always this thorough?'

'Almost never. The people who know me best would say I skate through life, engaging with it as little as possible.'

'Hard to believe,' he says. 'What else would they say about you? For instance, are you competitive?'

I consider this. 'That's situational. I am if I care about something, but not so much if I don't.'

'And into which category does today's competition fall?'

'That's difficult to say. Boat building doesn't interest me, but beating my sister definitely does.'

'I'll do my best,' he promises. 'Here's the lake. Is that the stretch of water where we'll be sailing our rafts this afternoon?'

'It must be. There are no other inlets. The water looks so beautiful – all calm and blue. I suspect it will look rather different when we're doing our best to keep our raft afloat longer than everyone else's.'

'There's no reason for it to sink if we design it properly,' he says. 'Is there any internet connection around here? I'd like to search for raft-building suggestions.'

I frown. 'I don't know what Kant would have to say about that. He was big on duty and acting according to the laws of honesty and integrity. And Aristotle would encourage us to develop good moral character by doing the right thing and striving for personal excellence without taking short cuts.'

'Do you want to win this race or not?' he asks.

'Definitely.'

'Then I suggest we consign all moral philosophers and their works to the bottom of the lake and get on with building the best possible raft in order to achieve that. Surely, at least one of those old codgers would support that aim?'

'Possibly, we should adopt the principles of Nietzsche,' I say after a moment's thought. 'He was all about rejecting traditional morality if it holds you back. He would tell us to create our own rules, be our own masters, and win on our own terms, without apology.'

'Do whatever it takes, and don't feel guilty about it?' he asks.

'That sums it up for me.'

'I can't get a good connection,' he says, waving his phone above his head as though it's some kind of dreamcatcher he hopes will locate and trap the elusive internet rays he's sure are lurking around here somewhere.

'Me neither,' I say. 'Should we walk back up the hill? We're bound to get better reception near the main building.'

'Or we could hunt in this forest for anything that might give us some ideas.'

'Such as what?' I ask.

'The important thing is to find something capable of being inflated,' he says. 'Like the inner tube of a bicycle tyre.'

I sink down onto the nearest log. 'If you expect me to spend the next hour puffing into an oily inner tube, you're mistaken. I don't want to be rude to my partner in crime before we start, but it's important we lower our expectations from the outset.'

'Do you think Jon and Isabella have planned something sneaky?' he asks. 'They're the only ones who knew about this task ahead of time.'

'It's possible,' I say, 'but not likely. If there's one thing I can say about my sister, it's that she plays fair. She may bend the rules, but she wouldn't break them entirely. She has her own code, and she lives by it.'

'So, you owe your knowledge of moral philosophy to Isabella?'

'Definitely not. I owe all that to my wide range of reading and my extraordinarily retentive memory. But we're getting away from the subject of this raft. We need to get a move on. The others may almost have reached the testing stage by now.'

'I doubt it,' he says. 'How do you suggest we should begin?'

'We could find a stack of similar length branches and tie them together.'

'With what?' he asks.

'Twine?'

His lips twitch. 'Twine?'

'There has to be something growing here we could use. Do you see anything rope-like hanging from the tree branches?'

'No, but that's because we aren't in a tropical jungle.'

'Do you have a better idea?' I ask.

'I suppose it's too late to order something for same-day delivery?'

'We aren't allowed to spend any money,' I remind him.

'How about guy ropes then? There are plenty of tents around here.'

'Now may be the time for me to remind you of our earlier conversation,' I say. 'We've decided to work within a loose moral framework.'

'I remember. But my grandmother always used to tell me if you don't ask, you don't get.'

I follow him over to a tent pitched a little way down the lake.

'Good morning!' he calls to a man crouched over a makeshift barbeque, trying to scrape something out of a pan. 'I wonder whether you could do us a favour?'

The man looks up and grins. 'We only started out with three eggs, and I've burned them all. But they sell them at the camp shop. That's where I bought these.'

'We aren't egg rustlers,' says Michael. 'We were hoping you might lend us a spare guy rope or a piece of cord.'

The man lays down the pan and stands up. 'Having some trouble with your tent?'

'Not exactly,' I say. 'We're trying to build a raft.'

'It's for a competition,' says Michael. 'We have until half past three this afternoon to produce something that will stay afloat for about fifteen metres and carry a small load. We can't buy the materials, but no one said we couldn't ask for help.'

'My tent doesn't have a guy rope,' says the man. 'And I can't remove the cords unless I want it to collapse in the night. But I may have an old tow rope in the boot of my car.'

'That would be amazing,' I say. 'We'll let you have it back the moment the competition is over.'

'No need,' he says. 'You're welcome to it. How are you going to make this raft?'

'We have no idea. We'll probably try to lash some branches together and hope for the best.'

He frowns. 'That won't work. I remember trying that when I was a child. You'll have to come up with something better than that.'

He raises his voice. 'Lisa!'

A woman pokes her head around the tent door. 'What is it? Are the eggs ready?'

'I'm afraid I've burned them,' he says. 'These people want to build a raft.'

She clambers out of the tent. 'Are they trying to escape? I don't blame them. If you'd told me in advance what this place would be like, I'd have stayed safely at home.'

'We aren't trying to escape,' I tell her. 'We're taking part in a competition.'

Lisa pushes her long, blonde hair out of her eyes and looks at me more closely. 'What sort of competition? Something like I'm a Celebrity – Get Me Out of Here?'

I give a choke of laughter. 'I hope not! And please don't suggest that to my sister if you bump into her. Apparently, this is her idea of a fun hen do activity.'

She points to Michael. 'Then why is he here?'

'I'm her bodyguard,' says Michael. 'Georgia is undercover this weekend. Her father wouldn't allow her to attend without her close protection squad.'

He sees her look of incredulity and adds, 'His Majesty was most insistent that –'

He breaks off and claps a hand to his mouth. 'I've said too much!'

She's laughing now. 'What's really going on?'

'I told you,' I say. 'It's all my sister's idea. She thought it would be a great idea to invite us to the back of beyond to build rafts that don't work, just so she can watch us fall into the lake. To make it even more exciting, she and her fiancé decided to combine it with his stag party. They drew lots to decide who should work together, and Michael and I have ended up as partners.'

'It sounds a lot more fun than what we're doing,' says Lisa. 'Ben insisted on bringing me here to test out his new tent. It seems exactly the same as his old one to me, but he doesn't agree.'

'It's the Stormlock 500,' says Ben proudly. 'It has state-of-the-art ventilation and stays dry in even the most violent storm.'

'It's a tent,' she says. 'Which means it's cold, draughty, and uncomfortable. Where are you guys staying?'

'In the cabins at the top of that path,' I say. 'They're surprisingly comfortable. If I were you, I'd book yourself into one of those the next time you come here.'

'I wanted to do that this weekend,' she says. 'But Ben insisted I enjoy the whole camping experience. Your trip sounds far more fun. Tell me more about your raft.'

'So far, it's only a mythical raft,' I say.

'It's more of an ontological thing,' adds Michael. 'It currently exists as a concept rather than an actuality.'

'Maybe we should start with proper introductions,' she says. 'I'm Lisa, and you already know Ben.'

'Georgia,' I say. 'And this is Michael.'

'So, you're the bride's sister?' she says to me. 'How about you, Michael?'

'I'm the best man. And Georgia is the chief bridesmaid.'

She gives us an amused look. 'So, the old cliché is true?'

'What cliché?' he asks.

'Nothing!' I say. 'Lisa's confusing it with things like saving the top tier of the cake. So, about this raft. Thanks to you and Ben, we now have a rope. But that won't get us very far on its own. We were planning to tie some branches together, but Ben doesn't seem to think that's a good idea.'

'It isn't,' says Lisa. 'The load-bearing capacity of loosely lashed branches is practically zero. The moment you apply lateral force, the structure will flex and break, and your raft will be making the closer acquaintance of that group of ducks before you can say catastrophic failure!'

'That's very impressive,' I say. 'Have you done this sort of thing before?'

'Lisa's a structural engineer,' says Ben. 'You've come to the right person.'

'We mustn't take up too much of your time,' says Michael. 'This is your weekend away.'

'I've kept my promise and slept in the tent for one night,' says Lisa. 'I've told Ben I'll be booking into a guest house tonight if it starts raining. But we didn't have anything particular planned for today. Now we do!'

'You're going to help us?' I ask.

'I most certainly am. I refuse to see you lose a competition on my watch when a little planning and technical know-how would do the trick. Pull up a log, and Ben can make us all a cup of coffee while we decide how best to proceed.'

Chapter Thirty-Five

Ben makes us some surprisingly good coffee, considering he only has a barbeque at his disposal. He heats the bottled water and scoops the ground coffee into a makeshift funnel, lined with layers of kitchen roll, then pours the boiling water over it. The resultant brew is slightly gritty, but it tastes like coffee, which is the object of the exercise.

I raise my cup to the other three. 'To teamwork!'

'To rescuing me from a day of Ben complaining he's forgotten to pack his fishing rod,' says Lisa. 'If you two hadn't come along, I'd have had to listen to him telling me how important it is for everyone to get away from civilisation as often as possible and re-connect with Mother Earth.'

Michael looks amused. 'There's a restaurant and a supermarket on site, and we're less than a mile from the nearest pub. I'd hardly call this getting away from civilisation.'

'I would,' she says. 'I had to sleep on a groundsheet last night, and there were pine needles sticking into my back. Then Ben forgot to buy enough eggs and bread for breakfast. In what universe does that count as civilised?'

'I'm not the most enthusiastic camper either,' I say. 'But my sister is. That's why we're here. I told her when she first mentioned this weekend that I refused to come if it meant sleeping in a tent. So, she booked cabins to make sure I couldn't get out of it.'

'Our cabin is very comfortable,' says Michael. 'If you discount the fact we were woken by a loud crash in the middle of the night. Apparently, one of the twins dreamed he was at the swimming pool and tried to dive in. It would have worked fine if there hadn't been a suitcase standing where the diving board was supposed to be.'

'That would be Ollie,' I say. 'I remember Isabella telling me he used to sleepwalk. I thought she said he'd grown out of it, but maybe the excitement of the trip has had an adverse effect on him. I know it has on me.'

'Our cabin door was locked, and Jon had the key,' says Michael. 'Ollie wouldn't have got very far even if he'd dreamed he was trying to swim the English Channel.'

'I'll have to remember that one the next time Ben takes me camping,' says Lisa. 'Where were you when I woke up this morning, darling? I'm terribly sorry! I was so overcome by the excitement of spending the night in a space no bigger than a telephone box, while fighting off earwigs and earthworms, that I sleepwalked to the car, then sleep drove all the way home. I'll see you when you get back to the house. Enjoy your hike!'

'It's a perfectly adequate tent,' says Ben. 'The man in the camping shop told me it had a surprisingly spacious interior for the weight and price.'

'He must have been an estate agent in a previous life,' I say. 'Did he also mention it had great natural light and stunning open-plan views of the undergrowth?'

'Not that I remember,' he says with dignity. 'Have you finished your coffee? We should get back to the raft.'

'It was delicious, thank you. An impressive effort, considering you haven't brought a cafetiere with you.'

'We aren't allowed to pack anything that might make our lives easier,' says Lisa. 'It isn't the point of camping. If you bring something useful, you might as well have stayed at home.'

'You just don't *get* camping,' says Ben. 'But you will.'

'Georgia's the actual coffee expert,' says Michael. 'She works in a bakery and makes all their hot drinks. Everyone says she's the best barista in town. Or rather, the village.'

'You can make the next one,' Lisa tells me. 'I'll have a half-cap latte – oat milk, extra hot, no foam, three-quarter shot.'

'Coming right up!' I say. 'Would you like cinnamon with that?'

'That's not a drink – it's a thesis,' says Ben. 'What's wrong with a nice cup of black coffee?'

'Nothing,' says Lisa. 'Unless it's served on a muddy riverbank after a broken night's sleep. In which case – everything!'

Michael looks at his watch. 'We only have an hour before we have to meet everyone for lunch. I suppose we could tell them we'd got lost on the way, and that's why we didn't arrive.'

'We could not,' I say. 'I have strong views about missing meals. An hour is plenty to make a start. The only question is – how?'

'No problem,' says Lisa. 'I love this type of thing. I spend a lot of my time doing load calculations and analysing stress points. It will be nice to put my expertise to good use doing something fun like this.'

'What do you do?' Michael asks Ben.

'I'm a computer programmer. I spend my days in a small room fixing code. That's why it feels so great to get out into the wild.'

'That makes sense,' says Michael.

'Please don't encourage him,' begs Lisa. 'Ben thinks he's Bear Grylls, whereas in fact he's the man you see on the news who's had to have the mountain rescue team called out.'

'How about you?' Ben asks Michael as they rinse out the mugs with the last of the bottled water.

'I'm a civil engineer. I spend most of my time inside too. That's why it's so nice to drive into the countryside for a weekend.'

'We need a plan!' announces Lisa, who's been busy scribbling notes on a piece of paper. 'What sort of raft are you planning to build? I need to know your requirements before I can come up with a blueprint. Let's start with the most important – load capacity. How much weight will this craft have to support? I must know that if I'm to calculate the minimum structural integrity without compromising stability. We need to assess buoyant force and water displacement, then factor in dynamic loads.'

She taps her pen against her teeth. 'We should also take shear stress and torsional forces into account, especially if the water's choppy. I recommend cross-bracing the slats to distribute the load efficiently.'

'Wow!' says Michael. 'I didn't realise raft building was so complicated.'

She doesn't appear to hear him. 'Ease of propulsion is a major factor. We have to consider hull geometry to minimise drag when you launch it. And it would be a good thing to build in some redundancy in the form of flotation devices to maintain positive buoyancy in case of any breaches. Any questions before we proceed to material sourcing and timeline estimation?'

I raise my hand. 'Just one. How are we supposed to do all this in three hours, using only what we can find in the local area?'

Ben slips his arm around her shoulders. 'Georgia's right. Your plan sounds excellent, but you may have to modify it to fit within the parameters available.'

'Think of us as particularly difficult clients,' says Michael. 'We've come to you with a tight budget, only the vaguest of expectations, and absolutely no understanding of basic engineering principles.'

'And don't forget to mention an unrealistic deadline,' I add.

'Fair enough,' says Lisa. 'I'll adjust the plan accordingly and simplify it.'

'We just need our raft to stay afloat for about five minutes,' says Michael. 'And it has to be able to carry three two-litre bottles of water.'

Lisa scribbles for a minute, then glances up. 'I've made you a best-case, a compromise, and a worst-case scenario.'

'Let's have the bad news first,' I say.

'Your payload falls into the lake the second you set sail.'

'I'd prefer one of the other options,' says Michael.

'All my clients would. The compromise scenario is that you get the raft at least halfway across the water before the bottles fall off.'

'We're the clients, and we aren't at all happy with that scenario,' I say. 'You need to up your game if you hope to retain our business.'

She sighs. 'Clients are by far the worst part of my job. It would be way more enjoyable without them. Ok – this is what I recommend.'

She shows us the piece of paper, and we study it.

'Where will we get those things?' I ask.

'Leave that to me and Ben,' she says. 'Meanwhile, I'd like you to gather plenty of small sticks. You two are going to make a truss grid.'

'I'd ask,' I say, 'but I doubt I'd understand the answer.'

'You'll be tying the sticks together in triangular formations. It's a simple concept of load dynamics.'

'Why didn't you explain it to me like that when we were discussing this earlier?' I ask Michael, who shrugs.

'It's all a matter of triangles. I thought that would have been clear to everyone. I shouldn't have to explain the most basic parts of the design to you.'

'I'd be surprised if you could explain them at all,' I say. 'But I'm happy to do as I'm told.'

'You'll have to keep the cargo's centre of gravity as low as possible,' says Lisa. 'Would you two like to work on some ideas for that?'

'Michael can do it!' I say.

'Not if you're hoping to win,' he says. 'Lisa has told us to collect sticks. Since neither of us knows what we're doing, and she clearly does, I think we should follow her instructions and do all the grunt work, while she focuses on the abstract concepts.'

'Try to find sticks of a similar size and weight,' says Lisa. 'About 20cm long, if possible. Ben and I will be back in a few minutes.'

'Where are you going?' I ask.

She raises an eyebrow. 'You don't want to know.'

'That works for me,' says Michael. 'Come on, Georgia! If there's one place we should be able to locate sticks, it's in a forest.'

Ben and Lisa climb into their car and set off up the stony track.

'Do you think they're coming back?' I ask Michael.

'They've left their tent here with all their belongings.'

'That isn't conclusive. I get the feeling Lisa would willingly abandon the lot if there were the faintest chance of Ben taking her home.'

'Not she!' he says. 'I've never seen anyone more enthusiastic about the idea of building a raft.'

I hesitate. 'Is this cheating? There's nothing in the rules to say we can't ask random fellow guests for help, but I'm not sure it's really in the spirit of the contest.'

'It very much is. Lisa and Ben are locally available resources, which Isabella was very keen on. And they aren't charging for their work. That falls well within the parameters of the competition rules.'

'Lisa didn't mention anything about not charging us,' I say. 'I hope she doesn't present us with a massive invoice at the end of the afternoon.'

He smiles. 'There's no risk of that. She's really getting into this thing. What a stroke of luck for us meeting someone who knows about structural engineering.'

'The rest of us aren't much help,' I say. 'We haven't prepared properly for this occasion. If only we'd had the foresight to select our educational qualifications according to what might be needed during a pre-wedding weekend.'

'I should have studied boatbuilding at university,' he agrees. 'And Ben won't be much help – unless he's expecting to program a sophisticated GPS system to make sure our raft doesn't get lost on its hazardous journey. Although I doubt we could forage the components for that in time for the competition. How about you, Georgia? What are your qualifications?'

Why did I start this conversation? It was bound to land me in difficulties.

'I don't have as many as I'd like,' I say. 'And none of them are relevant to today's task.'

'I can't believe you didn't pick up something during your education that we could put to good use.'

I shrug. 'Nothing comes to mind. Let's concentrate on what we're supposed to be doing. Lisa and Ben will be back soon, and I'd rather not tell them that you and I couldn't locate a set of matching sticks in the middle of a forest.'

'Jack has an unfair advantage,' says Michael. 'He has a degree in forestry. And Lily used to work as an office manager, so she must have plenty of organisational skills.'

'Can we please stop talking about qualifications and do some actual work?' I ask.

My tone must have been sharper than I intended because he glances at me in surprise.

Before I have time to apologise, he raises a finger to his lips. 'Do you hear that?'

'What?'

'Someone's coming this way. It may be one of the other teams.'

'So what if it is?' I ask. 'It isn't as though we've created some amazing prototype we'd prefer them not to see. We haven't done anything yet.'

'But we don't want them to notice us standing next to the tent and suspect we're getting outside help.'

There's another crashing noise, followed by the sound of Ollie's voice calling to someone. 'What will we use to tie it together?'

'Quick,' says Michael. 'In here!'

He makes a dart towards me and pushes me into the tent. I stagger and fall, and he lands almost on top of me.

'Ouch!' I whisper, and he gives a soft laugh.

'Shh! Enemy combatants approaching from the east.'

Ollie's voice grows louder. 'How about a frying pan? There's one in our cabin. Or a chopping board?'

'Good thinking,' shouts Isabella. 'You and Toby nip up there now and see what you can find. Be careful not to run into any of our competitors on your way. Pretend you're a ninja and melt into the shadows.'

'You're squashing me,' I whisper to Michael. 'No wonder Lisa doesn't enjoy camping. There's barely enough room in here to breathe.'

'Sorry,' he says, rolling off me and trying to sit up. 'That was a close call.'

We're still tangled awkwardly in the cramped space. His knee is brushing against mine, and one of his hands is resting on my hip.

I try to sit up too, but this space doesn't seem designed for two unrelated people, and my shoulder is pressed rather too closely against his.

I listen for the noise of Ollie returning, but there's only the faint sound of birds and the distant splash of something further along the lake.

'You have leaves in your hair,' Michael says softly, reaching over and pulling one out.

'A natural result of being forced to spend time in the great outdoors,' I say.

He smiles, and the space between us feels suddenly electric. His hand moves to my shoulder and rests there lightly.

'We're back!' calls Lisa's voice from somewhere outside. 'Where do you think they are, Ben?'

Michael gives me an awkward smile before opening the tent door. 'In here!'

Catching her look of surprise, he adds, 'We're hiding from the enemy agents skulking around the woods.'

'Quick thinking,' she says, raising an eyebrow at my flushed face. 'Ben and I have done better than I hoped. How about you? Have you collected those sticks yet?'

'We were about to begin when we heard the others coming,' I say. 'We'll look for them now.'

'That sounds good,' she says. 'As soon as you've finished that, I'll show you what we've found.'

Chapter Thirty-Six

We meet our fellow competitors for a quick lunch at the campsite cafe. It isn't a particularly friendly meal. Everyone is shooting suspicious looks at everyone else and nudging their partners to make sure they don't mention anything about their plans.

'Isn't this nice?' asks Jon as he hands his menu back to the server. 'A chance for us all to get together and really bond. Who'd like to go first and tell us what they've been up to this morning?'

'Not me!' says Toby. 'Isabella told me if I breathed a word about our raft, she'd blindfold me and force me to walk the plank.'

'Did she indeed?' I ask. 'So, are we to understand planks will be involved in your final design?'

'It was a figure of speech,' says Isabella, cramming a forkful of chips into her mouth and chewing briskly.

'But a telling one,' says Michael. 'Would anyone else like to give us a hint about their plans?'

There's complete silence around the table.

'What a shame,' I say. 'But don't feel bad. Not everyone is as resourceful and competent as me and Michael.'

'Or we're so confident of winning that we don't need to brag about it,' says Jon.

'I hope no kitchen implements are involved in any of your entries,' I say. 'Stealing something from the cabins might fall foul of the judges' rules.'

Isabella gives me a startled look. 'What makes you say that?'

I wink at Ollie. 'It just occurred to me it's the sort of thing our opponents might think is a good idea.'

'Where were you and Michael this morning?' asks Chris. 'We saw everyone else at some point, but there was no sign of you.'

'We were around and about,' says Michael. 'Watching and listening to everything that went on.'

'You're bluffing!' says Jack. 'I wouldn't be surprised to hear the pair of you spent the entire morning in the cafe and are planning to claim an injury at the last minute to avoid having to compete.'

'I'd prepare to be surprised if I were you!' I say. 'Are you ready, Michael? We should get going.'

'You have nothing!' says Isabella. 'This is exactly the sort of tactic you used when we were small and you wanted to persuade Mum you'd cleaned your room, when really you'd pushed everything under the bed.'

'Possibly,' I say with an enigmatic smile. 'And possibly not. You have no way of knowing.'

I walk out of the cafe as quickly as possible before she can reveal any more embarrassing secrets from my childhood.

We arrive at the appointed place a few minutes early that afternoon. Chris and Lily are already there.

'Where's your raft?' Lily asks me.

'Where's yours?'

'Behind that tree. We didn't want to risk one of the other teams realising how brilliant our raft was and taking the chance to sabotage it before we set sail.'

'Same here,' says Michael. 'I wouldn't put anything past half the people here. Isabella has a competitive streak, and I'm not sure what she'd stop at in her quest for a gold medal.'

'She has nothing on Georgia,' says Lily. 'I can't believe you haven't realised that by now.'

Michael smiles at me. 'I think you're mistaken. Georgia strikes me as the perfect competitor – invested enough in the project to make it a pleasure to work with her, yet mature and balanced enough to be a gracious loser if things should go that way.'

Lily rolls her eyes, and I give her a reproving look. 'You should listen to him. He clearly knows me far better than you do.'

'Here come Abby and Jack,' says Lily. 'What's that they're dragging behind them? Is it supposed to be a raft? If that's the standard of competition we're up against, you and I have no problem, Chris.'

'That's the love of my life you're talking about,' he says, and she laughs.

'Sorry. I got a little carried away there.'

'It's fine,' he says. 'I didn't get together with Abby because of her boat-building skills.'

By half past three, everyone has arrived. Isabella looks around at the assembled group.

'Now is the time for you to make your ridiculous excuses,' she says. 'I'm fully prepared to hear that several of you have come down with a bad case of raft-induced vertigo, or your horoscopes this morning advised against travelling over water.'

She scans the group. 'Anyone? No sudden fear of knots or reports of other boat-related injuries?'

When we all shake our heads, she carries on.

'Right – a short safety briefing. I'd like you all to listen carefully. Jon and I have taken out injury insurance for this weekend, but we'd prefer not to use it. If your raft sinks and you have to wade out to retrieve its cargo, you will get wet, and it will be your own fault for not designing a better raft. You should maintain your dignity and swim or flounder back to dry land and accept the fact you have been eliminated from the competition.'

'She sounds like my old PE teacher,' I mutter to Michael. 'She started all our lessons by warning us that if we got hurt, it would be all our own fault, and we shouldn't expect any sympathy from her.'

'Finally,' says Isabella. 'People always say that races are not about winning. They're about taking part and doing your very best. I'm here to tell you those people are talking nonsense. Second place is not "still very impressive." It tells the onlookers you aren't good enough and you've become nothing more than a footnote in someone else's victory speech.'

'The woman I plan to marry, ladies and gentlemen!' says Jon.

'I'm simply making things clear,' says Isabella.

'And you've done a wonderful job. But if you don't stop with your motivational speeches, the sun will have gone down and we'll be sailing around in the dark. Who's going first?'

Isabella consults her list. 'Lily and Chris. Prepare your craft, commend it to the gods of buoyancy, and let's see how far it gets.'

Lily and Chris drag their raft out from behind the tree. It's small, but at least it looks like a raft.

'We made this from a broken fence panel we found near one of the static caravans,' says Lily. 'We tied the loose bits of wood together with several pairs of socks. We may need to do some laundry later.'

They lower their raft into the water, and Chris gestures for Lily to load the cargo. She lowers the bottles onto the raft, which wobbles but doesn't sink.

'Why am I suddenly thinking of the film Titanic?' asks Jack.

'You mean the bit at the end?' I ask. 'When Rose wouldn't let the so-called love of her life onto the floating door in case she felt a teeny bit claustrophobic?'

'There's barely room on our boat for one bottle, let alone three,' says Lily as their raft tilts dramatically. 'I'm starting to feel more sympathy for Rose.'

'It's floating!' says Chris.

'Temporarily,' she says.

'Smile for the photo!' calls Isabella, pulling out her phone.

Chris takes the stick Jack hands him and pushes their raft away from the bank.

'I think it may work!' I say.

'You spoke too soon,' says Michael as the raft splits in two and upends itself.

Lily gives a shriek and makes a grab for the raft, but it's no good. Even as she lies down on the bank and tries to hold it up, it slips through her fingers and sinks out of sight.

'Good try!' says Isabella encouragingly.

'Oh, shut up!' says Lily.

Half an hour later, almost everyone is as wet as Chris and Lily. Isabella and the boys' raft gets halfway across the inlet before it gives up the struggle and dumps its bottles into the lake with an enormous splash.

Ali and Jon have made an impressive attempt at creating a triple canoe. If they'd had more time, they might have got it to work. They've hollowed out three large holes in a tree branch, but they haven't stabilised it with any side pieces, so it rolls over the second it leaves the shore.

Abby and Jack's attempt is even more impressive. They've found an old wheelbarrow from somewhere and constructed a raft using the barrow as the main body, supported on either side by bundles of wood tied together with what appears to be a pair of ripped up tights.

Their raft almost makes it to the finish line when it hits a patch of reeds and becomes tightly wedged. Jack tries to claim victory on the grounds their boat is strategically moored at a scenic point along the route, rather than stuck. But Isabella remains firm.

'You have to reach the far bank,' she says. 'Is that everyone? No, we still have Georgia and Michael. Would you like to admit defeat now or wait until your raft has sunk?'

'It won't sink,' says Michael. 'Help me carry it to the water's edge, Georgia.'

'It looks quite impressive,' says Jack.

'There's no need to sound so surprised,' I tell him.

'Who are those people?' asks Isabella, pointing towards a nearby clump of trees. 'They're showing a suspicious interest in the goings-on of a group of complete strangers.'

I look over in time to see Lisa duck behind a holly bush.

'I have no idea,' I say. 'Perhaps they're tourists.'

'American tourists, by the looks of them,' says Michael. 'I expect they're fascinated to observe our quaint English traditions up close.'

Isabella doesn't look convinced. 'Someone should keep an eye on them.'

'You'd be better off keeping an eye on us,' says Michael. 'I advise you all to watch and learn.'

Jack is studying our raft with admiration. 'Is this a catamaran?'

'Pretty much,' says Michael. 'We used a couple of bread delivery pallets salvaged from behind the cafe for the main body of our boat.'

'And what are these things underneath it?' asks Abby.

'Empty water containers,' I say. 'The kind people bring with them on camping trips.'

'They don't usually dump them in the forest when they leave,' says Jack.

I shrug. 'What can I say? Some people shouldn't be allowed to camp. You'd be surprised what Michael and I found just lying around the lake.'

'Including a flag!' says Jon.

'That's a tea towel,' I correct him. 'It's a pity it didn't have a skull and crossbones on it, but you can't have everything.'

'We made a lattice of sticks and inserted them between the two pallets to prevent them from drifting apart,' says Michael. 'Some of you omitted that step, with predictably disastrous results. You'll notice we used a triangular pattern for the lattice-work. It's by far the strongest structure.'

'Just get on with it!' says Isabella. 'And stop gloating. I'll freeze to the spot if you don't hurry up. The sun will be going down soon.'

'Fair enough,' says Michael. 'Before we start, I name this ship The Georgia!'

We push the raft away from the muddy bank. It barely even wobbles as it floats towards the far shore.

'It's a textbook example of proper load-distribution,' Michael informs everyone.

'I can't believe it's actually working!' I say as the raft passes the remains of Abby and Jon's wheelbarrow.

'It's a simple matter of engineering,' says Michael. 'I'm surprised by your lack of faith in your own creation.'

The late afternoon breeze fills Lisa and Ben's tea towel, which flutters triumphantly on its stick. A moment later, the raft slides into the reeds at the edge of the shore and comes to a stop against the far bank.

'Landed!' says Michael, holding out his hand to me.

We turn to face the others and raise our clasped hands in triumph.

'And that,' says Michael modestly, 'is how it's done.'

Chapter Thirty-Seven

'Where have you been?' Isabella greets me the next day when I reach the designated meeting point by the lake. 'Everyone's already here, and you know we can't start without you.'

'Sorry,' I say. 'I went back to the cabin after lunch and fell asleep. I only woke up a few minutes ago, and I ran down here as fast as I could.'

'Was it all the excitement from yesterday?' asks Jon.

'I'm not a child,' I say. 'I can handle the odd, unexpected victory without it keeping me awake all night.'

'She was reading in bed until late,' says Abby.

I pull a face at her. 'Tattle-tale!'

'What were you reading?' Isabella asks me.

'A recently published volume called Ten Ways to Deal with a Nosy Older Sister.'

'I haven't heard of that one,' says Jack. 'It can't have sold many copies.'

'On the contrary,' I say. 'It's a best seller. It appears to be a universal problem experienced by younger sisters world-wide.'

'You were supposed to be getting a good night's sleep in order to cope with today's jollities,' Isabella tells me.

'I'm here now. Would you like to discuss this further, or would you prefer to tell us without further delay what kind of waking nightmare you have in store for us this afternoon?'

'It's a treasure hunt!' she says with enthusiasm, and I only just stop myself from groaning.

'It's a wonderful idea!' she says. 'Jon and I spent a lot of time preparing this. I only hope no one else stumbles over one of our amazing clues and spoils the whole thing.'

'Like those American tourists?' asks Jack.

'They've left the campsite,' I say without thinking.

Isabella gives me a suspicious look. 'Who told you that?'

'I saw them driving away when I was walking down here.'

'How do you know they were actually leaving and not just going to buy food?' she asks.

I catch Michael's eye and see he's grinning at me.

'They stopped to ask me directions,' I say, trying to sound convincing. 'They're off to London today to see Buckingham Palace and Westminster Abbey. After that, they want to stand on Tower Bridge while it opens.'

'They won't be allowed to do that,' says Chris.

'I know, but there was no point in telling them that. They were determined to give it a go.'

'Perhaps they're interested in bridges,' says Michael. 'Plenty of people are keen to learn about load-bearing structures.'

'If I'd known you'd all be so fascinated by a couple of random American tourists,' I say, 'I'd have got their phone number for you.'

Isabella still looks suspicious, but she doesn't pursue the subject further.

'Toby and Ollie will be working together on this,' she says, 'which means there are effectively ten of us. Jon and I have made ten clues and hidden them around the campsite. The clues form a loop, so it doesn't matter where you start. You just need to collect them all, put them together, and work out the answer.'

'Everyone will start at a different point,' says Jon. 'Isabella and I will direct you to your first clue. Take a picture of the map segment on it, then follow the instructions to the next place. Rinse and repeat until you've found all ten clues. Put the pieces of the map together, and that will tell you where we're meeting after the treasure hunt. Keep a close eye out for your fellow competitors, and do your very best not to give them any hints.'

'Like tracking?' asks Ollie. 'Cool!'

'No one will track us,' says Toby. 'We're stealth experts.'

'Jon and I will be available throughout the competition if anyone needs help,' says Isabella. 'We'll give you all a whistle to attract our attention. You have your phones, but the connection is a little patchy down by the lake.'

'Can we work in pairs?' asks Michael.

'Not today,' says Jon. 'This is a test of your initiative, resilience, and advanced code-solving and survival capabilities. Essential skills for the members of any self-respecting wedding party.'

'None of this was mentioned when Isabella asked me to be her bridesmaid,' I say. 'I feel as though I was recruited under false pretences.'

'I was easing you in,' she says. 'You make such a fuss about everything that I was forced to adopt a more subtle strategy. You're number seven, by the way. We handed out the numbers while you were making your painfully slow progress down here.'

'Please wait here while Isabella and I escort the first set of victims to their starting point,' says Jon. 'We'll be back for the rest of you in a minute.'

They beckon to Ali and the boys to follow them and disappear in different directions – Isabella and Ali along the path leading to the swimming pool, and Jon and the boys towards the forest.

'This should be fun,' says Michael.

'You have a strange idea of fun,' I say.

'You don't like this sort of thing?'

'Sometimes, I do. But I'd prefer to be back in the cabin with my feet up and a bag of snacks at my side.'

'Reading a book?' he asks. 'Zen and the art of Annoying Sister Maintenance?'

'I read that last month. It was good, but not as helpful as Sisters for Dummies, or even The Seven Habits of Highly Irritating Sisters.'

He laughs. 'You two seem to get along just fine. My younger brother and I haven't spoken to each other for the past few months – ever since he told me the ending of Game of Thrones before I'd got around to watching it.'

'A serious offence,' I agree. 'Will you ever speak to each other again?'

He shrugs. 'Who knows? Our mother is trying to act as mediator. "You are brothers," she told us. "You may hate each other today, but the world is cruel enough without turning your back on blood. Make peace before winter takes one of you, and you regret every wasted chance to speak." My mother's quite a forceful character. She had to be if she wanted to hold the throne of Reynold against our enemies until we came of age.'

'She sounds almost as much to be pitied as our mum,' I say.

'She would scorn your pity. My mother comes from a noble and ancient lineage, and her heart is proud.'

'Georgia – you're up next!' Isabella calls as she trots down the hill towards me.

'That's my cue!' I tell Michael.

'It's wonderful to think I'm finally able to talk to you of my noble family,' he says. 'Few people understand the burdens that come with the weight of such an inheritance. Perhaps we can continue our discussion later?'

'Only if we solve all the clues. Otherwise, we may find ourselves wandering around until nightfall, growing colder and hungrier by the moment.'

'Don't you mean we'll be wandering this cursed place until the cold seeps into our bones, while hunger gnaws at our resolve?' he asks.

'If you like. See you later!'

I follow Isabella up the track towards the reception building.

'What were you and Michael talking about?' she asks.

'The kingdoms of Westeros.'

'Is he a fellow Game of Thrones fan? Yet another thing you have in common.'

'Another thing? What else is there?'

'Ship building,' she says. 'And befriending so-called American tourists.'

I give her my most guileless smile. 'Michael and I were just doing our bit to promote friendly relations between our two great countries.'

'Since when have you promoted friendly relations between anyone?'

'You have a point,' I admit. 'But the past is a shadow that chills the soul. Look to the vista before you and plant your feet there if you would stand once your enemies have fallen.'

'Excuse me?' says Isabella.

'Chains forged in old fires bind only those that clutch at them. Release them, and you may yet be free.'

'Sometimes, I wonder about you,' she says.

'I'm trying to tell you to let go of the past and concentrate on the present. What happened yesterday is over and done with. Accept your defeat with grace and move on.'

She sighs. 'Next time, say it in English. Your first clue is under that stone.'

I lift up the rock she indicates and see a laminated slip of paper underneath it.

'Take a photo, then replace the clue where you found it,' Isabella instructs me.

I study the picture. 'It's part of a map.'

'It is!' she says. 'Not Westeros, I'm afraid, but this campsite. You need to collect all the pieces in order to discover where we're meeting when this is over.'

I tap my screen to enlarge the photo. 'This bit looks like a poem.'

'It tells you where the next clue is hidden,' she says. 'It's a brilliant treasure hunt, even if I say it myself.'

'You should,' I agree. 'No one else will.'

She blows me a kiss and disappears to select her next hapless victim.

I look at my phone again. The piece of map doesn't tell me much, but the rhyming couplet is more informative.

I sway and creak where campers rest. Your eighth clue lurks where naps are best.

It isn't difficult to work out it's talking about a hammock. There may be hundreds of those around the campsite, but even Isabella wouldn't expect us to search for them all. There's a hammock slung between our two cabins. Jon told me the boys begged Ali to allow them to sleep in it while they were here. But she told them she didn't want to rescue them at two in the morning when they'd changed their minds about becoming a snack for the giant mosquitoes that patrol the campsite each night.

I set off for our cabins, wondering where the next clue will send me. This feels like a gigantic waste of the time I could be using for more important things. I spent most of my precious Saturday afternoon making a boat that will never be used again. And now it looks as though most of Sunday will be taken up with another pointless task.

I realise I'm doing this for Isabella, but couldn't she have organised a more traditional hen night? We could have drunk enough prosecco to overcome all our inhibitions, then paraded around a city centre wearing ridiculous sashes. We could have followed this up with a tragic couple of hours attempting to perform karaoke without having things thrown at us. It would have been painful and embarrassing, but the torture would have been confined to a single evening instead of taking up the whole of a valuable weekend.

I reach the cabins and locate the hammock. As I expected, there's another clue taped to its underside. I'm about to take a photo and attempt to decipher it when a thought strikes me. We're all doing this task separately, which means none of us knows how far anyone else has got with the hunt. Jon said it would take us about an hour and a half to retrieve all the pieces of the map and fit them together in order to work out where we're supposed to meet.

Instead of doing that, I could stay in my cabin for an hour, then locate one of my fellow participants and follow them to the meeting place. Failing that, I could message Michael and tell him I'm having difficulty with the treasure hunt and would like some assistance. Something tells me he would step in and help me out if I sounded pathetic enough.

I hesitate. This isn't really fair on Isabella. But she need never know about it. I can do what I have to do, then meet up with everyone and join in with tales of how I found and deciphered all the clues.

I slip my phone back into my pocket and let myself into the cabin, careful to lock the door behind me so no one will suspect I'm here. I pull a book out of my backpack, climb onto my bunk bed, and am soon lost to the world.

I'm not sure how long it is until a slight noise brings me back to reality. I put down my book and pull the quilt over my head. Maybe someone is here to use the bathroom or collect something they've forgotten. Or possibly, it's a burglar, seizing the chance to look around what they believe to be an empty cabin in case there's anything worth stealing. Whoever it is, I'd prefer not to come face to face with them.

I realise the sound I heard was a key turning in the lock. That seems to rule out an opportunist passer-by. It must be a member of our group. Hopefully, they'll find whatever it is they're looking for and leave. The best thing I can do is stay where I am and pretend to be an under-sheet. Even if it's Abby, she's unlikely to notice a lumpy quilt piled on the top bunk, as long as it doesn't move.

I shift my position to make sure the quilt is hiding me properly. As I do so, my elbow bangs against the wall. It sounds unnaturally loud in the silent cabin.

'Hello?' calls Isabella's voice. 'Is anybody there?'

I tell myself that quilts can't answer and stay as still as possible, trying not to breathe. I hear her footsteps walk down the passageway, followed by the sound of the bedroom door opening. I freeze, willing her to realise she was mistaken and leave. But this is Isabella.

She twitches the quilt off my bed and glares at me. 'What do you think you're doing?'

I toy with the idea of telling her I'm checking the thread count of everyone's sheets but decide against it. She looks absolutely furious.

'I'm reading,' I say when it becomes obvious she isn't going away without an answer.

'Reading what?' she demands.

'A book.'

She snatches it from me and glares at it. 'The Dialectics of Ethical Subjectivity?'

I could tell her it's a werewolf romance and I've covered it with a different book jacket to make me look smarter. But she only has to open the book to realise this isn't true.

'It's an interesting book,' I say. 'And I was feeling quite tired today, so —'

'Tired?' she explodes. 'It's one afternoon! You aren't making the slightest effort, are you?'

'Not true!' I flash back. 'It isn't one afternoon. It's an entire weekend. And I'm making far more of an effort than you'll ever know. I've done everything you've asked of me – and then some. I came here on Friday night, even though it was extremely inconvenient. I made a stupid boat and floated it across the stupid lake. I sat around the campfire last night and roasted marshmallows until almost one in the morning. And very soon, I'll meet everyone at some secret location and talk and laugh and pretend to have fun. So, why don't you cut me some slack and allow me to read my book for an hour?'

I expect her to snap back and give me a few home truths. I wouldn't blame her. I'd do exactly the same in her position. I brace myself for whatever she's about to throw at me. To my astonishment, she doesn't. She studies my face for a moment, then climbs onto the bed beside me and puts her arm around me.

'Why don't you tell me what's going on, Georgia?'

Chapter Thirty-Eight

The compassion in her voice sends me over the edge. Anger, I could have withstood. Petulance, I could have ignored. But kindness is the one thing I've never been able to cope with.

I open my mouth to tell her not to be so ridiculous, and nothing's going on, but the words won't come. I give a choking sob, and the floodgates open. Tears spill down my cheeks before I can stop them. I turn my face away from her, but it's no use. My whole body is shaking, and there's nothing I can do about it. It's as though that one kind sentence has given me permission to fall apart.

Isabella doesn't speak. She doesn't even make soothing noises. She just sits beside me and waits for my torrent of tears to subside. It takes a long time, but eventually I'm all cried out. I sit with my head on her shoulder while she strokes my hair.

She waits until the last hiccupping sob has left my chest, and the silence has settled around us. 'Better now?'

'A little.'

'Then why don't you tell me all about it?'

I shrug helplessly. 'I wouldn't know where to start.'

'Why not start from the moment I came in just now, and we can work backwards from there? Why are you hiding away in here while everyone is outside having fun?'

'Because I have to.'

I feel the sudden tension of her arm as it rests lightly across my shoulders. 'You have to? Georgia – has something happened? Has someone –?'

'Nothing like that,' I assure her. 'This has nothing to do with anyone else. It's all me. But I can handle it.'

'Clearly not or I wouldn't have found what I took to be a burglar lurking under your duvet.'

'I thought you were a burglar too,' I say. 'But it didn't occur to me to climb down and investigate. I decided to stay where I was and hope they went away.'

'Don't you have a phone?'

'I didn't think of that,' I confess. 'I was too busy trying to remember where you'd put the chocolate for the s'mores and hoping the burglar wouldn't find it.'

'It's in the top cupboard,' she says. 'Where I believed you wouldn't think to look for it. If you didn't come here to search for chocolate, why did you come back? Surely, not to read that book? I can't imagine where it came from.'

I take a deep breath. 'It came from my backpack.'

'Is that why it was so heavy when you arrived?'

'There are three more books just like it in there.'

Isabella looks horrified. 'It brought friends?'

I give a shaky laugh. 'Several of them. That kind of book always travels in packs.'

She looks at the title again. 'You'll have to explain.'

'I'm studying for my end-of-year exams,' I say. 'I'm taking them in a few weeks' time.'

'What kind of exams?'

'I'm doing a university access course. I didn't want anyone to know.'

'Why not?' she asks. 'I think it's fantastic!'

'It would be if I were eighteen, but it's just weird at my age.'

'No, it isn't! It's amazing. What made you decide to do this?'

'I started thinking about it soon after you took me on at the bakery,' I say. 'I realised that a lot of what you said to me when we were younger was right. I ought to want something more out of life. But until I came to work for you, I'd been feeling a bit trapped. I was working in a job I hated, but at least it was a job, and I wasn't qualified to do anything else. So, I went to work each morning and tried not to think about the fact that this would be my life for the next few decades. Then you offered me a job at the Sugarloaf, and I saw how much fun you and Lily had each day. It started me wondering about the kind of life I wanted for myself.'

She nods. 'I'm glad that working at the bakery has been better for you than your last job. But you've always told me it's a temporary thing.'

'That's true. I love working at the bakery, and I'll never forget what you've done for me. But it isn't what I want to do forever.'

She moves the book and pulls a pillow behind her back. 'There's no reason it should be. Running a bakery is the most fun I've ever had, but I wouldn't expect that to be the case for everyone. What do you plan to do with your life?'

'I haven't quite decided, but I've been thinking about teaching. It's been fun volunteering at the arts centre during the holidays. The children have been so cool. They're always excited to try out new things, and they don't let anything hold them back. I started wondering whether I might do something like that full time. So, I contacted the nearest college offering access courses and signed up.'

'That's wonderful!' she says. 'How long have you been doing this?'

'Nearly a year. I've almost finished the course. My final assignments are due in two weeks' time, and I have a few exams at the end of June.'

She picks up the book again and looks at the cover. 'What are you studying?'

'A bit of everything. English literature, history, philosophy, and some introductory social sciences. I haven't decided on my final direction yet, but it will something along those lines. I haven't ruled out social work either.'

'You'd be good at that,' she says. 'I don't know what to say! I'm so impressed with what you're doing. But that's a pretty heavy workload on top of working at the bakery.'

'It's been quite full-on,' I say. 'But I was anxious to get cracking with it. I didn't want to extend it into another year if I could avoid it. It feels bad enough that I've waited this long.'

'I don't agree,' she says. 'I'll bet you've been a far better student because you made a conscious decision to do this, and you've had to overcome quite a few obstacles to get there.'

'Better late than never?' I ask.

She frowns. 'What I don't understand is why you didn't tell anyone what you were doing. Lily and I could have done far more to support you. We'd have given you all the time off you needed.'

'I know you would, but I have to earn a living somehow. And I've been trying to save up my money in case I do well enough to be accepted for university this year.'

'You will!' she says. 'Anyone who can pronounce the title of this book, let alone understand what it means, is someone any university would be lucky to have.'

'I'm not sure it works like that, but thank you. The other reason I didn't tell anyone is because I always avoid the subject of qualifications when other people talk about theirs. It only reminds me of how far behind I am in life. So far behind that I'm still not sure I'll ever catch up. But I intend to have a jolly good try.'

'I don't believe your qualifications matter to other people half as much as you think,' she says. 'No one I know ever mentions theirs.'

'That's because they have them. It's like money. People with plenty of money don't need to discuss finances because they go through life secure in the knowledge there's a cushion there if they need it. And people with good qualifications don't have to think about them because they've already used them to get where they are in life. You can't imagine how inferior I feel knowing I've reached my thirties with nothing to show for it.'

'I wouldn't say that,' she says. 'You have plenty to be proud of. But I understand what you mean. People are terrible at realising their own privilege.'

'We were discussing our qualifications yesterday,' I say. 'Lisa and Ben were talking about their amazing engineering and IT achievements, and Michael joined in and talked about his job. And then he told them I make hot drinks. He didn't mean it in a belittling way, but that's how it felt. There's nothing wrong with making hot drinks for a living, but not when that isn't what you want to do, and you know it's all your own fault for not doing something about it sooner.'

'Who are Lisa and Ben?' asks Isabella.

'Just some people Michael and I bumped into. It isn't relevant to what we're talking about now.'

A slow smile spreads across her face. 'Would that be the American tourists, by any chance? The ones who were so fascinated by our darling English traditions that they couldn't help lurking behind a holly bush to observe them more closely?'

'Don't tell anyone about Lisa and Ben!' I beg. 'If you do, Michael will wonder why I told you, and he'll start asking questions. I can't face that right now. It was difficult enough telling you what I've been up to.'

'I promise,' she says. 'By rights, I ought to put an asterisk next to both of your names to let everyone know you cheated. But I'll let it go this time because of the effort it took for you to be here at all this weekend.'

'Thank you. And it wasn't really that much effort. I'm sorry I said your boat race was stupid. I didn't mean it. I was surprised by how much fun I had. And I'd have loved this treasure hunt at any other time. It's just that all I can think of at the moment is my exams. When I started this course, it felt as though I had plenty of time. But the final exams have snuck up on me without me noticing.'

'I haven't made things any better,' she says ruefully. 'I asked you to be my chief bridesmaid because I thought it would be wonderful for us to spend time together, organising everything.

You must have been wishing I'd never met Jon and had chosen instead to retire to a nunnery to live out the rest of my years.'

'I was delighted for you both,' I say. 'But the timing wasn't quite as ideal as it could have been. I've had to turn down so many things you've invited me to because of my evening classes. I knew you were annoyed with me, but there was nothing I could do about it.'

'Was that why you arrived here late on Friday evening?' she asks.

'Yes. I came straight here after my class.'

'I wish I'd been more understanding. I've been so wrapped up in this wedding planning that I've been suffering from tunnel vision.'

'You weren't to know,' I say. 'And weddings trump exams. I can retake those any time if need be. You only get one chance at this wedding. Or I hope you do. It will be a shame if you've enjoyed it so much that you intend to get engaged to someone new every year – just so you can plan another wedding.'

'Once is more than enough,' she says. 'In fact –'

'In fact what?'

She shakes her head. 'I've forgotten what I was about to say. I have to leave soon. Everyone will be meeting at the final destination – unless they've got the clues wrong and are currently marooned on that little island in the middle of the lake. Would you like to come with me or would you prefer to stay here? I can easily make some excuse for you.'

I push my damp hair out of my eyes. 'I'll come. I don't want Michael taunting me with my failure to follow simple clues and read a basic map.'

'I'll tell him you solved it all more quickly than anyone else,' she says. 'And then you decided to some back to the cabin and put your feet up while the slower members of our party struggled to crack the code.'

'Where are we meeting?' I ask.

'The ice cream parlour – Camp Chill.'

I laugh. 'I should have guessed. I was planning to follow someone closer to the time, but now I don't need to.'

'I'll show you the way. And I promise I won't give away your secret to anyone. You can tell them yourself when you're ready.'

'I appreciate that,' I say. 'Give me a minute to wash my face and make myself presentable, and then we can walk up there together.'

Chapter Thirty-Nine

Everyone except Chris is waiting for us when we arrive at Camp Chill.

'You took your time!' Michael tells me when I walk in. 'Did you have trouble with the clues? I struggled a bit with number nine. The one about the tall pine tree.'

'I got that one at once,' says Ali. 'But I thought number three meant the swimming pool, and I went chasing off up there. It set me back by about twenty-five minutes.'

'And yet you still arrived here before Georgia,' says Michael.

I could easily wipe the grin off his face by telling him I cheated – and with the enthusiastic connivance of one of the organisers. But that doesn't feel like the right thing to do, so I refrain.

'Georgia finished ages ago,' says Isabella. 'She and I have been chatting in our cabin while we waited for the rest of you to finish.'

'Ages ago?' asks Jack. 'That's impressive.'

She sits down opposite him and gestures for me to sit next to her. 'I suppose so, but it's no more than I expected. Jon and I discussed creating a supplementary set of clues to make it a bit more fun for Georgia, but we didn't have time. My parents used to do the same thing when we were small. Otherwise, Georgia would get bored waiting for us all to catch up.'

'Is that right?' he asks.

'Oh, yes! It became quite a family joke. Georgia was brilliant at solving puzzles. We went to her whenever we were stuck with anything, and she'd have it all worked out for us in seconds. It comes of having a genius level IQ.'

'I didn't know that,' says Lily, looking impressed.

'That's because she's so modest,' says Isabella. 'She doesn't like people talking about it. I remember once that she –'

We aren't destined to find out what I once did because Chris walks into the cafe at this moment. His face falls when he sees us. 'Am I the last to arrive?'

Abby waves to him. 'I'm afraid so. We've all been here for the past fifteen minutes, wondering what had become of you. Jon was about to send out a search party to rescue you.'

'We thought Georgia needed rescuing too,' says Michael. 'But apparently, she solved the whole thing quicker than anyone.'

'I thought some of those clues might be too obscure,' says Jon. 'I had to give the boys a hand with several of them.'

'Nonsense!' says Isabella. 'Georgia didn't have any difficulty with them.'

'But we don't all have genius level IQs,' Jack points out.

I nudge Isabella before she can get too carried away by thoughts of my brilliance and launch into a story about the time Stephen Hawking had to call me to ask for clarification about a few things that were puzzling him.

'Have you decided what you're ordering?' asks Jon. 'Isabella and I are paying. We want to thank you all for giving up your weekend to risk life and limb playing our ridiculous games.'

'It was quite a sacrifice,' says Michael. 'There were times during the boat building exercise when I was thought I might lose a thumb. But all my fingers and toes seem to have remained intact.'

'I hope that's also true of the American tourists after such a busy camping trip,' says Isabella, smiling sweetly at him.

Michael shoots me a suspicious look, which I meet with my blandest smile.

'Puzzles always make me hungry,' I say. 'I think I'll have a Knickerbocker Glory with extra whipped cream.'

'That sounds perfect,' says Lily. 'Especially as it's free. It will give Isabella the opportunity to realise how it feels for the rest of us when people hand out products without charging for them.'

Our ice creams arrive, and we dig into them.

'Chasing around a campsite after red herrings is hungry work,' says Abby.

'Not for Georgia,' says Michael. 'From what I hear, she treated the clues with the contempt they deserved and solved them without a second thought. She shouldn't need an ice cream as a reward.'

'I always need an ice cream,' I say. 'And Isabella was exaggerating. She has a tendency to do that.'

'Not at all,' she says. 'If anything, I was playing down your childhood achievements.'

'What's happening this afternoon?' I ask to prevent her detailing more of my mythical exploits. That's the trouble with Isabella – she never knows when to stop. I have to admit I'm touched by her loyalty. It's nice to know someone has my back, especially during this stressful period of my life.

'We didn't want to timetable things too tightly,' says Jon. 'Otherwise, it might feel more like attending boarding school than enjoying a relaxed weekend away in the countryside. There's plenty to do here, so take your pick. There's a tennis court and a swimming pool. There's also an outdoor badminton area and a miniature bowling alley. I'm sure you can all organise yourselves. Isabella and I will be leaving around five, but everyone else can do as they like.'

'That works for us,' says Lily. 'My parents are putting the children to bed at our house tonight and told us not to hurry home. I feel a bit guilty after they've given up their entire weekend for us, but Mum told me to take the help when it was offered. Jack and I plan to stop for dinner on the way home, if any of you would like to join us.'

Isabella scrapes the last of her ice cream out of her dish and picks up the cherry by its stalk. 'I always save these for last. It gives me something to look forward to. How many of you have cherries on your ice cream? We should take the stones and use them for that old rhyme – rich man, poor man.'

'If you're hoping it will land on rich man,' says Jon, 'I'm afraid you'll be disappointed. I'm a humble project manager, and I'll never be able to afford the sort of mansion you deserve.'

'I don't want a mansion!' she says. 'It's enough trouble trying to keep a one-bedroom flat relatively clean.'

'But if you were rich enough to live in a mansion,' I point out, 'you could afford to pay for housekeeping staff. And pool-cleaners, farriers, and whatever else you might want.'

She smiles at Jon. 'I'm very happy as I am.'

'Give me all your cherry stones,' says Lily. 'I'm going to do it anyway.'

She arranges the stones in a line on her plate. 'We need a new rhyme. The original one is out of date.'

Jack prods them with his spoon. 'Bakery owner, forestry employee, project manager, occupational therapist, civil engineer, school child, accountant, pastry chef …'

'We need a ninth one,' says Lily. 'Who haven't we counted?'

'Me,' I say.

'Of course. Where were we? Accountant, pastry chef …'

'Secret genius?' suggests Michael.

'Not so secret,' says Isabella. 'That last stone is for woman of the year. My sister may not have a boring job title, but I have no doubt she'll astonish us all in the not-too-distant future.'

'I'll do my best,' I say, embarrassed. 'Someone should take those cherry stones home and plant them. You never know what they'll turn into.'

'If they don't turn into cherry trees, I want my money back,' says Jon.

'Not everything is as predictable as you'd like to think,' Isabella tells him. 'I'm glad that some things still have the power to surprise us. People too.'

She smiles at me, and I smile back. It's nice to think that someone believes in me. I've been so stressed and exhausted over the past few months, I've almost lost the ability to believe in myself.

'Who's up for a game of tennis?' asks Jack.

'Me!' chorus the boys.

'You'll have to be on your best form if you want to beat those two,' Jon tells us. 'They've recently joined a tennis club, and they're very good.'

'Lily and I will take them on,' says Jack. 'She used to play a lot of tennis as a child.'

'That was a long time ago,' says Lily. 'I haven't picked up a racquet in years.'

'Now's your chance,' says Isabella. 'It's what this weekend is supposed to be about – the chance to let down our hair and get away from real life for a while.'

'Sounds good to me,' says Michael. 'What do you say to a game of badminton, Georgia?'

'I could take time out of my busy schedule to thrash you at badminton,' I say.

'How do you know I wasn't the school badminton champion?' he asks.

'I don't, but I'm willing to take my chances. Isabella and I used to play together in the garden when we were younger. We were extremely competitive, but I usually won.'

'It's true,' says Isabella. 'When my sister sets her mind on something, she achieves it. Beating me at every single game we played was one of those things.'

Michael pulls me to my feet. 'See you all later – if I'm still able to walk.'

'It will have to be a quick game,' I warn him. 'I need to be home by six.'

'It's only four o'clock. I thought we could join everyone for dinner on the way back.'

'I can't,' I say. 'I have things to do this evening.'

'Hot date?' Jack asks me.

'Something like that.'

It sounds better than announcing I have to write two thousand words on the subject of gender representation in 19th century literature.

'Don't feel you have to stay here at all if there's somewhere else you need to be,' says Michael, and I see Jon and Isabella exchange looks.

'I'm ok for an hour or so,' I say. 'Unless you're getting cold feet?'

'Not exactly. Just unsure whether I should remain in the game at all.'

'You can't back out now!' says Isabella. 'That would be most unsportsmanlike behaviour.'

'Maybe,' he says. 'But sometimes you have to know when to call it.'

'Nonsense!' she says. 'I've never seen such a defeatist attitude. Haven't you heard the saying you have to be in it to win it?'

'Everyone's heard that saying,' I say. 'But it won't come true in this case. Michael may be in it, but he won't win it!'

'That's what I'm afraid of,' he says quietly.

I give him a challenging smile. 'So, are you backing out and conceding defeat before we've even started?'

He opens the cafe door for me. 'Not quite yet. Perhaps I'll stay for a while longer and give it my very best shot.'

Chapter Forty

I almost arrive late for work on Monday morning. My essay took longer than I expected, and my brain was so revved up that I couldn't sleep for a long time after I'd finished. My thoughts were full of Jane Eyre and Catherine Earnshaw. I was trying to fathom what either of them saw in the annoying specimens with whom fate had seen fit to provide them.

In my opinion, both men would have benefited from a swift kick in the pants, followed by some extensive therapy. But their creators obviously saw something in them that I didn't, so I avoided mentioning that theory in my essay and focussed instead on their few good points.

I'm glad I don't live in those times. It isn't always easy juggling work and study while simultaneously being involved in wedding preparations. But I'm grateful for the opportunities available to me – rather than being confined to a lifetime of dreary, underpaid jobs and denied a university education like the heroines of old.

I have no idea whether I'll do well enough to be accepted onto my chosen course this autumn. If not, I'll try again next year. I'm determined to finish what I've started and find a career that will make me happy, rather than drifting aimlessly through life, never looking beyond the next few months.

Isabella messaged last night to tell me not to come into work this morning if it wasn't convenient. She offered to cover for me as often as I like. But I'll need time off for my exams, so I've decided to keep working my regular hours for now.

'Sorry I'm a minute late!' I apologise as I race in. 'It was a long night.'

'I'm happy you're here at all,' says Lily. 'I have to nip out to Daisy's school at ten o'clock. They're doing a show-and-tell of all the artwork they've done this year, and I'd hate to miss it.'

'Check whether any of the children have painted a picture that looks like Bernie,' I suggest. 'If so, offer to buy it from them. I'll go up to five pounds if they throw in the mounting paper too.'

'Don't get your hopes up,' she warns me. 'The last time I went to one of these things, the entire wall was covered with terrifying-looking tarantulas – all done in wax crayon and chalk. It was like walking into the set of a particularly gruesome horror film.'

'I would have loved that when I was at primary school. We had to draw endless vases of flowers, with the occasional sunset thrown in for variety.'

'Daisy's class went to the zoo last month,' says Lily. 'Anyone brave enough got the chance to hold a tarantula.'

'Was Daisy one of them?'

'Are you kidding? She was first in line. And now she wants Santa to bring her one for Christmas. I'm trying to give her thoughts a more proper direction by suggesting she ask him for a goldfish instead. But I don't fancy my chances.'

'Christmas is a long time away,' I say. 'She'll have moved on to something else by then. In the meantime, there's the wedding to take her mind off it.'

Lily sighs. 'That's what I told her, but she isn't too happy about it. She still wants to wear her favourite dungarees, and Chloe won't hear of it. She's provided a mood board with suggestions for suitable flower girl dresses, but Daisy isn't keen on any of them. She doesn't see why Ethan can wear trousers and a shirt, while she has to look like a china doll.'

'I'm with Daisy,' I say. 'It wouldn't hurt Chloe to back off a little and allow everyone to enjoy the day. I'm surprised Isabella hasn't said something. She's very protective of Daisy.'

'I haven't mentioned it to Isabella,' she says. 'It doesn't feel fair to add to her stresses. I don't think she realised what she was taking on when she booked her wedding at Willowmere Hall. If we all start piling in with complaints and demands, it will make things even worse.'

'That's been my approach too,' I agree. 'Isabella tells me what she wants, or what Chloe says she may have, and I smile and say it sounds wonderful. It seems the only way to get her to the big day in one piece.'

'Mum's promised to take Daisy shopping for a dress and finish up at the ice cream shop,' she says. 'That usually does the trick. But she's still disappointed about not being allowed to wear her dungarees.'

Ivy puts her head around the door. 'Are you open?'

'Of course,' says Lily. 'Why wouldn't we be?'

Mabel appears behind Ivy. 'We thought we'd better ask, since your opening hours have been so erratic recently. None of us knows what to expect from one day to the next.'

'We were closed for *one* day!' says Lily.

'But your staff is always changing,' says Mabel. 'We come in here expecting to find you and Georgia, only to be greeted by Victoria and goodness knows who else. Your customers like continuity, and they assume they'll get it.'

'What would you do if we all went down with the flu at the same time?' I ask.

She throws her coat over the back of a chair. 'If you weren't in the hospital, we'd suggest you worked in shifts. It isn't our fault if you haven't had your flu shots this year.'

'You've spoiled them,' I tell Lily. 'If I ran a small business, I'd make it clear to my customers from the outset how lucky they were to be served by me. There would be none of this constant complaining about the service.'

'You're very wise,' she says. 'But it's too late to do anything about it now. It is what it is, and we'll have to make the best of it.'

'I don't believe it's too late,' I say. 'But you're the boss.'

'We'd like our usual drinks, please,' says Ivy.

'Coming right up,' I say.

'How are you doing with your competition entries?' asks Lily as I spoon foam over Ivy's cappuccino and add a chocolate illustration of a syringe.

'I've finished mine!' says Mabel proudly. 'The judging is on Friday at four o'clock. I hope you'll both be there.'

'And leave the bakery unattended?' asks Lily, shocked. 'What would our customers say?'

Mabel ignores the jibe. 'Good point. I'll ask Barb to move it to five o'clock.'

'That works for me,' I say, handing Ivy her mug.

'What's this?' she asks, looking at the picture on the foam.

'It's a hypodermic needle for our flu shots.'

Mabel gives a rumble of laughter. 'You're a creative girl. I'll say that for you. Are you entering something in this competition?'

'I am, but don't ask what it is because I won't tell you. Lily's the one who surrenders to all our customers' demands, not me.'

I find Isabella waiting for me in the living room when I arrive home.

'I wasn't expecting to see you today,' I greet her. 'Have you come for dinner? I have a class this evening, so I'll eat later.'

'Mum called this morning to invite us,' she says. 'Jon will be along later, but I wanted to come over early to have a chat with you.'

'Something wedding related?' I ask, flinging myself into an armchair and stretching out my aching legs. 'Don't tell me Chloe has been offered a job as a prison warder and feels that could be a better match for her talents?'

'Not that anyone's told me.'

'It wouldn't be the worst thing in the world. They might replace her with someone a little more relaxed. Then you could stop stressing about everything and enjoy your day.'

'You and I have had this conversation several times,' she says. 'And we're unlikely to agree. I can't imagine what I'd have done without Chloe to guide me through this whole thing. It's been an absolute minefield. I had no idea how complicated it would be.'

'My feeling is that a wedding is only as complicated as you want it to be,' I say. 'But I'm not talking from direct experience, so I expect I'm wrong. If you aren't here to discuss the wedding, what did you want to talk about?'

'To ask whether you needed any help with your studies?'

'That's kind of you, but I'm not sure what you could do.'

'I could take your exams for you,' she says. 'That's one benefit of us looking so much alike. I could walk into the examination hall with my head held high and show them your ID. No one would be any the wiser.'

'Until they read your paper. Do you know anything about moral philosophy?'

'I know that it's wrong to tell lies – even about stray American tourists. And I know you shouldn't take something that belongs to someone else unless it has custard in it – in which case all bets are off.'

'I'm impressed by your ethical code,' I say. 'But I suspect the examiners won't be.'

'At least let me drive you over and wait for you while you're in there.'

'Most of the exams last for two hours,' I say.

'I'll bring a book. Or you can lend me one. I noticed you had several thick volumes in your backpack. I'd be bound to learn something from them.'

'If I were you, I'd bring something a little lighter,' I say. 'But thanks for the offer. I'd love to take you up on it. I doubt I'll be in a fit state to drive by then.'

'I hope you know how impressed I am with what you're doing,' she says. 'This can't have been easy for you.'

'But it's been very satisfying. And I've enjoyed many of the courses. If I'd known how interesting some of these subjects could be, I might have listened more closely in school.'

The doorbell rings, and she jumps up. 'That must be Jon.'

'It's sweet you're still so excited to see him, even after all this time.'

'It's been less than two years,' she says.

'True, but you've never had the longest attention span.'

The living room door opens, and Jon appears. Michael follows him into the room.

'Hello!' I say. 'I didn't know you were coming too.'

'I was with Jon when your mum called and invited him for dinner. She asked if I'd like to come along. I had nothing else to do this evening, and I hoped I might catch up with you.'

'That's very gracious of you after your humiliating defeat on the badminton court,' I tell him. 'I'd love to challenge you to a rematch after dinner, but I won't be here. I have plans for the evening.'

His face doesn't change. 'That's unfortunate.'

'I'd better get going or I'll be late.'

'Maybe I'll see you later?' he suggests.

'It's possible, but not likely. I rarely get home until late.'

He nods. 'That's what I thought. Enjoy your evening.'

Enjoyment isn't the word I'd have used. But I can't tell him that, so I wave and slip out of the room, all ready to face the joys of moral philosophy.

Chapter Forty-One

We close the bakery fifteen minutes early on Friday.

'I'd be worried about our customers complaining,' says Lily. 'But most of them will be at the arts centre by now.'

'It's been a busy week,' I say, 'and I'm dead on my feet. I'd love to go home and have a rest before I go out this evening. But I've promised to be there for the competition, so I have no choice.'

'You can't get out of it now,' she agrees. 'This was all your idea.'

'Not quite. It was my sister's feather-brained notion. I'm just picking up the pieces.'

She switches off the lights. 'I know how grateful she is.'

'Let's hope her gratitude takes some more tangible form than words. Such as a bonus, or an extra week's paid leave.'

'Hope is a beautiful thing,' she says, slinging her jacket over her arm and turning the shop sign to Closed.

The arts centre is packed when we arrive. We're using the downstairs room for what Mrs Ogilvie persists in referring to as 'Bernie's Exhibition.'

'As though he were a famous artist,' says Lily.

'At least she hasn't yet referred to it as a royal exhibition,' I say.

'Not in front of anyone, but I'm sure that's how she thinks of it privately. Bernie is her little prince. It's quite sweet really.'

I smile. 'Other opinions are available, as Mabel is so fond of saying whenever Bernie is mentioned.'

'You're here!' Barb greets us as we walk in. 'Now we can get started.'

'You could have started without us,' I say.

'No, we couldn't,' says Isabella. 'This is your thing, Georgie. None of it would have happened but for you.'

'But we've decided to forgive you anyway,' says Mabel.

To my amusement, I see she's wearing a dark blue artist's smock, topped off with a velvet, tasselled hat.

'You look great,' I tell her. 'You wouldn't be out of place in Leonardo da Vinci's studio.'

'Is he the actor who starred in Titanic?' she asks.

'That's the one,' says Isabella. 'He was very fond of painting.'

'I haven't painted the mutt wearing a French maid's costume,' says Mabel. 'I hope that won't count against me?'

'Who's judging this competition?' I ask Isabella. 'Not me, I hope. I don't know enough about art to make an impartial decision.'

'David has agreed to do it.'

She points to the far end of the room, where David is helping Bob to lift several canvases onto a trestle table.

I feel a pang of guilt when I realise I haven't been in contact with him since our dinner together. I noticed a couple of missed calls from him, but I had other things on my mind and forgot to call him back. With any luck, he's forgotten all about me too.

Isabella waves to him. 'We can make a start whenever you like!'

David catches sight of me and walks over to us. 'Hi, Georgia. I haven't seen you for a while.'

'Sorry about that,' I say. 'I've been busy with –'

'Work,' says Isabella smoothly. 'Her employer is highly unreasonable and expects far more from her than is either fair or legal. Certainly more than is compatible with any kind of a social life.'

David frowns. 'Doesn't Georgia work for you?'

'She does,' agrees Isabella. 'Which makes the way she's treated even more reprehensible. But that's always the way when people work for family members. Boundaries get blurred, and exploitation follows closely behind. I'm thankful we don't pay her enough to cover union fees.'

'Are we starting this thing, or what?' asks Mabel. 'If you stand around talking much longer, the ice sculptures will melt.'

'Seriously?' I ask. 'Someone's made an ice sculpture of Bernie?'

'Not to the best of my knowledge, but I remember Edie suggesting it when she first heard about the competition. I told her I wouldn't trust her anywhere near a chainsaw, but someone else may have had the same bright idea.'

Isabella waves her hand and calls for silence.

'It's a pity she can't be her own MC at the wedding reception,' I tell Lily. 'Her voice has a certain piercing quality that means she doesn't need a microphone.'

'Hello, everyone!' says Isabella when people have stopped chattering and turned to face us. 'And welcome to the Honeywell Arts Centre's first exhibition. We're delighted so many of you have agreed to demonstrate your artistic skills and display them for us all to enjoy today. If you'd like to wander around and look at everyone's work, David will announce the results in half an hour.'

'I'll have a quick look at them before I set up my own entry,' I say.

'Don't miss the watercolours,' says Isabella. 'Ivy told me Bob has spent weeks getting his painting just right.'

'I'll come with you,' Lily tells me. 'I want to see Mabel's interpretation of the wonder that is Bernie.'

'Let's hope it's flattering,' I say. 'Otherwise, she'll be looking for a new place to live by this evening.'

We wander towards the nearest table, where several members of the poker club are proudly displaying their entries. Doreen Wallage has created a sculpture entirely from poker chips.

'It's Bernie!' she informs us as we stare at it in admiration.

'Who else would it be?' asks Mary Palmer. 'He's the reason we're all here today.'

'I thought I'd better make it clear,' says Doreen. 'Steph Parker asked me if it was a dinosaur. The cheek of the woman!'

Julie Coleman has made a dog-shaped table mat out of felt – embroidered with tiny playing cards and marrow bones.

'In case Bernie ever wants to try his paw at the game,' she explains. 'It would stop him scratching the table.'

My personal favourite is a hand-drawn comic strip by Rose and Peggy Hollenbach, entitled Bernie's Big Bluff. It follows the tale of a cavoodle who learns to deal cards and calculate odds. It ends with him walking away with all the chips and cashing them in for dog biscuits.

'Mrs Ogilvie wouldn't approve of Bernie gambling,' I say. 'But this cartoon is inspired.'

'My mother and I have been taking a course on character art,' Peggy explains. 'We started with stick figures and built up to this.'

We move to the next section, where people have fixed their paintings onto a bare stretch of wall.

'I love that watercolour of Bernie looking hopefully up at the kitchen table,' I say.

'That one's mine,' says Lynn Radford. 'The brownish blob on the plate is supposed to be a roast chicken. It isn't very clear, but I did my best.'

Lily leans forward to study the caption underneath the painting. '*Moral Dilemma.* That's wonderful!'

'David suggested we all think of titles for our work,' says Margaret Le Breton. 'He told us the words can be almost as important as the image. Apparently, they guide and focus the viewer's emotional journey.'

'Or distract them from the dodgy perspective,' says Donna Collins, laughing. 'I've called my painting *Paws for Reflection*. Bernie's looking into a mirror.'

'Thank goodness for that!' says Mabel, who's standing at the next table. 'I wondered why there were two of him. For one awful moment, I thought you'd discovered one of his long-lost relatives and given them our address. I'd hate to wake one morning and find Bernie's second cousin waiting on our doorstep, expecting to be fed. Pensions don't stretch as far as they used to.'

'What have you made?' I ask her.

She gestures to a pottery figure on the table in front of her. 'It's for our back garden. Some people have gnomes, so I didn't see why we shouldn't have a Bernie.'

'I love it,' I say. 'What's he sitting on?'

'A toadstool. It would be easier to recognise if I'd painted it red and white like the ones in the fairy tales, but Edie wouldn't hear of it. She says that particular variety is highly poisonous, and she doesn't want me putting ideas into the mutt's head. So, I painted it brown. It makes it more difficult to tell which bits are Bernie and which are the toadstool, but it keeps Edie happy, so I don't mind.'

'You could call it *Not Mushroom*,' I suggest, and she gives a shout of laughter.

'You're as bad as your sister! Have you made something for the competition?'

'I'm about to,' I say. 'I'll see you all in a minute.'

I slip away to the kitchen, leaving Lily admiring Ali Uzzell's painting of Bernie lying underneath what looks like one of our bakery chairs, gnawing on a biscuit. She's labelled it *Crumbs!*

'I never realised the residents of Honeywell were so creative,' says Isabella, following me into the kitchen.

'I can't think why not. They come up with new ideas each day to trick you into giving them free cakes.'

'That's the Silver Surfers,' she says. 'They employ their own brand of tweed-wrapped cunning, and I've long since given up trying to get the better of them. It's lovely to see so many other people here, showing off their artistic achievements. Did you notice the table of knitted Bernies the Brownies have made?'

'I did. Apparently, they're killing two birds with one stone and using them for their craft badges too.'

'Even the bell-ringing club has sent in an entry,' she says. 'Suzanne Cowen's made a mobile for a baby's crib, complete with miniature brass Bernies that jangle in the breeze.'

'I'm impressed,' I say. 'Can you pass me that jug of milk?'

'Are you making yourself a drink? I wouldn't mind one if you are.'

'No one touches this coffee until after the judging,' I say, pouring foam into the cup and starting to trace a picture on it.

'Is that Bernie?' she asks.

'Unless my hand shakes too much, in which case I'll tell everyone it's an abstract representation of some unknown member of the canine species.'

'Mrs Ogilvie would still insist it looked like Bernie,' she says. 'Is that a cap on his head?'

'It's the tweed one he always wears. Mrs Ogilvie says it's his favourite.'

'I'm so glad we got to know her,' says Isabella. 'When Lily first met her, she was a crabby old thing who didn't approve of anything or anyone. But I think she was just lonely. Once we took over the bakery and she came to know us better, she thawed out, and we saw the real person behind the gruff exterior. Mabel arrived a few years later, and the pair of them have never looked back.'

'Your bakery has done a lot for this village,' I say. 'I wish I'd realised that years ago. I've missed out on a lot of fun.'

'You're here now,' she says. 'Better late than never. And you make your own unique contribution to Honeywell.'

Lily opens the kitchen door. 'It's about to start.'

I carry my mug through and place it on a table next to a group of mosaics depicting Bernie in various poses – ranging from half-asleep to frantically racing around, chasing his tail.

David smiles when he sees my latte. 'Proof that fine art is found in every walk of life.'

'If we could please have your attention!' calls Isabella. 'We're about to discover which of these wonderful works will receive this year's Honeywell Arts Centre and Sugarloaf Bakery Prize for Artistic Excellence. Without further ado, I'd like to hand the floor over to David.'

There's a polite ripple of applause as he steps forward. I hope he doesn't launch into a lengthy history of art – starting with the Italian Primitives and packed with information about the *arte magnifiche* hung in *musei famosi* all over the world.

To my relief, he merely introduces himself and says how honoured he is to be judging the competition.

'I'm impressed with the high standard of entries,' he adds. 'It's been a pleasure to spend time with you all this year, helping to unlock your inner creativity. After much thought, I've decided to award the prizes as follows. In third place, we have Gill Newman with her wonderful linocut print of Bernie jumping up to greet someone we can't see. The bold lines and careful carving perfectly capture his joyful energy, while the restrained colour palette enhances rather than overshadows the sense of dynamic movement. Altogether, a most striking piece.'

Gill steps forward to receive her rosette.

'David shouldn't have chosen that one,' Mabel tells her neighbour. 'It looks as though Bernie's about to attack someone. Awarding it a prize will only encourage him.'

'In second place,' says David, 'we have Dawn Brickley with her wonderful hand-stitched felt tableau of Bernie running through a field of wildflowers.'

'Probably trying to eat them,' says Mabel. 'Then he'd keep me up all night being sick on my carpet.'

'Dawn's meticulous embroidery and layered textures create a vibrant, tactile depiction of the subject, full of warmth and energy,' adds David. 'Whatever else art does, it should make us feel something. And this piece achieves that to perfection.'

'I know how it makes me feel,' says Mabel, and Ivy shushes her.

'And now, the moment you've all been waiting for,' says David. 'The overall winner of the competition. But first let me say —'

I groan inwardly. He's about to come out with the same thing everyone says at this point. Everything is completely amazing, and any one of the entries could have been the winner. Typical teacher stuff that no one takes any notice of. To my surprise, he doesn't.

'I have to tell you how moved I've been by the joy these works have brought to all of us,' he says. 'Each piece of art displayed here today tells a story, captures a moment, and reflects the spirit of this community. You don't know how lucky you are to live in a place like Honeywell, where people really see and connect with each other. And you celebrate that not only on occasions such as this, but all year round.'

'That's quite sweet,' I murmur to Isabella.

'Isn't it?' she murmurs back. 'It's nice when people really get us.'

'And now,' says David, 'it's time to announce the winner. It was a genuinely difficult decision, but there was one entry that stood out to me each time I walked past it.'

'That rules mine out,' I whisper to Lily. 'He only took one quick look at my awesome latte.'

David gestures towards the windowsill, and I catch my breath when I realise what we're looking at. Someone has lovingly created a piece of stained glass showing Bernie sitting underneath a large oak tree on a summer's day. The vibrant colours cast dancing patterns over the rest of the picture, causing Bernie's fur to look as though it's rippling in the breeze. It's stunning.

'Caroline Shields Forbes!' says David, looking around the room.

Caroline steps forward, blushing furiously. I recognise her as one of our customers, although I haven't seen her very often.

There's a burst of applause, and she blushes even more deeply.

'Speech!' calls Mabel.

'No!' hisses Phyllis. 'I'm keen to get at those refreshments.'

David comes over to talk to us as soon as the applause dies down.

'I have to go,' he tells Isabella. 'I have an appointment this evening.'

'An exciting date?' she asks teasingly.

'As it happens, yes. I've been seeing a teacher from our school for a while now. It's going very well.'

'Is she a language teacher?' I can't help asking.

'Geography. Why do you ask?'

'No reason. I'm pleased for you. I hope you have a lovely time.'

'See you around,' he tells us and disappears.

'He didn't even wish you *buona notte*,' says Isabella. 'How does it feel to watch the one that got away walk out of your life in favour of an evening discussing map-making and river tributaries?'

'Painful, but I'll recover and live to love again.'

'I hope so,' she says. 'You've had enough people trying to catch your eye over the years.'

'My focus is on the next few weeks. They'll have to catch someone else's eye if they're in a hurry.'

'Not everyone is as fickle as you imagine,' she says. 'I realise you're too busy to think of anything else at the moment, but don't become so wrapped up in your books that you forget to look up once in a while and see what's right under your nose.'

Chapter Forty-Two

Isabella picks me up after my final exam.

'I'm taking you out to dinner to celebrate!' she says. 'No excuses.'

'I rarely make excuses about dinner.'

'I'll take you home to change, and then I thought we could go to that new restaurant near the Priory. I've been meaning to try it for a while, and this seems like the perfect occasion.'

'It sounds great,' I say. 'Although I can't guarantee not to fall asleep in my bowl of soup.'

'I'll tell the server you're drunk,' she says. 'They'll have seen it all before.'

I climb into her car and sink back into the seat. The windows are open, and the warm summer air streams over my face as we drive.

'I don't think I was ever so relieved in my life as when the examiner told us to put our pens down at the end of the exam,' I say. 'Pass or fail – it's over!'

She turns her head and smiles at me. 'I'm very proud of you. But I know you hate people saying that.'

'I do when it's about something I should have done years ago.'

'You've been doing other things,' she says. 'And who's to say which is the best order in which to live your life? It's like eating dinner. If you decide tonight that you want to start with a lemon souffle and finish with deep-fried mushrooms, that's exactly what you should do. You'll still end up eating an entire dinner.'

'Two if I'm lucky,' I say. 'But you may have a point. Shall we try it and see how the server reacts?'

'If you like. What I'm trying to say is that each of us only gets one life. We should live it in the way we choose, not the way everyone else thinks is right for us. It will all work itself out in the end.'

'I hope so. Anyway, there's nothing more to be done until the results come out. It's wonderful to feel I've done everything I can, and now it's out of my hands.'

'Would you do it again?' she asks.

'I would. It's been hard work, but I've enjoyed almost all of it. And I've learned a lot about myself in the process.'

'Which is a good reason to do something like this when you're ready for it, and not before,' she says. 'I don't remember learning much about myself at school. I don't remember most of the facts I learned either. Which may mean it was all a gigantic waste of time.'

'I don't think so. It was the thing you needed to do to get you where you wanted to go. My philosophy teacher said something of the kind during a lesson about purpose and meaning.'

'We weren't offered the chance to study philosophy at school,' says Isabella. 'That's another benefit of doing it your way. What else did you learn during your course?'

'That sometimes it's ok not to have all the solutions right away; that questions are often more important than answers; and that meaning isn't found in a book – it's something you create for yourself.'

'I'm starting to wish I'd done things your way,' she says.

'You may not have enjoyed it as much as you think. I don't believe I've slept properly for the past twelve months.'

'And you won't for another six weeks,' she says. 'I can't manage the rest of this wedding all by myself.'

'Isn't that what Chloe is for? If I were you, I'd sit back and let her get on with it. She seems to know what she's doing.'

Isabella sighs. 'She's given me a timetable. You wouldn't believe how complicated it all is. There are seating plans to finalise, suppliers to contact, final dress fittings, last-minute reminders to the guests who haven't RSVP'd, the rehearsal dinner to arrange, transportation to double-check, and wedding favours to organise. Then we have to call the photographer to confirm our thoughts about the video and photos, sign off on the flowers and music, make appointments for our hair and make-up trials, choose a guest-book cover –'

'I get it!' I say. 'But surely Chloe is organising most of that?'

'She is, but she likes her brides to be involved every step of the way.'

'As long as they don't contradict her vision? I forgot to ask whether you've decided on a theme yet?'

She shakes her head. 'Chloe didn't like most of my suggestions. She finally suggested we go with timeless elegance and just make sure everything is as classy and tasteful as possible.'

'What do you and Jon think about that?'

'We're happy something's been decided. You can't think how overwhelming it's all been, Georgie.' She looks almost panic-stricken as she says this.

'It sounds perfect,' I assure her. 'A lovely blue-and-white colour theme, and a string quartet playing as you walk down the aisle. I'm sure Chloe will give you the wedding of your dreams. And don't forget what this is really about. You're marrying the man you love and beginning a new life together.'

'That's true,' she says, looking more cheerful. 'The wedding day is only the start of all that.'

'Exactly,' I say. 'It's the thing you need to do to get you where you want to go.'

She laughs. 'I knew your moral philosophy course would come in useful at some point.'

'Just like your menu-related analogy of life. Between us, we have all the bases covered.'

She pulls up outside the house. 'I'll wait for you here. If Mum sees me, she'll want to talk about Great Aunt Mary's latest demand for me to wear the lace collar from her wedding dress, or tell me that Gran has called for the fifth time to say a wedding without a harpist is barely a wedding at all. Everyone has an opinion, and they don't seem afraid to share it.'

'Too bad,' I say. 'They've had their weddings, so they should let you have yours. Mum hasn't been telling you what you should and shouldn't do, has she?'

'Not at all. She's been wonderful. But our other family members haven't been quite so restrained.'

'It's a pity you had to invite them,' I say.

'I don't mind. They'd be hurt if we left them out. But it meant we couldn't invite as many of our other friends as we would have liked. We've had to cap the numbers, or we'll be paying off this wedding for the rest of our lives. Mum and Dad have very kindly paid for the cake and the champagne, and Jon's parents are dealing with the flowers. But we didn't feel comfortable accepting any more than that. We're supposed to be adults, after all.'

We arrive at the restaurant forty minutes later.

'Reservation for two,' says Isabella. 'The Campbell sisters.'

'Why does he need to know we're sisters?' I ask as we follow the server to our table.

'He doesn't, but I thought I'd tell him anyway. I'm proud to be related to you.'

'Did you ever imagine you'd be saying that?' I ask.

'Quite the opposite. As you're probably aware, I used to pretend we weren't related.'

'I'm glad we worked things out,' I say. 'As sisters go, you could be considerably worse.'

'You too.'

'Plato says the family is a fundamental unit of society,' I add. 'And siblings are foundational to social development.'

'He sounds like a bit of a pill,' says Isabella, and I laugh.

'He was. I promise not to quote him again.'

She hands me a menu. 'There are far better quotes on this. "A gently spiced date sponge, served warm with a glossy toffee sauce. Comforting and indulgent." That's real poetry for you.'

I glance down the list of entrées. 'Or this. "Creamy arborio rice softly simmered with roasted squash and finished with parmesan and sage." The English language at its finest.'

'Forget ancient wisdom,' says Isabella. 'Nothing beats the cadence of a really well-written menu.'

'I had to study D. H. Lawrence for one of my course credits, and I agree. He could have learned something by eating out a bit more often.'

'When do you get your results?' she asks.

'August. I'm trying not to think about it.'

'It will be a big month for us both.'

'That's true,' I say. 'But my thing is less permanent than yours. If I don't do as well as I'd hoped, I can go back and try again next year. You don't have the luxury of adopting that attitude – or not if you want me to be your bridesmaid. This is a one-time offer, and you're lucky to have secured that.'

Isabella hands her menu to the server. 'I'll have the chicken chasseur, and my sister will have the risotto, please.'

She smiles at me. 'I know how lucky I am that you agreed to do this. Lily and Abby too. You all lead such busy lives. I didn't realise quite how busy when I first asked you, but I do now. And I don't expect to need your services again. This is a one-time thing for me too.'

'It had better be,' I say. 'For many reasons. But I'm not too worried. I don't see us all visiting Chez Colette any time soon.'

Her eyes are momentarily wistful. 'They were lovely champagne truffles.'

'Better a life of marshmallows with the man of your dreams than a lifetime of truffles with the woman you tortured for an entire afternoon with your horrible indecision.'

Isabella sighs. 'That's beautiful. Which of your philosophers said that?'

'Epicurus. He talked a lot about desserts. I quoted him in my final paper.'

'I never know when you're being serious. Were there really Greek philosophers who talked about desserts?'

'You'll have to take the course and find out. I've already forgotten most of what we studied, and I intend to keep it that way.'

'Good,' she says. 'From now on, I want your mind on my wedding. If you think you've been busy up until now, that's nothing to what I have in store for you over the next few weeks. There's still so much to do. I've made you a list.'

She hands me a piece of paper, and I study it for a minute. 'No problem. I can manage all these things. And my dress is almost finished. Angela says I only need two more fittings. I can't believe she's making all four of our dresses.'

'Angela Carson is a talented woman,' she says. 'I want to be just like her when I grow up.'

'Isn't it a little late for that? Getting married is a very grown-up thing to do.'

'I suppose it is,' she agrees. 'But I don't always feel very grown-up. I still can't fold a fitted sheet or cook rice without close supervision.'

'You can do lots of other things,' I console her. 'There are plenty of different ways of being an adult, and you're good at all of those. You show up for people. You're kind to them, even when it's inconvenient. You know when someone needs a cup of tea and when they need to be left alone. You apologise when you're wrong, and you keep secrets when you're asked to.'

'Really?' she asks. 'I do all of those things?'

'You do. I forgot to add that you notice when someone's struggling and you do something about it. That counts for a lot. I think we both know we wouldn't be sitting here today if it hadn't been for you.'

She's quiet for a moment, looking down at her hands. 'I didn't realise I made that much difference to anyone.'

'You do to me,' I say. 'And to lots of other people. You'd be surprised if you knew how many. And that's far more important than owning matching towels or having a favourite brand of washing-up liquid.'

'Thanks, Georgie. That means more than I can say.'

'Again, it's a one-time thing,' I warn her. 'I'm feeling sentimental because you're paying for my meal. Don't forget you're buying me dinner again in the middle of August. I hear it's going to be a good one!'

She nods, and I'm pleased to see the look of strain has left her face. 'It will be a great day, won't it?'

'The very best day of your life,' I assure her. 'Even one hundred Chloes couldn't ruin it!'

Chapter Forty-Three

Isabella wasn't joking when she said she planned to keep me busy until the wedding day. The final few weeks fly by in a whirl of seating charts, gift bags, place settings and dress fittings. On one particularly memorable day, I find myself drawn into a discussion about chair covers.

'How did I stoop so low as to allow you to drag me into a debate about striped versus plain fabrics?' I ask Isabella. 'Why does it matter what the guests sit on to eat their meals, as long as the food is good?'

She gives me a hunted look. 'It just does! Chloe messaged this morning to demand an answer by lunchtime, and I don't know what to tell her. I seem to have lost the ability to make any kind of decision.'

I pick up her phone and read Chloe's text. 'Is she always this abrupt?'

'She wants everything to be perfect.'

'She's a control freak. Someone should have put her in her place long ago.'

I quickly type a message.

Isabella: Chloe – I need you to do your job and make all these minor decisions by yourself. I have far more important things to be getting on with. Please don't

> *refer any but the most urgent queries to me from now on. Regards, Isabella.*

I hit send and switch off the phone. 'You should have done this from day one. Now, I want you to forget all about satin chairs and tell me what you'd like for lunch. If that's too big a decision for you at the moment, I'll choose for you.'

She smiles. 'Thanks, Georgia. You always help me keep things in proportion.'

'You helped me when I was stressing over my exams. I'm just returning the favour.'

'I'll do the same for you when it's your turn,' she tells me.

'If I ever do something as bizarre as getting married, no one will know anything about it until at least my tenth wedding anniversary. Even then, only if the witnesses are threatening to go public and leak it to the press.'

'Who do you plan to marry?' she asks with interest. 'The paparazzi are unlikely to be interested unless it's someone who's appeared on at least two reality television shows or gone viral for rescuing a celebrity's cat from a tree.'

'I'm not planning to marry anyone. But if I do, it won't be anyone stupid enough to climb up a tree after a cat. Everyone knows you should leave some food at the foot of the tree, and they'll come down when they're ready.'

'Much like you?' she asks.

'I'm happy for people to leave food out for me, but I rarely climb trees these days. I'm not as young as I used to be. Although it's a comfort to remember you'll always be a few years older than me. It may be a good thing you're getting married now, before you're too decrepit to walk down the aisle by yourself.'

I heat up a couple of quiches and put them on a plate for her. 'There you go. Decision made for you! Let's hope Chloe has finally got the message and leaves you alone until the wedding day.'

And, for a while, it appears that she has. Isabella shows me a few texts telling her that Chloe has put in the final orders for wedding favours and run the requested playlist past the band. But she doesn't ask Isabella to make any further decisions, and I start to hope we'll get safely to the big day with no more fuss and stress. Isabella seems a lot calmer these days, and I'm anxious that nothing disturbs that.

Which makes it all the more surprising when Isabella's phone rings four days before the wedding, and Chloe's name flashes up. Isabella's in the kitchen, so I answer it for her.

'Hi, this is Isabella Campbell's number.'

'Who's that?' says an agitated voice.

'Her sister Georgia.'

'Is Isabella there?'

'I'm not sure,' I say cautiously. 'Is this Chloe?'

'Yes. I need to speak to her at once!'

'Can you tell me what this is about?'

'No.'

'Then I'm not sure I can help you. You've already caused my sister enough anxiety for ten weddings. Why don't you tell me what's going on, and I'll decide whether I can assist you?'

Chloe's voice is filled with barely controlled panic. 'I have to talk to her in person.'

'If it's about the seating chart,' I say, 'we're all quite happy with it. Likewise, the flowers and the menu. And you're supposed to be dealing with my parents about the champagne.'

'You don't understand!' she says in a frantic tone. 'I must speak to Isabella directly. I've called Jon, but he isn't answering. There isn't a moment to be lost.'

She clearly isn't giving up, so I decide I'd better call Isabella.

'I'll hand you over to her,' I tell Chloe. 'But if this is about the calligraphy on the place cards or a discussion about changing the hashtags on your website for the seventeenth time, I'll block your number entirely.'

I open the kitchen door. 'Isabella – phone call for you!'

'Can't it wait?' she asks. 'Abby's invited me in here to conduct a most important taste test. She's about to debut her new line of savoury choux pastries, and she needs an expert opinion.'

'I'm afraid it can't. It's Chloe, and she seems to think it's urgent. I expect she wants to discuss a missing catering invoice or the most recent trends in napkin colours. But she insists on speaking to you personally, so it may be best to get it over with.'

'I'll be right back,' she tells Abby. 'Don't make any final decisions about these pastries without my input.'

'This, you can make decisions about?' I ask, handing her the phone.

She pulls a face at me. 'Hi, Chloe! I'm right in the middle of something important. Can we make it quick?'

She listens for a moment, as though unable to believe what she's hearing. She glances at me and Abby before saying in a choked voice, 'One second. I'll take this in my office.'

Abby gives me a worried look. 'What do you think all that's about?'

'I assumed it was some ridiculous question about cake forks or how long the speeches should be. I wouldn't put it past Chloe to stand in the background, holding a stopwatch and shooting daggers – or even BB pellets – at anyone who dares to go two seconds over their allotted time.'

'Those things wouldn't make Isabella look like that,' says Abby. 'She turned quite pale.'

I bite my lip. 'I know. You don't suppose it's something really awful?'

'I hope not, but it sounds as though it's quite serious. Should we go and find out?'

'Give her a minute,' I say. 'We don't know how long the call will take, and I don't want Isabella to think we're trying to listen in to it.'

We wait in silence for five minutes. At last, I can stand it no longer.

'I'll see what's happening,' I tell Abby. 'I'll call you if I need anything.'

She nods and returns to her baking. At any other time, I'd be tempted to demand she include me in the taste-testing team. But

I have a sinking feeling in my stomach, and my appetite has disappeared.

I walk quietly out of the kitchen and through the shop. There's no sound from the office, but there's no sign of Isabella either. Can she have rushed off to sort out whatever crisis Chloe has discovered – or more likely manufactured? It seems unlikely. I didn't hear the shop bell ring.

Several of the Silver Surfers are sitting at a table near the door.

'Did Isabella come through here a few minutes ago?' I ask Phyllis.

'Not that I noticed. Did you see her, Edie?'

Mrs Ogilvie shakes her head. 'I think she went into the kitchen.'

'Is something wrong?' asks Mabel. 'I'd ask whether the mutt has been causing trouble, but for once in his life he has an alibi. He's fast asleep under this table.'

'And he never causes trouble,' says Mrs Ogilvie. 'I've been meaning to ask you about the winning competition entry, Georgia. Have you thought about –?'

'I'm so sorry to interrupt you,' I say, 'but this is rather urgent. Isabella definitely hasn't left the shop?'

'We'd have seen her if she had,' says Mabel. 'And the mutt would have woken up and made his usual fuss. He has a ridiculously short memory, and he's convinced that whenever someone leaves a room, that's the last he'll see of them. So, he has to make his feelings clear by barking at the top of his lungs.'

'Thanks,' I say before Mrs Ogilvie can protest that Bernie almost never barks, and he has the longest memory of any dog she's ever met. 'I'll be right back.'

I tap gently on Isabella's office door. When there's no answer, I open it a crack and peep in. She's no longer on the phone. Instead, she's staring blankly at the wall, her face paler than ever.

I slip inside and close the door behind me. 'Isabella?'

It takes her a moment to realise I'm there. When she does, she doesn't speak – just looks at me. To my horror, I see tears sliding down her cheeks.

I kneel next to her. 'Issy? What's wrong? You can tell me. Is it Jon?'

She shakes her head.

'What, then?' I ask.

She swallows hard. 'That was Chloe.'

'I know. I answered the call. If she's said something to upset you, I'm driving over to that stupid hotel right now to demand her head on a plate. If that doesn't work, I'll fire her myself, even if I have to print myself a manager's badge to do it.'

Isabella pulls out a tissue and wipes her eyes. It doesn't help. Her tears are falling faster than ever, and the tissue is soon soaked.

I take it from her and hand her a new one. 'What is it, Issy?'

She gives another choking sob. 'It's Willowmere Hall!'

'What about it?'

She points to her phone as if the details of Chloe's call will magically appear on the screen and save her the trouble of answering. When it remains blank, she clears her throat and forces herself to speak.

'There's been some sort of gas leak. I didn't take it all in, but I heard enough to understand what Chloe was telling me.'

'A gas leak?' I ask. 'From an oven or something?'

'It's much, much worse than that. She said that an underground gas main ruptured in the hotel grounds last night and caused a minor explosion in the basement. It started a fire, which shorted out the electrics. The sprinkler system activated, and the fire brigade was called in. They put it out fairly quickly, but between the sprinklers and the fire hoses, there's been extensive water damage across all the lower floors.'

She takes a shaky breath. 'As if that wasn't enough, the explosion also damaged some of the old pipework. One of the main sewage lines cracked, and now there's some sort of backup. Environmental Health has been in and shut the place down. The hotel is closed until further notice. Chloe says it could take weeks.'

I stare blankly at her. 'It sounds like something out of a disaster movie. Were there asteroids involved too?'

I catch myself. This is not the time to be making jokes.

'I'm sorry,' I say, 'but it's almost unbelievable. No wonder Chloe was freaking out when she called. What are they planning to do – hold the wedding somewhere else?'

She reaches for the box of tissues again. 'There is nowhere else. Everywhere is booked up for the summer. No one can provide a venue for eighty people at three days' notice. I'd be surprised if they could provide one for eight people.'

'That can't be true,' I say. 'There's bound to be somewhere free. Maybe the hotel can provide the food for us, and we can transport it to a new venue.'

She shakes her head. 'Their kitchen is out of action. And Chloe's called everywhere she can think of. She says we're all out of options. I knew something would go wrong at the last moment. I just didn't expect it to be quite so catastrophic as this.'

'Does Jon know?' I ask.

'I called him as soon as I'd finished talking to Chloe. He's on his way over here, but there's nothing he can do. Chloe made it clear the hotel won't be available for the foreseeable future.'

She lifts her head from her arms and gives me a tragic look. 'It's nice that you want to help, but in this case, you can't. We both have to face it, Georgia – this wedding isn't going to happen!'

Chapter Forty-Four

Jon arrives ten minutes later. I point him towards the office and return to the bakery, thinking furiously. There must be some way we can persuade the hotel to honour its obligation to Isabella and Jon. Maybe they could put the tables outside on the lawn or hire a larger marquee. The weather forecast for Saturday is good, so it might not be too bad to have an entirely open-air wedding.

But Jon, when he returns from the office, disagrees.

'I called Chloe and had a long talk with her,' he says. 'She told me that members of the public aren't allowed in the grounds, let alone inside the hotel. I asked about holding the whole thing outside, but she said it wouldn't be possible. Their kitchen will be out of action for a while, so they won't be able to provide the food.'

I let out a long breath. 'So, we really are out of options?'

'I'm afraid so. I called the local register office. As you can imagine, it wasn't the first call they'd had today. Willowmere Hall has several weddings booked in the near future. The registrar was very nice, but she told me we'd have to start from scratch with the twenty-eight-day notice period if we wanted to be married there. The local vicar says he'd love to help us, but he can't legally do so. He's offered to do a pre-wedding blessing in the church if it helps, but Isabella doesn't seem keen. I can understand why. It's very kind of him, but it wouldn't be the real thing, and we'd still have to start all over again to get the knot properly tied.'

'So, what does Isabella want to do?' I ask.

'We haven't got that far. I've only just persuaded her to stop crying.'

'That's understandable,' I say. 'How about you? This is your wedding too. What do you want to do?'

'I want to marry Isabella. Other than that, I don't care. But I want her to have the wedding of her dreams. If that means waiting for Willowmere Hall to be rebuilt or repaired or relocated, that's what we'll do.'

'I wonder whether Isabella feels the same,' I say.

'I hope so! You don't think she's changed her mind about marrying me?'

I smile at him. 'You're safe there. I've rarely seen a couple so sickeningly in love. I was only talking about the hotel.'

'Isabella set her heart on it the minute we saw it,' he says.

'She said the same thing about you.'

He looks surprised. 'Really? I didn't care much either way. Willowmere Hall is a lovely place, but it's just a venue. The important thing is getting married, not where you hold the wedding. But I realise it's different for the bride.'

'Maybe. Do you think Isabella is up to talking to me yet?'

'She'll tell you if she isn't.'

'She usually does!' I agree. 'I'll take a chance and stick my head around the door and hope she doesn't throw something at me.'

Jon looks worried. 'Be gentle with her. She isn't in a great state. I'll take her home as soon as she feels up to it. She should have something to eat and lie down for a while. Then we can talk about how to handle all the arrangements.'

'I won't stay long,' I promise.

Isabella is sitting at her desk when I enter the office. She's still pale, but she looks much calmer than she did earlier.

'I've come to find out how you're doing,' I say.

'Surprisingly badly.'

'I'm sorry. That was a ridiculous question. I should have said I came to talk about your options.'

She wipes her eyes. 'That won't take long. We don't appear to have any.'

'The range is more limited than I'd like, but we shouldn't give up hope yet.'

'We don't have time to do anything but cancel,' she says. 'I have eighty people who need to know at once their presence is no longer required at the wedding of Isabella Campbell and Jon Peters.'

'Mum and I can take care of all that. How do you feel about waiting until Willowmere Hall has been declared fit for purpose again?'

'Chloe told me we'll be at the top of the list when that happens. She couldn't say when that would be, but she's promised we'll be their first booking the minute they re-open.'

'That's nice of her,' I say. 'To be fair, there's not a lot else she can offer. Much though I hate to admit it, none of this is her fault.'

She blows her nose. 'Chloe may have decided I'm such a difficult bride that her only option was to puncture the gas pipe. She may not have realised the extent of the damage it would cause.'

'You're a lovely bride!' I say. 'She doesn't deserve you, and she never did. I think we can rule out deliberate sabotage on her part. What I'd like to know is whether you want her to continue to organise your wedding at all.'

'Who else would do it?' she asks.

'Let me rephrase that. Is Willowmere Hall really the venue of your dreams? It's fine if it is. I just need to know.'

'I think so,' she says. 'And I'm very sure it's the venue of Jon's dreams. He was really keen to book it, and he was so excited when everything fell into place. When they called to offer us the booking, he was over the moon. He said it was clearly meant to be.'

'And you agreed with him?'

'I did at the time.'

'And now?' I prompt her.

Isabella wrinkles her brow. 'I'm not sure what you're saying.'

I perch on the edge of her desk. 'I'm asking how you feel about it all – something I think you may have forgotten about when you were in such a hurry to book it. You assumed it was what Jon wanted, and he assumed it was what you wanted. Neither of you seems to have realised that you both thought it was the place of the other one's dreams.'

She's silent for a moment while she considers this.

'You may be right,' she says at last. 'Willowmere Hall is lovely, but it's all felt a little surreal over the past few months – as though someone else is getting married there, not me.'

'That's the impression I've gained. But you didn't want me to mention it, so I tried not to.'

'It was too late,' she says. 'We'd paid almost half the costs upfront. That's an awful lot of money to lose when the most likely explanation is pre-wedding jitters.'

'All I need to know is what you want, rather than what anyone else wants. This is about you, Isabella. Don't overthink it. Deep down, you know what you'd like to do.'

'I want to marry Jon,' she says. 'I don't care about all that other stuff.'

'Good decision! But first of all, would you like me to take over and sort all this out for you?'

She frowns. 'You mean you'll cancel the arrangements?'

'That's right. You and Jon won't have to do a thing. I'll cancel the guests, arrange for the hotel to give you a full refund, and liaise with Chloe to undo everything. You can go away for a few days if you like. I'll even make a reservation for you if you can't decide where. Once you get back, and you're feeling a little better, you can decide when and where you want to book a new wedding and exactly how you want to arrange it. I know I told you this was a one-shot deal, but circumstances alter cases. I'll be there for your actual wedding, no matter when it is.'

Isabella lets out a long sigh. 'Would you really sort out the cancellations? I don't think I can face it. I feel like one of those brides in the movies who've been dumped at the altar. I realise that's not what's happening here, but it feels horribly similar.'

She gives me a shaky smile. Her face is still swollen with crying, but she seems much calmer. Despite her reddened eyes and blotchy cheeks, she looks far more like the Isabella I remember from before this whole wedding business began.

'Jon will take you home now,' I say. 'Abby and I can close up here. I'll drive over to your flat after work and you can give me any last-minute instructions that occur to you. After that, I want you to put the whole thing out of your mind. Go away for a few days and spend some time relaxing with the love of your life. If that doesn't put things into perspective for you both, nothing will.'

Her eyes fill with tears again. 'Thanks, Georgia. I don't know what I've done to deserve you.'

'Many people have said that over the years, although I'm not quite sure they meant the same thing.'

Jon taps on the door. 'Your ride awaits.'

He looks relieved when Isabella smiles back at him. It may not be quite her old sunny smile, but she's less tearful and more composed than I expected.

'I'm fine,' she says in answer to his unspoken question. 'Worse things happen at sea.'

'They do when you're in charge of the steering,' I say. 'Take her home, Jon. I'll be over as soon as we've closed up.'

He gives me a grateful look and steers Isabella towards the door. I follow them out and notice the remaining customers looking curiously at their departing backs. I step in front of their table to shield Isabella from view.

'Is everything alright?' Phyllis asks in a sympathetic voice.

'Not really,' I say. 'But it will be.'

'What can we do to help?' asks Mabel.

'It's kind of you to offer, but there's nothing anyone can do.'

'That's almost never true,' she says. 'However, I can see you don't want me interfering, so I'll break the rule of a lifetime and keep my nose out of things.'

'It isn't that,' I say. 'But there isn't a lot you could do. Isabella's wedding has been cancelled. The hotel has exploded.'

Ivy gives a gasp of horror. 'Exploded?'

'A gas leak,' I hasten to explain. 'But it feels like a game of dominoes.'

'You aren't making things any clearer,' says Mrs Ogilvie. 'What do dominoes have to do with Isabella's wedding?'

'Sorry,' I say. 'My mind's in a bit of a whirl. I was referring to people setting up hundreds of dominoes in a row, then knocking the first one down and watching the rest of them topple over. From what I can gather, there was a gas explosion, which led to an electrical fire, which led to the sprinklers going off and causing water damage. Then there was something about the drains, just to add to the confusion.'

'That's terrible,' says Phyllis. 'Was anyone hurt?'

'Apparently, everyone was safely evacuated, and the only damage was to the building.'

'That's the most important thing,' says Ivy. 'But poor Isabella. She must be devastated.'

'She was when she first heard about it. She was surprisingly calm by the time she left. I'll go over and see her as soon as we close.'

Ivy gestures to the other three, who jump to their feet.

'You'll go and see her now,' she tells me, walking over and turning the sign on the door to Closed. 'We're leaving, aren't we, girls?'

'You still have almost another hour to finish your food,' I say.

'Don't be ridiculous,' says Mabel. 'You need to help Isabella. You can give us doggy bags if you must, although please don't call them that. I don't want the mutt getting the wrong idea. He already has enough trouble distinguishing between the words yours and mine.'

She gives me a friendly nod. 'Please call on us at any time. We're free agents, and we're very fond of you and Isabella.'

The rest of the Silver Surfers nod their agreement.

'That means a lot,' I say. 'I don't think there's much any of us can do about what's happened. But if something occurs to me, I'll know exactly who to call.'

Chapter Forty-Five

I find Isabella packing a bag when I arrive at her flat half an hour later.

'We're taking your advice and going away for a couple of nights,' Jon tells me. 'If you're serious about your offer to dismantle what's left of our wedding?'

'No problem,' I say. 'It won't take us long, and I'll make sure Chloe does her fair share of the work. You two should have some time to yourselves. I'd tell you to relax, but I try not to hand out advice I know I wouldn't be able to take.'

'I think I will,' says Isabella. 'I was distraught when I first found out about what had happened. But I'm all cried out now, and I feel surprisingly calm. We're going back to Fernwood. Jon called and booked us a cabin for the next three nights.'

'I may try to extend it over the weekend,' he says. 'It won't do either of us any good to be here on what ought to have been our wedding day.'

'I agree,' I say. 'Far better to spend the day climbing along those terrifying-looking ropes they've strung between the trees than sitting around here thinking of what might have been.'

'We wanted you all to try those ropes,' says Isabella. 'But Ali hates heights, and she wasn't too keen on the idea of the boys being let loose on some of the more difficult ones. So, we did the raft building thing instead.'

'I'm glad you did,' I say. 'I still have my homemade medal.'

'So does Michael,' says Jon. 'He was wearing it around his neck the last time we met.'

'Does he know about any of this?' I ask.

'Not yet. I'll call him tonight. Unless you'd prefer to do it?'

'You know Michael better than me,' I say. 'I'll leave that one to you.'

'Aren't you in touch with him at all?' he asks.

'Not since the hen weekend. I half expected to bump into him at some point, but I've been too busy to think much about it. I imagined I'd see him on the wedding day, if not before.'

I catch Isabella's eye and grimace. 'Sorry, I shouldn't have mentioned your wedding.'

'Don't be silly,' she says. 'It's all anyone will be talking about for the next few days.'

I nod. 'All the more reason for you and Jon not to be here. Don't let me hold you up. You should try to reach Fernwood before dark. You know what your night driving is like.'

Jon waves his keys at me. 'All taken care of. The only thing Isabella needs to decide is whether we should stop somewhere for dinner on the way or get ourselves something when we arrive.'

'That's easy,' I say. 'I thought you knew her by now. Both.'

Isabella is looking more cheerful. 'I am quite hungry.'

Jon closes the flat door and hands me the key. 'Just in case there's an emergency. Do you mind?'

I slip it into my pocket. 'Not at all. Although we've had enough gas leaks and water damage to last us a lifetime.'

'Bad luck is supposed to come in threes,' says Isabella.

'Not this time,' I say more confidently than I feel. 'What happened at Willowmere Hall is your share of bad luck for the next few decades. Everything will go perfectly for you both from now on. You'll see.'

She gives me a watery smile. 'What would I do without you?'

'You'd cope just fine. You're a capable, confident woman. But why manage alone when you don't have to? I'm here, and I'm eager to make myself useful, so please don't stand in my way. It isn't an impulse that strikes very often, and it would be a pity to squash it.'

Jon gives me a quick hug. 'I'm looking forward to having you as a sister-in-law. I'm just not sure when.'

'Willowmere Hall will have everything fixed up in a few weeks,' I say. 'You'll be top of the list – if that's what you both still want.'

He glances at Isabella, who shrugs. 'I'm past knowing what I want. I'll think about it when we get back.'

I watch them drive away, then run upstairs to retrieve as much wedding paperwork as possible. Some of it may be at the bakery, but Isabella probably keeps most of it here. Despite her ditzy manner, she can be organised and efficient when things are important to her. I decide to start by making a list of all the telephone numbers she has on file. I'll begin with the suppliers in case Chloe hasn't got around to contacting them yet. Then I'll move on to the guest list.

Mum is finishing cooking dinner when I get home.

'I thought you wouldn't be long,' she greets me.

'I was at Isabella's flat. They've just left for Fernwood. Did she call you?'

'She did. What a dreadful thing to have happened! I wanted to go straight over there, but Isabella said she'd prefer to slip away quietly. She thought if she saw me, she might start crying again, and she didn't want to do that.'

'She didn't cry when she saw me!' I say, trying to sound offended. 'She seemed remarkably calm and resigned about the whole thing.'

'She'll be alright,' says Mum. 'She's far tougher than most people give her credit for. You both are. By this time next year, she'll barely remember it.'

I pull off my jacket and sink into a chair. 'That may be a little over-optimistic. Isabella hasn't just received a call to say the flowers she's set her heart on are out of season. Her entire wedding venue has exploded and is now nothing more than a heap of rubble.'

'The local news said there was no external damage,' says Mum. 'But I know how you girls like to exaggerate.'

'It's the internal part that's important. There's no functioning kitchen, which means no food. People aren't even allowed inside to use the restrooms. The fact that the exterior brickwork is still intact is neither here nor there as far as Isabella and Jon are concerned.'

She nods. 'Isabella told me they can't move the venue at short notice.'

'That was the first thing I asked her. I suppose it makes sense for the authorities to insist that marriage banns are announced in church or the notice of intent to marry is displayed in the register office. I looked it up, and it's designed to stop people marrying bigamously.'

'Like Jane Eyre?' she asks.

'Exactly, although there isn't much we can do if Jon has his first wife secretly locked in an upstairs bedroom. It isn't likely or the boys would have noticed her when they stayed over at his house. But if you secretly move your wedding venue at the last minute, it doesn't give the public the opportunity to jump up and object at the relevant moment.'

'Do you think anyone was planning to do that?' she asks.

'It's difficult to say. Who knows what dark pasts Isabella or Jon may be concealing? I admit it doesn't seem likely, but the fact remains they can't suddenly switch venues without renewing the notice of intention.'

'It's such a shame,' says Mum. 'Isabella says they can re-book Willowmere Hall after the repairs have been done.'

'She said the same thing to me, but she didn't appear too enthusiastic about the idea.'

'That's understandable,' she says. 'She's just had the bottom knocked out of her world. We can't expect her to be planning her new wedding quite yet.'

'I wonder whether she'll stick with Willowmere Hall when she does? They've offered her a full refund, so she may choose to be married somewhere else.'

Mum looks surprised. 'I hadn't thought of that.'

'I don't think this is the wedding she'd have chosen if she'd known how it would turn out,' I say. 'I won't call what's happened a silver lining, but some good may yet come out of it.'

She sighs. 'I don't think Isabella will see it like that. She told me when she called that she wished they'd just booked a register office from the start, because they almost never blow up, and at least she and Jon would have been married this weekend.'

'Did she?' I say. 'I wonder –'

I break off and stare out of the window, my mind working furiously.

'I'm not sure I like that look,' says Mum. 'What are you up to?'

I turn and smile at her. 'Possibly nothing. Possibly something. Could you plate me up some dinner and stick it in the fridge for later? There's someone I have to see as quickly as possible.'

'It's almost ready,' she says. 'Can't it wait half an hour?'

I shake my head regretfully. 'I wish it could. That moussaka smells delicious. But I need to go. I've had an idea, and there's not a minute to lose.'

Chapter Forty-Six

By Friday evening, I feel completely wiped out. I feel as though I've run several marathons, followed by making a surprise guest appearance in the Ironwoman Triathlon. I prop my chin on my hands, running over everything in my head for the hundredth time and trying to spot the flaws. I can't think of any, but I'm so tired that it's quite possible I've overlooked some glaring omission.

'Go home and get some sleep,' Lily tells me. 'Or you won't be fit for anything by tomorrow morning.'

'I don't want to waste precious time sleeping. It may make the difference between things running smoothly and some enormous error that ruins everything.'

'Nothing will be ruined,' she says. 'You've made sure of that. We all have.'

I fold my arms on the table and rest my head on them. 'Are you sure?'

'Perfectly sure. Would you like to stay here tonight? I could leave you where you are and throw a quilt over you.'

I look up at her hopefully. 'Would you?'

'No, because it wouldn't be good for you. Jack can drive you home if you're too tired.'

I push myself to my feet. 'I'll be fine, but thanks for the offer. Do you have all the lists? I've printed them off in triplicate. If one of us loses them, we'll still have two copies.'

'I have the lists,' she says. 'Not that they're needed. I've memorised everything. We've gone over it all a hundred times. I also have two children who will be waking up in about six hours' time, demanding their breakfast.'

'I'm going! I'll call you first tomorrow morning.'

'Isn't that a delightful thought?' she says. 'Don't hesitate to send me eighty-seven texts during the night if something occurs to you that has to be shared at once.'

'I won't. Are you sure –?'

'Get out of here!' she says, marching me to the front door and practically throwing me out onto the driveway.

I adopt my best Arnold Schwarzenegger pose. 'I'll be back!'

'Not if I've moved house in the meantime. Go home and get some rest!'

She closes the door and switches out the porch light. I climb into my car and briefly weigh up the merits of reclining the seat and spending the night on Lily's driveway. It would mean I was on the spot when their household woke up. But I would also risk tying several knots in my spine and being unable to walk for the next few days. I heave a sigh, turn the key in the ignition, and set off for Little Compton.

The birds do their very best to wake me early the following morning. Possibly, they believe I'm Cinderella, and they have a duty to help me perform those basic tasks most adults should know how to do by themselves. But I'm way ahead of them. I've been awake since dawn. I throw back my quilt and jump out of bed.

'You're welcome to make my bed for me,' I tell the sparrow sitting on my windowsill. He's obviously not a properly trained Disney bird because he gives me a disdainful look and flies away.

Mum is already downstairs when I arrive.

'I'm making bacon sandwiches,' she says. 'I insist on your eating at least one.'

'Fine, but strictly under protest,' I say, taking the largest one.

She watches me. 'Mind you finish that! I've been alarmed by the number of meals you've skipped over the past three days.'

'I've alarmed myself,' I admit. 'I didn't realise it was possible to go for so long without eating. I promise I'll make up for it when all this is over.'

'What's first on the list?' she asks, sitting down and pouring us both a cup of coffee.

'Making sure that Isabella arrives here on time. I've put Jon in charge of delivering her to our house at nine o'clock, but I'm prepared to drive over and collect her myself if there's any doubt.'

'There won't be,' says Mum. 'When Jon promises to do something, he does it.'

'But this is Isabella we're talking about. She may take it into her head to wander off somewhere without warning. Jon told me she was extremely disappointed when he had to tell her there were no cabins available at Fernwood last night. She wanted him to hire a tent instead. Sadly, there were no pitches available.'

'How did you manage that?' asks Mum.

'I drove over and talked to the manager myself. She seemed quite amused by the whole thing and promised to personally throw Isabella off the site if she didn't leave at the specified time. Jon called yesterday evening to say they'd arrived home. He said Isabella had a mild wobble when she realised they should have been setting out for the rehearsal dinner at that time, but he suggested they ordered themselves some pizza. He even made up a fictional three-for-the-price-of-one deal. I can't believe Isabella fell for that. She's memorised every takeaway menu in the area, and she's more than aware of what deals they offer and on which days.'

'Maybe her mind was elsewhere,' says Mum.

'It was stuck on the subject of stuffed crust versus thin and crispy. Anyway, she ate enough pizza to put most people in hospital, told Jon she was exhausted, and went to bed early.'

'She should be feeling well rested this morning,' she says.

'It sounds as though she's doing much better,' I agree. 'Jon messaged me half an hour ago to say she'd eaten some porridge. But it might be an idea to have something waiting for her after their strenuous half hour drive over here.'

'I've made plenty of bacon sandwiches,' says Mum. 'Jon will need something too.'

There's a ring at the front door, and I lay down my sandwich. 'I'll go!'

I pad along the hall and open the door. Isabella and Jon are standing on the doorstep.

'You look much better!' I greet her. 'How are you feeling?'

'I'm fine. What's this emergency that couldn't wait? I was worried you had a gas leak too, but the outside of the house looks fine.'

They follow me into the kitchen, where Mum lays down the spatula and hugs them both.

'Sit down!' she instructs them. 'You must be hungry.'

Isabella's eyes light up. 'I smell bacon sandwiches! This feels like old times. Has Georgia eaten them all?'

'Mum's made plenty for us all,' I tell her.

'I won't say no to a bacon sandwich,' says Jon. 'Isabella didn't leave me much porridge this morning.'

'You snooze, you lose!' she says, handing him a plate. 'How did you get on with the cancellations, Georgia? I'm sorry I disappeared like that. I wanted to come home and help, but Jon insisted you had it all in hand. He said he'd called, and you told him that between you and Chloe everything had been covered. I hope you know how grateful I am.'

'It was my pleasure,' I say. 'Lily and Abby helped too. And Mum and Dad, of course. Between the five of us, we managed to get it all sorted.'

'I don't know how to thank you,' she says. 'Did you contact all the guests?'

'Every last one of them.'

'Were they upset?'

'Not at all,' says Mum. 'Everyone was concerned for you, not themselves. They all sent their love.'

'That's kind of them,' says Isabella. 'But this must have ruined all their arrangements. Some of our guests were supposed to arrive yesterday, and they had their accommodation booked.'

'It's all sorted,' I say again. 'Don't give it another thought.'

She finishes her sandwich. 'So, what's this big emergency? Jon told me you called him this morning and insisted we came over as soon as possible. But everything seems fine.'

'It is,' I say. 'But I needed to see you. There's something I have to talk to you about.'

'Does it have to be right now?' she asks. 'I don't want to make too much fuss, but today was supposed to be my wedding day.'

'That's why I asked you to come over here this morning. It still could be.'

She lays down her second bacon sandwich. 'What are you talking about?'

'I told you we'd cancelled everything,' I say. 'But we haven't. There is no emergency, but I knew you wouldn't agree to see any of us today unless we pretended there was.'

There's a long silence.

'You didn't cancel the wedding?' she asks at last.

'That's right. I wanted to talk to you this morning and let you make the decision. Do you still want it to go ahead? Say the word, and we'll make it happen.'

Isabella gives me a stunned look. 'I can get married today?'

'That's right,' I say. 'But only if you want to.'

Chapter Forty-Seven

The silence stretches out for what seems like hours. I don't dare look at Mum or Jon. I can't bear to see their looks of disappointment if it turns out I've got this wrong. I'll feel disappointed enough in myself without any extra encouragement. Things have been so hectic over the past few days that I haven't had time to stop and think about anything except my plan. And I've dragged Lily and Abby – and goodness knows who else – into it. What was I thinking?

I glance at Jon. He looks the same as he always has – solid, dependable, and slightly amused. I feel a rush of relief to realise that, no matter how things go today, Isabella still has him on her team.

Mum is watching Isabella with the same expression she always wears when she looks at either of us. It's a mixture of affection and warmth, occasionally tinged with amusement or faint exasperation. I've always depended on her being there, looking at us both in just that way. It tells us there's someone in our lives who will never let us down. Dad is quieter and far less chatty, but I know there's nothing he wouldn't do for us either. Isabella and I are far luckier than we realise.

Isabella swallows hard and turns to face me. 'Am I dreaming, or did you just say Jon and I can be married today?'

'That's right,' I say. 'But it's up to you. No one expects you to do anything you don't want to. One word from you, and I'll cancel all the arrangements. You can plan another wedding at the time and place of your choosing.'

'Did you know about this?' she asks Jon.

He smiles at her affectionately. 'I did. We wanted to offer you as many options as possible and allow you to make the final decision. But Georgia's right – one word from you, and none of this needs to happen. This is your wedding, and I want it to be right for you. I don't care when or where it takes place, as long as I end up married to you.'

Isabella turns to Mum. 'You knew about this too?'

'To save time,' I say, 'you can assume everyone in our family knows about this. And a few other people too. But that isn't important. The only thing that matters right now is what you'd like to do. I hate to press you, but we have less than five hours, so we'll need a decision either way.'

'But how can we possibly –?' she begins.

'Don't worry about that. Just tell us what you want.'

She turns back to Jon, who's looking at her with an expression that makes my heart turn over.

'Is this ok with you?' she asks.

He kneels down next to her chair and takes her hand. 'I want to marry you, Isabella. I don't care whether that's in a hot-air balloon or down a coal mine. But I want us both to look back on our wedding day as one of the happiest days of our lives. So, whatever we decide to do needs to be right for both of us.'

Isabella gives a tiny gasp, then flings herself into his arms. 'I can't believe it! We're getting married today!'

'Please don't start crying!' I beg her, although I'm so relieved I almost burst into tears myself. 'I don't allow my brides to walk down the aisle with red eyes.'

She lifts a radiant face to me. 'I'm not crying. But what aisle? Tell me what's going on!'

I assume my best wedding co-ordinator expression. 'I believe it's best if you don't think too much about the details. Allow me to do my job while you do yours.'

'Which is?' she asks.

'To obey all my instructions without question and get married to the love of your life.'

'I can do that!' she says. 'Just tell me what you want me to do.'

Jon drops a kiss on the top of her head. 'I have to go now, but I'll leave you in Georgia's more than capable hands.'

Isabella nods, the familiar look of mischief returning to her eyes. 'I thought you weren't supposed to see me on the morning of my wedding day?'

'That breach of protocol was inevitable,' I say. 'I can assure you there will be no further deviations. Off you go, Jon! We'll meet you there at two o'clock. Don't be late!'

'Meet him where?' demands Isabella, but I only shake my head as I shepherd her towards the stairs.

'Have you had a shower this morning?' I ask.

'I have. I even washed my hair!'

I look at my watch. 'That gives us an extra half hour to play with. I'll call Lily and let her know.'

'Lily is in on this too?'

'I'm afraid so. I wouldn't have mentioned that if you'd decided against going ahead today. I told her I'd take the entire blame. But yes, both Lily and Abby know.'

'Who else?' she asks as we reach the top of the stairs and I direct her towards her old bedroom.

'That doesn't concern you right now. What did I tell you only three minutes ago about obeying instructions and keeping questions to a minimum? I hope you aren't planning on being a difficult bride. I don't want a Bridezilla on my hands after all my hard work.'

'I'm sorry,' she says. 'It's just that I didn't expect to be a bride at all today, let alone a Bridezilla.'

I open her door and usher her inside. 'Welcome to the centre of operations!'

She stands stock-still, surveying the room. Her wedding dress is hanging on the far wall, with the other three dresses next to it. Her veil is draped over a chair. The air is lightly scented with vanilla and roses, and there's soft music playing in the background.

'This is exactly like –' she begins.

'Chez Colette? That's the general idea. You seemed to enjoy that afternoon so much, I thought you might like me to recreate it for you.'

'I did enjoy it,' she says. 'It was one of the best afternoons of my life. Now that I come to think about it, it's the last time I remember having fun making plans for my wedding. Things became more serious after that, and I felt as though I was walking through a minefield without instructions. I can't tell you how many times I've woken in the middle of the night, worrying about place settings and silverware.'

'I can imagine,' I say. 'It's been a lot of pressure for you. Chloe is sincerely sorry for that and will try to do better in future.'

'You've spoken to Chloe about it?' she asks.

'Once or twice. I felt someone should make her aware that her technique, although efficient, isn't calculated to put her more sensitive brides at ease.'

'Her brides!' says Isabella. 'Each time she called me that, it felt as though it was her wedding rather than mine. I should have spoken up earlier, but I was so overwhelmed by the number of things everyone expected from me that I didn't dare.'

I nod. 'The first thing people like Chloe need to learn at wedding co-ordinator school is that the aim of a wedding is for the bride and groom to get married. Everything else is just an added bonus – nice, but not strictly necessary. Understanding that might help them to calm down and relax their rules about matching the ribbon on the cake to the groom's tie or ensuring the vicar's socks are the regulation length.'

'Vicar?' she asks. 'I'm getting married in church?'

'It was a figure of speech. In this case, the vicar is entirely fictional.'

The doorbell rings. A minute later, we hear footsteps on the stairs.

'In here!' I call.

Lily appears, followed by Abby and Angela Carson.

'Perfect timing!' I say. 'Isabella is asking far too many questions.'

'What have you told her?' asks Abby.

'Nothing, except that we'll get her married today if it's the last thing we do.'

'Doesn't it look lovely in here?' asks Angela. 'It smells nice too.'

'It isn't quite Chez Colette,' I say. 'But it's as close as we could manage.'

'She had champagne truffles,' says Isabella, a reminiscent gleam in her eye.

I pick up a bowl from the bedside table and offer it to her. 'So have we. Help yourself. I don't want to upstage Colette too much, but we also have a bottle of real champagne. The glasses are over there, if someone would do the honours.'

'Shouldn't we keep clear heads?' asks Abby.

'I should,' I say. 'The rest of you can drink as much as you like. I've arranged for us to be chauffeured over there in style.'

'Wherever "there" turns out to be,' says Isabella.

'Just a small glass for me,' says Angela. 'I may have to make some last-minute adjustments to your dress, Isabella, and I'll need a steady hand.'

'You look very nice,' I tell her. 'That raspberry colour suits you. Did you make the dress yourself?'

She looks pleased. 'I did. It was our ruby wedding anniversary last year, and we held a lovely garden party to celebrate. I didn't think Isabella would mind my wearing it again today.'

'I wouldn't care if you wore your oldest pair of jeans,' says Isabella. 'I'm just happy you're here at all.'

'Jeans would have taken care of the something old and something blue in one go,' says Lily. 'You should have thought of that, Mum, before you got all dressed up.'

'As your wedding co-ordinator,' I say, 'I'm offended you don't believe I have all that in hand. My brides –'

Isabella groans, but I ignore her.

'My brides,' I continue, 'can rely on me to make sure everything is correct and as it should be – right down to the tiniest detail.'

Abby pulls a slip of paper out of her pocket and hands it to Isabella. 'The very first written warning you ever gave me. That counts as something old.'

Lily gives her a pink ribbon. 'Daisy's favourite hair ribbon. She wants you to tie it around your bouquet. That takes care of the something borrowed.'

I hand Isabella a small box wrapped in silver paper. 'And this is from Jon. It's something new and something blue in one fell swoop. I do like my grooms to be efficient.'

Isabella tears off the paper and opens the box inside. 'They're perfect!'

Lily leans past me to look. 'Sapphire earrings? Aren't they gorgeous? They exactly match the colour of your eyes!'

'I'm glad that's all sorted,' says Angela. 'I'm not superstitious, but it's nice to follow some of these old traditions. Now, let's get down to business. I'd planned to do a last-minute fitting of all your dresses yesterday, but Isabella wasn't here for hers.'

I pass Isabella a damp cloth. 'You've been eating truffles. I don't allow my brides to get chocolate all over their wedding dresses. Frankly, it's sloppy, and not the standard I expect from either them or me. It isn't as easy as you might think being a wedding co-ordinator, but there's no reason not to make an effort.'

Isabella pulls a face at me but obediently wipes her hands and mouth. 'What about the champagne?'

'I can't allow you to drink that once you're in your dress,' I say.

'I don't plan to. I'm going to drink it now. I'd like to propose a toast.'

She lifts her glass and looks around at us all. 'I don't know what my sister has forced you to do over the past few days, and this is not the time to ask. But I want to thank you all from the bottom of my heart. I can hardly believe this is happening.'

'Abby and I haven't done much at all,' says Lily. 'It was almost all Georgia.'

'Not true,' I say, 'but I'll let it pass. So, what should the toast be – to getting married?'

'To the best wedding day ever?' suggests Abby.

'To happily ever afters?' adds Lily.

'To the best friends a woman could ever hope for,' says Isabella. Her eyes soften as she turns to me. 'And to the very best sister.'

Everyone raises their glass and drinks.

I set down my glass and smile at Isabella. 'You once told me that no one would forget exactly where they were or what they were doing on the joyful day Isabella Campbell got married. It looks as though you were right, after all!'

Chapter Forty-Eight

By one o'clock, everyone is ready. I'm not sure how, but we are. Isabella is standing by the window in her wedding dress while I take a picture of her on my phone. The sunshine is streaming in and turning her curls a delicate pale gold. Angela, who should be nominated for a prize for all-round craftswoman of the year, has arranged Isabella's hair for her. She's swept it away from her face and fastened the veil with a circlet of white roses from Martin's garden. She's allowed the rest of Isabella's hair to fall in cascading waves behind her shoulders and left a few loose tendrils to frame her face.

I saw the finished wedding dress two days ago, but I hadn't anticipated quite how perfectly it would fit Isabella or how utterly beautiful she would look in it. She and Angela have selected an ivory silk, which exactly suits Isabella's creamy complexion. The dress is fitted through the bodice, with a sweetheart neckline and long sleeves, each one fastened at the wrist with a single row of silk-covered buttons. The skirt is softly pleated, yet heavy enough to fall in a graceful, unbroken line to the floor. Whenever Isabella moves, it flows around her like water.

Angela must have spent days on the delicate embroidery that traces the bodice and waist. She's stitched tiny roses in the same soft ivory as the dress and the flowers holding Isabella's veil in place. The hand-stitched flowers are almost invisible from a distance, but up close, they're mesmerising.

Lily catches her breath. 'I've never seen you look so beautiful.'

'That's because you usually see her wearing a tabard and covered with cake crumbs,' I say in an effort to hide my emotion.

'No, it isn't,' she says. 'There's something about her today that makes her look as though she's shining from the inside.'

'I haven't swallowed a light bulb, if that's what you're all thinking,' says Isabella.

Dad appears in the doorway and clears his throat. 'I wonder whether there might be time for Isabella to spend a few minutes with her parents?'

I look at my watch. 'I can give you seven minutes and forty-eight seconds. Make each one count.'

I follow the others onto the landing, where we let out a collective sigh of relief.

'I wasn't convinced we'd make it,' says Lily.

'Nor me,' says Abby. 'I didn't think Isabella would go for it at all.'

'I did,' I say. 'I think she realised when everything seemed to be cancelled that she wanted to marry Jon, not have the perfect wedding.'

'It seems to me she's about to have both those things,' says Angela. 'I can hardly believe what you three have achieved in such a short time.'

'We had a lot of help,' I say. 'Not least from you, Angela. You're an absolute genius. Isabella's dress is gorgeous, and so are ours.'

'Not that anyone will notice them when Isabella walks in,' says Lily. 'We may as well be wearing potato sacks.'

'Well, there's gratitude for you!' says her mother.

Lily laughs and kisses her cheek. 'You know what I mean. That wedding dress is sensational. You've made Isabella look exactly like herself, only more so.'

Angela gestures to the three of us. 'I wouldn't run yourselves down. The three of you look beautiful too.'

I have to agree she's done a great job. Our bridesmaids dresses are simple, yet beautifully crafted. I love the way the fabric drapes in smooth, clean lines, the softly scooped necklines, and the satin ribbons that tie neatly at the waist. The dresses are understated and elegant, and I was surprised to discover during our final fitting yesterday how well they suited us all.

'I'm impressed with what you've done with these,' I tell Angela. 'I always thought bridesmaids' dresses were flouncy and fussy.'

'Me too,' agrees Abby. 'And they're usually in colours that seem as though the bride has chosen them specifically to make her bridesmaids look as awful as possible. But you've found something that suits us all.'

'The colour helped,' says Lily. 'Georgia and I are fair-haired, and Abby is dark, but this gentian blue works for everyone.'

'Isabella was adamant you all had to look as good as she did,' says Angela. 'If there's one thing you can say about her, it's that she's generous.'

'She is very warm-hearted,' agrees Lily. 'I intended to hate her when we first met, but she made that impossible, and I gave up trying after five minutes.'

'And now she's fallen in love with Jon,' says Abby. 'I could never decide what sort of man would suit her. Then he came along, and it was obvious he was perfect for her.'

'Speaking of whom,' I say, 'he's just messaged to say he's arrived at the venue, and everything is on track.'

The bedroom door opens, and Isabella walks out, followed by Mum and Dad. I have no idea what was said in there, and I don't intend to ask. It's none of my business. But Mum's eyes are suspiciously damp, and even Dad looks a little choked up.

I hand Isabella a tissue and frown at her. 'My brides know better than to allow their mascara to run. Think of the pictures! I always say a wedding lasts for a day, but the photos hang around on the internet forever.'

'Do you expect to channel Chloe all day?' Lily asks me.

'I'm just getting the last of her out of my system. I've finished now.'

'No more "my brides do this"?' says Isabella.

'I promise. Are you ready to go?'

She hesitates. 'Is there time for a quick snack first?'

'No!' says Lily. 'Do you want to get married today or not?'

'I do!' says Isabella.

I run downstairs and turn to face everyone. Isabella takes Dad's arm, and they walk down the stairs together while I take several pictures with my phone.

'Your original photographer got himself a new booking the moment he heard about the catastrophe,' I say. 'But we'll do the best we can for you.'

Lily and Abby are travelling with Angela. I help Isabella into the back of Mum's car and carefully arrange her dress and veil. Then I climb in beside her and settle into my seat.

'Drive carefully!' I tell Mum. 'I don't trust Isabella not to have snacks in her pockets. I don't want you going too fast over a pothole and squashing them.'

'I don't have any snacks,' says Isabella. 'Although I would have brought some if I'd had more notice. What's the point of having lovely pockets in your wedding dress if you don't put anything in them?'

'You can put your hands in them if they're cold,' I say. 'And Abby's written warning. Nothing else.'

We wave to Angela, who trundles off down the drive at a snail's pace. She's obviously keen not to crush her passengers' dresses either.

'If she doesn't speed up a little, we'll be late,' I say. 'Sound your horn and overtake her if need be.'

'We have plenty of time,' Mum assures me. 'And I'll do no such thing. The Highway Code applies just as much on a wedding day as at any other time.'

'I'm not sure you're right,' says Isabella. 'Chloe would know, but unfortunately she isn't here to give us the benefit of her wisdom. Instead, we're stuck with a wedding co-ordinator who's mistaken today for a tactical invasion of a neighbouring county and prepared her military plans accordingly.'

'Georgia's done wonderfully,' says Mum. 'I'm lost in admiration for the way she's handled this whole thing.'

'As am I,' says Dad. 'You're lucky to have her, Isabella.'

Isabella smiles at me. 'She appears to have done an adequate job.'

'Turn left up there!' I tell Mum.

'I know,' she says. 'Dad has the map open on his phone in case of any diversions.'

'Should I be wearing a blindfold?' Isabella asks me.

'I thought about that, but I couldn't source an embroidered silk one at such short notice, and I'm determined everything should be co-ordinated on your big day.'

Mum turns off the main road into a smaller lane.

'Perhaps you should cover your eyes anyway,' I tell Isabella. 'It may as well be a surprise. What a pity I didn't think to hire a limo with blacked-out windows.'

'And you call yourself a wedding planner!' says Isabella, obediently closing her eyes.

'We're almost there,' says Dad ten minutes later. 'Just a few more minutes, unless a herd of cows wanders out into the road.'

'You'll have to drive through the fields if they do,' I say. 'This wedding needs to run like clockwork, or it won't be happening at all.'

'Don't say that!' says Isabella in a muffled voice.

'I told you to cover your eyes, not your entire face,' I tell her. 'Don't you listen to a word I say?'

'Not if I can help it.'

I sigh. 'I hope Jon has better luck at managing you than I've ever had. Although I don't hold out much hope.'

'Jon doesn't need to manage me,' she says. 'He's so lovely that it encourages me to be a better person.'

'You're fine as you are, but don't tell anyone I said so. It looks as though we're finally here. Are you planning to keep your hands over your eyes all day? If so, you run the risk of ending up married to the wrong person.'

Isabella doesn't move. 'Why am I suddenly scared?'

'Because you're taking a leap of faith,' I tell her. 'Most people have a similar reaction when their life is about to change forever.'

Lily walks over and opens the car door. 'You made it! What's going on with Isabella?'

'Last minute wedding jitters,' I say. 'I hear it's very common with brides. I can give her ten seconds, but no more.'

Isabella takes a deep breath and lowers her hands.

She looks out of her window. 'But this is –'

'It is,' I say. 'Lily will help you out.'

She takes Lily's hand and allows herself to be handed out of the car. 'I don't understand. I thought there had been an explosion.'

'There was,' I say.

'And no one was allowed near the place?'

'Also true. But I happen to have a man on the inside.'

Isabella straightens her skirt and takes the bouquet Lily hands her. 'I still don't understand.'

'Actually,' I say, 'it was less of a man and more of a woman. Here she comes now.'

I wave to Chloe as she makes her way over the gravel towards us. 'We made it!'

'I can see that,' she says. 'Hello, Isabella. You look beautiful.'

Isabella still looks bewildered. 'Chloe! What are you doing here? My wedding was cancelled.'

'It's been uncancelled,' I say. 'But only temporarily. We'd better get a move on.'

'We only have about half an hour,' says Chloe. 'Is everyone here?'

Another car pulls up on the gravel drive. Jon's parents climb out and wave to us. The back door opens, and Ali and the boys tumble out, followed by Daisy, who's wearing her flowered dungarees and clutching a wicker basket.

'Is that everyone?' asks Chloe.

'Is Jon here?' asks Isabella. 'And Michael?'

Chloe gestures towards the rose garden. 'Jon is waiting for you over there.'

'What about Michael?' asks Mum.

'Any minute now,' I say, hoping to goodness I'm right.

There's the noise of an exhaust pipe backfiring, and a moment later, a van comes into view. It creaks up the drive and stops next to ours.

Isabella peers at the writing on the side. '*Cartwright and Sons Meat Business – We bring home the bacon!*'

'Why is there a butcher's van parked on my drive?' Chloe asks me.

'I assume it was the best Michael could do at such short notice.'

Michael jumps out and opens one of the sliding doors. A woman wearing a mid-length blue dress climbs down and turns to face us.

'Grace?' says Isabella in a stunned voice.

'And me!' says Natalie, scrambling out after her.

'Me too!' says Meghan, turning and holding out her hand to Olivia, who almost tumbles out on top of her.

She's a lot larger than the last time I saw her, which is only to be expected. Alix and Victoria follow her, and the six of them beam at Isabella. They're all wearing dresses in various shades of blue. Each of them has a sash slung over their shoulders with the words *New Girl* printed on it in gold letters.

Isabella gives a piercing shriek and launches herself at them.

'Mind her dress!' says Chloe in alarm.

'I think we're well past that,' I say. 'Take a deep breath and go with the flow. It will do wonders for your blood pressure.'

Isabella emerges from the group of bridesmaids at last, laughing and crying.

'What are you all doing here?' she asks.

'Giving you the wedding you deserve,' I say. 'You couldn't have the fancy hotel and the string quartet, but we saw no reason not to have as many bonus bridesmaids as we could muster to accompany you to the altar.'

'Which we need to do in the next half hour or there won't be an altar at all,' says Chloe. 'Do you have any more surprises in store for us, Georgia?'

'That's the lot,' I say. 'From now on, we're in your capable hands.'

She looks relieved. 'In that case, would you please follow me to the rose garden, and we'll get this show on the road!'

Chapter Forty-Nine

We follow Chloe up the gravel drive towards the hotel. Just before we reach the main entrance, Chloe turns and points to a strip of wooden boards laid out across the grass.

'It's the best we could do,' she says. 'The ground is all churned up from the lorries that have been arriving all week.'

Isabella shoots me a questioning glance, and I smile back at her. 'Think of it as your own personal red carpet. Now let's get you married before the rest of the lorries arrive. Would the parents of the bride please process in single file up the aisle, followed by the parents and sister of the groom?'

Mum and Dad make their way slowly along the wooden planks to where Jon and Michael are waiting at the far end. Jon's parents and Ali follow them.

'It's your turn next,' I instruct the boys. 'Don't leave the path, whatever you do. I know you're wearing jeans, but there are no showers or laundry facilities available.'

They grin back at me and set off.

'And now for the main event,' I say. 'Thank goodness you didn't decide on a train, Isabella. Imagine if you'd chosen the dress Colette described as Mediaeval Muse? We would never have got the mud out of it. It will be challenging enough as it is.'

'No, it won't,' says Isabella. 'I can easily hold my skirts up. You lot should worry about yourselves.'

I nod to Lily and Abby. 'You two walk behind her and make sure she doesn't get lost. You know what Isabella's like with directions, and we don't want her ending up in Scotland. Everyone else can follow in any order they choose. I'll bring up the rear.'

'No!' says Isabella.

'What's wrong?' I ask. 'It's too late to change your mind now. The time for any last-minute indecision was back at the house.'

'I'm not having you walk at the back of the line,' she says. 'None of this would have happened without you. I want you to walk as close to me as possible.'

'Of course, you do,' says Lily. 'You've got her this far, Georgia. Don't give up at the last moment.'

'Are you sure?' I ask. 'Chloe and I had the order all worked out.'

'As you have so frequently reminded me,' says Isabella, 'this is my wedding, and I get to call the shots.'

'My mistake. Next time I won't lay quite so much stress on that point.'

'There will be no next time,' she says. 'So, let's make sure we do this one right.'

Lily squeezes Daisy's hand. 'This is your big moment, sweetheart. Remember how we practised it?'

Daisy nods and takes the basket of rose petals Lily hands her. She turns to beam at Isabella before setting off up along the makeshift path, scattering the petals as she goes.

'Don't you dare cry!' I tell Isabella. 'No matter how cute you think your goddaughter is. If you arrive at the altar in tears, Jon will think you don't want to marry him.'

She nods and bites her lip. I wave to Chloe, who's standing to one side of the rose arbour. A moment later, the violin music stops, and the first chords of Handel's wedding march float across to us.

'They're playing your song!' Lily tells Isabella. 'Time to go.'

Isabella sets off up the makeshift aisle, holding her skirt a few inches off the planks of wood.

'Anyone would think she'd been practising this for ages,' I tell Lily before following Isabella's example and stepping onto the first plank. 'Someone keep an eye on Olivia in case she loses her balance.'

'Go!' she says. 'Or Isabella will be married before the last bridesmaid arrives.'

I follow Isabella, balancing carefully on the wooden walkway. We reach the rose arbour, and she turns and hands me her bouquet. Chloe gestures for me to stand on a nearby patch of grass. The other bridesmaids arrive without mishap, and we all turn to face the celebrant.

'Good afternoon,' she says. 'What a charmingly unusual wedding. I won't waste time by saying more, as I understand we are under a certain time constraint. So, if you're ready, let's move straight to the vows.'

Everyone falls silent. There's no sound except for distant birdsong and the gentle hum of a tractor in the fields below us. Jon and Isabella turn to each other, and he takes her hands in his. I swallow hard. This is not the moment to burst into undignified tears. Michael, who's standing next to Jon holding Ethan's hand, catches my eye and grins at me. I smile back, and the danger passes.

I hardly hear the words as Jon and Isabella exchange their vows. I'm too busy watching their faces. If I'd ever had the slightest doubt about Jon's feelings for Isabella, it would have been swept away the moment he started speaking. He's looking at Isabella with such love in his eyes that my own eyes fill with tears. She's looking at him in exactly the same way. They're both lost in their own moment, and for the next few minutes I'm not sure either of them realises anyone else is here.

'Do we have the rings?' asks the celebrant.

Ethan steps forward, holding out a small velvet bag, and Michael shoots me such a relieved look that I almost laugh out loud.

Jon slips a ring onto Isabella's finger, and she does the same for him.

The celebrant smiles at them both. 'It is my very great pleasure to announce you are now legally married. May your future together be filled with happiness and love.'

Jon bends down to kiss Isabella, and there's a burst of spontaneous applause from the onlookers. I cast a quick glance at Chloe, wondering whether this is a breach of protocol too far. To my relief, I see she's joining in.

I nod to her, and she switches the music back on.

'I'm afraid we can't stay here for long,' I tell everyone. 'We need to return to our cars as quickly as –'

My words are interrupted by the deafening sound of a jackhammer.

I gesture to Jon and point towards the gates. He nods and takes Isabella's hand.

The noise stops, and I take advantage of the temporary silence to shout to the guests, 'Our time seems to be up! We should get going.'

We file back across the planks. Isabella and Jon come last. When I step off onto the grass and turn to make sure everyone is alright, I see him sweep her up in his arms and carry her over the narrow walkway.

'It's certainly a new twist on the tradition of carrying your bride over the threshold,' says Mum.

'And yet the rest of the wedding was so traditional!' I say.

Jon sets Isabella down on the grass next to us.

'I was convinced you were going to drop her,' I tell him. 'It wouldn't have been the greatest start to your married life.'

'I didn't want my wife to get her beautiful dress muddy,' he says.

'Your –?' I ask. 'Oh!'

Somehow, amid all the frantic last-minute preparations, I've almost forgotten what this is about. I've been so focused on getting everyone to the right place at the right time that it's slipped my mind what all this has been leading up to. Jon and Isabella are now husband and wife. It's a bitter-sweet feeling. Isabella and I are no longer the children who played together, the teens who squabbled incessantly, or even the adults who somehow found a way back to each other against all the odds.

Isabella seems to realise something of what I feel. She walks over and hugs me.

'Nothing's changed,' she says. 'You're still the little sister who drives me to distraction almost every day – the one I'm sure I couldn't live without.'

'And now you have a brother-in-law who's duty bound to come to your rescue if you get into any kind of trouble,' Jon tells me. 'Isabella made that quite clear when she accepted my proposal.'

The jackhammer has started up again, and I can't hear myself speak. I point towards the cars, and everyone nods.

'Just in time!' says Chloe as several more vans trundle down the lane and pull up outside the gates. 'You should get going. I'll see you all later.'

Isabella opens her mouth to ask a question, but it's drowned in the clatter of the pneumatic drills, which have now been augmented by a high-pitched whining noise that sounds like a squadron of fighter jets zooming past.

Jon helps Isabella into the front seat of his car. The bridesmaids have already climbed into the butcher's van. I hope someone found the time to clean it before Michael commandeered it. I must ask him later where he got hold of it.

I walk over to Jon's car and lean in to talk to Isabella. 'We're going to the Red Lion for a celebration meal. Is that alright with you?'

'It's perfect!' she says. 'I'm starving.'

'Naturally,' says Jon. 'It will be almost three o'clock by the time we arrive.'

'See you there!' I say and run back to where Mum and Dad are waiting for me.

'We must get moving,' I tell them. 'I want to get to the Red Lion before Jon and Isabella.'

'You should have re-programmed his sat-nav,' says Dad. 'You could have sent the happy couple on a wild goose chase around the local countryside. That would have ensured we arrived at the reception first.'

'You should have planned this wedding, not me!' I say admiringly. 'But it won't work in this case. Jon knows exactly where Honeywell is. And I'm convinced Isabella has some sort of internal homing system that would lead her to Shelley's game pie, no matter where in the world she was.'

Mum starts the car and sets off down the lane.

'How does it feel to have a daughter married?' I ask them.

'It's a tremendous relief,' says Dad. 'But only because I wasn't sure you'd pull this off, and I know how much you'd set your heart on it.'

'It was a beautiful wedding,' says Mum. 'The nicest I've ever attended. But I can't think how you persuaded the hotel to allow it, Georgia. Weren't they worried about their insurance if anything went wrong?'

'Chloe sorted all of that. She really came through for us.'

'I doubt it was what she really wanted,' she says.

'Not at first. But I drove over to see her after the gas explosion, and we had a long talk. I explained how Isabella had been feeling, and she seemed genuinely taken aback. I don't think Chloe had ever stopped to think about it like that before. She said most of her brides were delighted to leave most of the details to her. I told her Isabella wasn't your run-of-the-mill bride, and she said she'd started to realise that.'

'I hope Chloe wasn't too upset?' asks Dad.

'Maybe a little at first, but she quickly got into the spirit of the thing. It was her suggestion for us to hold the ceremony at Willowmere Hall, but she said we'd be on a tight schedule. The repairs were due to start this afternoon, and the insurance company had laid down tight restrictions for when and how the work was to be done. But Chloe isn't a top-notch wedding co-ordinator for nothing. She's used to negotiating and making last minute arrangements. She spoke to the site manager and persuaded him not to start the noisy part of the work until after the wedding. We weren't able to move it any earlier because the registrar was booked up all day and couldn't get here until two o'clock, which only gave us a forty-minute window at the most.'

'It all worked out perfectly,' says Mum. 'The bridesmaids were a lovely touch.'

'I wanted to add a little extra something to make the wedding ceremony special,' I say. 'There wasn't time to do much, but we had a group chat set up for the previous employees. They were already booked to come down early for a surprise afternoon tea. Lily messaged and told them what had happened and asked whether everyone had a blue dress they could wear. Luckily, they all did. They agreed to meet at the bakery at one-thirty today so that Michael could pick them up and drive them over here. We didn't want to risk losing any of them if they travelled separately. For all I know, they may be as directionally-challenged as Isabella.'

'Here we are,' says Mum, pulling into the car park of the Red Lion and parking next to the butcher's van. 'As promised, we've beaten the bride and groom to the finish line.'

'What a good idea to mark these spaces,' says Dad. 'We'd have had to park behind the bakery if this place was full.'

'Parents of the bride,' I say, pointing to the sign. 'Parents of the groom. Bride and Groom. Bridesmaids. Nathan has promised to monitor the car park and enforce the rule if necessary.'

'Chloe isn't the only one with an eye for detail,' Mum tells me. 'Or a strong desire of getting her own way.'

'That isn't how I'd put it. I prefer to be described as strategically assertive.'

'There's no question about that,' says Dad. 'If your career in the bakery doesn't work out, there's an opening in the wedding industry with your name on it.'

'Not a hope!' I say. 'This was a special guest appearance on my part. Isabella can count herself fortunate that I've set aside my scruples about encouraging the bridal industrial complex and decided to participate.'

'Here comes the happy couple!' says Mum. 'Right on time.'

'I expect Isabella instructed Jon to put his foot down and get her here before she passed out from hunger,' I say.

Jon opens the passenger door and helps Isabella climb out.

'Reserved parking spaces!' she says, looking impressed. 'How did you persuade Shelley to approve that?'

'Haven't you realised by now that your sister is very talented at getting people to do what she wants?' asks Dad.

'All in a good cause,' I say. 'Are you ready to eat?'

'I've been dreaming of Shelley's game pie for the past few miles,' says Isabella. 'Or Victoria's. I don't mind which.'

'I hope you aren't too set on ordering that particular dish,' I say. 'There are a few alternatives we'd like you to consider.'

'Why mess with perfection?' she asks.

'Have a look at what else is on offer, and then decide.'

'This way,' says Jon, taking her arm.

'The main entrance is over there,' Isabella tells him. 'Everyone talks about me being directionally-challenged, but I've never once got lost on the way to the Red Lion.'

'We have to make a quick stop first,' I say. 'Will you walk, or would you like your husband to carry you?'

'Maybe later,' she says. 'It depends on how many toasts we decide to drink.'

We reach the arts centre, and I pull open the door. It's so dark and silent that I start to wonder whether we've come to the wrong place.

Isabella and Jon follow me inside.

'What are you looking for?' she asks me.

'This!' I say and snap the light on to reveal the room packed full of people.

Everyone cheers when they see Isabella, who for once seems bereft of words.

Ivy pulls back the curtains, and the afternoon sunshine floods in, making us all blink. There's a huge banner stretched along the far wall saying *Congratulations – Jon and Isabella!* in swirling red letters. Every corner of the room has been decorated with silver and gold balloons – some floating freely and others tied to chairs with curling blue ribbons.

Garlands of fairy lights have been strung across the ceiling, and vases of roses and sweet peas sit on every available surface. None of the vases match, and the flowers haven't been professionally arranged. But I know they've come from half the gardens in Honeywell and have been contributed with love to make this day a success.

At the far end of the room, sitting on its own table, is the most beautiful three-tiered wedding cake I've ever seen. I can't imagine how Abby and Chris found the time to make a work of art like this at such short notice, but they've managed it somehow. Maybe this is one of the occasions when teamwork really comes into its own.

However it was achieved, they've done an incredible job. They showed me the finished cake last night, telling me they'd decided to create each tier in a different flavour in Isabella's honour. As Abby pointed out, Isabella isn't a woman to choose only one cake when she can have several.

The bottom layer is a chocolate sponge, filled with white chocolate and raspberry cream. Curls of dark chocolate spiral gracefully down its frosted sides. The middle layer is a lemon sponge, filled with lemon curd and decorated with tiny sugar daisies and crystallised lemon peel. The top layer is a vanilla sponge with a caramel filling. They've decorated this one with a scattering of golden edible pearls and cream sugar roses in honour of the occasion. It may not be the most traditional looking wedding cake, but Isabella isn't the most traditional bride – despite all Chloe's efforts.

Jon puts his arm around Isabella. 'Say something!'

'I'm lost for words,' she says in a choked voice.

'Finally!' I say. 'My work here is done.'

Everyone surges forward to congratulate the newlyweds, while I stand for a moment, taking it all in. This may not be the wedding of Chloe's dreams, but in my opinion, it's something far better. The entire building is humming with joy and the kind of organised chaos I've come to associate with Isabella over the years. This just feels right. And, judging by the expressions on Isabella and Jon's faces, they both agree.

Chapter Fifty

'What now?' asks Mum, and everyone turns to me.

'I've done my bit,' I say. 'The rest is up to you. We have a bride and a groom and more bridesmaids than anyone could reasonably expect. We have a venue until midnight and enough food and drink to feed a small army. If none of you can work out what to do with them, that's your problem.'

Isabella's eyes shine as she looks around the room. 'This is it! This is the theme! I spent so long trying to find one and feeling a failure because I wasn't able to. And all the time, it was right under my nose.'

'I couldn't agree more,' says Jon. 'This is exactly the sort of wedding we should have planned all along.'

He and Isabella make their way through the crowd, pausing as they go to receive everyone's congratulations. I follow them towards the top table.

'Are we allowed to eat yet?' asks Mabel as I pass her. 'Sarah True has brought some of her famous samosas, and I don't want them all disappearing before I can get to them.'

It looks as though, contrary to my expectations, my work here isn't quite finished. I join Jon and Isabella and wave to everyone for silence. The noise and chatter die down as everyone turns to face us.

'First,' I say, 'a very warm welcome to everyone who's joined us this afternoon to celebrate this special occasion. You've all worked so hard to make this day perfect for Jon and Isabella. We couldn't have done it without your generous contributions of food and flowers and decorations. In true Honeywell spirit, you've helped to turn a potential disaster into a resounding triumph. I used to wonder why Isabella loved this village so much and why she spent most of her time here. I no longer wonder about that.'

Mabel breaks into a chorus of *For She's a Jolly Good Fellow* and is quickly hushed by Phyllis.

'I don't have much more to say,' I go on. 'Only that, against considerable odds, we've managed to get my sister safely married to the only man I've ever met who's up to the task of being her husband. And now it's time to celebrate that fact. As you can see, we have a buffet here with more food than one small village could reasonably consume in a week. We're hoping that will keep everyone going until this evening, when we'll be providing you with a hot meal. If you could visit the buffet in order, according to your table number, that would be very helpful.'

'Can I get you something to eat?' asks Michael, appearing next to me. 'You must be starving.'

'For once in my life, I'm too relieved to be hungry.'

'If I thought that state of affairs would last, I might be concerned,' he says. 'But it doesn't seem likely. Can I bring you some food, anyway?'

'Why not?'

He returns a few minutes later with two plates and sets one in front of me.

'I've been wanting to see you to thank you for everything you've done for us,' I tell him. 'I was so grateful that you offered to help the moment I messaged you. Lily and I were worried some of the bridesmaids might get lost, but you did an amazing job of rounding them up and delivering them exactly on time. I wasn't expecting the butcher's van, but who am I to complain?'

'It isn't a butcher's van,' he says. 'It used to be, but the owner sold it when he went out of business. A friend of mine bought it and fitted seats in the back because he plans to use it for family camping trips. He was happy to lend it to me and apologised that he hasn't yet got around to painting the outside.'

'I'm kind of glad he hasn't. It was the perfect slogan for today. You really did bring home the bacon.'

'I think that was mostly you,' he says. 'But I wanted to do my bit. And there was the added bonus of seeing the expression on Chloe's face when I drove up the lane.'

'She seemed a little taken aback, but she recovered. She isn't half as bad as I thought. She may not have been the right wedding co-ordinator for Isabella, but no one can deny she's good at her job. And she's excellent in an emergency. Once I'd been to see her and told her how things were, she really stepped up. She had to call in a lot of favours to persuade the manager to allow us onto the site at all. Then she had to talk the workmen into starting work half an hour later than they were supposed to.'

'I'm glad she was so helpful,' he says. 'But let's not pretend we don't know who was the real brains behind the operation. That was all you, Georgia.'

'I had an excellent team at my disposal. Everyone I contacted went the extra mile to make it happen. This village loves Isabella.'

He smiles. 'I think they're pretty fond of you too.'

'I hope so. I'm very fond of them.'

'And here we all are today,' he says, looking around at the tables of wedding guests.

'Here we all are,' I agree.

'Are you here with anyone?'

I drag my eyes away from the table by the window, where I've been watching Bernie standing on his hind legs, begging for a piece of quiche. Is that really a tuxedo he's wearing?

'I'm sorry,' I say, turning back to Michael. 'Did you ask me something?'

'Whether you're here with someone.'

'I'm here with lots of people. It's a wedding.'

'I meant a plus one,' he says. 'More specifically – David.'

'David?' I repeat blankly. 'Why would I be here with him?'

He shrugs. 'I thought you might be seeing him.'

'You thought wrong.'

'I'm sorry. I didn't mean to offend you. Some of the Silver Surfers were talking a while ago about you dating him.'

'It was one dinner!' I say. 'And that was because I was attempting to talk him into doing us a favour. I've only seen him once since then, and he was keen to tell me all about his geography teacher girlfriend. The Silver Surfers are lovely, but they're great ones for getting hold of the wrong end of the stick.'

Michael looks more cheerful. 'So, you and he aren't …?'

'Not even a bit.'

'And you and anyone else?' he asks.

'Why don't I make things easier for us both by saying there is no me and anyone? If you hear any wild rumours to the contrary, I'd be grateful if you'd put a stop to them. Otherwise, they'll be all around the village before you can say pound cake.'

Mum leans over to speak to me. 'You've done a wonderful job, Georgia. I still have no idea how you pulled all this together at such short notice.'

'I had plenty of help. You know how they say it takes a village to raise a child? In this case, it took a village to rescue a wedding. Everyone's contributed something. The Silver Surfers emailed the directions to get here, and they designed and printed all the banners and the place cards. And the gardening club stripped their gardens bare to provide the flowers. I'm fairly sure half of Honeywell is now a rose-free zone.'

She laughs. 'They'll grow back. And it's been worth it. The arrangements are beautiful. They smell lovely too, which flower shop roses rarely do.'

'Chloe didn't want scented flowers at the original wedding,' I say. 'Isabella told me she had some sort of complicated scent plan involving candles. Apparently, it was layered.'

Mum raises an eyebrow. 'Layered?'

'Top notes of orange blossom, with middle notes of freesia. And a base of something called tropical musk, which sounds like a body spray for teenage boys. I'm afraid I didn't have time to source any scented candles, let alone worry about the risk of them being knocked over in the stampede for the buffet. Anyway, Lily and I thought fresh roses would smell much better.'

'Poor Chloe,' she says. 'I hope she wasn't too disappointed when she heard your plans.'

'Once she realised there was no saving the original wedding, she was surprisingly flexible about the whole thing. She made several useful suggestions, such as asking the Red Lion to produce a signature cocktail and putting disposable cameras on all the tables so the guests can take lots of pictures.'

'Did you say we're having a signature cocktail?' Isabella asks me. 'I've always wanted one of those! What is it?'

'It's called the Sugarloaf Spritz. Nathan's been working on it for the past two days. Victoria has been enthusiastically assisting him to get the recipe just right. I'm surprised she managed to wobble her way across those planks today after testing all the various versions.'

'Not many brides have to walk the plank to get to their own wedding,' she says. 'It will be something to talk about in years to come if Jon and I run out of things to say to each other. So, what's in this cocktail?'

'According to Nathan, it's a sparkling blend of prosecco, elderflower cordial, a splash of pink grapefruit juice, and a twist of candied lemon peel. All perfectly balanced to be light, fresh, and just a little offbeat.'

'Like me!' she says with a delighted smile.

'That's the general idea. He'll be serving them later this evening. Not too early because you need to keep your head clear for the speeches. I assume you still plan to make one?'

'I haven't decided,' she says. 'I didn't plan on getting married at all today, let alone making a speech. Chloe wasn't keen on me breaking with tradition by giving a speech at the wedding I was supposed to have.'

'Chloe isn't here,' says Mum. 'So, you can do as you please.'

'As a matter of fact, she is,' I say. 'She's over there, sitting at the Silver Surfers' table. I'm not sure what she'll make of them, or they of her.'

'I'm glad you invited her,' says Isabella. 'She was only trying to do her best.'

'I know she was. But she was trying to do her best for the person she wanted you to be, not the person you really are.'

'Did you tell her that?' she asks.

'I told her quite a lot of things. And then I felt terrible when she apologised and asked what she could do to help. She came through for you beautifully. She spent all yesterday evening filling tiny silk bags with lavender from Martin Carson's garden for everyone to take home with them tonight.'

'That was nice of her,' says Isabella. 'I'm glad you included her in the reception. It sounds as though she deserves it.'

'We thought we'd show her how a real wedding should be organised,' says Abby. 'It will do wonders for her professional development.'

'Did you invite Colette too?' asks Isabella. 'She was very nice to me as well.'

I roll my eyes. 'Don't you think that poor woman has had enough to put up with without being reminded how much better Angela Carson is than any of her wedding dress designers?'

'My dress is beautiful, isn't it?' she asks. 'I'm almost tempted to get married again just so she can make me another one.'

'May I remind you that I'm sitting right next to you?' says Jon.

Isabella leans over to kiss him. 'I said almost!'

'You need to decide,' he says. 'It's nearly time for my speech, and I need to know whether to introduce myself as your husband or merely your first husband.'

'Both!' she says. 'But you can add the word "last" if you like. I'm quite happy to keep you for the rest of my life.'

'I'm delighted to hear it.'

He rises to his feet and clinks his knife against his champagne glass. 'Ladies and Gentlemen – if I could have your attention, I'd like to say a few words!'

Chapter Fifty-One

Half an hour later, the speeches are nearly finished. Jon's is short and very touching. He's obviously so happy to have married Isabella that it's almost taken the power of speech from him. Dad's is slightly longer, but he's a man of few words at the best of times, so he contents himself with telling us a little about Isabella as a child and how proud he and Mum are of the woman she's become.

Michael talks about what a privilege it was to be asked to be Jon's best man and how happy he is that the wedding went ahead against all the odds. He finishes by proposing a toast to all the bridesmaids – especially Abby, Lily, and me – who he says have risen to the challenge in an incredible way and, in three short days, have managed to create one of the most memorable weddings he's ever attended. The applause goes on for an embarrassingly long time, but it dies away at last.

I breathe a sigh of relief. Wedding speeches aren't my favourite thing, and I'm feeling rather exposed sitting at the top table in full view of everyone. I'm about to signal for Nathan to push the tables to the side of the room so the dancing can start when Isabella taps her glass with her spoon.

'I've decided to say something after all,' she says, rising to her feet.

She catches my eye and grins. 'You're the one who keeps telling me I should do exactly as I like at my own wedding! And what I want to do is make a speech.'

I smile back at her. 'Go ahead.'

She looks around at the assembled guests. 'When Jon asked me to marry him just before Christmas, all I could think of was saying yes as quickly as possible before he changed his mind. I didn't consider how or where we'd get married. I assumed it would all sort itself out. But it quickly became clear there's a lot more to planning a wedding than I realised. And I got lost. Not literally – although I'm aware of my reputation for being unable to find my way out of a phone box without the aid of a map and a flare gun. But I lost sight of what we wanted. I started worrying about chair covers and colour schemes and whether to fold the napkins into lilies or swans.'

She pauses and smiles at Chloe. 'What I didn't realise was that I was planning a wonderful wedding, but it wasn't *my* wedding. It was someone else's – a person who's elegant and sophisticated and not only knows the difference between a souffle and a sabayon but also understands the intricacies of damask and jacquard. And I wanted to be that person because I thought that was the sort of woman Jon deserved to marry. It took me far too long to understand the important thing was never the wedding day – it was marrying the man I love. If I could do that, I didn't care where or how we did it. And just when I'd come to my senses, it seemed it was all too late and the wedding would have to be postponed.'

She looks over at me. 'But I was reckoning without my sister. Most of you know Georgia, and you'll have realised by now she's one of the most stubborn and single-minded women you'll ever have the privilege to come across. When she decides something is going to happen, nothing gets in her way.'

Her smile widens. 'But it isn't only weddings she refuses to give up on. Very few people here know that Georgia has spent the last year studying for her exams so she can go to university this autumn. She's had to do all that alongside working at The

Sugarloaf Bakery. Lily and I are the most exemplary employers anyone could dream of, but we still expect our employees to work as hard as we do. And Georgia is the hardest-working member of staff we've ever had.'

'Hey!' says Grace, and everyone laughs.

'And then I got engaged,' says Isabella, 'and I asked Georgia to be my chief bridesmaid and become involved with the wedding planning. Even then, she didn't breathe a word about all the other things she was doing. She agreed to help me, and she's been as good as her word every step of the way, even though it's meant her having to study until late at night and on all her days off.'

I feel my face flame as everyone turns to look at me.

'As if all that wasn't enough,' Isabella goes on, 'four days ago we heard that our wedding had been cancelled, and all our hard work had been for nothing. But Georgia rarely takes no for an answer. She set out to make sure this wedding took place despite everything, and that it took place in style. To absolutely no one's surprise, that's exactly what happened.'

Bernie gives an encouraging bark, and everyone laughs.

'Georgia received her results yesterday,' says Isabella. 'She wasn't planning to tell me until after the wedding because she didn't want to overshadow my day. But Mum told me just now that she passed with top marks, and she's been offered a place at university this September to study for an arts degree.'

She turns to me. 'I can't believe you thought your achievement would overshadow my day. I couldn't be prouder of you, and hearing how well you've done has only made this day better. So, if everyone could raise their glasses, I'd like to propose a toast. To Georgia – the best chief bridesmaid and sister a woman could ever have!'

It takes a long time for the toast to be drunk and the applause to die away. I briefly consider slipping under the table and crawling towards the door. But the tablecloths are too short, so everyone would be able to watch my progress. Besides, it wouldn't be fair to Angela's lovely dress. She's put a huge amount of work and love into it, and it deserves a better fate than being covered in dust and cobwebs.

Chloe switches on the music, and the first notes of *Single Ladies* blast out.

'Are you and Jon really having your first dance to this?' Mum asks Isabella. 'It doesn't feel terribly appropriate.'

'I can ask Chloe to switch to something more romantic,' I say. 'Bob offered to make me a playlist of his favourite songs, and I didn't have time to check it first.'

Isabella grabs Jon's hand. 'No, this is perfect!'

'I agree,' he says. 'From now on, when anyone asks us, we can tell them this is our song!'

'I knew I'd get something wrong,' I tell Mum. 'And I made so many lists.'

She watches Jon and Isabella walk onto the dance floor. 'I think it's just right. Isabella isn't really a *Moon River* sort of girl, is she? This is much more her.'

'I agree,' says Michael. 'Would you like to dance too, Georgia? I'm almost certain the best man is supposed to dance with the chief bridesmaid at some point during the reception.'

'In case you hadn't noticed,' I say, 'we've thrown almost every single tradition out of the window today. Most weddings don't have Christmas lights strung everywhere and no formal seating plans.'

He holds out his hand to me. 'Then would you like to dance with me just because?'

'I would – if only because I'll feel less conspicuous on a crowded dance floor if Isabella takes it into her head to make another embarrassing toast.'

The song switches to The Proclaimers' *I'm Gonna Be* just as we reach the dance floor.

'Even better!' says Michael. 'I like this one.'

He pulls me into his arms, and we do our best to keep time to the music, although without much success.

'I think you're supposed to dance more energetically to this song,' I say, pointing to Mabel, who's pulled her sister into the crowd of dancers and is doing her own unique version of the Twist, while Bernie runs in circles, tangling his lead around their legs.

'I think he's doing the Berniehop,' I say.

He smiles. 'It doesn't matter, as long as he's having fun.'

The song finishes, and *Wonderful World* starts to play.

'This one's better,' says Michael. 'I'm too old for breakdancing.'

'Maybe, but I'd like to see you try.'

He shakes his head and draws me closer. 'This is good enough for me.'

We dance in silence for a minute before he asks, 'Was that the reason you were never free when I asked you out?'

'Was what the reason?'

'Your studies.'

To my surprise, I realise I've almost forgotten about those. They seem so long ago now.

'I suppose it was,' I say. 'I was attending evening classes three times a week, and I had a mountain of homework to fit in during my free time. Perhaps I should have taken the course over a longer period. But once I'd decided to do it, I wanted to finish as quickly as I could.'

'I can understand that,' he says. 'And you couldn't have realised when you started that there would be a wedding happening right in the middle of it all.'

'No, but I was delighted when I heard about it. Just look at them!'

I gesture towards Isabella and Jon, locked in each other's arms and swaying to the music, oblivious to everyone around them.

Michael nods. 'I'm very happy for them, but I'm even happier for myself.'

'Because?'

He tightens his hold on me. 'Because I thought the reason you kept turning me down was that you were seeing someone else.'

'You could have asked me. I'd have told you I wasn't.'

'I asked Jon,' he confesses. 'He said he was sure you weren't dating anyone. But that made it worse because the only other explanation was that you were avoiding me because you didn't want to see me at all.'

'I wasn't avoiding you,' I say. 'I was just too busy for anything else. And you only mentioned us having dinner a couple of times.'

'But I gave you a selection of dates, and you told me none of them worked for you. I couldn't keep asking you out when you'd made it clear you weren't interested. It wouldn't have been fair to you.'

'I didn't realise you'd taken it like that,' I say. 'If I'd thought about it at all, I would have assumed you enjoyed dinner as much as I did and were always thinking about it. That's very understandable.'

'I'd have been happy with bread and water,' he says.

I pull a face. 'For dinner? I can't agree with you there.'

'It was a figure of speech.'

'I'm glad to hear that. Is this why you haven't been around much for the past few weeks?'

'Partly,' he says. 'It didn't seem fair to keep pressuring you if you didn't think of me in that way.'

He pulls away and looks down at me with a smile in his eyes. 'So, if I were to ask you now about dinner, what would you say?'

'That I've booked a fish and chip van to arrive at seven o'clock. It was the best I could do at short notice, and everyone likes fish and chips.'

He sighs. 'I'm not making myself very clear, am I? Let me try again. Would you have dinner with me one night this week – just the two of us?'

I smile back at him. 'I think I'd like that.'

'So would I.'

He hesitates, then leans in, brushing his lips against mine. I tilt my face up towards his, my hand sliding to the back of his neck. The dance floor swirls with colour and movement, but it feels as though we're in a quiet bubble. The noise around us – the music, the chatter, the clinking glasses – blurs into the background as he kisses me again with more certainty. I feel his hands slide to my waist, steady and sure, and I catch my breath as my pulse quickens in response.

'Well, it's about time!' says Isabella's voice, and I come back to reality to see her beaming at us.

'I knew you believed in some wedding traditions!' she tells me. 'No one could be as cynical as you pretended to be. And the chief bridesmaid and the best man is the perfect example of such a tradition. It's far too late to pretend you don't know what I'm talking about. Half the village is watching you.'

Michael doesn't release his grip on me. 'I'm delighted to go along with any tradition that means I get to kiss your sister. And the rest of the village can mind their own business.'

'That's a very rude thing to say!' calls Mabel. 'If people start kissing each other in the middle of the dance floor, what do you expect us to do? Pretend we haven't noticed?'

'Sorry about that,' I tell her. 'It won't happen again.'

Michael looks at me with a lurking smile in his eyes and draws me back into his arms. 'I wouldn't be so sure about that.'

Chapter Fifty-Two

The wedding reception goes on until late in the evening. No one wants it to end – least of all Isabella. Gone is the pale, quiet, unfamiliar figure of the past few months. In her place is the bride everyone expected – dancing every dance and, at Mabel's urging, leading a conga line around the room after Nathan has brought in the cocktails.

Jon is at her side through it all. He doesn't seem fazed by anything she does. He's just content to be a part of her life, and for her to be a part of his. I'm happy to know he'll never want Isabella to be anyone other than exactly who she is. She'll continue to march to the beat of a different drum, and he'll march right alongside her. They're both so lucky to have found each other.

I spend most of the evening dancing with Michael, but I find time between dances to talk to most of the guests. The Flour Girls all introduce me to their partners. I met a couple of them a few years ago, but I didn't take much interest in the bakery in those days. It seemed so far removed from anything that was going on in my world. But now I'm genuinely interested to meet them all and hear their stories.

At Olivia's request, Will is busy making a professional wedding video and taking photographs. He shepherds us outside around five o'clock to pose for some formal pictures in the garden. But he mostly concentrates on taking unobtrusive pictures of the guests and bridal party enjoying themselves.

I'm surprised to see him and Mrs Ogilvie greet each other like old friends. She and Mabel tell him about the competition to portray the spirit of Bernie, and he laughs when he hears about the poker cartoon and the mosaics. To Mrs Ogilvie's delight, he offers to pop into the bakery the next day and replace one of the smaller panes of glass with the stained-glass picture of Bernie sitting under a tree.

'I was planning to suggest that when Isabella was less stressed out,' says Lily. 'It will look lovely when the sun shines through it. Caroline used so many beautiful colours.'

'It will make it more difficult to see the cakes from the street,' grumbles Mabel. 'I like to know what's available before I decide to come in.'

'You always choose the same thing,' says her sister. 'And if you don't know what a plum slice looks like by now, there's no hope for you.'

'Do you hear how she talks to me?' Mabel asks Will. 'To think I came all the way back from Australia for this! Isn't it enough that I have to put up with that photograph you took of Bernie misbehaving himself when I'm at home, without having to see another picture of him each time I walk along the high street?'

'That photo was one of my best pieces of work,' says Will. 'Everything came together in one perfect moment.'

'From what I hear, it was a sheer fluke,' says Mabel. 'As usual, the mutt was doing something he wasn't supposed to be doing. And, again as usual, he ended up being rewarded for it. It goes against all the established codes of morality.'

'Isn't it about time you let that one go?' Lily asks her. 'It was years ago, and a lot has happened since then. Bernie is an older and wiser dog these days.'

Mabel snorts. 'You didn't see him on the dance floor earlier. I think he fancies himself as a young Fred Astaire – when in fact he's more like a scarecrow on roller skates.'

The fish and chip van arrives at seven and stops in the pub car park. There's a rush towards the door, and a line quickly forms.

'You'd think we hadn't provided anything for our guests to eat since they arrived,' I tell Michael. 'Whereas our generously loaded buffet table was stripped bare within half an hour. Granted, Isabella was present, but I thought it would take longer for the food to disappear than it did.'

'You were here too,' he reminds me. 'The Campbell sisters' reputation precedes them.'

'I had to make up for a stressful few days. I don't want to shock you, but I almost forgot to eat breakfast yesterday morning. Luckily, I remembered in time, so disaster was averted.'

Isabella taps me on the shoulder. 'Could I have a quick word?'

'Of course. But I didn't expect to see you in here. I thought you'd be heading up the queue at the van.'

'No need,' she says. 'Jon's gone for me. He told me it's one of the perks of being married. I knew I'd enjoy having a husband, but I didn't realise it included this sort of thing. I hope he doesn't take too long. I'm starving.'

'I'm off to get some fish and chips myself,' says Michael. 'Can I bring some for you, Georgia?'

'Good idea,' says Isabella. 'I've been wanting to catch her alone all afternoon, but every time I get near her, she's with you.'

'I'm afraid you'll have to get used to me being around in the future,' he says. 'I'll be as quick as I can, Georgia.'

'I'd almost given up hope of you two getting together,' Isabella tells me when he's gone.

'I thought you were only joking when you teased me about him.'

'I never joke about serious things. There have been so many times I've wanted to tell you to stop messing around and see what was right under your nose. It was difficult to restrain myself when the pair of you were obviously so right for each other. I could see that Michael realised it the first night you met. But for such a bright woman, you remained remarkably obtuse.'

'I had a lot on my mind,' I defend myself. 'And I wasn't looking for a relationship. You were keeping me far too busy to think about anything else.'

'And you had your studies too,' she says. 'Which is what I wanted to talk to you about. Where are you planning to live once you start university?'

'I haven't given it much thought. I wasn't even certain they'd accept me.'

'I was,' she says. 'I'm sure Mum and Dad won't kick you out of the house if you want to stay where you are.'

'So am I, but I'd rather not keep living at home when I'm a student. It's time I spread my wings a bit. I suppose I'll look around for a house share.'

'You could do that,' she says. 'Or you could live in my flat. I was planning to rent it out once Jon and I were married, and I can't think of a better tenant.'

'That's very kind of you, but I'll be on a reduced income until I graduate, and I'll still need a loan for my fees. I'm hoping you'll let me stay on at the bakery part-time so I can pay my living expenses, but I'll still have to watch the pennies for a while. Private rentals will be way out of my reach for quite some time.'

'Not this one,' she says. 'I'm willing to offer it to you at a more-than-affordable rate. I'll only charge you the interest on the mortgage.'

'You could earn far more each month by letting it out to a real tenant.'

'But I wouldn't have any peace of mind. The truth is that I've recently become the proud possessor of several houseplants that need specialist attention. Martin gave them to me as a wedding present, with strict care instructions. I'm terribly worried about leaving them alone in the flat with just anyone. I'd feel so much better knowing someone responsible was in charge of their welfare.'

'Can't you take them with you to Jon's place?' I ask.

'My new husband won't allow them in the house.'

'The day Jon doesn't allow you to do something is the day the sun forgets to rise.'

She gives a mournful shake of her head. 'I'm sorry to say that ever since we got married, Jon has changed into someone I barely recognise. He's adamant that if any of my houseplants come into his home, he and I are over. Apparently, he hates having any green things in his living space, and it's non-negotiable. It's left me in a real quandary. If you don't agree to move into my flat and look after my plants for me, my marriage may not last. What do you say, Georgie – will you help me out?'

'Are you sure?' I ask.

'Perfectly sure.'

Jon appears carrying two white paper parcels. 'Double portion for you, Isabella! What are you two talking about?'

'Houseplants,' I say.

'What kind?' he asks. 'I've just bought myself some peace lilies, and I'm not sure which room I should put them in. I'm hoping Isabella will advise me. She's a dab hand at horticulture now that Martin has given her some advice.'

I look at Isabella, who smiles back at me. 'It's too late. You've given me your word.'

Michael makes his way through the crowd and hands me a similar parcel. 'I took a chance and asked for a double portion.'

'I told you he was perfect for you!' says Isabella. 'Let's sit down and eat these before they go cold.'

The evening slowly winds to a close. I never want it to end. Some memories stay with you forever, like a bright shining light, and this is one of them.

Mum comes over to us at eleven-thirty. 'Nathan says your going-away car will be ready when you are.'

Isabella looks at Jon. 'I thought we were taking your car?'

'I made certain contingency plans,' I tell her. 'I wasn't sure what Jon's car would look like by now. Don't forget all the Silver Surfers are here today, and they aren't exactly known for their subtlety and restraint.'

'We're driving off on our honeymoon tomorrow morning,' Jon reminds Isabella. 'I thought you might prefer to go incognito.'

'He's right,' says Michael. 'I noticed your car while I was waiting in line for our fish and chips.'

Isabella's eyes light up. 'I want to see it!'

'You're the boss,' I say. 'Would you like to throw your bouquet before we go?'

'I'll do it out there,' she decides. 'It will be more fun in the dark. Anyone who wants to catch it will have to really work for it.'

She takes Jon's arm, and Michael and I follow them outside. The Silver Surfers have really gone to town on Jon's car. They've strapped two garden gnomes to the roof rack. One of them is dressed in what looks like a white pillowcase, with holes cut out for its head and arms. The other is wearing a black T-shirt with a spotted bow tie. I'm almost sure I recognise the second gnome as Sir Grudgewick.

'They're supposed to be bride and groom cake toppers,' explains Ivy.

'They're not topping any of my cakes!' says Abby.

The car itself has been decorated like a wedding cake, with swirls of foam piped along the edges of the windows to represent royal icing. Someone has tied a string of whisks, wooden spoons, and cookie cutters to the bumper with pink ribbons, and there are cupcake wrappers strung across the back window, surrounding a large sign that says 'Whisked Away!'

'It's perfect!' says Isabella. 'I want to keep it like this forever.'

'The plan is for you to take my car home tonight,' Dad tells Jon. 'I'll clean yours up and drop it at the flat tomorrow morning before you leave.'

Isabella looks disappointed, but Jon breathes an audible sigh of relief. 'I wasn't looking forward to driving all the way to Wales in this.'

'Are you going back to the place where you first took Isabella camping?' I ask him.

'Yes, we thought it would be romantic.'

'I'm hoping they'll let us zipline down the mountain together,' says Isabella. 'Jon insists it would contravene health and safety laws, but I haven't given up hope. And he's promised to take me whitewater rafting and watch me climb the rock wall each morning. I forgot to ask you to look after my houseplants while I'm away, Georgia. Would you mind? It will be good practice for you. Don't forget to talk to them each day.'

'As long as you don't expect me to sing to them,' I say. 'That would be a step too far, even for you.'

'I hope you like houseplants,' she tells Michael. 'I suspect you'll be seeing quite a lot of them over the next few years.'

'Are you planning to throw this bouquet or not?' I ask her.

'Will you catch it?'

I place my hands behind my back. 'I will not.'

'I'll throw it underarm,' she says encouragingly. 'Stand over there next to the fence, and I'll send it in that direction.'

'No, you won't!' says Mabel. 'You'll do it properly and give us all a chance. I've been in training for this ever since I arrived in Honeywell. I've thrown so many balls for the mutt over the years that I have great hopes of catching your bouquet.'

Isabella turns her back on us, closes her eyes, and throws the bouquet high into the air. Several people make a dive for it, and Isabella turns around just in time to see Chloe clutching the bouquet, looking startled.

'I came out to see whether you'd left yet,' she says. 'And this hit me in the face.'

'It still counts!' says Isabella. 'It means the next wedding you arrange will be your own. I hope you aren't as difficult a bride as I was.'

Chloe steps forward and hugs her. 'You weren't difficult. You were just … unusual. I'm so happy you had the wedding day you wanted in the end.'

'I always thought you'd be the one to catch it,' Isabella tells me.

I shake my head. 'I'm afraid that's a tradition too far for me.'

She looks from me to Michael and smiles. 'I get the feeling this relationship doesn't need any bouquets to go the distance.'

Michael slips his arm around my shoulders, and I relax as I feel his solid warmth against me.

'I hope you're right,' he tells Isabella.

She gestures towards the Flour Girls, most of whom are still wearing their New Girl sashes.

'I was right about all of them, and I'm right about this. Just you wait and see!'

Thank you for reading!

If you would like to read a free short story telling you how Lily and Isabella came to buy the bakery, go to this link to request your free copy.

rosemarywhittaker.com/a-new-start

A Tale of Two Christmases

Annie never comes home for Christmas. There's too much chance of running into Alex. He broke her heart, and she never wants to speak to him again. Alex always comes home for Christmas. He's desperate to talk to Annie about what went wrong between them.

Join the fun in the first book of the *Christmas in Honeywell* series.

A Tale of Two Christmases is available now in paperback and Kindle e-book.

Books by Rosemary Whittaker
All available now in paperback and Kindle e-book

The Sugarloaf Bakery series

A Sugarloaf Valentine
A Sugarloaf Mix-Up
A Sugarloaf Surprise
A Sugarloaf Christmas
A Sugarloaf Easter
A Sugarloaf Secret
A Sugarloaf Summer
A Sugarloaf Appeal
A Sugarloaf Adventure
A Sugarloaf Wedding

The Christmas in Honeywell series

A Tale of Two Christmases
A Boxful of Christmas
The Christmas Cookie Club

The Year Away series

The Cinnamon Snail
Sunshine State
The Wattle Birds
The Feijoa Tree
The Villa Mimosa

Short Reads
Available now in Kindle e-book

Making the Effort

Printed in Dunstable, United Kingdom